J.D. STANTON

VANISHED

Also in the J. D. Stanton Mysteries series

A Ship Possessed *(Book One)*

J.D. STANTON MYSTERIES

VANISHED

ALTON GANSKY

ZondervanPublishingHouse
Grand Rapids, Michigan

A Division of Harper Collins*Publishers*

Vanished

Requests for information should be addressed to:

ZondervanPublishingHouse
Grand Rapids, Michigan 49530

Library of Congress Cataloging-in-Publication Data

Gansky, Alton.
Vanished / Alton Gansky.
p. cm. — (J. D. Stanton mysteries ; bk. 2)
ISBN: 0-310-22003-3
I. Title. II. Series: Gansky, Alton. J. D. Stanton mysteries ; bk. 2.
PS3557.A5195V36 1999
813'.54—dc21 99-39342
CIP

Interior design by Melissa M. Elenbaas

Printed in the United States of America

99 00 01 02 03 04 /DC/ 10 9 8 7 6 5 4 3 2 1

To my three amazing children:
Crystal, Chaundel, and Aaron

Prologue

22 November 2000; 0255 hours
Edwards Air Force Base, California

The colonel plowed through the open door and marched with determined steps through the crowded, dimly lit room. People parted before him like water before the prow of a ship. His eyes were narrow and flint hard, his expression stern and sour. Mark Bettleman tensed.

"Let's have it, Master Sergeant," the colonel barked as he came to an abrupt stop six inches from where Bettleman stood. Colonel Marcus Brooks was shorter than average, with a barrel chest and a thick jaw. His hair was cut close to the scalp and looked the color of sand. His air force uniform was sharply pressed and it hung on his solid body as if it had been tailor-made. The early morning hour had dulled neither the creases in his uniform nor the edge in his voice.

"Yes, sir," Bettleman began, then hesitated as he looked down at the round screen in front of him. Planted before the electronic display was a young airman who sat in wide-eyed disbelief.

"Well?" Brooks prodded. "Spit it out."

"Yes, sir!" Bettleman responded quickly. He began his briefing, spilling his comments out in a torrent of words. "At 0245 hours, Airman Lenick called my attention to several aberrant targets. Initially there were three . . . craft; one at 36,000 feet, another at 22,500, and the third at 18,200. Targets were verified on other units to rule out electronic artifacts. We began tracking them—best we could."

"What do you mean, the best you could?"

"They're unlike any targets we've ever tracked, sir, and as you know, we've seen everything there is to see." Bettleman was not exaggerating. Edwards Air Force Base was one of the premier installations for the testing of new military aircraft. Everything from the X-15 to the space shuttle had been flown in the desert air over the base. "These don't play by the rules."

The colonel looked down at the display and watched as an orange band of light swept clockwise around the face of the radar monitor. "I don't see anything."

"Just wait, sir."

On the next pass, the monitor painted one small dot. "I see it." He studied the blip. "Search only?"

"Yes, sir," Bettleman answered, scratching his head. "Search only. As you can see, there's no transponder identification. Two minutes before you arrived, there were three targets."

"I only see one. Where are the other two?" Brooks demanded. "Did they fly off?"

"No, sir. That's just it. They didn't fly off, they flew *into* each other. They didn't crash. I don't mean that. I mean they just . . . just melted into one. As you can see, it's still airborne."

"And by the looks of it, it's just hovering there."

"Yes, sir, but there's more. Before the three became one, we tracked two of them into a sudden descent. They dropped like rocks—no, that's not right—they didn't drop, they *flew* straight down at an incredible speed."

"Nearly one thousand miles per hour, Colonel," Lenick added, speaking for the first time. "One thousand miles an hour, straight into the ground."

"It was as if they wanted to crash," Bettleman added. "At that speed, they would have left craters the size of a city block."

"Are you saying they didn't crash?"

"No, sir . . . er, yes, sir. They didn't crash." Bettleman said, flustered. "Ten seconds later they climbed to the level of the third contact and stopped abruptly. Then they melded into one."

"Do you know what you're saying, Master Sergeant?" the colonel asked sternly. "An up-and-down flight like that would represent at least forty Gs, both negative and positive. No one could survive that. The G forces would tear a man to pieces."

"Yes, sir. I know that. I can't explain any of this. I can only report it."

"You make radar contact with three unknowns flying at different altitudes when two of them power themselves into the ground at one thousand miles per hour without crashing, rise again to high altitude, and then combine with the third object. Do I have that right?"

"Yes, sir."

"Do you know how crazy that sounds? Do you expect me to believe any of that?"

"Sir, I don't know what to expect. And that's not all. The objects are only on the radar screen every other pass. We can't get a definitive lock on them. One moment they're there, the next they're not. It's as if they are blinking in and out of existence."

Colonel Marcus watched the radar screen. Where once the bright orange dot of the contact had been there was now nothing. On the next pass, the dot reappeared.

"It's doing it again," Lenick said. "It's split back into three."

The colonel spun on his heels and picked up the closest phone. "This is Colonel Marcus Brooks. Get me the base commander."

"May I ask what the colonel is doing?" said Bettleman.

"I'm going to ask for an air recon, Sergeant. Maybe the jet jockeys can eyeball that thing for us. Exactly where is it?"

"Hovering over the Roanoke compound, sir. Dead center over Roanoke." Bettleman could see his commander stiffen.

N

PART 1

ARRIVAL

Chapter 1

23 November 2000; 1715 hours

3,000 feet above the Cajon Pass, California

The thunderous thumping of the fifty-three-foot main rotor reverberated through the fuselage of the SH–60B *Seahawk* helicopter and deep into J. D. Stanton's bones. He had started this trip with a mild headache which, with the help of the 1,662 horsepower General Electric engine, had painfully blossomed in magnitude. He raised a hand to the bridge of his nose and squeezed.

"Are you feeling all right, sir?" The voice sounded distant and electronic over the speakers in Stanton's flight helmet.

Stanton dropped his hand and looked across the aircraft at the uniformed man who sat in the jump seat opposite him. "I'm fine, Chief. Just a little headache."

The helicopter pitched, then dropped a few feet.

"Sorry, Captain," another voice said. It was the pilot. "It's a little more windy out there than I like."

"No need to apologize, Lieutenant," Stanton said evenly. "You're giving up your Thanksgiving dinner to cart my fanny up here."

"Any excuse to fly, sir," the pilot said flatly. "I wish I could tell you that the ride is going to get smoother, but I can't. I have a sister who lives up here; she says it's windy all the time. Had the shingles blown off her roof once."

"No problem," Stanton replied. His churning, acid-filled stomach disagreed. He hated flying. Something about whizzing through the nothingness of air seemed wrong. Leaning forward, he strained to see out the pilot's window. Darkness was quickly consuming the sky, leaving only shreds of salmon-colored clouds. Below him, the sparse and drab canvas of desert scrolled by at a brisk 150 miles per hour. He sighed, forgetting the sound would be carried to the earphones of all on board. Everyone aboard the *Seahawk* wore a helmet equipped with microphone and speakers. The earphones did double duty, protecting the crew's hearing from the intrinsic noise of the helo and aiding in communication.

"You don't much like flying, do you, Captain?" The chief's words were a statement more than a question.

"It's that obvious?" Stanton replied.

"We see it all the time," the chief said. "Besides, those dolphins I saw on your chest tell me that you're more comfortable under the water than over the ground."

"You're an observant man, Chief." Stanton had spent most of his naval career in or around nuclear submarines, a duty for which he was ideally suited. Not everyone could endure being locked inside a long metal tube for months at a time, but Stanton found the duty challenging, even thrilling. Now retired, he missed the sea greatly. Retired. Perhaps he should say semiretired. Although he had officially left the navy eighteen months ago, he had been called back to duty twice. The first time was a little over a year ago, when the USS *Triggerfish*, a World War II Gato class submarine, mysteriously ran aground on a San Diego beach, fifty-six years after it had gone missing in the Atlantic. It was an event that forever changed his life, especially spiritually. The second recall occurred one hour and fifteen minutes ago.

"Don't worry, Skipper," the chief said. An embryonic smile creased his face. "We'll get you there in one piece."

The helo lurched, pitched up slightly, and then down again. The chief was unfazed. The gyrations seemed of no consequence to him. Apparently this was a smooth ride.

"If I'm not being out of line," the pilot began, "exactly where are we going, sir? I mean, I know the coordinates, but I didn't know there was a base there."

"Neither did I, Lieutenant," Stanton said. "My guess is that we weren't supposed to know. Just look for a small community of tract homes."

"I've got Hesperia and Victorville off to my right, and I can see the lights of Barstow north of us."

"Then we're getting close," Stanton said. "Just fly us to the coordinates."

"Aye, sir."

The speakers in Stanton's helmet fell silent for a moment, then the pilot's voice returned. "If this is none of my business, sir, then just say so, but what is so important that we all had to be yanked away from our turkey dinners?" Then he quickly added, "Not that I'm complaining, sir."

The pilot's account was correct. Stanton had just placed the first forkful of stuffing in his mouth when the front doorbell rang. Before he had answered the door, he had known something was wrong. His intuition had been dead on. Standing on his front porch were two of the navy's finest—military police. Their expressions were grave and stern. Stanton had swallowed his stuffing and said, "I don't suppose I could talk you gentlemen into waiting until dinner is over."

"No, sir," one of them had replied.

Turning back to the table, he faced his wife, brother-in-law and his wife, and the rest of the assembled family. No one spoke. There was nothing to say. Ten minutes later, Stanton was in his khaki uniform and seated in the backseat of the dark blue sedan used by the MPs. On the seat next to him was a bag containing two turkey sandwiches, a gift from his wife. In an act consistent with her nature, she had also made sack dinners for the two escorts. *Heaping burning coals upon their heads*, Stanton had thought. The Bible verse brought a short-lived smile to his face.

The trip from his Point Loma home to the North Island Naval Air Station on Coronado had taken only twenty minutes, but they slipped by languidly. Once on the base, he was ushered in to see Captain John Hollerman, the base commander. The conversation had been short.

"I feel horrible pulling you away from your family, Captain," Hollerman had said sincerely. "I wish we could have waited until tomorrow, but I don't have that option."

"I understand," Stanton replied, knowing that something significant must have happened.

Before Stanton could say anything else, Hollerman had walked around his desk. "I'll explain as we walk. I have a helicopter warming up." He led Stanton through the door and into the hall.

"Helicopter?"

"Yes, you're taking a short hop up north to the high desert." The base commander was being cryptic.

"High desert? China Lake?" China Lake was a naval air warfare center near Ridgecrest, California.

"No, someplace different. Someplace secret." Hollerman hesitated, then said, "I don't know much more than that. Actually, I'm in the dark. I've got orders to get you underway as soon as possible."

"May I ask who issued the orders?"

"Admiral Kaster of the Pentagon," Hollerman replied crisply. "I don't know what's going on, but something has put a bee in their collective bonnets, and they want you to fix it. Here," he had said, thrusting an envelope at Stanton. "This landed on my desk forty minutes ago. Arrived by special courier—an F-16 pilot to be exact. It's straight from the Pentagon. Apparently, someone thinks you're pretty special."

Stanton took the file. It read "Eyes Only" on the front and bore his name. The file was sealed.

"Wait until you're on the chopper," Hollerman said. "The file doesn't look very thick. You should have time to read it on your flight."

Apprehension began to boil in Stanton's mind. "You mean this was hand-carried from the Pentagon?"

"Exactly," Hollerman stated. "I know what you're thinking. There are a dozen ways to send secret material electronically. We do it all the time. As you know, it's not unusual for a ship or sub to receive secret flash messages. All that's done through satellites and advanced crypto."

"Then why the special courier?" Stanton wondered aloud.

"That really says something, doesn't it?" Hollerman answered. "My guess is that the Pentagon is keeping secrets from the Pentagon. It's one of those left hand not knowing what the right hand is doing situations."

As they emerged from the administration building, Stanton saw the same sedan and the same men who had ferried him from home. One of them opened the door to the backseat and Hollerman climbed in. Stanton followed.

"I am to see you to the helicopter," Hollerman said once he was seated. "From there, you're on your own. I wish I could offer you more help."

"I wish you could offer me more information," Stanton said.

Five minutes later, the car pulled up to the *Seahawk*. Its rotors were already spinning. Both men exited. Pausing, Stanton took in the sight of the fifty-foot-long, seventeen-foot-high craft. His stomach dropped. How anything that looked like a mutated grasshopper could fly was beyond him. Ships made sense, helicopters did not.

"Good luck, Captain," Hollerman said, offering a salute. "Somehow, I have a feeling you're going to need it."

Stanton returned the salute, ducked his head against the artificial wind created by the spinning rotor, and jogged to the *Seahawk*. Two minutes later he was airborne with the file in one hand and the sack dinner in the other.

"Sir?"

The voice jarred Stanton back to the present. "Sorry, Lieutenant. What was your question?"

"What's going on, sir? I mean, this was rather quick."

Looking back at the file he had been studying, Stanton wondered how to answer. The information was classified, so he was prohibited from directly speaking to the question. "I'm supposed to find somebody," he finally replied. *Actually*, he thought, *I'm supposed to find a whole bunch of somebodies*.

Gazing out the window, Stanton saw the glow of gold-yellow emanating from the high-pressure sodium streetlights of the small high desert cities of Hesperia and Victorville. They would be landing soon. The map in the file had told him exactly where he was going, and it was near. The sky was now dark with stygian gloom. The night seemed thick, ominous, disconcerting. His thoughts returned to the information in the file. It was fantastic, unbelievable. But he had been in the navy his entire adult life, a length of time measured in decades, and of one thing he was certain—the navy had no sense of humor. No matter how much he wished it so, this was no joke.

Now a middle-aged former submarine captain, he was being called upon to solve a very landlocked mystery. And he had no idea where to begin.

N

"There it is," the pilot of the *Seahawk* said, nodding forward. "Just where they said it would be."

"Can you set down on the parking lot?" Stanton asked. The folder he had been given contained a map of the top-secret Roanoke II compound. It also contained a detailed satellite photo. On the photo an area had been highlighted in yellow and marked "Golden Grain Supermarket." It was part of a small strip mall.

"There are quite a few cars, but the northwest corner looks clear enough," the pilot responded. "If you don't mind me saying so, Captain, this place doesn't look like any military base I've ever seen. Even the houses look better. Are you sure we've got the right spot?"

"You're the pilot, Lieutenant," Stanton said. "Did you stay on course?"

"Yes, sir, I did."

"Then this must be the place."

"If you say so, sir." Stanton could feel the helo slow and then hover. A moment later, it began its slow descent. Stanton's stomach turned. "It looks like you have company, sir."

"How's that?"

"A small group, about seventy-five yards from the landing zone."

Stanton thought about the file he had just read. This must be the team he was told to expect. Somehow they had arrived before him. "Any military?"

"Yes, sir. Looks like three marines. There are two Humvees also."

"They're mine, all right," Stanton said. At least there would be no waste of time.

The chief turned and slid open the door on the side of the fuselage. The cold night air rushed in, carrying with it the resonant thundering of the rotor. Stanton could see out the door and down the last one hundred feet of descent. As they neared the ground, the chief leaned his head out the door. Stanton felt the wheels of the helicopter touch the asphalt parking lot.

"Wheels on the ground," the chief stated perfunctorily. Immediately, the mighty engine began to slow as the pilot powered down the craft.

"There you go, Captain," the pilot said, with humor. "Safe, sound, and ten minutes early. Thank you for flying Air Navy."

"The pleasure has been all mine," Stanton said. "I can't remember when I had more fun."

"That's not sarcasm, is it, sir?"

"Maybe."

"Anytime you need a cab, just give me a call," the pilot rejoined. "Good luck, Captain."

Stanton thanked the pilot and crew and exited the *Seahawk*, lowering his head to protect himself from the rotor blast, and quickly walked to the small gathering of people who stood a short distance away. No sooner than Stanton was clear of the helo, he heard the engine throttle up. A minute later, the large helicopter was airborne and headed south toward San Diego. Stanton watched as the craft climbed higher and higher, the throbbing of its engine diminishing with distance.

"Captain Stanton," a firm voice said behind him. Stanton turned. Before him stood three marines in full urban BDUs—battle dress uniforms. Unlike the drab green fatigues shown in movies, these were black and mottled with four shades of gray. The three men came to attention and offered a salute.

"As you were," Stanton said, returning the gesture.

"Sir, I am First Lieutenant Alex Dole," the closest marine said. "With me are Sergeant Marc Ramsey and Staff Sergeant Penny Keagle."

Dole was tall and thin, and his face was pockmarked from what Stanton assumed had been a severe case of adolescent acne. His eyes were dark and narrow; his mouth thin and taut. He looked to be in his late twenties. Ramsey, on the other hand, was as large as Dole was thin. His skin was dark and fleshy. Despite his very American name, Stanton could easily see the man's Samoan heritage. He was large enough to play linebacker in the NFL. Despite his size, there was a peace in his round, pudgy face, a serenity that escaped definition. Penny Keagle was another matter. Nothing about her seemed peaceful. Her blue eyes were fixed intently on Stanton as if she could suck all there was to know about him through the invisible umbilical of her gaze. A small wisp of thin, brown hair hung loose from her cap. It was the only thing out of place. All three marines carried M-16 automatic rifles and holstered nine-millimeters.

"Good to meet you, Lieutenant," Stanton said. "Surely, you're not the sum total of security here."

"No, sir." Dole's words were sharp and crisp. "I have forty others, sir. I've set up a perimeter guard."

"Has there been any contact with outsiders?" Stanton asked.

"No, sir. The entire compound is tight as a drum. There is an eight-foot-high chain-link fence around the compound's perimeter. Perhaps you saw it as you flew overhead." Stanton had not. "No one has tried to make ingress since our arrival."

"Or egress," came another voice. The words were as chilly as the night wind. A man stepped forward. He was handsome and rugged, with gray eyes and thick brown brows. On his head was a blue baseball-style cap with the letters FBI emblazoned on it. He also wore a blue work coat with the same initials over the left breast.

"You must be Pierce Tulley," Stanton said, holding out his hand.

"That's right," Tulley responded coolly, ignoring Stanton's gesture. "Special Agent Tulley. I'm here to solve this little riddle, and I would appreciate being cut loose to do my job."

"Cut loose?"

"The gestapo won't let me work." Tulley pointed at Lieutenant Dole. "Every minute we let pass makes my job more difficult."

"I appreciate your enthusiasm," Stanton said evenly. "But Lieutenant Dole is following orders."

"I don't care," Tulley spat. "I'm not in the navy or the marines or any other service. I'm FBI and I demand the right to do my job."

Stanton felt his patience evaporating. While he was home, seated before the Thanksgiving meal that his wife had labored over all day, he was just another man, living in a typical house in a familiar neighborhood, and happy to be just that. Even after the military escort had arrived at his door, and he had donned his uniform, he still felt quite average. But things were changing rapidly. He was now immersed in a mystery that made no sense, and to make things worse, a member of his team was developing into an annoying twit. Tulley was pushing him, and Stanton didn't like being pushed. It was time to make a statement of leadership. Not just for Tulley but for the sake of the men under his command.

"Mr. Tulley," Stanton said stiffly, his voice a half octave lower. "Where are you?"

"What?" Tulley was nonplussed, confused by the sudden change in Stanton's demeanor. It was the response Stanton was seeking. He wanted the FBI man off guard.

"Where are you?" Stanton repeated.

"I . . . I don't understand." Tulley leaned back involuntarily.

"Then let me help." Stanton leaned closer to Tulley. "You are in a navy housing area associated with a naval research facility. A great many navy personnel and their families are missing. Are you with me so far?"

"Yes, but—"

"This is a naval investigation. I am a navy captain, and I have been charged with finding out what has happened."

"Of course, but—"

"I intend to fulfill that mission as I have fulfilled every mission assigned to me. I am in charge. I am in control. I will call the shots. You have been assigned by your superiors to help me with that task. Therefore, you will follow my lead. We will do this the right way. Is that clear to you, Mr. Tulley?"

Tulley frowned deeply and his eyes blazed, but he had understood. "Yes, *Captain*. I understand perfectly."

"If you are unable to work under my command, then say so now, and I will have the good lieutenant here drive you off base. I'm sure your superiors have another man who would be happy to help our cause."

"There will be no need for that," Tulley replied. The bitterness in his voice was unmistakable.

"Very well." Stanton straightened and turned to the others. "Are we all clear on this?"

The other two civilians nodded, but the marines came to attention. "Sir, yes, sir!"

"Mr. Dole," Stanton said to the marine lieutenant. "I assume you have a place for us to meet."

"Yes, sir, I do, sir." There was a small, tight grin on his face. Clearly he had enjoyed the tête-à-tête he had just witnessed.

"Lead on, Lieutenant. It's getting cold out here."

"Yes, sir. Please follow me."

As the team turned to follow the three marines, Stanton took a moment to make eye contact with the two members of the team he had yet to meet. One was a distinguished elderly man, whom Stanton recognized from his briefing folder as Mason Eddington, civilian consultant to the navy; the other was a woman dressed in the same blue FBI jacket and cap as Tulley—she was smiling at him.

Diverting his gaze from the woman, Stanton quickly took in his surroundings. Light standards spaced evenly through the parking lot cast an eerie penumbral sulfur light, carving shadows from the night. Stanton was not a superstitious man, but the night seemed unusual, heavy, augural, oppressive. It was as if the night sky knew something—something secret, something sinister. Above him glittered the frozen flecks of starlight and the ivory half moon.

Gathering his thoughts, he marched through the rows of empty parked cars that waited patiently for their owners—owners who were gone. Lined in neat rows, the autos reminded Stanton of headstones in a graveyard.

Stanton shuddered involuntarily.

N

The makeshift command post was set up in the small banquet room of the Quail Wing restaurant. The eatery was typical of many such establishments and looked as if it had been modeled on a Denny's or some other franchise. Since form followed function, that was to be expected. What was unexpected were the tables set with food and drink. A plate of meatloaf and mashed potatoes rested on the table of one booth. Opposite, where the diner's companion had been seated, was a chef's salad and a glass of water. A paper napkin lay on the green carpet. Every booth told the same story of meals served, but unfinished; drinks poured, but never consumed.

As Dole led the group through the dining area toward the back to where the banquet room was, Stanton noted other disturbing things. The drawer of the cash register hung halfway open, resting on its metal tracks. Twenties, tens, fives, and ones could be seen in their respective slots. *Who would leave a register drawer open like that?* Stanton wondered.

"Everything was left as we found it," Dole said loudly. "Not a plate of food has been touched. We did, however, turn off the burners on the stove and grill. That was necessary."

"Why necessary?" Stanton asked.

"Because food had been left cooking on them. Or what used to be food."

"Left cooking?" Stanton was having trouble believing what he was hearing.

"Yes, sir," Dole said. "Three steaks and six hamburger patties, as well as soups, potatoes, and the like, on the stove. We also turned off the coffeemakers."

"Doesn't make much sense, does it?" Stanton said. "Food left on plates, burners left on. It's as if the people left in a panic, but all the cars are neatly parked outside."

"They didn't leave in a panic," Tulley said with authority. "Silverware still sits on the table, and not a single drink, not a single coffee cup has been toppled. At least we know it was evening when it happened. Whatever 'it' is."

"How so?" Dole asked.

"The meals, Lieutenant," Tulley said, sounding like a teacher with a slow student. "They're all dinner meals: meatloaf, steak, hamburgers, and so on. It's obvious, really. If we were seeing oatmeal, fried eggs, and toast, then we would know that whatever happened, occurred in the morning."

Once in the banquet room, Stanton said, "All right, everyone take a seat. I think we all share Agent Tulley's desire to get to the bottom of this, but I want to make sure we're all on the same page. Let's begin with you, Lieutenant. Start from the beginning."

Dole started to stand, but Stanton motioned him to remain seated. The man had probably been on his feet for the better part of twenty-four hours.

"Yes, sir. At 0315 hours my security team was ordered from Camp Pendleton. We were given very little information, other than to search and report. Forty of us arrived by helicopter at 0425 hours. I ordered two squads to do a perimeter search and secure the area. The rest of my team began a house-to-house search. There are six hundred and fifty private homes, forty-five commercial establishments, and four research buildings. We have not gained access to those. Four hours ago, I was told that someone from the navy would arrive to take charge of the mission. I guess that's you, sir. Two hours later a helicopter arrived with the others. I restricted their movements until your arrival."

"That's an understatement," Tulley sniped.

"You'll have your turn, Agent Tulley," Stanton said firmly. "Continue, Lieutenant."

"There isn't a great deal to report, sir. We have found no one. Not a single person. Everything else seems in order. Just like this restaurant. It looks like there were people here, and then they just evaporated."

"People don't evaporate," Tulley said. "They have either left of their own free will, or been forcefully moved out, maybe abducted. We can be sure of that. We can also be certain that they have not evaporated."

"All right, Mr. Tulley," Stanton said wearily. "Since you insist on being heard, let's hear from you."

"Since I have been prevented from doing my work, I have nothing to offer. I've been cooling my heels for two hours."

"My briefing paper says you're an evidence specialist," Stanton said.

"That's right. I specialize in abductions. I was ordered here from the Los Angeles office. The navy provided a plane and I was flown to Edwards Air Force Base in Palmdale, then here."

"*We* were ordered here," the woman corrected, speaking for the first time. "Someone in the Department of Defense contacted someone in the Department of Justice who contacted our L.A. office—and here we are." She removed her FBI cap and set it on the table. Thick black hair, previously held back by the hat, hung over her ears and down to the middle of her neck. Her face was round and the color of alabaster. She smiled again. "I'm Special Agent Loren Wendt," she said. Stanton already knew this from the briefing folder. "I specialize in evidence recovery. I'm AIC Tulley's partner."

"AIC?" Dole asked.

"Agent in Charge," Wendt said. Dole nodded.

"We've been assigned to help you in your investigation," Wendt offered. "The FBI is at your disposal."

Tulley grumbled and shifted in his chair.

"From Mr. Tulley's complaints, I assume you have nothing to offer at this time."

"That's correct," Wendt said.

"You must be Dr. Mason Eddington," Stanton said to the silver-haired man to his right. He was stoutly built and, according to the briefing folder, sixty-two years of age. His silver hair was worn straight back and long to the collar. He reminded Stanton of an orchestra conductor: stately, professional, confident, in control.

"That's correct, Captain," Eddington replied. His voice was deep and richly resonant.

"My file says that you're a consultant to the navy," Stanton prodded.

The man offered a small smile and dipped his head in a slight bow. "Guilty as charged."

Stanton waited for more, but Eddington offered nothing else.

"And on what do you consult for the navy?" Stanton asked.

Eddington hesitated before answering, as if he were weighing each word before allowing it to issue past his lips. "Most of it is classified, Captain, but I can say this: I built Roanoke II."

"You built it?" Stanton inquired.

"Perhaps I should say that Roanoke II is my project. I supervised it for the navy. And before you ask, I have no idea what is going on. This is as much a mystery to me as it is to you. In fact . . ." He trailed off and his expression soured.

"In fact, what?" Tulley asked.

"I live here for part of the year. Had I not been gone to my daughter's in Ventura, I would be one of the missing." He took a deep breath and let it out. Stanton could see the thought frightened him. "I had friends here, Captain. Dear friends."

"Had?" Tulley snapped. "You sound like they're all dead."

Eddington spoke no words, but the fear on his face said a great deal. He studied Tulley with a piercing gaze, then finally said, "I hope not, Mr. Tulley. I hope not."

Chapter 2

Winter, 1500 B.C.

Oya stumbled and fell. The harsh and sharp shards of decomposed granite pierced the skin of his knees and hands. Blood began to run freely. Oya was oblivious to the scorching pain of the fall, and to the icy cold of the snow which continued to fall from the high, black clouds. Tears poured from his eyes and fell to the white-covered ground, joining the blood that dripped from his fingers.

Rising to his feet again, he began to run. It was foolishness. The full moon was barely visible through a rift in the thick clouds. The dark of night blanketed him like the snow blanketed the earth. But he ran anyway. And he fell again. Rose. Fell. Rose. Fell. With each tumble, he injured himself all the more. Once he barked his shin on an unseen boulder; another time, he tripped over a fallen Joshua tree, its spiky trunk piercing and ripping the skin from his legs.

Pain no longer mattered. Nothing mattered. So he ran up the mountainside until he stumbled again; and when he could run no longer, he staggered; and when he could stagger no longer, he crawled; and when he could crawl no farther, he collapsed on his back, staring through wet eyes into the distant, slate-dark sky.

Flakes of snow fluttered down in the still night like tiny white leaves.

He lay without moving in the frosty snow, uncaring about the heat that flowed from his body. This was a good way to die. Numb, cold, and alone. He wondered, how had his family died? If they were dead. What else could they be? He had seen no bodies, but then he had seen the unbelievable. The village was gone. His friends, his family gone. Everything they owned remained: clothing, blankets, arrows, everything still in its place. Cooking fires blazed. Handmade children's toys lay scattered about. But the people were gone.

He had arrived late, having underestimated the time it would take for him to return from the day's hunting. He had killed two rabbits late in the evening and was bringing them home. Darkness had fallen and more clouds had poured in. The walk was treacherous, but possible if he was careful. By the time the clouds had blotted out the moon, he was in sight of the village, his feet crunching through a snow that had begun that morning. He could see the cook fires, but something was wrong. As he approached, using the fires as his guide, he heard nothing. The gentle breeze should have carried the noise of conversation and children playing to his ears, but there was nothing. Just silence.

Then he saw them: the dancing white fires that flew like giant glowing hummingbirds, darting from place to place over the village. It was as if three stars had fallen from the sky and were swooping like vultures over his home.

Oya began to run.

Empty. Horrible emptiness. Every abode empty. His friends, gone. His family, gone. Like the dew after the first rays of sun, they had just ceased to be.

At first, Oya had assumed that they had walked off, or worse been taken captive, but the snow proved him wrong. There was only one set of tracks coming into the village—his own. With torch in hand, he had searched every abode, as well as the surrounding area. He cried out the names of his young wife, his child, his brothers and sisters, but was answered only by the yammering of distant coyotes.

The flying stars had left before he made his way into the village. He had watched them rise higher and higher in the sky, floating upward like smoke on a windless day. He begged them to come back and bring with them his people. He cursed them, caring not if they were gods.

Surrounded by his own footprints, Oya came to know that he was alone. Miserably alone.

He wept.

He ran.

He fell.

Now, lying on his back in the cold snow, sharp rocks pressing their way into his muscles, Oya continued to weep. Alone. Lost. Empty. He had no idea how he knew this, but he knew that whatever had taken his people would never return them.

Slowly, Oya sat up and stared at the village fires that were now several hundred strides away, and mourned his loss. His father had been there, an old but respected elder. He longed to see him, his brothers, his wife and his child.

Overhead, the clouds parted again, and the white light of the moon set the landscape aglow. Looking to his left, he saw something that brought more tears to his eyes: a scraping—images etched into a large stone by his father. His father had been the storyteller, and his stories were etched onto the flat surface of rocks for others to see. They told of hunting expeditions and myths. When he had become too old to hunt, his father had brought the young children here and told them the stories of their ancestors, pointing to the images abraded onto the stones.

Here the children learned the wisdom of those who had lived here before.

At his feet lay a palm-sized rock, broad on one end, narrow on the other. Oya picked it up and turned to the story stone. A blank place remained at the top. Slowly and lovingly, he began to scrape and rub the face of the rock with the stone he held in his bloody hand.

First, he drew a stick image of his wife, then one of his son, then his father. He chipped and scraped, scraped and chipped until the image of his village could be seen. Lastly, he added the three flying stars. He did so with anger and hatred, pounding at the rock face more than scraping it.

Finally, the story was told. Oya lay down in the snow and waited for death.

Chapter 3

23 November 2000; 1755 hours
Roanoke II, The Quail Wing Restaurant

"That was the first place we looked, Captain," Dole said. "After we realized that the houses were empty, I sent teams out to investigate any building large enough to hold fifteen hundred people. There aren't very many of them."

"Schools, too?"

"Yes, sir. But I imagine the schools were already closed by that time. As Agent Tulley noted, the disappearance seems to have taken place around dinnertime. Maybe later."

"That's what's confusing," Stanton said. "My file says that radar at Edwards picked up their first anomaly at 0245. That's a long time after supper."

Dole turned to Eddington. "Mr. Eddington, we have found three buildings we couldn't enter. Each of them has a security fence around them and the doors are made of steel. Each entry point has a camera above it and a keypad lock. I assume that these are research buildings."

"You assume correctly, Lieutenant."

Dole looked at Stanton.

"What about it, Eddington?" Stanton asked. "Could the people be in those buildings?"

"I don't see how, Captain," Eddington replied. "Certainly not all of them. There wouldn't be room to breathe. The buildings are rather small."

"I think we should check them out," Dole remarked.

"I agree," Stanton said.

"Captain, the research done here carries the highest D.O.D. security level. I can't allow soldiers to walk willy-nilly through the halls. The Pentagon would be most upset."

"It was the Pentagon that sent me here," Stanton countered. "We need to see those buildings." Eddington leaned back in his chair and crossed his arms, lowering his head as if in deep thought. Stanton decided on a different tack. "The anomalous objects picked up by radar, are they associated with the research done here?"

"I really can't talk about our research, Captain."

Stanton was nonplussed. "Why not?"

"I've told you, this is a secure area and the work is above top secret."

Stanton stood and leaned over the table. His words were hushed but heavy, laden with intensity. "Dr. Eddington. We are not a tour group. We are a specially selected team charged with the finding of fifteen hundred missing people. I carry a top-secret clearance, and the Department of Defense has granted the same clearance to everyone on this team."

"It's all need to know," Eddington said flatly. "Security clearances mean nothing."

"What?" Tulley said. "What kind of logic is that?"

"Need to know," was all Eddington said.

Tulley looked at Stanton. "What's he mean?"

Stanton sighed. "The D.O.D. grants three levels of clearance based on the perceived threat to the country: confidential, secret, and top secret. But possessing a top-secret clearance doesn't mean that you can look at everything classified top secret. It's all on a need-to-know basis. If there's no reason for you to have that information to carry out your job, then you can be denied access to material, regardless of any clearance you possess. You have to be able to show that the information designated top secret is instrumental to your mission."

Tulley sniggered. "Finding fifteen hundred people isn't reason enough?"

"They can't be in those buildings," Eddington said. He was looking down at the table, avoiding eye contact.

"Can you open those buildings?" Stanton asked, straightening his stance.

"Yes, but the people can't be there, so I won't."

"Perhaps a call to the Pentagon will help," Stanton said. "To whom do you answer there?"

"That's secret, too."

Stanton was becoming irritated. Time was accelerating at race-car speeds, and Eddington was being obstinate and obtuse. "How can that be? Surely you have a superior."

"Not really," Eddington said. "I've been given carte blanche on this project."

"What about your superiors?" Tulley said. "We can't be sitting on our fannies in some restaurant while James Bond here stonewalls us."

"It wouldn't do any good," Eddington said. "Even the Pentagon has its secrets. Departments keep secrets from one another. This is a black project, Captain. The blackest."

"Black project?" Wendt asked. "I don't understand."

"It's a term used to describe secret research and development. The projects are secretly funded, their monies concealed under other projects, or through inflated billing."

"You mean like the military paying $300 for a hammer, or $500 for an ashtray?" Wendt asked.

"Exactly," Stanton replied.

"So, how about contacting your superiors, Captain?" Tulley asked. "How long would that take?"

"Not long to contact them, but it could take hours to find out who is really in charge of this project."

"That's too long," Tulley snapped.

"I agree," Stanton said and turned to face Dole. Dole was glowering at Eddington, his eyes fixed and his mouth pulled tight. Stanton could imagine Dole's eyes glowing red with anger—too much anger. "Lieutenant?"

Dole continued to stare.

"Lieutenant!" Stanton said more loudly. This time Dole snapped his head around, his face still stone hard with hostility.

"Yes, sir. Sorry, sir." He took a deep breath.

"Are you all right, Lieutenant?"

"Yes, sir!" he said crisply. "I'm just a little concerned about this . . . delay."

"As I am," Stanton agreed. "You said your men did a search of the secured buildings?"

"The outside, sir."

"Are they still there?"

"Yes, sir. I left men at each of the three buildings."

"Can you make ingress on your own?"

Dole's face lightened with a smile. "Yes, sir," he said enthusiastically. "We came ready for bear. It will take a little time, but my men can have the necessary tools to the sites in short order."

"Very well," Stanton said. "Make it happen."

"Yes, sir." Dole was on his feet and talking into his radio. His commands came quickly and efficiently. Dole, Stanton decided, was a man who knew what he was doing. No doubt, he was the best in the area.

"You can't do this!" Eddington objected. "You don't have the right."

"Sometimes, Dr. Eddington, it is easier to get forgiveness than permission."

"You may find the Pentagon a very unforgiving bunch," Eddington countered.

"I was pulled from a Thanksgiving meal with my family and flown out here with a simple set of orders. Get to the bottom of Roanoke II. I plan to do just that. And from this moment on, I expect your full cooperation in all matters."

Eddington said nothing, but his frustration was evident on his face.

"What now?" Tulley asked.

"Now we get to work," Stanton answered quickly. "Now we find our people."

"It's about time," Tulley stated.

Choosing to ignore the jibe, Stanton asked, "What do you need to see to start your work?"

"That's the hard part," Wendt said before Tulley could respond. "This isn't a typical crime scene. Best we can tell so far, there is no incident point. In a murder there is a body which is usually found at the place of the killing. Even if the body has been moved, we still have a body and know there is a site where the killing took place."

"Or in the case of a kidnapping," said Tulley, seizing the conversation back, "we have a place of abduction, family, and friends to question. Here we have none of that."

"So what do you propose?" Stanton asked.

"If we don't have a place to start, then we can start anywhere."

"Got it," Stanton said. "Lieutenant, I want to see what you've seen. Take me to a house, then to a store or shop. When your men pop the lid on the research building, tell them to hold their ground. No one is to go in until we are all there. Clear?"

"Perfectly, sir."

Stanton looked out the window. The light from the restaurant fell on a small cottonwood tree which was bending in the wind, its leaves fluttering like a thousand little flags. The weather was turning bad. Wind blew from the north, and he recalled seeing dark clouds moving in from the same direction. He wished he had thought to bring a coat. The others seemed ready for the weather. The marines wore heavy urban camouflage BDUs, the FBI agents had their blue field jackets, and even Eddington had a thick coat. Perhaps they had had more warning than he. San Diego had been warm for the season, and all he wore were his khakis and a navy blue ball cap with the name of the USS *Maine*, the submarine he formally skippered, emblazoned on it.

"Begging the captain's pardon," Dole said, "we have an additional battle dress uniform in the Humvee. I'm sure it will fit." He paused and surrendered a small smile. "Of course, Captain, it is a marine uniform. You will be warmer, however."

Although the marines were a division of the navy, it was truth written on paper and not on the heart of any marine. Their mission was different, as were their ratings and rank. Only their pride was the same. "Freeze or wear a marine uniform, is that it?"

"Yes, sir."

"I'll try not to get it too dirty."

"That's all right, sir," Dole said. "Marines aren't afraid of dirt." Dole motioned to the big Samoan, who stepped from the restaurant and returned a moment later with a canvas bag.

Stanton took it. It felt heavy in his hand. "I'll be back in five, and then we move out."

"Yes, sir."

The others had risen to their feet, but not Eddington. He chose to remain planted where he was, but he knew he could not stay there. They would require that he accompany them. *Idiots. Fools.* Eddington closed his eyes. He had to think, to reason. It would take time for Dole's men to find a way into any of the three secured labs. He had seen to it that no one could get in easily. The doors were solid steel and rode along on tracks instead of swinging on hinges. All the windows had been mounted high and were made of three-inch Plexiglas. Anyone who thought they could climb a ladder and break out a window to gain access would be sorely disappointed. Then there were the walls. Each unit was constructed of concrete tilt-up partitions. Six inches of solid ferroconcrete—concrete and steel bars molded into a single unit.

Still, a squad of men with the right tools and enough patience could create a way in. There had to be a way to see that that never came to pass. Too much was at stake; there was too much to lose. He had devoted his life to such projects and had created many such facilities. He, Dr. Mason Eddington, was one of the few civilians who could walk down the corridors of the Pentagon and be recognized by nearly every admiral and general. And he knew them. He knew them by their first names and had met their families, kidded their children, flattered their wives.

They came to him for advice, for ideas, and he had provided them with everything they needed. He was a legend in every "skunk works" factory in the country, and here he was being treated like an ogre. They couldn't understand. They didn't know the cost. Sure, there were people missing—a lot of people. He understood that, but he had to remain true to his cause. His work was important, even world-changing. Nothing would be the same when he and his crew were done.

The last thought stopped him. He no longer had a crew. He alone was left with the project. He alone knew of its full power and capabilities.

Eddington drew in a deep breath. He was alone. He was confused. He was puzzled. Just what had happened? Where were his team of researchers and their families?

"Let's move." It was Stanton. He was standing at the entrance to the banquet room, dressed in black and gray fatigues, his navy ball cap covering his brown hair. He was looking directly at Eddington.

Slowly, Eddington rose and walked behind the others as they left the restaurant. He would have to do something. The project must be protected, no matter what had happened.

N

The wind gusted angrily, carrying with it small bits of dust and sand that stung the skin. The team walked briskly across the macadam parking lot, and then split into two groups, each entering one of the large, green Humvees. Stanton crawled into the passenger seat, while Dole sat behind the wheel. In the back sat Dr. Eddington and Agent Loren Wendt. Tulley rode with the other marines in the second vehicle. The division was not an accident. Stanton wanted Eddington and Wendt in his car.

No sooner had the vehicle pulled out than Stanton asked, "Why Roanoke II, Dr. Eddington?"

"What do you mean?"

"The name. Why Roanoke II?"

Eddington chortled. "Politics, Captain. Politics and money."

"How so?"

"As I said earlier," Eddington replied, "this whole facility is a black project. That means that money is hard to come by.

Politicians are becoming less likely to earmark funds for such things. The end of the cold war was wonderful in many ways, but devastating to military research and development. It takes some rather creative approaches to make congressmen open their budgetary purses."

"And?" Stanton prompted.

"There was one senator standing in our way. So we had to finesse him. He's from California, so we initially proposed that the site be constructed in North Dakota. We knew he'd protest, so we went ahead with plans for the current location. That way it would look as if we were making concessions. You know, making him feel like he was in control."

"I don't see what that has to do with the name Roanoke II," Wendt said.

"We all have egos, Agent Wendt," Eddington said. "Senator White was no different. He has an ego so thirsty for recognition that it takes a tanker truck of praise to satiate it. Knowing his lineage, we changed the site name to Roanoke II."

"Ah," Stanton said with understanding. "John White."

"I don't get it," Wendt said, puzzled.

"John White," Stanton began, "was the one who discovered that the one hundred plus colonists on Roanoke Island had disappeared. Early 1590s, I think. The colony was founded in 1587 by Sir Walter Raleigh, who left the next year. He sent John White back with provisions. The plan had been for White to return to the colony years earlier, but he was delayed by the war between Spain and England. Anyway, Senator White is related through a series of brothers, cousins, and grandparents to old John White himself."

"And that made him throw his support behind you?" Wendt asked Eddington.

"Not that alone," Eddington admitted. "It was just one of the straws that broke the camel's back. Ultimately, it was the wisdom of the project that swayed him, but the name helped. Ironic, isn't it?" Eddington paused. "Another Roanoke with empty houses."

"Eerie is more like it," Wendt said.

"Stop!" Stanton ordered. Something had caught his eye. "Pull over there."

"Where?" Lieutenant Dole asked, his head snapping back and forth, scanning for whatever it was that had caused Stanton to issue the sudden command.

"The gas station," Stanton answered, pointing off to his right.

Dole directed the large Humvee off the road, up the concrete apron, and onto the grounds of the Unocal service station. "What is it, Captain? What do you see?"

Without answering, Stanton stepped from the vehicle and briskly walked toward the pumps. Dole followed, M16 in hand. He thumbed off the safety.

A car was parked next to the pumps; its front door hung open. Stanton peered in. The vehicle was a late model Lexus with tan leather seats. The interior was immaculately clean. Keys hung from the ignition, like a stilled pendulum. Looking in the backseat, Stanton saw something that chilled him—an empty child's car seat.

"Captain?" Dole prompted. "Did you see something?"

"The car caught my attention. The nozzle is still in the gas port and the door is open." Stanton studied the nozzle. "The trigger is still locked in the open position." He turned to the pump. It was one of the devices that took credit and debit cards. A small narrow screen flashed blue letters: PLEASE REPLACE NOZZLE. PLEASE REPLACE NOZZLE. The LCD display on the pump read 11.25 gallons, $15.30.

"More proof that whatever happened, happened quickly," Wendt said. Stanton watched as she peered in the car. "Woman driver," she said flatly.

"How do you know that?" Stanton asked, wondering what he missed. "A whiff of perfume?"

"That would only tell us that a woman had been in the car," Wendt responded. "The key chain is the real giveaway. It has a small pom-pom on it. Something like what an alumnus might receive."

"They teach you that in FBI school?" Dole asked as he peered into the front seat.

"I learned a great deal at the Academy, but not that. I learned about pom-poms from John Quincy Adams high school in Oregon."

"You were a cheerleader?" Dole said with surprise.

"Don't look so shocked, Lieutenant. Cheerleaders have ambitions too." She reached in and pulled the keys from the ignition. "You can tell a lot about a person from their keys. In addition to the pom-pom, there is a tiny flashlight. She probably arrives home after sundown most nights and needs the flashlight to find the keyhole. That means that she's returning to a dark house. Hubby must work nights, or perhaps she's divorced." She examined the other keys more closely. "Not divorced," she corrected herself. "There's another set of car keys here. Late model Ford if the stamp on the key is to be believed. There are several other keys with the words 'Do Not Reproduce' marked into the metal. I would guess that she works in a school or at one of the research sites."

"That's a lot to assume from a few keys," Stanton said. He was impressed with her confidence.

"You couldn't build a case on it, but it says something about the owner." Wendt opened the door to the backseat and froze. Her expression of concern was instantly replaced by profound consternation.

"What is it?" Stanton asked, stepping forward. He looked in the backseat and saw only a child's car seat. It was the same seat he had noticed before. "What do you see?"

"The car seat, Captain," Wendt replied quietly, reverently. Stanton watched as she leaned into the vehicle, brushed something into her hand, then stood erect again. She held her palm out, as if someone had poured gold dust into it. Centered in her cupped hand was a small pile of white chips.

"What's that?" Dole asked.

"Crumbs," Wendt answered. "Saltine cracker crumbs, to be exact. The kind of thing you give to a hungry child who is noisily impatient for dinner."

"I noticed the car seat, too," Stanton offered. "It's shocking to think that children are missing. It doesn't seem right."

"It isn't right, Captain. And that's not all that's wrong." Wendt brushed the crumbs from her hand, then pointed at the car seat. "That's a bigger problem."

It took a few moments of study before Stanton picked up on Wendt's point. The thought made him all the more uneasy. "I see," he said softly.

"I don't," Dole confessed.

"The child's seatbelt," Wendt explained. "It's the typical three-point restraint used on most car seats."

"So?" Dole said.

"So, it's still latched," Wendt said numbly. "The seatbelt is latched. There's no way the mother could have pulled her child out of the seat without first unbuckling him . . . or her."

"Couldn't she have just buckled it again?" Dole said.

Wendt shook her head. "Could, but wouldn't. What's the sense in it? She would only have to unbuckle it again to put her child back in. Not likely."

"Are you saying that the child just disappeared from the seat?" Dole was doubtful.

"That's what it looks like," Wendt said. "It doesn't make sense, and there certainly isn't anything here to prove it, but still . . ."

Her voice trailed off and her brow wrinkled. "Where's her purse?"

"Her purse?" Stanton said. "I have no idea."

Wendt returned to the front seat, bent over, and ran her hand under the seat. Nothing. Putting one knee on the driver's seat, she stretched across the interior of the vehicle until she could reach the glove compartment. A moment later she had it open and removed a small black leather handbag.

Snapping open the bag, Wendt removed a thin wallet. Stanton and Dole stepped next to her. She tossed the handbag on the front seat and pulled open the wallet. The first thing Stanton saw was a family photo of a man in his mid twenties, a woman of similar age with wavy blonde hair, and cuddled in her arms, an infant dressed in blue. *A boy*, he thought.

"This picture is at least six months old," Wendt said. "The car seat is too large for an infant." She flipped through the wallet until she found the woman's driver's license. "Mary Fenton, born July 15, 1974. Now we have a name."

"One name out of fifteen hundred," Dole said.

Wendt cut him a stern glance. "Never overlook a victim's name, Lieutenant. Everyone has a right to an identity."

Stanton understood her sentiment. Something was terribly wrong, and whatever "it" was, had absconded with an entire town. He stepped back from the others, intent on crossing the concrete bay and entering the small store located in the service station's metal building, when he saw a movement, a glimpse of something small and white just beyond the little mart. "What—hey!" He broke into a run.

"Captain?" Dole said. "What is it?"

Stanton took a few steps, then shouted to Dole, "You're with me." Out of the corner of his eye, Stanton saw that Dole was on the move, the muzzle of his M16 pointed into the air. As Dole ran, he pulled the microphone of his radio to his mouth and keyed it. "Ramsey, I want you and Keagle here on the double. Unocal gas station."

"Take the far side," Stanton said, motioning to the other end of the small building. "I think I saw someone, but I can't be sure. Just a glimpse of white." Dole jogged back around the building as Stanton came to the right rear corner. He stopped, inhaled deeply, and started to peek around the edge when he heard something behind him. With a start, he snapped his head around and saw Wendt, her hand on the grip of her pistol which was still snug in its holster. He had not seen the gun before and assumed that it had been hidden beneath the field jacket.

"What—" she began, but Stanton silenced her with an upraised hand.

Sensing that Dole had had enough time to round the front of the shop, Stanton slowly peered around the edge of the building. Nothing. A stack of old tires was piled against the wall. A pay phone was mounted to the exterior, its receiver hanging loose by its cable. At the rear property line was a three-foot-high concrete block wall in front of which grew feeble juniper bushes.

Dole emerged from around the far corner. His motions were slow, deliberate, guarded. Stanton stepped away from the building and onto the asphalt drive that separated the building from the block wall. Wendt followed, her hand still ready to draw her weapon.

Walking to the wall, Stanton stared over the other side. Again, nothing. Just another asphalt patch like the one on which he stood, except this one spanned the distance between the block wall and a doughnut shop. Looking to his right, he saw an auto parts store and, to his left, a hardware store. Typical suburban businesses in what looked like a typical suburban neighborhood.

"I was sure I saw something," Stanton said.

"You didn't see it full on?" Dole asked.

"No. Just a glimpse out of the corner of my eye." He pursed his lips with frustration. "It's not here now."

"Could it have been a dog or something?" Wendt asked.

"I suppose, but that wasn't the sense I got. I thought maybe it was somebody, but why would they run?"

The sound of a speeding vehicle rolled through the night air. A moment later, the other Humvee pulled alongside them. Both Ramsey and Keagle were out of the vehicle the moment it stopped.

"Take a drive around," Dole said. "The captain saw something. Possibly small and white. Let me know if you see anything." Seconds later, the Humvee with Ramsey, Keagle, and Agent Tulley was gone. Dole turned back to Stanton. "What now, Captain?"

Drawing himself up, Stanton said, "We carry on." He was uncertain of exactly what that meant. Overhead, the last star blinked out as a thick, funereal shroud of clouds congealed into a mass of tangled blackness. The first raindrops began to fall.

Chapter 4

23 September 1880; midafternoon
Farm outside Gallatin, Tennessee

"Faster!"

Sarah Lang stopped abruptly, dropped the wooden handle of the wagon to the ground, and turned to face her brother. "George, do I look like a horse to you?"

"Yes," he said with a shrill laugh. "A big, old plow horse."

Closing her deep blue eyes, Sarah inhaled deeply. Her eight-year-old brother was a growing source of irritation. When would he grow up? She, at the mature age of eleven, had already put away such childish behavior. But it seemed that George never would. A breeze, still warm from a lingering summer and heavy with the smell of hay, caressed her face and tousled her long black hair—hair just like her mother's, except Mama's was now streaked with silver.

"Yup," George said between giggles. "A big, lazy plow horse."

"I'll have you know," Sarah said seriously, propping her hands on her hips as she had seen her mother do so often, "that I am not a horse, and I am not old. Besides, it's my turn. Papa said that we had to play fair, and I've already pulled you around the yard twice. It's my turn to ride in the wagon."

David Lang had brought the small wagon home from Nashville just yesterday. It had been too dark to play with then, and there had been a few chores left to do. Today was the first time she had been able to play with the toy.

"Once more around, Sarah," George pleaded. "Just once more, then it'll be your turn."

"That's what you said last time."

"Pleeeese. I promise. This will be the last time for me, then it will be your turn."

"Not until you say you're sorry for calling me a horse."

"Just pull the wagon, Sarah."

"No."

"I'll tell Papa," George said.

"Go ahead. See if I care."

"There's no need to tell me anything." The strong, deep voice startled Sarah, and she spun around. Her father, tall and thin, stood on the porch. Next to him was Mama. His skin was dark and leathery from the sun. Deep wrinkles, like irrigation ditches, surrounded his eyes. Brown and gray stubble covered his chin. He had spoken loudly, but then he always did. "I didn't bring that wagon home so you kids could fight over it. You want me to take it back?"

"No, Papa," Sarah and George said in unison.

Sarah knew that her father would never take the wagon back. He was a stern man, but he was always fair, always loving.

"I was thinking of taking a little ride in it myself," David Lang said. His mouth parted into a grin that revealed large, yellow teeth. "Your ma wants me to take her into town. I was thinking of using the wagon."

"Oh, no, you don't," Mary Lang said, playfully punching her husband's arm. Mary was large, with blue eyes a shade paler than her daughter's, and smooth pink skin. "I'd sooner ride into town on your back than get in that little bit of a thing."

Sarah laughed. It always pleased her to see her parents tease each other. Many of her friends at school had parents that were humorless and harsh. Always demanding, always yelling. Sarah was thankful for the home she had.

"Are you really going into town, Papa?" Sarah asked excitedly. The thought of a trip, short as it was, had made her forget her selfish brother.

"Yes, ma'am," David Lang said. "Got to. Your mama won't make supper tonight if I don't. She's holding a chicken hostage and threatening not to cook it unless I take her."

"Can I go with you, Papa?" Sarah asked.

"Me, too?" George added.

"I don't know. I barely have enough room on my back for your ma."

"Oh, Papa," Sarah said with a laugh. "We could take the buggy."

"The buggy?" Lang ran a rough hand across his stubble-laden chin. Sarah could hear its rough scratching from where she stood in the yard. "Take the buggy, eh? I suppose we could do that. It sure would be more comfortable. But then again . . ."

"What, Papa?"

"You and George have been making quite a ruckus out here. I don't know if I want all that noise in the buggy with me."

"I'm sorry, Papa," Sarah said quickly. "But George called me a horse."

"Is that true, George?" Lang asked seriously, an effect that was rendered powerless by a wink.

George lowered his head. "Yes, Papa."

"Well, that's the silliest thing I've ever heard," Lang said as he stepped down from the porch and walked toward the children. He stopped at Sarah's side and with callused fingers pushed back her stringy black hair from one of her ears. "You see here, George? No horse has ears that big."

"Papa!" Sarah pulled away. Her father laughed loudly, then picked her up in his powerful arms. "You ain't no horse, dear. You're the most beautiful young lady in Tennessee. You and your mother, that is." He spun around with her in his arms.

Sarah laughed. "Put me down, Papa. You're gonna drop me."

"I'd never drop you, honey. Never in a million years. Ain't never goin' to let anything happen to you." He set her down, leaned forward, and kissed her on the forehead. "Of course you can go to town with us. I wouldn't have it any other way."

"Now? Are we going now?" Sarah asked.

"In a few minutes," Lang answered. "First, I'm going to check on Chester." He started toward the split-rail fence that separated the front yard from the adjoining pasture.

"I swear," Mary said with a laugh. "I think you love that animal more than you love me."

"Naw," he replied. "Chester can't cook a chicken."

"Hurry back," Mary said. "I want to get to town before the stores close."

"I will," he said with a wave and marched on toward his prize quarter horse.

"We're going to town," Sarah said to George. Excitement filled her, and she wanted to dance a little jig, but she was eleven now—too old for such childish behavior.

"Who's that?" Mama asked. Sarah turned to her mother and saw her pointing toward the road that ran by the farm. "Sarah, your eyes are younger than mine, can you make out who it is?"

Turning, Sarah squinted through the glare of golden sunlight. It took a moment for her to make an identification. "It's Judge Peck," she said with excitement. Judge August Peck was always a welcome visitor because he brought presents whenever he stopped by. Today he had someone with him. Sarah raised a hand to shield her eyes. "I think that's Mr. Jacob Pullman with him."

"Well," Mama said. "I wonder what the judge and his brother-in-law are up to today."

Judge Peck shouted hello and waved at Sarah's father. Sarah shifted her gaze toward her father to see if he had heard. He had, for he raised his hand and waved back. "Hello," he shouted, turned and—

The scream came from behind her. It was loud and long. So much so, that Sarah could only barely recognize the voice as belonging to her mother. As Sarah turned, she heard her mother scream again, her hands drawn to her face in disbelief. She had seen it, too—just like Sarah.

"Papa?" George said softly. "What happened to Papa?" He climbed out of the wagon, his face pale with fear, his eyes wet with a sudden stream of tears. Mrs. Lang's screams were unnerving him.

Sarah felt sick. Inside her, her stomach churned and leaped. Fear had sent a piercing cold through her, deep into the marrow of her bones. "Papa!" she cried. "Papa!" Sarah ran. She ran across the yard and through the gate. She ran into the brown stubble of pasture land, backed by the summer sun. Behind her, she heard a voice.

"Sarah, wait. Sarah, no!" It was her mother, but the voice wasn't distant. Her mother must be running behind her. Sarah had never disobeyed her parents, never resisted their commands, but this time she could not obey. She could not stop. She ran. Beneath her feet the dry hay crunched with each panicked step.

Out of the corner of her eye, she saw something. It was Judge Peck and Mr. Pullman. Both were running to the same spot as she. Sarah got there first. "Papa! Papa!"

But there was no Papa, just an empty field.

"Where are you, Papa?" No answer. The gentle breeze suddenly stiffened, blowing through Sarah's hair and stinging her face with bits of loose debris. A dust devil swept over her, but she took no notice of it. "Papa. Where are you?"

A hand seized her arm. "Sarah, wait." It was her mother. Her normally pink face was pale with fear; her eyes were wide and darted about. "Where is he?"

"I don't know, Mama. I don't know!"

Heavy footfalls caught Sarah's attention. Judge Peck had arrived. "Did he fall?" he asked breathlessly. He was a rotund man, and the jog across the field had winded him.

"I don't know," Mary said. "I don't see him."

"What was that light, Mama?"

"David!" Mary Lang called. Her voice was saturated with fear and confusion. "David, answer me!"

"Mama?" Sarah said with alarm. "What happened to Papa?"

"Hush, Sarah. I think I hear him."

Sarah strained her ears and closed her eyes, listening with all her will, might, and heart. She heard the chirps of birds, the rustle of wind through the leaves of nearby oak trees, but she heard nothing of her father. Opening her eyes, she faced her mother and knew that Mama heard the same nothing. Tears began to trickle down Mary's cheeks. The sight of her mother crying brought hot tears to her own eyes and made her heart race.

"He just disappeared," Judge Peck said. "I was looking right at him and he just disappeared."

"That can't be," Pullman said.

"You saw it for yourself," Peck countered. "He was right here, then he was gone."

"Such things don't happen," Pullman insisted. "A man can't just walk off the face of the earth."

"Do something," Mary said with desperation. "Stop arguing and do something. I want my husband. I need my husband." She began to sob.

"Okay, okay," Peck said, raising his hand to his forehead and rubbing it in deep thought as if he could massage an idea into his brain. A second later he said, "Are we all agreed that this is where David was when he disappeared?"

"I . . . I think so," Mary said.

"Let's assume that we're wrong," Peck went on. "Maybe he just fell down and is unconscious." He looked around and saw what he was searching for. "Sarah. Do you see that rock over there?"

She followed the direction of his gaze and saw a gray lump of granite the size of an apple. "Yes, sir."

"Go get it and bring it here." Sarah did as she was told. Judge Peck took the rock and set it at his feet. He then removed a small knife from his vest pocket and scratched an X on the stone, then set it on the ground at his feet. "This will keep us from losing our place. Now everyone spread out. Mrs. Lang, you stand by the rock. Sarah, you walk ten paces out from the rock. I'll walk out twenty paces, and you, Jacob, go out for thirty. We're going to walk in a circle around Mrs. Lang. He has to be here somewhere."

"Shall I get George?" Sarah glanced back toward the house. Her young brother sat unmoving in the new wood wagon.

"No," Judge Peck said. "I don't want to lose a minute."

Sarah walked carefully, her eyes cast down to the ground in front of her and then looking side to side. There was nothing. Nothing and nothing and nothing. When they had completed one full circuit, they expanded their search. Nothing.

After the third circuit, Mary Lang collapsed and had to be revived. Sarah walked her mother back to the house—a house the young girl instinctively knew would never hear the loud, loving voice of her father again.

The hours had oozed by in a slow procession of agony and fear. From the porch, Sarah could see the townspeople and neighbors holding lamps high as they searched the field. She could hear their voices calling out for her papa. After Mr. Pullman had spread the word and the crowds began to arrive, Sarah had gone back into the field, leaving the care of her distraught mother and brother in the hands of neighbor women. The women had told Sarah to stay close to the house, but she had refused. Her father was gone, and she was going to find him.

Darkness had settled upon the farm, but still the friends of David Lang searched, stomping on the ground, looking, hoping to find some hole into which David may have fallen. There were no holes. And despite a thorough search of the field, there was no David Lang. He was gone, having disappeared on a clear September day, in sight of his family and two men.

As the hours passed, the darkness deepened. Not even the moon rose to offer its light to help. Overhead, a spangled sky watched the search as an audience would watch a play.

Sarah walked back to the house and sat on the porch swing. The seat, held to the porch roof by an old rusty chain, squeaked with each movement. Voices from inside the house wafted out the open window. Two neighbor women were talking.

"The poor dear," old Mrs. Maple said. "She's exhausted. Sound asleep she is now, and who can blame her?"

"Not me," Mrs. Leighton replied. "Have you ever heard of such a thing before? It ain't right. I can tell you that much. And he was such a good man."

Sarah cringed at the last statement. It was said with such finality, such certainty. Her father was not coming home.

"But what could have happened?" Mrs. Maple asked. "A man just don't up and disappear right in front of all his kin like that. No, sir, something strange is afoot, I can tell you that."

Why couldn't they just be quiet? Sarah wondered. *Why couldn't they keep their opinions to themselves?*

"I'll tell you what I think it is," Mrs. Leighton said. "It's the Devil's work, it is. Pure and simple, it's the Devil's work. None other than the Prince of Darkness has come a callin' at the Lang farm. We best pray that we're not next."

Sarah looked out from the porch and watched the light of the lanterns held by the searchers. The lights danced above their heads like ghosts haunting a cemetery.

"Papa," Sarah whispered. "Come home, Papa."

The front door opened, and George stepped from the house. He saw Sarah and quietly joined her on the swing. She could tell that he had been crying. Minutes poured slowly by like cold molasses. Neither spoke.

An hour later, or a minute, Sarah could no longer tell, George broke the silence. "I'm sorry I called you a horse."

Turning to her brother, Sarah studied him for a moment. There was an ache in him—a deep, cold, piercing ache. The same pain she felt. Offering a weak smile, she put her arm around his shoulders. A second later, the shoulders began to shake as George began to sob with the kind of sorrow and fear that only a child—a fatherless child—could experience.

Sarah had no words, not a single comforting thought. So she did the only thing she knew how to do: She joined his weeping.

N

10 April 1881

The Lang Farm

"I'm scared," George said as Sarah and he crossed the gate between the pasture and the front yard.

"There's nothing to be afraid of, George," Sarah said as she led the way. George had changed greatly since that day seven months ago. His boyish arrogance was gone, replaced by fear and timidity. He clung to Mama now, seldom leaving her side. "I've been out here every day. No need to be scared. I'm with you."

George just nodded with unconvincing resolve.

Everything had changed, not just George. Without Papa, there was no one to run the farm. Mama had had a nervous breakdown. She was nothing like she had been before. Now she was skinny. Refusing to eat but the barest of minimums had caused her to drop pounds. She had always been a large, corpulent woman, but now to Sarah she looked like a skeleton loosely dressed in skin.

Judge Peck had rented out the farm to help support the family. They got to stay in the house, the renters got use of the land—all except this field. The one in which Papa had disappeared. Mama had insisted that it be left just the way it had been those long months before.

"Why do you keep going there?" George asked. "It's been a long time."

"Time doesn't matter. I *have* to go. I *want* to go." Sarah continued. George followed close behind. A few minutes later, Sarah said, "Here it is." She leaned down and touched the small gray rock. The cross that Judge Peck etched into it with his pen knife could still be seen.

"What's wrong with the grass?" George asked. "It's all yellow."

Sarah looked around her. She had seen it so often that she failed to notice it this time. The circle of dead, yellow grass was new to her brother. "I don't know. It's been like that since Papa disappeared."

"Where is he?" George asked. It was a question he asked often.

"I don't know," Sarah admitted. "I don't know."

Tears were beginning to roll down George's face. He had not cried for months now, but Sarah knew that seeing the actual spot had brought back the terror of that horrible day.

"I miss him," Sarah said. "I miss him so much." Her eyes began to burn. She sniffed and took a deep breath. "I keep hoping that he'll come back, but I know he never will." Seven months of separation had not healed the scar in her life, or in George's. The sorrow was heavy, suffocating, like a wet wool blanket.

"Papa!" George cried out. It was a cry of desperation, a volcanic eruption of emotion. Sarah understood it. She had made the same attempt herself many times. At first, she had come to the site of her father's disappearance daily, then weekly, but she always came. Always called out for him.

Sarah put a hand on her brother's shoulder. The gesture achieved what words would have failed. The pain was real, but life would go on. The sun would rise; the stars would flicker at night like distant candles. They would go on, emptier and confused, but they would go on.

Something touched Sarah's attention. Something distant, yet close; something quiet, yet perceptible. It was a shout no louder than a whisper, a plea no greater than the beating of a dragonfly's wings. George fell silent. His head snapped up. He had heard it, too.

"What—" George began.

"Shush!" Sarah demanded, then closed her eyes. The sound had been familiar. She strained to hear as if by the sheer act of her will, she could raise the volume of the sound. But the sound was gone, replaced by the singing of birds in distant trees and the lullaby of the breeze as it rolled past her ears. She concentrated harder, trying to eliminate all other sounds.

Heeel . . .

It was back. Distant, vague, weak, but it was back.

. . . lpppp.

It made no sense.

Saraaaah.

Familiar, close, yet far. Recognizable, but undefined. Haunting, pleading, longing. Pained.

Sarahhhh. Heeel . . . lpppp. Louder this time. Louder than before, but still so very weak. It was a hint of a voice, but not a voice.

Ice ran down Sarah's spine. Her eyes snapped open.

"Papa?"

Weeping sounds. Pleading sounds. Distant sounds.

Sarah. Help me. Please, please, help me.

"Papa!" George screamed. "Papa, Papa, Papa!" He was running in circles, looking into the sky and then down to the ground. "Where are you, Papa?"

There was no answer.

"George, be quiet. I can't hear."

But George refused to be quiet. He screamed and then cried. "Papa, Papa, Papa." He was beside himself with confusion.

Seizing him by the arms, Sarah pulled him toward her in a bear hug. "Quiet! We need to listen. We need to hear." George took several ragged breaths and then stilled himself. Sarah strained her young ears to listen, but the wisps of words were gone. Only the sound of nature remained. Minutes passed, maybe an hour, but the distant, haunting, breathless words never returned. Slowly, holding George by the hand, she walked back to the house.

"It was Papa, wasn't it?" George asked softly.

"No," Sarah said, saddened by the lie. "It was just the wind. It tricked our ears. That's all. Just the wind."

"But I know it was Papa," George protested.

"Papa's been gone for seven months, George. It couldn't be him. It was just the wind."

Sarah understood that George knew different, but he was a smart boy. He would soon understand that no one would believe them, no one would understand. And any such talk would only make their now invalid mother worse. It would have to remain their secret.

"Will we go back?" George asked in a breathy whisper.

"Every day," Sarah replied. "Every day."

Chapter 5

23 November 2000
1600 Pennsylvania Avenue, Washington, D.C.

Admiral Philip Kaster closed the door behind him. His slow, smooth motions belied the raging storm of anger inside. What he really wanted to do was slam the office door so hard the hinges would bend and the plaster walls would crack. But a man of his position did not do such things—especially to the door of the Oval Office. Still, the urge was there, held beneath a tough, but weakening skin of discipline.

Such breaches of etiquette could only lead to further regrettable actions. Still, the mental picture of him holding the president by his long aquiline nose and lecturing loudly until the commander in chief understood the seriousness of the problem had played frequently across the screen of his mind.

"Good night, Admiral," the secret service agent at the door said as Kaster finally released his grip on the doorknob. He stared at the agent for a moment, then grunted. *Probably heard everything*, the admiral thought, as he walked down the plush carpeted corridor. *How could he not hear?* In stewing silence, he made his way out the front of the building to a waiting limo. The night sky was made all the darker by a thick coagulation of sable clouds. Black as it was, the evening was no darker than the admiral's mood.

Climbing in the backseat, he ignored the navy chauffeur who shut the door and walked quickly to the driver's seat. Admiral Kaster aimed his gaze out the side window. Carefully placed decorative lighting cast bright beams on the white painted sandstone exterior of the president's mansion. Within a month, a large Christmas tree would be erected on the White House grounds, adding its lights to the eighteen-acre compound. It would attract tourists from all over—tourists who had no idea of what decisions were made in the building a few yards away.

Rain splashed down on the metal skin of the limousine as it pulled out from beneath the large, protective portico at the front of the building. "It's a miserable night, sir," the driver said. He was a young second lieutenant assigned to the admiral's staff. "And cold enough to make your teeth ache."

Kaster said nothing.

"Back to the office, sir? Or home?"

"Home," he growled.

"Yes, sir. I imagine you're ready to put an end to this day. You've been at it"—he paused as he looked at his watch—"fourteen hours. That's a long one."

Kaster responded by reaching for a button on the console of the car door and pressing it. A glass partition closed the small window that separated the front seat from the back. Kaster was in no mood to talk. He had to think, to reason. His mind drifted back to the meeting he had just had.

"Mr. President, I can't emphasize enough the danger we face in this situation."

"Admiral Collins and General McCormick assure me that no danger exists."

"Sir, I requested this special meeting because I strongly disagree. We've already lost well over a thousand people. I have fears for the surrounding communities."

"The situation is contained, Phil. There's nothing to worry about."

Kaster stared across the teak coffee table between the sofa upon which he sat and the plush chair of the president. They were meeting in the informal sitting area of the Oval Office. Kaster hated to be called by his first name. He was, after all, a vice admiral and had served his country for twenty-six years. Respect to protocol was not too much to ask, not even of a president. "Is it, sir? We can't know that until we first know what happened at Roanoke II, and as it stands now, we know nothing."

"We will. I understand your man in the field is good. He'll have something for us soon." The president was placating.

"Sir, I have reviewed the situation, the men assigned, the resources available to them, and they are insufficient for the task. Those men may be in danger."

"Your friends at the Pentagon think otherwise."

Kaster wanted to assure the president that most of his "friends" did no thinking at all. Especially when budget items were at stake. "Sir, if I may—"

The president raised his hand, then stood to his feet. "I'm sorry, Phil, but you're overreacting on this one. Let's stay the course and everything will be fine and dandy. We're going to keep a lid on this. We don't want our enemies to get hold of this technology."

"Not to put too fine a point on it, Mr. President, but if this thing gets out of hand, then our enemies won't have to do anything but wait for us to wipe ourselves out."

"You see there, Phil? That's the kind of overreaction I was talking about. That's why I didn't put you in charge of this. It was your project to begin with, but you've let your emotions get in the way."

"No such thing, sir," Kaster protested, standing to join the president. "I'm just willing to tell you the truth about the matter. We've made a terrible, terrible mistake."

"No," the president said loudly. "*You've* made a mistake. How dare you ask to meet with me, then impugn my decision-making ability. I may not have served in the military like you, Admiral, but I still know a few things, and one thing I know is that I am your commander in chief."

"But, sir, our investigator is undermanned and out of the loop. How can we expect him to do his job, if he doesn't know what we've been doing down there?"

"He has Mason with him. That's all he needs."

"Mason Eddington is the one who insisted on secrecy. I can understand not releasing this to the newspapers, but to keep hidden any information vital to the work of our investigator is ludicrous. In fact, it is stupidity, dressed in hubris." Kaster immediately regretted the words. The president was known for his temper. Unfortunately, Kaster had a temper, too.

"How dare you!" the president snapped. His words came out guttural, like a growl. "Don't you forget whom you're addressing. You're the one who sent him in there in the first place. I didn't authorize that."

"It was in my purview, sir. We needed to know what happened, and Captain Stanton was qualified and close. I assumed you would want to know what went wrong."

"Of course, I want to know. But this has to be done right. I'm the only president in recent years who believes that our military has become too weak. If word of this gets out, future R and D money will be impossible to get. Not to mention the devastation it could cause to my run for a second term." The president suddenly raised a finger and pointed it at Kaster like a knife. "And don't you dare assume that that is what all this is about. The military needs me for another four years. If I'm voted out of office, your precious research will go with me."

"Mr. President," Kaster said, unable to fully mask the disdain in his voice, "I am only concerned with the men in the field."

"You are only concerned that your perfect image is not tarnished. Well, too late. This whole thing is your fault. This was your program. You made great and grandiose predictions. 'It will forever change the face of warfare.' Isn't that what you said?"

"It is, but—"

"I didn't make those people disappear, Admiral. Your project did, and now you've sent more people into the area. It's too late to pull them out. I would have preferred the privilege of selecting my own team to investigate—people who are qualified, safe, and loyal."

"There is no better man than Stanton," the admiral countered loudly. "He has served his country with distinction and honor."

"I know all about your man Stanton," the president said. He walked to his mahogany desk and sat down on the deeply padded leather chair behind it. Kaster watched as his commander in chief studied him. It was as if the admiral had his thoughts and emotions written inside him and the president was reading them word for word. "Sit down, Admiral." He motioned to a chair opposite the desk.

"I prefer to stand, sir."

"I prefer you sit."

Kaster clinched his jaw so tightly it felt as if his tendons would snap. He sat down.

"I read Stanton's file. He seems a bright enough guy: Annapolis grad, worked his way up the ranks, skippered a nuclear sub, taught history at the Academy, even wrote a couple of books. And, of course, there was the USS *Triggerfish* incident. He did well with that. Saved a few hundred lives."

"Those are the very reasons I chose him for this investigation."

"You got ahead of the game. You should have consulted others before committing to a course of action. You certainly should have consulted me."

Kaster had considered that, but dismissed it immediately. He knew that he would be opposed at every turn. His decision to compile the Roanoke II team and send them in without discussion had been premeditated. It would have been better if he had had time to meet with them personally, to brief them on the problem and what to look for, but there were forces working against him. He did what he had to, and he had done it quickly. "Perhaps so, sir, but we're beyond that now. I need to be free to provide additional information to my team."

The president shook his head. "Not now, Admiral. I need time to think about this; time to listen to others from the Pentagon. You are to do nothing more. Is that clear?"

"I can't ignore them. They deserve better."

"You are to do nothing more," the president repeated firmly. "No contact, no communication." There was a long, electric pause. "Don't make me relieve you of duty, Admiral. Your career is impeccable. Let's make sure it stays that way."

"If you think I'm unfit for duty, then relieve me. Otherwise, stay out of my way." It was not the way a military man spoke to the president of the United States, but Kaster could no longer contain himself.

The president was instantly on his feet, his face red with rage. "You will do as I say, or so help me, I will have you brought up on charges of treason."

"I don't think you can do that, sir."

"I will find a way," the president shouted loudly. "Now get out of my office. Go! Get! Now! Leave!"

Admiral Kaster rose to his feet, turned, and walked from the Oval Office, certain he was leaving his career behind.

"Here we are, sir." The military driver stepped from the limo and opened the door for Kaster. Rain was falling in large, pebble-like drops. Without words, he left his driver and walked to his spacious Georgetown home. "Same time tomorrow, Admiral?"

"Yes," was all Kaster said. Entering his house, he closed the door behind him, blocking out the rain, but not the world—that he carried on his shoulders.

"You're home," Martha Kaster said cheerfully. His wife walked over and kissed him on the cheek. "You're also wet. This storm is going to wash us all away."

"I'll be in my study," Kaster said solemnly. His fury had settled into anger and his anger into despondency. Normally he was a man of few visible emotions, seldom shaken, imperturbable.

"Are you all right?" Martha asked with concern.

"No, and I don't want to talk about it." He started toward the door, then stopped. Turning, he returned to his wife. She was tall, with striking gray hair and blue eyes. Always the love of his life, she had endured the trials of a navy wife for well over two decades. "I'll be fine," he said softly and then kissed her lightly on the lips. "I just have some thinking to do."

"Shall I wait up for you?" Anxiety was etched into her face.

He shook his head. "No. I may be working late."

"Can I get you anything?"

Kaster chuckled involuntarily. What was there to get? "No, I don't want anything. I'll come to bed later."

"Okay," she said without conviction. She never could conceal her worry. "You let me know if you need anything."

"I will." He kissed her again, and turned toward his study. On the way, he stopped at the liquor cabinet and removed a bottle of Chivas Regal and a glass. At first he had planned to pour himself a drink of scotch. Instead, he carried the bottle with him.

One drink was not going to be enough to exorcise the ghosts of fifteen hundred people.

23 November 2000; 1820 hours
Roanoke II

The house was simple in every fashion with a beige stucco exterior, brown composition shingle roof, and a front yard of barren dirt. The only thing that distinguished the grounds from the surrounding desert was a lack of weeds. Even in the artificial light of the streetlamps, Stanton could see that the grounds and the desert were the same monochrome brown. All the houses that he had seen during their brief drive looked the same, as if they had been stamped out by a huge machine rather than built by craftsmen. The fact that the roof shingles and the color coat of stucco were similar shades of dun was not wasted on him.

"Camouflage colors?" Stanton asked Eddington, who stood next to him on the front step.

"Yes, to limit the effectiveness of spy satellites. We couldn't conceal the buildings, so we chose to make them indistinct from high altitude. It's far from foolproof, but it helps."

"Shall we, sir?" Lieutenant Dole asked.

"Try the handle before you kick it in," Stanton said, as he took a step back, motioning for Eddington, Tulley, and Wendt to do the same. Dole had ordered Ramsey and Keagle to remain by the vehicles.

Tulley had already protested the number of people entering the house. "We might as well let a football team scrimmage on the crime scene."

His point was well taken by Stanton, but he thought it more valuable that they all see the same thing, at least at first.

Dole twisted the doorknob. It was locked. He took one step back and kicked the door just to the side of the knob. It flew open explosively.

"I'll go first," Stanton said.

"Sir, maybe I should take the point."

"Whatever has happened has already happened. I doubt there's anything in there to threaten us."

"Still, sir . . ."

Dole was just doing his job, Stanton realized. "Very well, Lieutenant."

The marine stepped over the threshold, weapon at the ready. He found a light switch and turned it on. Tulley started forward, but Stanton held out his arm, blocking the way.

"What the—" Tulley started.

"Just wait," Stanton answered.

"I thought he said that his men had searched the area," Tulley protested.

"He did," Stanton replied. "But there are a lot of houses here. Let the man do his job, then you can do yours."

"If he doesn't destroy all the evidence."

"I don't think you'll find any evidence, Agent Tulley. I don't think this is a crime scene. At least not as you would use the term."

"Why don't you let *me* decide that," Tulley stated flatly.

"I shall."

"Clear," Dole called from inside the house.

Stanton was the next through, followed by the others. Tulley was close on his heels. Inside, Dole had shouldered his weapon.

"It looks normal to me, Captain. Just like any house, except without the people."

"Very well," Stanton said. He looked around and estimated that the house was sixteen hundred square feet. He was standing in the living room, and since the house was designed in an open floor plan style, he could see directly into the dining room and kitchen. Inexpensive artwork, the kind purchased at department stores, hung on the wall. The carpet was a bright blue, and the walls an eggshell white. Like all homes, this one had an odor, a smell unique to those who lived in it. Stanton thought he detected a whiff of perfume, the lingering aromas of a dinner, and the unmistakable hint of talcum powder. The last sense troubled him.

"They had . . . or have a child," Dole said sullenly. "Got kids of my own. When they were young, the house always smelled like baby powder."

Stanton nodded. He and his wife had never had children, and at times he regretted it. They had wanted a family, but it never came to pass. It was something he now accepted as God's will.

Walking down the narrow hall, Stanton peered in the first door he came to. It was the hall bathroom. A fiberglass tub and shower were on the far wall; a water closet and sink were in their positions, like in so many millions of other bathrooms.

In the next room, Stanton saw Wendt on her knees, looking under the bed. The bed was small, the kind a child would use. It was painted a dark blue, and stickers of airplanes were stuck to the headboard. On the wall was a large poster of the SR–71 Blackbird. On the floor was a baseball glove, the kind worn by first basemen. An older child, Stanton surmised. A boy, if the glove and color scheme meant anything. On a battered nightstand next to the bed rested a child's Bible. On the cover was an artist's rendition of a happy, smiling Jesus. "Find anything of interest?"

"No. Somebody kept a neat house. Not a single dust bunny under the bed, and in a child's room, at that. Everything looks in place. No sign of a struggle."

"Where's your partner?" Stanton asked.

"Master bedroom."

Two other doors were at the end of the hall. Stanton stepped through the one on the left. It was a nursery. An oak crib stood near the far wall; a mobile of brightly colored jungle animals hung over it. Next to the bed was a changing table. The table was made of metal but was covered with a decorative plastic pad and skirt. Laughing clowns beamed their smiles from the bright fabric. On the floor rested a tightly bundled disposable diaper. Attached to the crib was an electronic device, an intercom that many parents used to monitor their infants at night.

Stanton noticed something on the crib, a carefully hand-lettered card that read, "Let the little children come to me, and do not hinder them, for the kingdom of heaven belongs to such as these. —Jesus. Matthew 19:14." The Scripture verse tugged at his heart.

The next door led to the master bedroom. Tulley was inside, intently examining the window.

"Any luck?" Stanton asked.

"I've only been at it a few minutes, Captain. These things take time."

"It's just a question, Tulley, not a demand for speed."

"Nothing, Captain. Everything is what one would expect in a house like this, except this one is unusually clean. Neat freaks lived here."

"Nothing wrong with tidiness," Stanton replied. "Have you looked in the baby's room?"

"No, why?"

"There's a diaper on the floor."

"Okay, so maybe the lady of the house is not a neat freak."

"No, I think she is. The diaper is on the floor because she dropped it and never had the opportunity to pick it up. Another indication that things happened quickly."

"As interesting as that is, Captain, we already knew that. Your observation is a fine confirmation, but it is no revelation."

"I just thought you should know."

"Thank you, Captain," Tulley said without conviction.

"Are you going to dust for prints?" Dole asked the FBI man.

Tulley chuckled. "Hardly, Lieutenant. If I had some indication that a struggle took place, or a window or door had been forced, or even if the jewelry had been stolen, then I might. All I'd get right now is a bunch of fingerprints from Mom, Pop, and the older child."

"Wouldn't that tell us who lived here?" Dole inquired, his voice slightly deepened by anger he felt at Tulley's words.

"No problem there," Tulley said. He walked over to the nightstand that stood next to a king-size waterbed and picked up a magazine. He handed it to Dole. Stanton noticed that Tulley was wearing latex gloves. As he thought about it, Wendt had been, too.

"What's this?" Dole asked.

"*Time* magazine, Lieutenant. The big red word *Time* is the giveaway clue."

Dole narrowed his eyes. Tulley had no inkling what the lieutenant could do to him. Stanton decided to intervene. "A little more respect would be appreciated, Agent Tulley."

"Whatever," Tulley snipped. "The magazine has a label on it. Tony and Julie Ignazio. Italian is my guess. Their picture is over there." He pointed to an oak and hunter green dresser.

Stanton picked up the picture and examined it. An olive-skinned couple were centered. To the father's right was a dark-haired boy of six. The mother held an infant. "Artifacts of a onetime life."

"Excuse me, Captain?" Dole said, confused.

"Oh, nothing, Lieutenant. I feel like an archaeologist. We know people lived here; we just don't know what happened to them. This picture, the furniture, everything, are artifacts of lives that used to be."

"I see," Dole said.

"You're touching things, Captain," Tulley admonished.

"You said that you weren't going to dust for prints," Stanton countered.

"There's more to investigating than tracking down fingerprints. Now put it back and let me return to work." A moment later, he added, "Please."

Stanton set the picture down where he had found it, took the periodical from Dole's hand, and tossed it on the bed. "Here's your magazine. You have fifteen minutes, then we're leaving."

"I need a lot longer than that."

"That's all you get. I want you and Agent Wendt with us when we gain access to the labs. Hopefully, things will prove more promising there." He motioned for the lieutenant to follow him, then stopped. Turning, he stared at the bed.

"What is it, sir?" Dole asked.

"The headboard," Stanton said pointing. "It has a baby monitor on it."

"So?" Tulley said. "Thousands of parents use baby monitors. That's not going to help us."

"No, but it gives me an idea."

"It's a monitor, Captain, not a recorder," Tulley said with exasperation. "It lets Mom and Dad hear Junior when he cries, but it certainly doesn't record events in the house."

"Perhaps not, Mr. Tulley," Stanton replied slowly. "But I'll bet you there are things around Roanoke II that do."

Dole's eyes widened in understanding. "Of course."

"I think it's time we have another talk with Dr. Eddington," Stanton said.

"Yes, sir," Dole replied with enthusiasm.

Both men left the room, but Stanton returned alone seconds later. "I am serious about leaving in fifteen minutes, Agent Tulley. See that you're ready."

Tulley offered a limp salute and said, "Aye, aye."

Stanton stepped back into the room, walked around the bed to where Tulley was, and leaned forward so that his face was just inches from the FBI agent. "Henceforth you will address the people under my command with respect. I have only known you a short time, but I have already grown weary of you. Do you understand?"

"What are you going to do, Captain?" Tulley said with disregard. "Tell my superiors? I am a pain to work with, Captain, but I have a one hundred percent solve rate. No one else can say that. My superiors tolerate me because they recognize my genius."

"Mr. Tulley, if you choose to stand in the way of my work here, I will find someplace with very thick walls and have you locked away until I am done with my mission."

"You can't do that."

"I can, and I know three marines who would love to help me."

Tulley took a step back.

Stanton spun on his heels to march out of the bedroom but was forced to stop. Standing in the doorway was Loren Wendt. She was smiling again.

"You didn't stay in the house very long," Stanton said as he climbed into the backseat of the Humvee where Eddington was sitting. Eddington had produced a pipe from somewhere and was puffing nervously on the stem. Billows of scented smoke poured from the pipe and wafted out the side window, which had been opened just enough to let the smoke out.

"I'm just dead weight in there," Eddington replied.

"Couldn't be a troubled soul, could it?"

"My conscience is clear, Captain. I have nothing over which to be troubled."

"Fifteen hundred missing people sounds like a good reason to me," Dole said. He had taken a seat in the driver's position. Rain dripped from his helmet.

"I am very concerned about them, Lieutenant. I considered many of them my friends."

"We have a problem here, Dr. Eddington," Stanton said firmly and a little louder than he intended. Eddington stiffened. "I have orders to find those missing people, or at least the cause of their disappearance. You have orders to help, but also to keep certain information secret. It seems that our orders are at cross-purposes."

"Neither one of us can be blamed for that," Eddington said.

"I've asked this before, but I'm going to ask it again. Who gave you those orders? Maybe I can convince him that we need all the information we can get."

"My orders come from a higher level than yours, Captain." Eddington put the pipe in his mouth for a moment, then withdrew it. "The Pentagon is a multiheaded beast. I'm accountable to a different taskmaster than you. I can tell you this. He outranks anyone you're talking to."

"My orders came from Admiral Philip Kaster. There aren't too many people who can outrank him."

"I know Vice Admiral Kaster and his wife, Martha. Lovely woman. Tells a good joke. Puts on a good party, too. Nonetheless, there are those who outrank the good admiral."

Stanton sighed heavily. This was useless. "Let me see your wallet," he said suddenly.

"What?" Eddington said, surprised by the conversation's sudden change. "Why do you want my wallet? There's nothing in it."

"I'm not going to steal anything, Dr. Eddington," Stanton replied. "I just want to see something."

"There's nothing in there to help you."

"Please, humor me."

Eddington reluctantly pulled his wallet from his back pocket and handed it to Stanton. "I'm starting to wonder about your sanity."

"Wait until you get to know me." Stanton took the black leather billfold, opened it, and immediately saw what he was looking for: the tiny clear plastic envelopes that held photos. He flipped through them. There was a family photo of Eddington, his wife, two adult children, and just what Stanton was hoping to find. He showed the picture to Eddington. "Your family?"

"Yes. What is this?" Eddington asked with agitation. "If you think you can intimidate me by threatening my family—"

"No threat. Just a question." Stanton pointed at the baby being held by the young woman. "Is that your grandchild?"

"What if it is?"

Stanton closed the billfold and then handed it back to the engineer. "The mind is an unusual thing, Dr. Eddington. We humans have a tendency to contextualize information based on our experience. When I was flying up here, I read the briefing file that had been given to me in San Diego. Not much in it really, mostly information about you and the others—training, specialties, that sort of thing. But I was shocked to read that so many people had disappeared. I kept thinking, 'Fifteen hundred men and women can't just disappear into thin air.'"

"So?" Eddington asked suspiciously.

"Don't you get it? I don't have any children. It never worked out for us. I view the world through the eyes of an adult. That's pretty much all I know. So I keep thinking about the men and women who are missing. But when I went in that house"—he pointed to the home he had just left—"I saw a crib in one of the rooms and children's toys in another."

"And?"

"Until that moment, I had visualized all of this happening to adults, not to children. Even after seeing the child's car seat back at the service station, I was still thinking in terms of adults only. But that crib brought it home, Dr. Eddington. It isn't just men and women who have gone missing—it's infants, and toddlers, and school-age children. Boys who play catch with their fathers, and girls who play with dolls. Little children, Dr. Eddington. Infants like your grandchild."

Eddington fingered the bowl of his pipe, rubbing it like it was a worry stone. "I'm touched by your observation, but I still can't help you."

"This can't stay under wraps forever, Eddington," Stanton said. "Those children have grandparents, too, and those folks are going to want to know what happened."

"Still . . ." His voice faded off.

Stanton continued, "If your family went missing, your children and grandchildren, wouldn't you want to know that the very best had been done on their behalf?"

"Stop it, Captain," Eddington said loudly. He shifted his weight and cut his gaze out the window. "I can't betray my oath."

"I'm not asking you to do that. What I want you to do is to take us to the monitoring site."

"The what?"

"Look up there." Stanton pointed out the window at a tall streetlight. "Up there, on top, do you see it?" He was pointing at a white cylinder mounted to the top of the light standard.

“The . . . the camera.” Eddington seemed surprised. “I hadn’t thought about that.”

“You’re a busy man,” Stanton said. “I bet someone else was in charge of setting up surveillance equipment. Cameras like that are used all over the country. Police use them to monitor high crime areas and dangerous traffic locations.”

“Yes, that’s right. I assigned that work to someone else. All I had to do was verify its functionality.”

Stanton leaned forward and spoke in a whisper, “Take us to the monitoring room. There may be a tape that shows what happened. The monitoring room is not in the labs, is it?”

“No. It’s operated separately.”

“Then take us there. You won’t be betraying your trust or defying orders.”

Eddington furrowed his brow as he thought.

“Help me find those children, or at least give some meaning to their disappearance.”

Nodding slowly, Eddington said, “I can do that.”

A second later, Dole started the Humvee.

“What about the others?” Eddington asked.

“We’re in radio contact with them,” Stanton said. “Dole’s team will remain on scene with Tulley and Wendt. Tulley wanted more time anyway. This will give him a few more minutes.”

As Stanton leaned back in the seat, he felt a wave of warmth roll over him. He was making progress. But, like the tide, the warm wave receded and was replaced by the cold current of reality.

Somewhere inside him, Stanton could feel the odd mix of excitement and dread. He needed to know what happened—he just wasn’t sure he *wanted* to know.

Chapter 6

June 1872
Vicksburg, Mississippi

Barely past breakfast and we're already sweltering," Captain Joshua Beecher said. He dragged a large white handkerchief across his brow. A breeze, too slight to make any difference in the June temperature, rolled through the open doors of the wheelhouse.

"It's the humidity, sir," the pilot John Waverly said, as he stood behind the large wooden wheel of the steamer. "Don't much matter the time of day, the humidity saps the strength out of a man. At least we ain't tending to the boilers."

Captain Beecher nodded. It took a special breed of man to work in the heat of the boiler room. Shoveling coal was no easy task any time of the year, but was hellish in the summer months. Replacing the cap on his head, Beecher stepped from the wheelhouse and onto the *Iron Mountain*'s upper deck. Below him, on the dock, a workman was untying the thick ropes that held the steamboat in its moorings. As he did, a crewman pulled in the wooden gangplank. Beecher stepped back into the wheelhouse. "Let's get underway, Mr. Waverly. We're ten minutes behind, and I don't like to be late."

That was true. Captain Beecher had a reputation for arriving on schedule, sometimes early, but never, ever, late.

Waverly stepped to the large wheel, reached above his head, and pulled the cord that dangled nearby. A shrill whistle sounded twice, warning nearby craft of the *Iron Mountain*'s departure. The wood floor beneath Beecher's feet shuddered as the powerful West Point Foundry steam engine began to do its work. The large paddlewheel at the stern began to turn, churning the muddy Mississippi into a boiling froth. Black coal smoke belched from the twin smokestacks and billowed into the clear June morning. Even in the wheelhouse, Beecher could imagine the walking beam rocking as the engine's steam-driven piston plunged back and forth in its cylinder.

From the decks below came the shouts of the passengers as they waved good-bye to family and friends. There were only fifty-five souls on board beyond the crew complement. The *Iron Mountain* was used primarily for the transportation of goods. On her decks were bales of cotton and barrels of molasses destined for Cincinnati and finally Pittsburgh.

Beecher eyed Waverly for a moment. They had worked together for five of Beecher's twenty-two years on the river, and he had proven himself an able pilot. Today was no different. Waverly's eyes danced about as he took in the traffic on the river, the current and shallows. This would be another safe trip with passengers and cargo delivered to the right place at the right time.

Again, Beecher stepped from the wheelhouse and into the open air. This time he strolled along the upper deck toward the stern, his hand gliding along the smooth, polished wood rail. A dozen steps later, he was gazing back over the paddlewheel at the barges loaded with consumer goods. They were dutifully following along through the brown-green river water, like ducklings behind their mother. The exit from Vicksburg had gone just as it should. The 180-foot-long *Iron Mountain* was on her way up the Mississippi toward the Missouri, just as she had done year after year. There was little to do now but endure the tedium. Nothing exciting ever happened to Captain Joshua Beecher.

N

"They're all secure, Captain," the brawny *Iroquois Chief* crewman said.

"Thank you, Mr. Bell," Captain Wright said, pulling a well-worn pipe from his mouth.

"What do we do now?"

"You keep an eye on the barges. Whoever lost them will be back looking for their missing cargo. Any idea who they belong to?"

"Yes, sir. The barges are marked *Iron Mountain*."

"*Iron Mountain*," Wright repeated. "That makes sense. She's out of Vicksburg about six miles up river. I expect she's on her way right now. We'll just hang onto the barges until she gets here. No sense in doing away with river courtesies, now is there?"

"No, sir. If I may say so, Captain, you did a fine job getting us out of the way. It would've been bad if we had collided with the likes of them."

The helmsman of the *Iroquois Chief* had been the first to notice the runaway barges coming downriver. Wright had had to call for emergency power to move the riverboat out of the way, avoiding a collision that would have been nothing short of disastrous. "You are right, there. Please tell the rest of the crew and the passengers that we will be delayed awhile."

"Yes, sir. Oh, and sir, there is one more thing. The towlines didn't break. It looks as if someone cut them."

"No captain orders barges cut away unless his boat is in trouble."

"Yes, sir, that's why I thought you should know."

Captain Wright raised a rough hand and rubbed his weary eyes. The sun had set an hour before, and he was now making port in Vicksburg for the second time that day. The first had been to unload the runaway barges he and his crew had salvaged. After releasing the barges and giving a report to the local authorities, he ordered the *Iroquois Chief* back up the river. The *Iron Mountain* had not returned to Vicksburg as was expected of every vessel who suffered the loss of barges. That truth coupled with the cut towlines had prompted the *Iron Mountain*'s owner to request Wright's help. Wright, a professional and a gentleman, quickly agreed.

The unspoken was being thought. Something untoward had happened to the *Iron Mountain*.

"Captain Beecher is a fine and honorable man," the owner had said. He was a thin, well-dressed, nervous man. "He's one of the best captains I have known. It is impossible to think that he has become irresponsible now. No, something has happened."

"Perhaps he's aground on a shoal," Wright offered, unconvinced of his own words.

"Perhaps, but not likely. He's been on this river for more than two decades."

"The river changes."

"Of course, but either way, we need to know."

It was then that Wright directed his steamer out onto the river again, following the course of the *Iron Mountain*. Although he could not know precisely, Wright could guess how far the missing steamboat had traveled. It was a simple matter of multiplying the elapsed time from the departure of the *Iron Mountain* to his discovery of the free-floating barges by the maximum speed of the steamboat.

With every available crewman standing watch, the *Iroquois Chief* worked its way up the Mississippi. Other vessels were hailed, but no one had seen the missing steamboat. There was no smoke from fire or from the stacks of the missing riverboat. No wreckage. No bodies. No debris. No witnesses. There was nothing to indicate that the *Iron Mountain* had ever navigated the river waters.

The *Iron Mountain*, with her crew and fifty-five passengers, had steamed around the bend north of Vicksburg into oblivion.

As Wright stood in the wheelhouse, his pilot directing the *Iroquois Chief* into port, he saw a crowd at the docks. Raising a spyglass to his eye, he could see in the ivory light of a full moon men, women, and children, many of whom were weeping. Wright knew that they were the family of the crew and passengers, and they were waiting on any word he might have for them.

News traveled fast. Telegraph operators had sent messages back and forth from the towns that populated the Mississippi River. He was sure they had heard nothing. For there was nothing to hear. The *Iron Mountain* had, under full steam, sailed out of sight—forever.

Chapter 7

23 November 2000

1600 Pennsylvania Avenue, Washington, D.C.

The hum and whirring of the treadmill filled the small white room. Norris Crane, president of the United States, plodded along easily, his athletic shoes making dull thumping sounds with each footfall. Only a tiny rivulet of perspiration that ran down his right temple betrayed the effort the exercise machine was demanding of him. At fifty-two he was as trim and fit as men half his age, but where physical stamina came naturally to him in college, he now had to work at it. Still, a half-hour on the treadmill every day was considerably easier than the effort he had expended as captain of the Harvard lacrosse team. His flat stomach and thin frame made him look twenty years younger.

As he jogged on the treadmill, Crane kept an eye on the television in the entertainment center across the room. *News with Jim Lehrer* played in the background. At the front of the treadmill was a stand upon which the latest issue of *Newsweek* magazine rested. Crane paid attention to neither the magazine nor the PBS news report. His attention was fixed on the corpulent man who sat on a bench in the private exercise room.

"What did you find out?" Crane asked easily, despite his exertion.

"Not much more than what we already have," Mark Adler said. Adler was chief of staff to the president, a sharp man with a keen mind. An academic turned politician, the former college professor won a seat in Congress, then ten years later, a seat in the Senate. When Crane won election to the White House, he did so because of the campaign genius of Adler. He was a man who knew huge amounts of information about anything, but especially about every man and woman on the Hill. He was invaluable. "Stanton is Windex clean. Spotless military record. Commendations enough to fill a good-sized storage bay. Top-secret clearance. Exemplary service on several fronts. He could be a poster boy for the navy."

"We have his military history, Mark," Crane said. "I want to know about the man, not the uniform."

"What's to know? He seems to be an average guy with a great military record."

"What about his family?"

"Married, no children, no divorces, and one sister, a woman married to a navy chaplain."

"Chaplain?" The president contemplated that. Without thought, he punched a button and the treadmill sped up. "Is Stanton a religious man?"

"His personnel jacket lists him as Protestant, but that's all we know."

"I need more."

"That's all we can learn without putting him under surveillance."

"Well, we can't very well do that with him in Roanoke II," Crane said tersely. "I want to know about him, Mark. I want to know what he eats for breakfast and the kind of paper towels his wife buys at the store. But most of all, I want to know about his morals. A man with too many morals can be a problem—especially in this situation."

"I don't see how," Adler said. "Men of his caliber are hard to come by."

"In most cases, I would agree, but this is too important. We are between a rock and a hard place here, Mark. If what happened at Roanoke II is related to the research being done there, then nothing can save my administration."

"Sir, you stand higher in the polls than any president in the last thirty years. The people love you."

"They do now," Crane said, "but the voting populace is fickle. You know that as well as anyone. After the Gulf War, George Bush was a hero. Had the highest ratings in the polls ever. By the time the election rolled around, all that anyone could remember about him was his statement that the country had no financial problems. The voters knew different. In the end, Bush was out and Clinton was in. And it's not just the voters, Mark. It's the press. If they get wind of this, they'll be all over it. We are on the hot seat here, and I don't have any intention of letting things get out of control."

"Why not just replace him?"

"That could make things worse. He already knows of the problem. If it doesn't come out, he may decide to talk about what he knows."

"Would he disobey a direct order?" Adler asked. "This man is military all the way. An order from an admiral, or you, would shut him up."

Crane stopped the treadmill and stepped down. He took a towel from a nearby rack and began to dab at his perspiration-soaked hair. "Maybe, but things have a way of getting out to the public. Remember the My Lai massacre in 1968. Lieutenant William L. Calley was found guilty of killing unarmed civilians.

Do you think he would have done the deed if he thought word might get out? But word did get out, didn't it." Crane stepped to the mullion windows overlooking the White House grounds. The rain had grown worse. A little later in the year and there would have been snow falling. "Moral men are moral because they answer to a higher power. That power may supercede all Stanton's training."

"But aren't we stuck with him?" Adler asked.

"Thanks to Admiral Kaster, we are—at least for now."

"How far do you want me to go?"

"Do what it takes, just don't set off any flares. I want this kept quiet. In the meantime . . ."

"Sir? In the meantime, what?"

"In the meantime, I need to be thinking of a contingency plan. A tight, well-thought-out contingency plan."

23 November 2000; 1905 hours
Roanoke II

"This is it?" Lieutenant Dole said with surprise, as he directed the large Humvee off the street and onto a small parking lot. Rain poured from black clouds made invisible by the night and splattered hard against the metal body of the vehicle. To Stanton it sounded like gravel was falling from the sky. "Doesn't look like much."

"That's the idea, Lieutenant," Mason Eddington answered sharply, like a father scolding his son. "We thought of erecting a neon sign that read Security and Surveillance, but it didn't get much support."

Stanton ignored Eddington's sarcasm. He was gazing at a small, drab building that looked more like an auto repair shop than a high-tech security operation.

Eddington continued, "This is more than a military research and development site, Lieutenant. People live here, kids go to school here. Families get together to play cards and gossip about their neighbors. Do you think all that would be possible if there were guards, cameras, and checkpoints everywhere? I designed Roanoke II with two goals. First, to be the most productive facility of its kind in the world. Second, to be as comfortable for the families of the research staff as possible. Happy researchers do better work."

Stanton turned just in time to see Dole stiffen. They made eye contact. "Let's see what's inside," Stanton said.

Without words, the three men exited the military vehicle and started toward the adobe-colored building. Rain pelted them, and cold wind lashed at their faces. The storm was intensifying. A sheet of lightning shot across the sky, and a peal of thunder ripped through the air like a cannon blast. Stanton caught himself tensing.

The building was constructed of brown concrete block and was the size of a community post office. The small macadam parking lot in front of the structure deliquesced into gray as streetlight melded with the sheets of runoff.

"Would people have been on duty when the ... event occurred?" Stanton asked.

"The building was always manned," Eddington said. "The work here is as secret as it gets. Surveillance is ... was conducted twenty-four hours a day."

Stanton turned and studied the street. They were in a small commercial section of town. A fast food restaurant was situated across the way. A drugstore and hair salon bracketed the building. Each of those was constructed of the same brown concrete block.

Eddington pulled a plastic card from his front pocket and stepped to the door. The doorknob was similar to those in large hotels: metal handle and metal plate with a slot. Eddington inserted the card and quickly removed it. A soft click could be heard. Turning the knob, he and the others entered.

Inside, Stanton found himself in a small foyer enclosed by floor-to-ceiling partitions. He touched one of the walls and found it cool to the touch. Plastic. High tensile plastic, he assumed, the kind used by banks to separate tellers from would-be robbers. The enclosure was bullet-proof and, for all Stanton knew, bomb-proof.

On the wall opposite the entrance was another door. It was featureless, gray, and made of steel. "Quite a place you have here," Stanton said.

"It does the job," Eddington replied. Facing the door, Eddington reinserted the card in another slot. This time a small panel next to the door opened. Eddington stuck his hand in. A bright light shone from the cavity in the wall.

"Fingerprint identifier?" Stanton asked.

"Nothing so mundane, Captain," Eddington said. "This device reads four biometric indicators: palm print, vein map on the back of my hand, hand size, and skin effluvia."

"Skin what?" Dole asked.

"Effluvia, Lieutenant," Eddington explained. "Body odor. In addition to that, there is this." He removed his hand and pointed at a small dark dot that looked like the head of a nail. "Fiber optic camera. A computer is comparing my face to a database of approved personnel."

There was a slight, almost imperceptible beep. Eddington spoke: "Dr. Mason Eddington." The door slid open.

"Voice imprint?" Stanton asked.

"Exactly," Eddington said. "At the moment we have the most sophisticated, computer-controlled biometric security devices in the world. Several of them will be obsolete within twelve months. There's a business tip, gentlemen. Invest in security companies. It's one of the fastest-growing industries in the world. It's a good way to make your future finances bright."

"I have other matters on my mind at the moment, Dr. Eddington," Stanton said, stepping through the second door. "I'm more concerned with the present than the future."

The small foyer gave way to an expansive room filled with television monitors and other electronic devices. A clear plastic wall with a map of the compound was to one side, and reminded Stanton of flight-status boards on aircraft carriers. There were six desks, each with a computer and a monitor. All the desks faced the same wall, a wall upon which had been mounted row upon row of monitors placed in a unified grid. Each screen displayed a different scene of the compound. Stanton could see the entry gate, the intersections of streets, and what he assumed was every significant building on the site.

Movement caught his eye. "What's that?" he asked, pointing at a monitor near the middle of the grid.

"Let's see," Eddington replied. Stepping to one of the computers, he tapped a key. Suddenly the mosaic of pictures on the monitor melted into one giant image. Clearly displayed was a green Humvee and several men in BDUs, standing around smoking cigarettes. Stanton glanced at Dole, who stiffened and frowned deeply.

"Excuse me a moment," Dole said with a growl and walked to one corner of the room. Stanton was unable to make out the exact message Dole transmitted over his radio, but a half-second later the men with the cigarettes had extinguished them, grabbed their weapons, and began to march along the perimeter of the fence.

"Kind of gives one the feeling of omniscience, doesn't it, Lieutenant?" Eddington said with a smile. "I'll bet your boys will be talking for weeks about their all-seeing commanding officer."

Stanton studied Dole, who was clearly not amused by Eddington's comments.

"Care to check up on the rest of your men, Lieutenant?"

"That won't be necessary," Dole answered sharply. Stanton would have bet money that Dole would love to verify his men's locations and activities, but he was not about to do so in front of Eddington.

"You're sure?" Eddington inquired with a smile. "There are cameras strategically placed in and around the compound, including the road in. We can watch the entire perimeter fence and the surrounding area to a distance of three miles."

"This would have been helpful information to have had earlier, Dr. Eddington," Stanton said with irritation. There was more to Eddington than he was letting on.

"Not really," Eddington said defensively. "Dole's men were already in position when I arrived."

"It would help in communications between teams," Stanton said. He turned to Dole. "Lieutenant, I assume that you could make use of this equipment."

"Yes, sir."

"Then bring in whatever personnel you see fit."

"Yes, sir." Dole was on the radio again.

"Now, Dr. Eddington," Stanton said coolly. "I assume that what is seen here is also recorded."

"For a while. It's too much information to keep complete records. There are a lot of minutes in a day, and a lot of cameras.

Once a week, the digital optic disks are cleared and reused. Unless, of course, there is an incident that needs to be saved for future use."

"Can you call up the event time?" Stanton wondered.

"The Event," Eddington said. "That's a good title. This technology isn't my forte, but I should be able to handle it. Give me a couple of minutes." Eddington sat down at one of the computer consoles and began clicking keys.

"I have a team coming in to man this post, sir," Dole said softly.

"Very well, Lieutenant."

"We'll have to stay here until they arrive," Eddington said over his shoulder. "Your men can't get in without me. For that matter, they can't even get out without me."

"There's no manual override to the security system?" Stanton asked.

"None, and that's by design." Eddington said.

Stanton felt that Eddington was lying. "Can your men disable the doors, Lieutenant?"

"Yes, sir. My men will pull the building off the foundation if ordered to do so."

"Let's hope it doesn't come to that. I want you to secure those doors open. I don't want your men trapped in here if we need them. Clear?"

"Crystal clear, sir."

"I found the files list, Captain," Eddington said. "I suppose you want me to—" He stopped abruptly and gazed at the monitors on the wall. "What the . . . ?"

Following Eddington's gaze, Stanton saw that the wall of monitors had returned to their mosaic presentation of Roanoke II scenes. It was the upper right screen that caught his eye. "Where is that, Eddington?" Stanton demanded.

"I'm not sure."

"Get sure," Stanton said. "I want a precise location."

Eddington looked down at the computer screen and then punched a few keys. The entire wall of monitors morphed again into a single image—the image that had captured their attention. Another keystroke and words appeared at the top of the screen: SECTOR 3, FIRST AND D. "That's near where we were before. When you caught a glimpse of something. Is that what you saw?"

"I don't know," Stanton admitted. "But I know what I'm seeing now. Let's go."

"You two go," Eddington said. "I'll stay here."

"Like you said," Stanton said forcefully, "no one gets in or out of this place without you. You're our key back in, so you're coming with us."

"Captain—"

Dole was suddenly standing next to Eddington. Startled, Eddington jumped to his feet. "It's time to go," Dole said.

Stanton looked back at the monitor. His heart pounded with excitement and his brain buzzed with confusion. How? When? Why? He had a thousand questions and no answers. Somehow, someway, there had been a survivor. On the screen was the image of a boy and a dog walking down the middle of a street. Stanton watched as the boy came to a stop in the golden wash of a streetlight. As if he could sense he was being watched, the lad looked directly into the camera that Stanton assumed was mounted in a tree or on a rooftop. The child wrapped his arms around himself and shuddered against the cold night and harsh rain.

"Lieutenant, have Ramsey and Keagle join us. I don't want him getting away this time."

"Yes, sir."

"Dr. Eddington, I want those doors open now."

Eddington complied, and Stanton led the way out of the building and into the driving rain.

Chapter 8

23 November 2000
Georgetown, Maryland

The glass of golden fluid sat untouched in the center of Philip Kaster's desk. Surrounded by the walls of his study, the admiral gazed at the tumbler which, like the room, was illuminated by a single bulb in a banker's lamp that sat on the desk. He tried to redirect his attention to the bookshelves filled with tomes on history and biographies, or to the pictures hung in custom wood frames—pictures of aircraft he had flown as a naval aviator, carriers he had served on, award ceremonies at which he had been honored—but his attention always returned to the glass of scotch.

He had entered the study an hour before with a bottle Chivas Regal in one hand and the glass in the other. He wasted no time in sitting down in his leather executive desk chair and pouring the strong liquor into the glass. He had even brought the fluid to his lips, inhaling the pungent aroma, but he could not drink it.

He wanted to drink it, to gulp the first glass in a display of machismo that only he would see, then slug back another, and another, until the magic of the alcohol made the regret go away;

the regret, and the fear, and the fierce anger which burned inside him like molten steel. But he could not tip the glass.

The words of the president swam around in his head like a school of barracuda. The more he thought of the conversation the more angry he became, but he still could not consume the liquor. So he set it in the middle of his desk and stared at it.

Kaster had never been much of a drinker, not even in his younger days, and was unable to recall a single time when he had been drunk. Drunkenness was unacceptable, a violation of his iron will, a surrender of his intellect to an addictive chemical.

Still, it did have the power to bring on momentary oblivion, a fog of delusion that would allow him to escape his problems, at least until the morning, when the anesthetic quality wore off. So why couldn't he down the fluid?

A knock, soft and tentative, came at the door. It could be only one person. "Come in."

The door swung open slowly, and the concerned face of his wife peeked around its edge. She was the light of his life. Silver haired, tall, thin, and stately, with the kind of blue eyes that men fell helplessly into. She was the linchpin of his existence. No longer young, her skin had surrendered to wrinkles and the occasional age spot. Lines spread from her eyes. But all of that was just the outer layer, just the thinnest veneer of appearance, the level at which most people judged the attractiveness of others. Kaster knew better. Just below the sheen of the visible was the most remarkable woman he had ever met. Her intellect was keen; her wit sharp. She carried herself with the dignity of royalty, but without the airs. Men of all ages fawned over her at parties. She was to people what a magnet was to iron.

Other men had left their wives for younger women in a vain attempt to prove to themselves their own attractiveness. Kaster had never entertained such thoughts. No woman could make him happier than Martha; no woman could have been more understanding of his career, the only mistress he had ever known.

"I was worried about you," she said softly, as she entered the study. Kaster watched her as her eyes darted from the bottle of Chivas, to the full tumbler, to him. He knew that she had assessed the situation in those few brief moments. "I didn't know you were having a party."

"Some party," Kaster said, leaning back in his chair. "No one is drinking. It must be the host."

"In a party of one, it is always the host."

Kaster chuckled unconvincingly. "Yeah, I guess you're right."

With amazing grace and meticulous movement, Martha removed the glass of scotch from the desk and poured it back into the bottle. Not a drop was spilt. "One should not drink when one is depressed." The words struck him as odd. She had never tasted booze of any sort.

"Depressed? Is that what I am? Depressed?"

Martha came around the desk and sat on one corner. He looked up at her, and the love she felt for him cascaded down like a waterfall. Somehow, her presence made him feel better. "Yes, dear, you are depressed—big time. So what won't they let you do?"

"What?"

"What won't they let you do?" she repeated. "The only time you ever get depressed is when the Washington Rednecks lose, or you feel helpless."

Kaster laughed, his melancholy unable to restrain him. "Redskins, dear. The Washington Redskins, and they don't depress me."

"So then, you're feeling helpless."

"I suppose I am, but I can't talk about it." He placed a hand on her knee. Just touching her made him feel better.

"Ah," she said. Martha had been the wife of a navy man long enough to know not to ask questions that could not be answered without breaching security protocols. "One of those things, is it? So what's the plan? Shall I join you in your depression?" She smiled.

She would do exactly that, Kaster knew. If he wanted to sit in the dark study, lit only by a desk lamp, and feel sorry for himself, for his mistakes, then Martha would sit next to him without complaint. He did not want that. "Thank you, no. It's not very pleasant down here in the dumps."

"Am I right?"

"About what?"

"You're feeling helpless," she explained. "Am I right about that?"

He thought for a few moments, reviewing his bitter conversation with the president, the problem of Roanoke II, and the crescendoing sense that he was to blame for it all. "Yeah, I guess I am."

"I see," she said as she slipped off her perch on the desk. Leaning forward, she kissed him on the forehead. "Is there nothing you can do about it? All avenues are closed to you?"

"Whatever I do will cause a stink, Martha. It's complex, convoluted."

"And the situation smells better if you do nothing?"

He shook his head. "No, not really."

"So the situation stinks no matter what?"

"That's about the size of it." He paused, wishing he could tell her more, but knowing that he couldn't. "My career may be over."

"Maybe? There is some doubt?"

"Yes. Nothing's final. But when the dust settles, it's going to settle on me."

"Haven't you been thinking of retirement?"

"We've talked about it. You know that."

Martha thought for a moment, then resituated herself on the corner of the desk. "There's something you want to do, isn't there? About the situation, I mean."

"There are lots of things I'd like to do."

"Have you been told not to do them?"

Kaster smiled. Martha had an innocent but piercing logic about her. "Not directly."

"Let me see if I have this right," she said. "As you sit here now, you feel your career may be over. If you do what you think you should, it may end your career. Either way, it's over. I guess it all boils down to what is right and what is wrong."

"I don't know, Martha, this is big and involves a lot of people. It could ruin my reputation. You could end up married to a former admiral."

"I didn't marry an admiral, dear. I married you. It has never mattered to me if you were a stockbroker, schoolteacher, football coach, or admiral, as long as it was you."

"How did I ever luck into marrying you?"

"Daddy always said you married above yourself. Besides, it wasn't luck. I chased you until you caught me."

Kaster smiled. "Maybe there is something I could do. But I might have to go out of town."

"As if that has never happened."

"You're not trying to get rid of me, are you?" asked Kaster.

She slid off the desk corner and sat on Kaster's lap. "Sweetheart," she said softly, "the navy has separated us many times, but it has never parted us."

He embraced her, holding her tight, smelling her hair, feeling the warmth of her cheek next to his. "And it never will." They kissed, long and passionately. The kind of kiss that only those who have traveled years of life together can share.

When the embrace ended, Admiral Philip Kaster said, "I need to make a phone call and pack a few things."

N

23 November 2000; 1930 hours
Roanoke II

Rain fell in silver sheets and slapped against the Humvee. The wind, which had been present but moderate when Stanton arrived, howled, its invisible hands pushing the rain sideways. "Lousy night to be out," Stanton said.

"Roger that," Dole replied. "The kid didn't look dressed for weather like this."

"Does it rain like this all the time?" Stanton asked Dole.

"I've been stationed in the low desert for three years, Captain, but the high desert isn't much different when it comes to weather like this. It seldom rains, but when it does, it can turn angry: flash floods, lightning storms, high winds. Up here it even snows in the winter. It seldom lasts more than a day, then it's gone."

Stanton looked out the window and up to the black marble sky. He could see nothing but the albescent rainfall which turned lemonade yellow as it passed under the glow of the sulfur streetlights. "Slow down," Stanton commanded. "Let's keep the engine noise to a minimum. If we go roaring in there, we'll frighten the child. Kids are resourceful. If he runs, we may never find him."

"I have my team coming up the south side," Dole said.

"Have them come the last two blocks on foot. I want them to approach quietly."

"Will do." Dole radioed the command.

"How do you explain this, Dr. Eddington?" Stanton asked of the man in the backseat. He had been taciturn since leaving the surveillance building.

"I can't explain any of this, Captain. I have no more ideas about what's going on than you do."

"Did you recognize the boy?"

"No, but then that's to be expected. Roanoke isn't a major city, but it is large enough to make it impossible to know everyone on sight."

"We're close," Dole said. "Do you want to go in on foot too?"

"That's the idea, Lieutenant." Stanton replied. "This spot looks as good as any."

Dole brought the vehicle to a stop in the middle of the road. "If he hasn't moved in the last five minutes, the boy should be around that corner and a block and a half away."

Stanton studied the intersection before him. They were in a residential area, surrounded by adobe-colored homes. The windshield wipers slapped back and forth in a vain rhythm.

"You two don't mind if I wait in the car, do you?" Eddington asked. "No sense in all of us catching pneumonia."

"I'd prefer it that way, Doctor." Stanton pulled his cap tightly down on his head. "Tell your team not to approach, but to keep the lad in sight."

"Yes, sir."

Stanton threw the door open. Wind, cold and wet, assaulted his face and cut through his battle dress uniform. An involuntary shiver ran up his spine as if ice water had been poured down his back. He was thankful for Dole's foresight in bringing the BDU for him to wear.

The world seemed surrealistic: black sky, wet wind, yellow lights, empty houses, vacant streets. Squinting against the wind, Stanton felt his face begin to sting. Raising a hand, he wiped at the skin. Sand. The rain was mixed with sand. The wind was carrying small grains of sand and dirt with it. It was raining mud. He and Dole, who had come around the Humvee, exchanged glances. "Let's move out."

Rocking. Rocking. Back and forth. Rocking.

Wet. Wind. Cold.

The dog whimpers and licks the boy's hand. The boy stares silently ahead. Water drips from his nose and falls to the ground. His skin is raw to the touch but he makes no effort to cover his face.

Tired. Tired of walking. Tired of standing. Hungry. Slowly the boy lowers himself to the ground and sits cross-legged in the middle of the street.

"Don't play in the street," his mother had told him more times than he could count. "Never, ever, play in the street. It's dangerous." But that had been when there were drivers, when there had been people, when there had been Mother.

He wanted to weep, but he had been weeping for two days. There were no more tears. He was becoming as numb to his loss as he was to the driving, pelting rain.

The dog licked his face, then lay down on the wet street, resting his large head on the boy's knee.

Rocking. Rocking. Back and forth the boy oscillated. Now side to side, he swayed. Rocking, swaying, staring.

Gone. All gone. There, then gone.

Lights in the sky. Roaring in the air. The smell, the colors. Gone. All gone. Alone. Deserted.

Rocking. Rocking. Back and forth. Rocking.

Wet. Wind. Cold.

Shiver.

A sound.

He was sitting in the street, his head down, resting in his hands. And he was rocking back and forth in time with unheard music. Stanton felt a wave of compassion wash over him like a tidal wave. Dressed only in a short-sleeved shirt, pants, and sneakers, the boy looked pathetic. Stanton felt miserable and wet in his utility uniform; he could only imagine how uncomfortable the child was. "Stay here," he said to Dole.

"But, sir. If he runs—"

"Stay here," Stanton repeated as he started forward. The boy had to be frightened. He had run before and he could run again. At least Stanton assumed that what he had seen earlier, and what he and the others tried to chase, had been this boy. That, somehow, did not seem right. He could understand how a clever boy might evade a group of adults, but concealing the dog would be another matter. Maybe the dog was a recent addition.

The dog was another problem. How would the creature respond? Growl? Attack? Run away? Stanton was about thirty yards away and standing in the dark. The best he could tell was that the dog was an Irish setter. An adult by the look of it. Slowly, Stanton advanced, walking down the center of the street. He walked softly so as not to frighten the boy. Beyond where the child sat, he could see Ramsey and Keagle, one on each side of the roadway. They were in position to pursue the boy if he bolted.

Step by step, Stanton approached, feeling as if he were walking miles instead of yards. When he was thirty feet away, the dog looked up, cocked its head, whimpered, and then sat up. The boy didn't move. Taking a few more steps, Stanton crouched down in front of the lad, who kept his head down, face in his hands. The dog stood and wagged its tail.

Stanton studied the sad figure. Muddy rain continued to fall, peppering the child's blond hair with brown. Gently, Stanton reached forward and touched the boy on the knee.

The child's head snapped up, terror painted across his dirty face. His blue eyes widened and he scrambled back. He screamed, and then screamed again. The ululation rose in a crescendo of terror. Turning, the boy started to his feet, but Stanton was on him before he could find his footing. He snatched the child up in his arm, but it was like holding a giant, wriggling octopus. Legs and arms were flying. A knee caught Stanton in the ribs, a foot on the inner thigh, and a fist to the side of the head, but he would not let go. Instead, he pulled the boy tightly to his chest.

"Easy, son, easy," Stanton said softly. A knee caught him in the stomach and he doubled over, still holding the boy. "Ouch. That was a good one."

Stanton put a hand on the boy's head and pressed it into his own shoulder. "Relax, son, no one is here to hurt you." The boy continued to thrash. The setter at his feet pranced, then stood on his hind legs and nuzzled the boy.

Footfalls echoed off the surrounding homes. Dole and his team were closing in. "Stay back," Stanton ordered, fearful that the sudden appearance of more men in uniform might further upset the child.

"But, sir," Dole began.

"As you were, Lieutenant," Stanton said firmly. Then for the boy to hear, he said, "My new buddy and I have to get acquainted."

The boy suddenly stopped struggling, and his screams melted into deep sobs. Stanton hugged him, then began to rock side to side. "It's all right, boy. It's all right. I'm going to take care of you. You're not alone anymore."

Stanton stood with the boy in his arms for five minutes. Neither said a word, but Stanton's strength flowed into the frightened child. When the sobbing stopped, he leaned forward and set the boy down. It was a painful act. Bruises were already forming where the child had kicked and punched Stanton. Tenderly, he brushed away the muddy splotches on the child's face. Then he took his cap off and placed it on the lad's head. The boy touched it tenderly, obviously confused. Stanton smiled and said, "I think we're getting wet. Let's get out of the rain." He offered his hand. The boy hesitated and looked at the dog questioningly. "Yeah, sure, son. The dog can come along."

As if understanding the words, the dog barked and then pranced in a circle. The boy took Stanton's hand. The two walked back to the Humvee. Dole followed behind.

Chapter 9

15 March 1947
Mt. Rainier, Washington

The Bell 47B helicopter moved slowly over the crash site. The pilot, Steve Petersen, guided the new helicopter in a lazy circle over Tahoma Glacier. The wind off Mt. Rainier was gentle and forgiving, something for which Petersen was thankful. He was one of the few certified helicopter pilots in the world, and he wanted to live to enjoy that distinction. Still, despite the danger and the difficult duty he had been hired to do, he was enjoying himself. Helicopters were the wave of the future, and his Bell 47B—the first model to be certified—was going to lead the way.

"Over there," his passenger shouted. Petersen looked in the direction that Sheriff George Grant was pointing. He found the site immediately.

"It doesn't look good," Petersen responded.

"Fly over it."

Petersen nodded, adjusted the collective, pushed the stick, and guided the craft over the site. Below them were the remains of a twin engine marine plane. One wing was broken off and lay a hundred yards south. The tail section pointed skyward in an unnatural way, like a leg with a compound fracture. "Doesn't look like it burned," Petersen said.

"No, but it sure hit hard. Looks like it may have traveled on its side before coming to rest on its belly."

Petersen lapped the helicopter around the site again. "No footprints in the snow. That's not good."

"They've been up here for two days," Sheriff Grant said. "The same bad weather that brought down the plane kept us from finding her. If anyone did survive the crash, they'd be dead from the cold."

Petersen nodded, then shuddered at the thought of what might be in the wreckage.

"Can you set us down?" Grant asked.

"What? That's a glacier, Sheriff. A steep one at that."

"Let's find a flat place. We can walk in."

"We? I'm a pilot, not a mountain climber."

"Come on, Petersen. Back at the airport you told me these new contraptions could land anywhere. Besides, there might be someone still alive."

"Not likely."

"If it were you hurt and freezing in that plane, wouldn't you want someone to at least try?"

"The ground search team can do it."

"It will take them too long to get here. Minutes count. Find a place and set us down. You can stay in the helicopter if you want."

Petersen groaned. This was the last thing he wanted to do, but Grant had a point. The least he could do was look for a flat rocky area to set down. He found one. A hundred yards east of the crash site was a jut of granite, bare of snow.

"If I can't get my bird out of here after we land," Petersen said, "the county is going to buy me a new one."

"I'll put a good word in for you," Grant said with a wry smile. Then he returned his attention to the crash site.

Grant had a good reputation. He was tall and thin, with a dark, pencil-line mustache. Quick to laugh, he was an easy man to get to know. Yet, despite his easy-going manner, he was a tough man in a fight and took his duty seriously. Duty and honor were things he had learned in the infantry during World War II. Once back home in Washington, he ran for, and won, the office of sheriff.

As Petersen hovered the craft and then slowly decreased power to begin his descent, Grant radioed the airplane's position. Ground crews would begin making their way up the treacherous glacier.

The chopper set down hard, harder than Petersen had wanted. He swore under his breath. "There you go, Sheriff. Don't ever say that Steve Petersen doesn't deliver the goods."

"You're a good man, Petersen. I don't care what the rest of the town says about you."

"Cute. I risk my life and livelihood, and I get cute comments from you."

Grant looked out the side opening toward the wreckage. He could see the dark fuselage in the distance. He unbuckled his safety belt and turned back to Petersen. "You coming?"

That was the last thing he wanted to do, but he felt uncomfortable letting Grant go it alone. "I'll have to shut the engine down. Although the weather has cleared, it's still cold. I can't stay gone too long, or I might not be able to get the engine started again."

"Then let's do it." Grant was out of the helicopter as the last word issued from his lips.

Petersen quickly cut the power to the rotor and joined the sheriff. He had to scamper across the rocks and onto the ice to catch up. This part of the glacier was nearly flat, with only a slight grade down the mountain. If it had been anything otherwise, they would not have been able to cross the ice without rope and climbing gear.

"I'm not looking forward to this," Petersen admitted. His heart was pounding hard from fear and exertion at seven thousand feet of altitude.

"This isn't something anyone looks forward to," Grant responded, his breath emanating in wisps of condensation.

Movement on the glacier was perilous, but they made it to the wreckage without incident. They paused a few yards from the metal hull. Both struggled to catch their breath. Although the plane went down in bad weather just two days ago, it appeared scarred and battered, as if it were a derelict from a generation before.

With an anxious sigh, Grant moved forward with Petersen close behind. Snow, freshly fallen from the storm that downed the plane, lay before them like a white wool blanket, disturbed only by the wreckage. No footprints were to be seen.

"How are we going to get in?" Petersen asked breathlessly.

"The tail section," Grant answered. "It looks like there is a gash in the fuselage big enough for a man to get through."

A chill, unrelated to the cold air, coursed through Petersen's veins. "It won't be pretty."

"No, I don't imagine it will, but I have to check for survivors. It's my job, and it's the right thing to do. If I had a family member on board, I would want to know the truth."

"Let's get it over with."

The snow scrunched under the weight of each step and covered Petersen's foot to the ankle. He hated snow; always had. It was pretty in pictures, but was cold enough to kill skin cells. Frostbite was ugly and destructive. The sooner he was out of the snow and back in the helicopter, the better.

The tail section of the craft was twisted and bent skyward, like a tin can torn in half. A gaping and ragged tear ran along the beam. The metal skin was serrated along its edge, like the business end of a saw. A small breeze rolled by, causing the whole tail section to shudder.

"That thing could come down any minute," Petersen said.

"I'll go in first, you follow behind."

Avoiding the jagged edges of metal, Grant pushed his way into the open maw. Petersen watched him disappear into the bowels of the airplane, took a deep breath, and followed him in. At first, Petersen kept his eyes down, fearful that he might see something horrible: broken and bleeding bodies, severed arms and limbs. But when he looked up, he saw something far more disturbing—emptiness.

Inside the twisted wreckage were seats enough for thirty-two people, all of them empty. "What? I thought the plane was supposed to be full," Petersen said. His words echoed in the metal cavern.

"That's the word I got. There are supposed to be thirty-two people back here."

"Where are they?"

"Maybe they never boarded. The plane was flying empty."

"That's a relief," Petersen said. "That leaves only the pilots."

Grant turned and carefully made his way forward. A thin bulkhead separated the pilots from the passengers. The door between the pilot's cabin and the passenger area was sprung open. Grant peered in.

"Well?" Petersen called.

Grant turned back, his face ashen. "There's nobody here."

"What? That can't be. This thing didn't fly itself."

"Maybe they walked away."

Petersen shook his head. "We would have seen their footprints."

"It was snowing. Maybe the snow covered up the tracks."

"Maybe." Petersen was unconvinced. Light, bright from reflecting snow, poured in through broken windows. So did a bone-chilling wind. "They wouldn't have made it very far. Not in this cold."

"Still—" Grant stopped abruptly.

"What? What's the matter?"

Granted pointed at the seats. "The belts. The seatbelts."

Petersen looked down at the seats to his left. Each one was equipped with a wide nylon belt, and they were all fastened. He also noticed a brown stain near the window, a smear that looked like blood. All the seats had similar splotches of blood. "They were here," he said with disbelief. "They were here and they were dead, and now they're gone. How can that be, Sheriff?"

Instead of answering, Grant peered back into the pilot's compartment. "There's blood in here, too. And the yokes are bent like a steering wheel in a car after a head-on collision. They were here, all right."

Petersen let his eyes dart about the cabin. There were several paperback books, magazines, and coffee cups strewn about. The cabin had been occupied. "They couldn't have all walked out, Sheriff. Not all of them. Some would have to have been too severely injured. This doesn't make sense. This doesn't make sense at all."

Chapter 10

23 November 2000

1600 Pennsylvania Avenue, Wahsington, D.C.

Gone? Gone where?" The president was dressed casually in a chocolate brown polo shirt and beige slacks. He rose from his seat on the Oval Office sofa and began to pace along the thick pile blue rug. "Where did he go?"

"Back to the Pentagon." The man standing before him was Mark Adler. "As you requested, I assigned a couple of men to keep an eye on the admiral. He went home, stayed a few hours, then his driver showed up. Next thing we knew, he was on his way. Our men followed at a discreet distance."

President Norris Crane looked at his watch: 10:45. "He's keeping late hours."

"It makes sense," Mark said. "This research was his baby from the beginning, and he's a man who takes responsibility seriously. He wouldn't be in the Pentagon if he weren't."

"I know that," Crane snapped. "I don't have a good feeling about this. This whole thing is too sensitive, and we had a pretty good row here a few hours ago. He doesn't see my position, and he got ahead of the game. Now we have others involved. We're on thin ice here. If it hits the fan, then I'll be left alone. I'll be twisting in the wind, with Congress using me for a piñata."

"I doubt it will come to that," Mark said. "There are some key senators and congressmen involved."

"And they will jump ship the moment the waters get rough." Crane lowered his head in thought, then raised it again. "Is he in his office?"

"I don't know. Our men couldn't follow him into the Pentagon."

Stepping to his desk, Crane tapped a key on his computer, bringing it back to life. A moment later, he picked up the phone and dialed out. "Admiral Collins, this is Norris Crane. I'm sorry to be calling so late." He paused while he listened. "Thank you, Admiral. I need a favor. Kaster may have gone back to the office. Is there any way for us to know, short of ringing him on the phone, I mean?" Another pause. "Okay, that would be great. You'll call me back then?" Listening. "Excellent. I'll wait to hear from you." Crane hung up.

"You think he's up to something?" Mark asked. "Going to the office at night isn't a sin. Half of Washington works until the wee hours. Look at us."

"Normally, I wouldn't give it a second thought, but my instincts tell me something's afoot. I've learned never to ignore my instincts. They helped get me here."

There was nothing to do now but wait. Ten minutes later, the phone rang. Crane picked up and listened to Admiral Collins, then: "Thank you, Admiral. What? No. No problem at all. Just checking on a couple of things. You have a good evening, and please give my best to the family." Crane set the receiver down in the cradle. His mouth was pulled taut. To Mark he said, "He's not there."

"But our men saw him go in."

"He went in all right. Security checked him in. Fifteen minutes later he checked out."

"But our operatives said that his car and driver were still at the Pentagon."

"Apparently he left by other means."

"Why would he do that?" Mark asked, confused. "Unless . . ."

"Unless he knew, or at least assumed, that he was being observed. He's up to something, all right. But what?"

"This is bad," Mark commented quietly.

"We can't wait to find out," Crane said forcefully. "We have to be proactive on this. I want to know what Kaster is up to. He holds our collective lives in his hands. Get the FBI in on this. Intimate that we have reason to believe that Kaster may be a security risk, but that we could be wrong. I want them to tread softly and report directly to me."

"That's more people in the mix, Mr. President," Mark said. "The FBI is a huge organization with less compartmentalization. We need a smaller action team, one who answers only to you."

"Do you have something in mind?" the president asked.

"Yes, I do."

23 November 2000; 1950 hours
Roanoke II

The mosaic screen in the surveillance room changed again, revealing a floor-to-ceiling view of a single-story concrete building. Four men in military dress were attempting to cut through a metal door with a blowtorch. Eddington chuckled.

"What's so funny?" Stanton asked.

Motioning with his head, Eddington, who sat at one of the terminals, said, "Them. They'll be there all week trying to cut through that steel."

"It would be a lot easier if you just opened the facility for us," Dole said.

"I've already told you, I can't do that. The area contains information that is vital to the security of this country. I've been asked to help, but I have not been released to allow access to the labs by unapproved personnel. And, Captain Stanton, I recommend that you cease this vain attempt. You will have to answer for your actions."

"I look forward to it," Stanton said evenly. He was determined that Eddington would not get to him. "Likewise, you'll have to give an answer for your resistance."

"It's out of my hands," Eddington said with a shrug. "But I can show you the inside of the lab through the surveillance cameras. At least—" He stopped short.

"At least what?" Stanton asked.

"Nothing," Eddington replied. "Here." He quickly punched in a few keystrokes, and the large composite monitor changed. They were now viewing the inside of a building. "This is the foyer your men are trying to gain access to. Not much to see here." He tapped on the keyboard again. The scene changed to a large room filled with drafting tables, desks, and computers. "This is the design room. The drafting tables are just for layout. The real design is done on computer, printed on a plotter, and then reviewed and discussed here." After a moment's pause, he changed the scene again, and again, giving brief descriptions of each. Stanton saw a lunchroom, individual offices, some small, others much larger and fashionably decorated. There were even cameras in the rest rooms. "As you can see, Captain, there is no one in the building. No gathering of frightened people. These rooms are as empty as the houses. You can call your men off. There's no need to get into the building."

Something was wrong, but Stanton couldn't put his finger on it. He had seen something that registered in his subconscious, but his active mind missed it. He struggled to bring the thought forward.

"Coffee?" a woman's voice asked.

Stanton turned to see Sergeant Keagle. She was holding two steaming mugs of coffee. To Stanton, who was still wet and chilled, the cup looked marvelous. "Thank you, Sergeant," he said. It occurred to him that this was the first he had heard her speak since arriving in Roanoke II. "Where did you . . . ?"

"I found a coffeemaker in the small kitchenette," she answered, then handed the other cup to Dole, who took it gratefully.

"I also found some hot chocolate mix," Keagle said. "With your permission, I would like to make some for the boy."

Stanton turned to the lad, who stood quietly in one corner, his damp clothes clinging to him. Next to his feet lay the Irish setter. They had done their best to dry him off, but had found only a roll of paper towels to work with. "Sergeant Ramsey should be back with Tulley and Wendt in a few minutes. He'll be bringing towels and a change of clothes for the boy." FBI agents Pierce Tulley and Loren Wendt had remained at the house looking for evidence. Their latest radio report had been discouraging. Remembering the bedroom he had examined, the one with the boy's baseball glove on the floor, he had ordered Ramsey to drive to the house and bring whatever warm clothes he could find that might fit the lad.

"Has he said anything?" Stanton asked. Despite kind and gentle coaxing from Stanton, the child had been silent during the trip back.

Keagle shook her head. "No, sir. Not a single word. He's been traumatized."

"I wonder what he saw," Stanton said. "I would also like to know why he's here when everyone else is gone. Keep working with him, Sergeant. I'm hoping he'll open up to you."

"I'll do my best, sir." She turned and walked back to the boy. "Come on," she said. "I bet some hot chocolate will fix you right up."

"Is there anything you want to see here, Captain?" Eddington asked. "Or are you satisfied that I'm not concealing people in the lab?"

"Yes. I want to see what happened at the time of the disappearances. You said that images were stored for a number of days before being used again. Is that right?"

"Yes, but—"

"I want to see those," Stanton said firmly.

"What day? What time?" Eddington replied. "We could be sitting here for hours looking at digital images."

"We know the time that Edwards Air Force Base picked up the anomalous radar images. We can start a little before that, then skip forward or back in half-day increments, until we stop seeing people."

"I suppose that would work," Eddington said.

"Can you call it up through the computer, or do you have to find video tapes to plug in?"

Eddington chuckled again. "This is a state-of-the-art facility, Captain. The information is saved on rewritable CDs."

"Where are they?" Dole asked. Stanton could see the lieutenant's patience ebbing from him, like the tide from the shore.

"I can access them all from here." The pride in Eddington's voice was noticeable.

"0245 hours, November 22," Stanton said. "Let's start there."

"Well, that may prove to be a problem," Eddington said, leaning back in the chair.

"Why?" Dole demanded.

"Because, Lieutenant, 0245 is two forty-five in the morning. The lab would be closed and the streets empty. Our work was important, but it was also ahead of schedule. We didn't operate around the clock."

"Everything would be closed down?" Dole asked with exasperation. "This building would be operational. Someone had to watch these monitors."

Eddington shook his head slowly. "While it is true that security would have been on duty at that hour, there are no cameras in this building. Surveillance people don't surveil themselves."

"Maybe not this room," Stanton interjected, "but I'll bet you there's a camera at the guard shack at the entrance to the compound. Try that one."

Eddington leaned over the keyboard, punched the menu that listed all the camera locations, and then selected the one labeled, ENTRANCE POINT GL1. An image appeared on the screen. Two marine guards were standing their posts. "This is real time," Eddington said. "Those are Dole's men." Again he punched up the menu and selected Archives. A series of dates appeared. He selected 22 November. A box appeared on the screen that read: Enter time here. Eddington did, and a moment later the screen filled with a new image. "I'm starting a full half hour before the Edwards' time," he said. "Hopefully, that will give us a baseline from which to work."

The real-time image had been replaced by the video archive. Instead of Dole's men holding position, there appeared men wearing white shirts, blue pants, and blue caps. Each displayed a small badge over the left breast pocket of the dark coats they wore.

Dole was incredulous. "You use rent-a-cops for security? You must have slept in great comfort."

"Sarcasm doesn't suit you, Lieutenant," Eddington said, unperturbed by Dole's comments. "Those two men are some of the navy's best. The uniforms are part of the presentation."

"Presentation?" Stanton said. "I don't follow."

"Everything about Roanoke II is designed to blend in. The houses are typical subdivision style. The school looks like any other school. Even the lab is designed to look like a simple industrial building. The goal was to look like a gated community. The guards at the front gate are supposed to look like hired security and not military."

Something new was puzzling Stanton. "When you called up the menu, it identified the guard shack as Entrance Point GL1. What does the GL1 stand for?"

"It's just a designation, Captain," Eddington said with a dismissive tone. "You know how the military is. Everything has to have a label."

"There's a reason for that, Dr. Eddington. I would like to know the reason behind the GL1."

"Ground Level 1," Keagle said. She had returned from the kitchenette. With her was the boy. He was holding a cup of hot chocolate. "That's a guess, of course, but it opens up some interesting ideas."

"Such as?" Dole asked.

It was Stanton who answered. "If there is a GL1, there must be a GL2. True?"

Eddington fell silent.

"And why the 'ground level' designation?" Stanton continued. "Could there be some way in and out of the compound other than at ground level?"

"Do you mean like an airfield?" Dole asked.

"Possibly," Stanton said thoughtfully. The same feeling of uncertainty, of something overlooked, washed over him again. In his mind, he replayed the rooms in the lab which had been displayed on the composite screen. They seemed out of balance, as if their sum did not equal the whole. Then it hit him. "Eddington, can you call up the real-time image of the lab again while letting this archive run?"

"That's why the composite screen is there, Captain. We can look at one image or thirty-six at a time."

"I want to see the lab again, but let the archive run."

"Why, Captain?" Eddington asked. "You've seen that there is nothing of interest there. Just computers and desks."

"That's the point, Doctor," Stanton replied. "One does not spend millions of dollars to build a compound like Roanoke II just to support what little we saw in the lab. There's more there than meets the eye."

"This is a waste of time, Captain." Eddington walked away from the keyboard. Dole started toward him.

"As you were, Lieutenant," Stanton said. "When you were showing us the lab, I noticed a wide door. It didn't strike me as relevant at the time, but there were no hinges on it. It slides open, doesn't it, Dr. Eddington?"

"And if it does, so what? Many doors slide instead of swinging on hinges. I have one in my house. They call it a pocket door."

"I know what a pocket door is, Eddington," Stanton replied. "But this was no pocket door. I'm betting it's an elevator."

Eddington stiffened.

"Of course," Dole said. "That would explain the GL1 designation. There must be an underground installation."

"You watch too much television," Eddington said.

"It makes sense," Keagle said, joining the conversation. "There are many underground installations. NORAD in the

Rockies, Mount Weather in Virginia. I have even heard that there are some here in the high desert: in Llano and Helendale. The Helendale sight is supposed to be a COG site—continuation of government site."

Stanton was nonplussed. "You certainly seem to know a lot about underground bases, Sergeant."

"Not really, sir," Keagle replied. "I have a brother who is big into conspiracy theories. He told me that some believe that there is a huge tunnel that runs from Edwards Air Force Base into the Tehachapi Mountains. There's supposed to be a secured airfield there."

"I can guarantee you that that is nothing more than rumor," Eddington said flatly.

"Perhaps so," Stanton said, "but underground bases are not out of the question. I personally know of a site near Seattle where submarines can be hidden from view. So how about it, Doctor? This place have other levels you're not telling us about?"

"I've already told you—" Eddington stopped abruptly. He was staring at the monitor. "What is that?"

Stanton turned in time to see something indescribable. "Back it up," he ordered. "I want to see it from the beginning."

Eddington returned to the computer console and punched at the keys. The image disappeared for a moment, then returned. The guards stood outside the small white guard shack smoking cigarettes. One must have told a joke, for both began to laugh, but the laughter stopped abruptly. The men looked up. A second later, one pulled a pair of binoculars from the hut and raised them to his eyes. He lowered them, shook his head, and then handed them to his partner.

Out of nowhere it came. It was amorphous and pulsating. At first Stanton thought it was a giant bubble but quickly dismissed the idea. Like a bubble, this was spherical, but its surface writhed and vibrated. It shimmered yellow and blue. Its surface was not smooth, but was nodular and rippling, like the surface of the sun he had seen once on video.

The bubble changed in an instant. One moment it was round, the next it was flat, like a sheet of boiling glass.

Light, blue and yellow, exploded from the thing. The next instant it was gone, and so were the guards. Only their cigarettes remained smoldering on the ground.

Dole and Eddington swore.

"Time," Stanton snapped. "Get the time."

"What was that?" Dole asked.

"I have no idea, Lieutenant," Stanton said.

"More importantly," Keagle said in awe, "is it coming back?"

The boy's mug of hot chocolate crashed to the floor, exploding in fractured glass and brown liquid. A second later the boy began to scream.

N

PART 2

DESCENT

Chapter 11

23 November 2000; 2010 hours
Roanoke II

They had all been the same. Every camera in every location recorded the identical scenes: a multihued light, a morphing, pulsating orb, an explosion of light, then emptiness. Because of the late hour in which the event had taken place, only a few cameras recorded people. A street video showed a man exiting a mini-mart when he disappeared, leaving behind his small bag of groceries scattered on the pavement of the parking lot. In another, a car moved slowly through a residential area; a moment later, it drifted to the side and crashed into a light standard. No one came out to investigate. No one exited the car.

The team watched in stunned silence as each unbelievable scene was played out before them.

"There must be a rational answer to all of this," Special Agent Tulley said. He and Wendt had arrived with Sergeant Ramsey shortly after the first archived video was played. Stanton had ordered the video to be played again for their benefit, and because he could not make his rational mind believe what he was seeing.

"I'd love to hear it," Stanton said.

"So would I," Wendt agreed. "It's like a giant magic act."

"Except the beautiful assistant doesn't reappear," Stanton added. He asked the group, "Any ideas as to what we are seeing?"

There was no response. No one had any ideas.

"Well, it's not magic," Tulley said. "I don't believe in such things. Therefore, it's a physical event, either manmade or natural."

Dole looked at Stanton and raised an eyebrow that said, "That's the best he can do?"

"Doctor Eddington," Stanton said, "can you explain what we've just seen?"

"No," Eddington replied tersely.

"This has nothing to do with the research that goes on here?" Stanton pressed the issue.

"No."

"I don't believe you," Dole said. "I've never heard of anything like this happening, anywhere. Do you want me to believe that someone else is responsible?"

"I don't care what you believe, Lieutenant," Eddington said, standing up and stepping away from the computer console.

Dole tensed and took a step toward Eddington. "As you were, Lieutenant," Stanton said. Dole froze in place, his eyes fixed on the engineer. "This is getting us nowhere." He turned to the others. "Anyone here familiar with computers and technical equipment?"

"I am," Sergeant Keagle said. "I'm no expert, but I can get around most systems pretty well."

"Good," Stanton said. "Please help Dr. Eddington secure the videos. We'll need them for analysis."

"Yes, sir."

"So what do we do now, Captain?" Wendt asked.

"Sitting here won't help," Stanton said. He thought for a moment. His team was anxious and concerned, and for good reason. While no one said so, he knew they harbored the same fear: the event could happen again. This time they would be the victims. "We're moving out."

"To where?" Tulley asked.

"The lab," Stanton answered. "Maybe we can figure out a way to gain access. The answer must be in the lab."

"Maybe it's a weapon of a foreign country," Ramsey said. His voice was a rich baritone that matched his size.

"We don't know that," Stanton said to the big Samoan. "It's possible, I suppose, but unlikely."

"There's nothing in the lab," Eddington said. "I must protest your efforts to get into it. National security is at stake."

"That's exactly why I plan to see what's in the building."

"You'll be defying orders, Captain," Eddington countered. There was fear in his eyes. Stanton knew the man was holding back, keeping a secret.

"Only your orders, Doctor. My mission is to find out what happened. I'm going to do that, with or without your help."

"But, Captain—"

"Lieutenant," Stanton said, cutting Eddington off midsentence. "Ready the vehicles and notify your men at the lab that we are on our way."

"Yes, sir."

"Captain!" Eddington screamed. "I will not let you enter my lab. I will have you court-martialed. I will see that you never have a command of any kind again. Do you hear me?"

Stanton started for the door without a word. Eddington sprang forward, interposing himself between Stanton and the doorway. "I won't allow it, Captain. Do you hear? I won't allow it."

The muscles in Stanton's jaw tightened like spring steel. He was tired and confused, sure that he was facing a problem beyond his understanding. The last thing he needed was a physical confrontation.

"If I may, Captain," Ramsey said. The big man stepped forward and placed one of his giant hands against Eddington's chest. The motion was slow, deliberate, and delivered a message unmistakable in any language. Then with a soft but profoundly solid voice, Ramsey said, "Please move." It was worded as a request, but everyone who heard it knew it was a command.

Eddington's breathing quickened, his fist clinched, and his eyes darted from Stanton to Ramsey, and then back to Stanton again. "You can't treat me this way. This is not right."

Stanton raised one eyebrow in response.

"Please," Ramsey reiterated. "Move aside and let the captain through."

Reluctantly, as if the very act caused him extreme pain, Eddington yielded and stepped to one side. Stanton looked at Ramsey, nodded, and said, "Thank you, Sergeant."

"My pleasure, sir," he replied with a thin smile.

"Now, let's see what we can see." Stanton marched through the door, into the secured lobby. The entrance/exit door had been propped open at the suggestion of Dole. Stanton, driven by his mission and concern for the missing, yet fearful of what he might find, advanced into the street.

"Lieutenant Dole," Stanton said, as they walked away from the building, "I want to make a call. A couple of them. Can you hook me up through your communications?"

"Yes, sir. Who would you like to reach?"

"I'm bringing another man in," he replied.

"Another officer?"

"No, a civilian."

"Is that wise, sir? I mean, the civilians we have are . . . well, what I mean is . . ."

"Making things a little difficult?" Stanton finished the sentence for Dole. "You're right, but Eddington is stonewalling us, and we need someone with a science background. Someone who studies things that others don't." He paused, then continued, "There's a division of orders here. I have one set, and apparently Eddington has another. It doesn't make any sense, but that is the lay of the land. This thing is beyond my experience, and probably beyond the experience of all but a handful of people."

"And those people are gone," Dole added. "You know a man who can help?"

"I do, indeed. We worked together once before. This type of thing is right up his alley. His name is Hawking Striber; he's a physicist. Maybe he can identify what we just saw."

"We could deliver the CD to him, rather than bringing him here," Dole suggested.

"Nothing leaves the compound until we know what's going on. Especially anything that can slip from our fingers. I want Hawking here. I don't even know what questions to ask. We need Hawking right away."

"Where does he live?"

"San Diego. If we get hopping, we can have him here within the hour. Maybe a little longer."

"What about Eddington?" Dole asked.

"We keep the pressure on. He's holding out. He knows something, something that has him afraid."

"I'll set it up," Dole said, and then jogged off.

"I hope you have some ideas, Hawking," Stanton said softly to himself.

When Hawking Striber arrived, he was green, and his forehead and bald head glistened with a film of perspiration. He was a thin, balding man, with a large forehead and eyes that looked as if the blue had been bleached out of them. Stanton shook his hand. "I take it that helicopters don't agree with you," Stanton said with a warm smile. They were standing in the same parking lot where Stanton had arrived a few hours before.

He and Hawking had been friends for just over a year. Stanton's brother-in-law, a chaplain in the navy, had introduced them when Stanton was working on the *Triggerfish* mystery. Hawking had proven insightful, helpful, and unfazed by the unfriendly welcome Stanton had first offered. Initially, Stanton had believed that no two men could be more different. Although both were academicians in their own right, Hawking in physics, he in history, they had gotten off on the wrong foot, and it had been entirely Stanton's fault.

Hawking, despite his frail, professorial appearance, had not been intimidated in the least by Stanton's rank or directness. Instead, he stuck to his beliefs and challenged Stanton on his. It had been Hawking who had moved Stanton from being a casual Christian to one with a dynamic, daily faith. For that, Stanton never ceased to be grateful. It had, after all, saved his life.

"It's that obvious?" Hawking asked weakly.

"Only to those with eyes," Stanton answered.

"There's a reason I don't avail myself of carnival rides, J. D.," the physicist said. "And the wind and rain made the flight here very much like one of those rides."

"I'm sorry about that, Hawking, but I needed you here right away." Stanton had made contact with Captain John Hollerman of North Island Naval Air Station in San Diego, who had arranged to have Hawking picked up, brought to North Island,

and flown to Roanoke II. The whole thing had taken less than sixty minutes. "I didn't get you out of bed, did I?"

"Not even close. I'm a night owl. I do my best work after the sun has gone down."

Stanton was thankful for that. He knew what it was like to have men in uniform come to your door and ask you to take a drive. At least, Hawking had had some warning. Stanton had seen to that. He tried to imagine the middle-aged physicist, sitting alone at his desk or computer, toiling away at his work. Hawking had never married, and in the year that he had known him, Stanton had not seen him date. He was a man consumed with his work.

"I'm glad I was in town for you." Hawking paused as he took several deep breaths of the cold desert air. His color was slowly returning.

"I'm afraid things don't get more secret than this, Hawking. I'm stretching things much farther than I should having you here, but I have a problem and you're the only one I can think of who can help."

Hawking pulled his dark leather jacket closed and zipped it up. "At least you had the foresight to warn me about the weather." He shivered. "There's a reason I live in San Diego."

Stanton smiled and patted his friend on the shoulder. "Let me fill you in, then I want to introduce you to my team." Stanton led Hawking to the Humvee. He had driven there by himself, wanting to spend a few moments alone to brief his friend. As they drove, Stanton explained the enigma they faced.

At first, Hawking was speechless, then he said reflectively, "Fifteen hundred people. And no sign of them at all?"

"None. All we have is the video of the bright light."

"I need to see that."

"That's the plan, but first I need to make a stop. The team is at the central lab trying to break in."

"Break in? You don't have a key?"

"Actually, we do, but he won't work."

Hawking looked puzzled, and Stanton explained the problem with Eddington.

"And this is Eddington's project?"

"Yes. It's his baby, all right, but I think he's hiding something."

"I don't imagine he'll be happy to see me."

Stanton chuckled. "You can bet the farm on that. He's done a few things to help, but he's really dragging his feet about the lab."

"Could he really have orders that conflict with yours?" Hawking asked.

"It doesn't seem reasonable, I know," Stanton replied, "but, yes, it is entirely possible. The military and political structure is extremely complex. In most cases, it works flawlessly; other times it is filled with infighting and competitive agendas. Everyone has something to promote or protect."

The ten-minute drive ended with Stanton pulling the Humvee into the parking lot of the lab. Three men stood hunched near the door of the building. He could see the bright glow of the torch being used on the entrance door. Others stood about waiting impatiently for something to do. Exiting the vehicle, Stanton called the team together.

"Everyone," he said, "this is Dr. Hawking Striber. He's here to help us." Several nodded and said hello. He turned to Hawking. "Hawking, this is Lieutenant Dole, Sergeants Ramsey and Keagle, Agents Tulley and Wendt of the FBI, and Dr. Mason Eddington."

"Ph.D.?" Eddington snapped, a scowl etched in his face.

"That's right," Hawking replied firmly but with a smile. "Physics."

"Earned?"

Stanton and Hawking exchanged glances. "Yes," Hawking replied. "I did my undergrad at Stanford. My master's and Ph.D. are from M.I.T. Last I heard, their degrees were still good."

"What kind of physics?" Eddington's words were clipped and cold.

"Quantum mechanics."

"So you're a theoretician?" Eddington asked. "I preferred the practical world of engineering. Pie-in-the-sky speculation seems a waste of time to me."

Stanton started to object to Eddington's tone, but Hawking was too quick. "I don't do formal research any longer."

"So you're a teacher."

"Part of the time. I'm an adjunct at UCSD, but I spend most of my time in my ministry."

"Your . . . your what?" Eddington seemed astounded. "Your ministry? Like a church or something?"

"Not a church. I research biblical miracles from a physics perspective. I write books and lead seminars."

"Well, now," Eddington said cynically to Stanton. "I see that you have successfully rounded out the group. We now have a religious fanatic. Well done, Captain. Well done." Eddington didn't wait for a reply. Instead, he turned and marched toward the Humvees.

Stanton looked at Hawking and raised an eyebrow. "Welcome to Roanoke II."

N

"That's it, sir." The man was holding an oxyacetylene torch. Scorch marks surrounded the high-tech door handle. "I can't seem to make any progress."

Dole turned from his man to Stanton. "I don't think we're going to get in this way."

"I told you that," Eddington said.

The rain had stopped, and the atmosphere was filled with smells of wet pavement and desert plants. The air was cold, and getting colder, but the wind had quieted. It was as if nature itself had paused to watch the strange goings-on at Roanoke II.

"The walls are eight inches of concrete, Captain," Eddington said. "Steel reinforced. The door is a steel alloy. The same one they use to make armored vehicles. Better actually. No stolen blowtorch will cut through it."

Stanton looked up. A row of windows ran the length of the wall. Eddington saw Stanton's gaze.

"As I said earlier, the windows are composed of a force-resistant plastic. You couldn't shoot a bullet through them."

"How about popping them out of the frame?" Dole asked.

"Thought of that too," Eddington said. "It's never going to happen. Bottom line is, you're out, and you're going to stay out."

"Just why are you here?" Dole asked sternly. "You're more a hindrance than a help."

"I'm here for the same reason as you," Eddington replied with a disingenuous smile. "To find out what happened to my people and my facility. I just happen to know that our research has nothing to do with the problem. We're wasting our time here. We should be looking in other areas, searching for more clues."

"The windows are fixed," Stanton said, ignoring the tense conversation around him.

"What?" Eddington asked.

"The windows," Stanton repeated. "They're fixed. They don't open for ventilation."

"Of course not. It wouldn't make much sense to put in security glass, then have windows that open so someone could climb through."

"Interesting," Stanton said.

"I don't follow, sir," Dole said.

"Lieutenant," Stanton said, "didn't you tell me that your men found the torch in a garage?"

"Yes, sir. A service station not far from here, to be exact."

Stanton said, "Do you suppose they could locate a ladder or two?"

"Yes, sir," Dole said enthusiastically.

"Then do it."

"May I ask what the captain is planning?" Dole inquired.

"The desert gets hot in the summer and cold in the winter. There have to be heating and air-conditioning units on the roof. I don't see any units on the ground, so I'm guessing they're topside. I want to take a look. Maybe we could remove one of the units and lower someone through the ductwork. There may be some wire or bar barricades, but I bet they're easier to cut through than that door."

Dole brightened. "Good idea, sir." He was beaming.

Both men looked at Eddington, who stood in rigid silence. He made no protests, offered no reasons why the task was impossible. Stanton took that as a good sign.

"The best I can tell, he looks fine," the corpsman said to Stanton. "He's cold, tired, and a little dehydrated. We've taken care of those things."

"Has he said anything?" Stanton had ordered the medic to examine the boy while he supervised the work on the roof. Now back on the ground, he was eager to hear about the child's condition.

"No, sir. Not a word. He won't tell me his name or where he lives. I told him jokes, and even tried being firm with him, but got nothing."

"Is he capable of speech?" Stanton asked. "He's not mute, is he?"

"I don't think so, Captain," the medic answered, shaking his head slightly. "At least not that I can see. There's no scarring on the neck that would indicate surgery, but there must be a hundred reasons why a person won't or can't talk—both physical and mental. He needs a more thorough exam than I'm qualified to give, especially here in the field. All I can tell you at the moment is that he has no physical problems."

Stanton turned to the boy, who was standing next to the medic. The child seemed small and withdrawn. His clothing had been changed with those found in the house Stanton had investigated earlier. A blue baseball cap with *LA Dodgers* embroidered on it sat awkwardly on his head. He also wore a thick blue Dodger coat that seemed to swallow the lad whole. Seated on the wet ground next to the lad was the Irish setter.

A sadness filled Stanton. The boy looked as lost and lonely as an orphan, which he probably was. What was it like to be suddenly alone, not knowing where Mother or Father went, wondering if they would return? Then, to add insult to injury, to be surrounded by men in uniforms carrying guns.

"What am I going to do with you?" Stanton said as he squatted down to be eye level with the boy. He straightened the child's cap. "Do you like baseball?"

The boy nodded slightly.

Stanton smiled at the response. At least the child was responsive.

"That's more than I got out of him," the medic said.

Ignoring the medic, Stanton kept his gaze on the boy. "I like baseball, too. I'm a big Padres fan. How about you? Do you like the Padres?"

The boy scrunched up his face and shook his head.

"Everybody's a critic," Stanton said with a laugh. "Well, I can't go around calling you 'boy,' so you need a name. How about . . ." His voice trailed off as he thought. A passage of Scripture came to mind. "You know, son, there was a man in the Bible that lost the ability to speak for a while. It was John the Baptist's father. His name was Zechariah. That's a good name. We could call you Zach. How's that? The mighty Zach. I think that's a good name for a baseball player."

The boy smiled a crooked smile.

"Okay, then. Zach it is." He turned to the dog. "How about you, fella. Do you have a name?" The dog chuffed and wagged its tail. Turning back to Zach, he said, "What say we call the dog Red? That's what an Irish setter should be called, don't you think?"

The boy nodded.

"Zach and Red, friends forever," Stanton said with a broad smile. Then, in a soft fatherly tone, he said, "Zach, I'm your friend, too. Okay? I want you to know that. No one here is going to hurt you. That's a promise."

Zach cut his eyes away, then moved slowly to Stanton. He could see the fear and uncertainty on the boy's face. The child had witnessed something that he could not explain, that no one could explain, and it left him alone in the cold wind and frigid rain. Zach wrapped his arms around Stanton's neck and began to cry softly. Taking the boy in his arms, he stood, hugging the child firmly. "It's all right, son. You're safe now. I won't let anything happen to you."

The boy answered with muted sobs. Stanton felt tears well in his own eyes. He prayed that he wasn't lying.

From the rear seat in a nearby Humvee, Eddington watched Stanton with keen interest through the rain-speckled side window. Stanton was the key to all of this. He was the leader and had already shown that he possessed an iron determination. The whole situation was unfair. Eddington had built this compound and had done so with the highest approvals. Now the same people to whom he owed his living, and his very lavish lifestyle, were demanding that he protect the secrets of Roanoke II. It was something he would do. He was, after all, a man of some determination. He was a patriot as much as any one of those buffoons in uniform. Their lives, and the lives of their compatriots, might one day depend on research done at installations like this.

Where did they think that high-tech weaponry came from? A catalog? A department store? No, it had to be designed, created from genius that lay in just a handful of men like himself. The safety of the country rested in technological advances brought into being by engineers, not gun-toting Neanderthals. The B–1 bomber, the stealth fighter, pulse engines, smart bombs, silent submarines—all of it came out of the minds of dreamers and doers. Men just like him. He was as patriotic as any man in a uniform. He just did his part differently.

He pulled his pipe from his coat pocket, and after following a pipe-smoker's ritual of loading tobacco and tamping, he lit it, sending billowing clouds of blue smoke into the cabin of the Humvee. He cracked the window to let the smoke drift into the cold night. He studied the dark sky for a moment. There were no stars, and the best he could tell the clouds were thickening. Soon it would begin raining again. But at least for the moment he was comfortable.

He watched as Stanton crouched down to talk to the boy. *Now there is an enigma*, he thought. *How could an entire population disappear and yet this boy still be here? What was special about the lad?* That was important information, but how to obtain it? He was far from being in good favor with the captain and the others. To them, he appeared to be dragging his feet, hindering the progress of the investigation. But he had no other choice. He was under obligation to the highest ranking officer in the country. Sure, Stanton had his orders, but he had orders, too, and he knew who it was that buttered his bread. There was no way he would betray his benefactors.

Such were the vagaries of government: one arm locked in combat with the other. There were many dark and secret hallways in the world's largest democracy. There were secrets kept not only from the American people, but from anyone who could not or would not help the cause. Eddington knew every corridor, every secret door, every person involved. He prided himself on that fact. Knowledge made him what he was today, not just knowledge in his field, but knowledge in the field of human studies. He could judge a man in a minute, determining his strengths and weaknesses. And that was what bothered him at the moment.

Stanton was a man of depth and conviction. He followed orders, not just because he was told to, but because he believed he should. Despite his rank, there was no air of superiority surrounding him; but neither was there any indication of moral or mental weakness. That frightened Eddington. Men with vices were easier to control than men without them.

Then there was Dole. Eddington shifted his gaze from Stanton, who was now holding the boy in his arms, to Lieutenant Dole, who stood like a statue at the parapet of the roof. Behind him, his marines were busy dismantling the HVAC system for the lab. Soon they would have the heavy machinery pulled to one side and would be cutting away the iron bars that were meant to keep intruders out. He hated himself for not making the duct system more secure, but who could have guessed the events that would lead to a team of marines with torches cutting away at the lab's security?

Dole was staring back. Even at the distance of fifty yards in the black of night pierced by the yellow light of streetlamps, he could see Dole scowl. Dole had a problem with him, that much was evident. It was the source of the problem that perplexed Eddington. He seemed too reactive to Eddington's refusal to grant them access to the lab, entirely too hostile. There was something at stake with the man, something more than the fulfillment of his assigned duty.

Now what? Eddington wondered, as he watched Dole point in his direction. He was shouting something down to Stanton, and then to his men, but he was too far away to be heard through the small opening left in the window.

First there was the vaguest of shadows in the corner of his eye, just enough movement to catch his attention. He turned to his right and there it was: black and looming, eyes wide, pupils dilated, medusa hair waving in a sudden gust of wind.

Eddington screamed and backed away, his heart pounding like a piston in a race car. His stomach turned. He pushed himself along the seat until his back touched the cold metal of the door.

"What the—" His own thoughts interrupted him, a realization: the door was unlocked. The creature slapped the window and emitted a sound Eddington was unable to recognize. It slapped the window again, and again, then stopped. With terror rippling through his body, Eddington watched as the creature looked down toward the handle of the door—the unlocked door.

"No!" he shouted and leaned forward to hit the latch. He missed, and the door swung open. The wind pushed past the thing, bringing a pungent, acrid stench with it. With a quickness that belied his age and size, Eddington shot backwards until his spine was once again pressed against the door. "Stay back!" he shouted.

He had to escape, to get away. He fumbled for the handle of the door behind him. Found it. Pressed it. He fell backwards to the wet ground, hitting his head on the door.

Rolling onto his stomach, he pushed up and attempted to get to his feet. Suddenly he felt himself pulled up. He glanced around him wildly. Two marines had grabbed him by the coat and pulled him to his feet. For the first time that night, he was happy to see them.

"The other side of the car," he shouted. "It's after me. It's after me."

Neither marine said a word. They simply dragged Eddington away.

Chapter 12

23 November 2000; 2135 hours
Roanoke II

"What you mean a-yellin' at ol' Josie dat a way?" The wild-eyed woman took a step back as armed marines slowly approached her. "I ain't done nothin' wrong. No need for you to haul off and go ta screamin' at me." She was pointing at the terrified Eddington.

"I . . . I . . . ," Eddington stammered. "You startled me."

"Me?" The woman replied with astonishment. "Why, I ain't been no trouble to nobody, all my days."

Stanton watched the exchange with curiosity. Eddington was red-faced and panting like a man who had run up several flights of stairs. He stood behind the marines who had picked him up off the ground after he had fallen out of the vehicle.

The woman was another matter. Tall, slightly hunched, she looked to be in her early seventies. Lines scored her black face deeply, and her hair was a mass of dirty, matted tangles. She spoke with a deep rural Southern accent and punctuated her words with wild gestures. She was nothing if not animated. At first, Stanton had trouble believing his eyes. The woman was like a cartoon character come to life. Her appearance and odor made it clear that she lived on the streets. Except there were very few streets in Roanoke II. She wore faded jeans, men's sneakers that were two or three sizes too large, and an oversized brown leather coat that had clearly belonged to someone twice her size. The coat was stained with brown blotches, as were her trousers.

How had she made entrance into a secured facility? There was only a short time from when the people disappeared until Dole's men arrived on the scene. Perhaps she had wandered in. Stanton had no way of knowing.

"We're sorry if we frightened you, Ms. . . . ?" Stanton said.

"Frightened me? Frightened me?" she yammered. "Why, ol' Josie ain't never been afraid of nothin', nothin' at all. And that's God's truth." She looked at the uniformed men around her, guns at the ready. "Course, these pretty boys with them guns ain't makin' ol' Josie feel none too welcome. No, sir. None too welcome at all."

"Have your men stand down, Lieutenant," Stanton said. Dole, who had raced down the ladder at the first sight of the woman, stood next to him.

"Yes, sir." Dole gave the orders, and his men lowered their weapons and took a few steps back. None took their eyes off the wild woman.

"Lieutenant—"

"I have no idea," Dole answered, anticipating Stanton's question. "There was no breach in the perimeter fence, nor did my men find any holes underneath it. As much as I hate to admit it, I'm at a loss."

The woman laughed loudly. "Don't you know that you can't keep ol' Josie outta nowhere? I comes and goes as I please. Ain't nobody but the Lord hisself can tell ol' Josie what and how to do."

A deep sigh escaped from Stanton's lips. The day had been long and was getting longer. Missing people, an arrogant FBI man, a stubborn and uncooperative engineer, a mute boy and his dog, and now a crazy, homeless woman. He was beyond the point of being surprised anymore.

"Josie," Stanton began in a soft tone. "How did you get here?"

"Same as I gets anywhere. I walked."

"No, what I mean is, how did you get onto this facility?"

"Facility?" she said, puzzled.

"Here, on the grounds," Stanton explained. "How did you get onto this property?"

"Why, I lives here." Her tone was confident, determined.

"That's impossible," Eddington said. "No one lived here without my approval."

"Ain't nothin' of thc kind, Mr. Too-Good-to-Talk-to-Ol'-Josie. I been living in these parts for the better part of thirty year."

"Ever since you came from . . . " Stanton prompted.

"Alabama," Josie answered frankly. "I like you. There's something special about you. I knows these things."

That explained the accent. "But how did you—"

"I done told you, Mister. I lives here."

"Desert rat," Dole whispered to Stanton.

"What?" Stanton said.

"Desert rat, sir," Dole explained. "There used to be a lot of them in the high desert. They're people who live some distance away from the towns. They have a small piece of property and put up a shack, or trailer, or something. No plumbing, no power. They're sort of homeless, with homes. If that makes any sense."

Stanton nodded. "Do you have a home somewhere around here?"

"Sure do, Mister. I got a place about three miles from here. Due north, as a matter of fact."

"Why are you here?" Stanton asked.

"Came to investigate," she answered. "Saw them lights in the sky last night and thought maybe the world was comin' to an end, like the Good Book says. When it didn't, I came a lookin' for them lights. Maybe aliens landed, or somethin'. I wanted ta see."

Aliens, Stanton thought. Any other time and any other place, the suggestion would have sounded ridiculous, but here in Roanoke II, it almost made sense.

"I seen that man there"—she pointed to Eddington—"sittin' in that fancy automobile. I figured he musta knowed somethin', so I decides to ask 'im. Next thing I know, he's a huffin' and puffin' and screamin' like a girl child, or some crazy man or somethin'. It was almost enough to scare me, ceptin' I don't get scared."

"Scared you?" Eddington said pointedly. "My heart nearly stopped."

"It's that pipe there you been smokin'," Josie admonished. "Ain't good for you. Take it from ol' Josie. I've lived a lotta years, and I'm healthier than a ox."

Several of the men chuckled. Dole cut them to silence with a single look.

"Josie," Stanton said. "I'm Captain J. D. Stanton, and—"

"What's the J. D. stand for, honey?"

"That doesn't really matter," Stanton said. "What I want to know is—"

"Sure it matters, honey. Everybody's gotta have a first name. Mine's Josie. I done told you that. Now you tell me yo' name."

"Josie," Stanton began, "I really don't have time for this. What we're doing here is important."

The woman frowned deeply and crossed her arms in defiance. Stanton knew he was going to get nowhere this way. If he wanted anything from the old woman, he would have to give something in return. "Julius," he said. "Captain Julius D. Stanton." He hated his first name.

"Well, now, that weren't so bad," Josie said, beaming a near-toothless smile. "What can ol' Josie help you with, Julius?"

"How did you get here?" he asked, cringing at the sound of his name.

"Walked, just like I said."

"You walked three miles through the desert in the dark?" Stanton asked in disbelief.

"Sure. Why not, honey? I been living out here a real long time. I knows every rock and bush. Ain't nothin' ol' Josie don't see. And the rain, it don't bother me none."

"But how did you get here, in the compound?" Eddington chimed in. "There's a fence around the entire complex and only one road in."

"I know dat," Josie snapped at the engineer. "Don't you think I know dat? I walked up that very same road you're talkin' about. Weren't nobody at the guard shack, like dere is most days. Gate was opened so I invited myself in. Been wanderin' and wonderin' ever since. Where are the people?"

"That's what we're here to find out, ma'am," Stanton said. "Did you—"

"Ain't no need to call me ma'am," Josie said. "No need for formalities between friends, Julius."

Stanton cut his eyes to Dole, who had been watching him. Dole quickly took his gaze away.

"Very well, Josie. Did you see anything besides the lights in the sky?"

"No, sir, not a thing. Just those bouncing balls of light."

"You say you've been wandering around the houses?"

"I didn't take nothin' excepting some food here and there, but that's all. Ol' Josie ain't no thief. Stealin' is against the commandments, and ol' Josie don't break no commandments."

"Can I have a word with you, Captain?" The voice came from behind him.

Turning, he saw Tulley. "What is it, Agent Tulley?" The FBI agent and his partner had spent the last half hour in one of the Humvees, waiting for Dole's men to break into the lab.

"Over here," Tulley said, motioning with his head. "You too, Lieutenant." The men followed Tulley until they were out of earshot of the old woman. "Listen, Captain. This woman is clearly crazy, and she can only be a detriment to our work here, not to mention a security risk to your people."

"My people?" Stanton said.

"Yes, the military complex. The people who built this place. Anyway, I suggest we get rid of her as soon as possible. The last thing we need is a loony desert rat getting in the way."

"Why do you think she's crazy?" Stanton asked.

"It's obvious, isn't it? All this religious talk, living alone in the desert, and just look at her. She looks like she climbed out from under a rock."

"Religious talk, huh?" Stanton said firmly. "That's why I don't think she's crazy. She's odd, I'll give you that, but not crazy. Still, your point is well taken. We do have our hands full."

"I can have a couple of my men drive her off the grounds, sir," Dole said.

"The boy has to go, too," Tulley said. "He's just going to be in the way. Him and that dog."

Tulley was right, but for some reason it galled Stanton. Maybe it was Tulley's attitude; maybe it was just the late hour, the adverse conditions, the inscrutable mystery he faced. The boy needed to be somewhere warm and safe, and the woman might be a bother. But . . .

"They're the only witnesses we have," Stanton said. "I agree with you in principle—"

"Witnesses," Tulley interjected bitterly. "What kind of witnesses are they? One is a psychotic woman and the other is a mute boy." His tone turned sarcastic. "I'm sure they're loaded with vital information." He shook his head then continued, "I'm sure the woman knows nothing. By her own testimony, she arrived after everyone was gone. She's an outsider who can add nothing to the investigation. The boy's affliction can only slow us down."

"Back off, Tulley," Stanton said sternly. Tulley's tone rubbed against his grain. "This is my call." Tulley fell silent, his face a mask of disgust. Stanton turned to Dole. "What's your opinion, Lieutenant?"

Dole straightened. "Well, sir, there's another problem. Whatever happened here could happen again. If we keep civilians here who are not involved in the investigation, then we may be endangering their lives."

It was a thought that had already occurred to Stanton. "Very well," Stanton said. "Lieutenant, have one of your men drive the woman back to her home. Make sure he takes note of its location. I want to be able to talk to her when we have a better feel of what is going on here. When he returns, he can take the boy to a local hospital. I'm sure your medic did a fine job examining him, but I would feel better if a doctor had a look at him."

"If I may, sir," Dole said, "our mission is secret. If we take the boy to a local hospital, there will be a great many questions. Especially if he is brought in by a man in uniform. There would be no way to keep such a thing out of the local papers."

"A military hospital then?" Stanton suggested.

"Yes, sir," Dole responded. "I suggest taking him to Fort Irwin in Barstow. Round trip will take my man about ninety minutes."

"That's what we'll do then, but it won't be a round trip." Stanton said. "Choose a man who will be sensitive to the boy's fear. Have him try to engage the lad in conversation. Also, I want him to stay by the boy's side until I relieve him. Better send two men; they can work in shifts. The boy is not to be left alone for a moment. I want the doctor's report as soon as possible as well as anything they can learn from the child."

"Yes, sir," Dole responded.

"Let me tell the boy. I think he trusts me."

"What about the dog?" Dole asked.

"He goes with the boy," Stanton answered. "The child needs any friend he can find."

Suddenly Dole raised a hand to his ear, touching the headset he wore. "Say again," he said into the microphone. "My men have made entrance into the lab, Captain. They have sprung the door from the inside. We can now make entry."

"Finally some good news," Stanton said. "Have your men hold their positions at the door. I want Tulley and his partner to survey the area first. I don't want us treading clues underfoot."

"Very wise, Captain," Tulley said. "Now maybe we can make some progress."

"Hold it," Dole said sharply. "I'm getting another report." He stiffened. "Captain, one of the sentries reports an aircraft headed our way."

"What kind of aircraft?" Stanton demanded.

"Unknown," Dole said. "A slow mover." Dole held up his hand. "Best guess is a private plane."

"The press?" Tulley asked.

Striding to the closest Humvee, Stanton snatched up a pair of binoculars. "Direction, Lieutenant."

Dole responded by pointing. "Due south and low, sir. Very low."

Raising the glasses to his eyes, Stanton scanned the area. The powerful lenses found the craft quickly. The plane's red and white collision lights flashed. "Low is right, Lieutenant. That guy's almost on the deck. Looks like a small private craft. A Cessna or something like it."

Just as he finished speaking a dark object flew across his field of vision. "What was that?"

"Sentry reports another craft in the area, sir," Dole said. "It shows no anti-collision lights."

"That's illegal, isn't it?" asked Tulley.

No one answered the agent. Stanton was trying to locate the dark object that had raced across his view. He had a bad feeling about this. Once again, the other mysterious craft zoomed in and out of Stanton's sight. "I can't get a lock on this guy," he said with frustration.

"Sir?" Dole said.

"The second craft is much faster," Stanton said. "But it's too dark to make out anything. The plane, however, is coming right for us."

"Sir," Dole said loudly, "someone is on our frequency. He wants to talk to you."

"Someone? Not one of your men?"

"No, sir," Dole said, clearly puzzled. "He says he's Admiral Philip Kaster."

"Kaster?" Stanton was shocked beyond words. According to his briefing file, Kaster was the Pentagon official who had ordered Stanton to Roanoke II. "What is he doing out here? We're a long way from the Pentagon."

"I don't know, sir, but he wants to talk to you, right now."

Stanton took the headset from Dole.

Until five minutes ago, Admiral Kaster felt he had made the trip free and clear. It had been a simple matter to have his driver drop him off at the Pentagon and then, instead of going to his office, make his way to the car pool where he checked out a fleet vehicle. From there it was a short drive to Naval Air Station Oceana in Virginia. Before flying a desk in Washington, Kaster had been an active navy pilot with more hours in the air than he could count. Using the weight of his rank, he requisitioned and flew an F–111 Aardvark cross-country, balancing his need for speed with the jet's fuel usage. The sleek General Dynamics attack aircraft gave him the high speed necessary and the range required. At 1,450 miles per hour, he had crossed the continent in just over two hours. The perfect plan would have him landing at Roanoke II, but that was impossible. The facility had a small airfield, but nothing big enough to land a military jet. Instead, he had flown to the China Lake facility and requisitioned another aircraft: a T–3A Firefly trainer. The propeller-driven plane was slow, but capable of landing on a short runway.

Kaster checked his airspeed again: 150 miles per hour. He tried to will the airplane to move faster. Raindrops streaked across the cockpit's windshield. Below him the desert raced past.

Twisting the dial on the radio, he tuned in to the frequency the Roanoke II investigation team was using. He offered a silent prayer of thanks that he had remembered to bring the briefing file with him. Otherwise he would have had to land without notifying Stanton and his men.

The streetlights of the tiny Roanoke II facility gleamed in the moist night air. He was getting close. Things were looking up; he had made it this far, and he was able to raise Lieutenant Dole on the first try. Now he waited for Stanton to get on the line and—The black object raced past him on the left side and then banked hard right. Kaster shouted with alarm and instinctively pushed the plane's yoke forward into a nosedive, then immediately pulled up. At only three hundred feet of altitude, he had little room to play with. Because of power lines, he could fly no lower, but wanted to fly no higher to avoid radar.

"What the—" The object pulled alongside Kaster's plane. It was a helicopter gunship. There were no markings to identify it, but Kaster recognized an AH–64A Apache when he saw one.

"Stanton here," Kaster heard over his headphones.

"Stanton, this is Admiral Kaster; I'm ten miles from your location."

"We weren't expecting you, sir."

"No time for that now, Captain," Kaster said sharply. "Just tell me that Apache off my wing is one of yours."

"Apache?" There was a pause. "No, sir. It's not ours."

"It has no markings, and it just buzzed me." A sinking feeling filled the admiral. The helicopter was faster, more maneuverable, and armed with a 30mm chain gun and eight Hellfire rockets. If the copter was unfriendly, then Kaster knew he had seen his last day. "Captain, I may not have much time, so let's get to it. This whole operation is dirty. You must watch your backside. Have you got that? The problem is deeper than it appears—"

The Apache suddenly buzzed over the plane. Kaster reacted by diving again, then pulling up suddenly. The copter was trying to force the plane down.

"Admiral, are you all right?"

"No," Kaster shouted. He began to swear. "He's trying to put me in the ground, Captain. I'll never make your location in time."

"Who's doing this, Admiral?"

"They don't want the secret to get out. They want to keep Roanoke II under wraps. It will ruin hundreds of people. Word has to get out. It's too dangerous. The whole thing has to be stopped. I thought they would support that, but they're protecting themselves. I'm sorry."

The T–3A began to vibrate, then pulsate. He was losing altitude. Looking up, he saw the helicopter flying directly over him. The downdraft of the rotor was tearing the plane apart. The vibration was painful, piercing his body and his ears. He could no longer hear, no longer speak. In desperation, Kaster plunged the right rudder pedal down and banked hard. The helicopter followed.

Kaster tried evading left, but the Apache stayed with him. His heart pounded hard, tears, not of fear, but of physical exertion, ran from his eyes. He tried to speak again, forcing the words from his mouth. "Be careful who you trust."

The helicopter continued its descent, forcing him down. *Why doesn't he just shoot me?* Kaster wondered. He knew the answer. The plane wreck was to look like an accident. They had thought of everything, anticipated everything.

It was hopeless. He would die, and it would look like it was his fault. They would have a full military funeral, present a flag to his wife, salute, and then bury the truth in his grave. His life would be over, his dreams, his goals, his work gone.

For a moment, Kaster thought of giving in, of putting the plane into a power dive and ending it, but the idea was a mere flicker in his thoughts. He had never surrendered anything. It was not part of his nature. If it had been, then he would be home warm in bed next to his loving wife, and not having his bones shaken to dust.

"You want to fight?" he said through clenched teeth. "You want me dead? All right, come and get me."

He banked sharply to the left again, then back to the right, but the helicopter stayed above him, anticipating each move. He throttled down, but the helicopter slowed with him. He followed that with a sudden lunge forward, the engine screaming as it was pushed beyond its design limits, but the Apache stayed closer than a shadow. Kaster knew there was no maneuver he could make that would shake the more sophisticated aircraft. The thunder of the rotors grew louder, as the helo slowly closed the gap between them.

With his mind spinning like the gears of a race car, Kaster weighed his situation. It was hopeless. Desperate acts were all that were left. They had anticipated his every action and countered it with skill. He had done what any military pilot would have done. Perhaps that was the problem—he was reacting in a predictable manner. It was time to be unpredictable.

Thrusting the yoke forward, Kaster put his aircraft in a power dive. The ground, which was now less than 300 feet below, raced toward him—250 feet, 200 feet, 150 feet, 100. The craft shook and rattled. "Now," he shouted to himself, and he pulled back hard on the yoke. The plane shuddered and groaned at the strain of the maneuver. It was an unreasonable act, but reason was not working. It was his hope to shake the Apache, forcing it behind him, then to fly as low as possible. With luck, the helicopter might hit power lines, or simply back off long enough for him to think of something new.

The propeller of the plane dug deeply into the fuselage of the war bird. The pilot of the helicopter had followed Kaster's dive, but had not reacted to his sudden change of direction. It was a mistake that took a fraction of a second to make, and it was fatal. At the moment of impact, the airplane twisted and its wing jutted into the Apache's main rotor. Both the wing and rotor shattered.

Both aircraft plunged to the ground a hundred feet below.

Stanton lowered the binoculars slowly. His stomach turned and his head throbbed. He had never met Admiral Kaster, but he knew that a noble man had just died. Through the binoculars, he had seen the flashing collision lights of the plane dip left, then right, then up. The lights went out, but were replaced a split second later with a ball of fire. There was silence on the radio.

"Did you hear all that?" Stanton asked Dole. His words came out hot and fast, fueled by a sudden rush of adrenaline.

"Yes, sir," Dole said. "I used Sergeant Ramsey's radio. I don't know what to make of it."

"Me either, but the man just gave his life to give us a warning. I plan to take it seriously."

"What now, sir?"

"I want this area cleared. Post more lookouts. I want everyone else in the lab. Now. Let's move, Lieutenant."

Dole was already on the move, shouting orders and reassigning his men. Stanton reached down and picked up Zach. "Let's get inside, son."

"What about the old lady?" Tulley asked.

"Her too, Agent Tulley. I need time to figure out what's going on."

"That many people on the scene may destroy important evidence," Tulley protested.

"I can't worry about that right now. Now, go!" Stanton started toward the building. In the distance, he heard the unmistakable thrumming of helicopters.

Chapter 13

24 November 2000
1600 Pennsylvania Avenue, Washington, D.C.

Slowly, President Crane set the phone down and rubbed his eyes. It should never have gone this far, never come this close to getting out of control. What else could he do? The whole thing was Kaster's fault. If only he had been more careful with the project, if only he had remained calm and not sent Stanton and his team in so quickly. He should have at least consulted the president of the United States.

Acid churned in Crane's stomach, boiling, seething like a witch's cauldron. Kaster should have turned back. That's all that was supposed to happen, simply turn and fly back to China Lake. But no, he had to play the hero, don the mantle of a martyr, and not only kill himself, but the crewmen of the helicopter.

"It couldn't be helped," Mark Adler said. "You're not responsible for Admiral Kaster's death, any more than you're responsible for the disaster at Roanoke II."

Crane looked up from his desk and stared at his chief of staff. The man was as loyal as they came. "This office carries a heavy burden with it, Mark. I knew I would have to make tough decisions when I decided to run for president."

"We had to stop him, sir," Adler offered evenly. "Once you knew that Kaster was on his way to Roanoke II, which, I might add, was done in total disregard to your orders, you had to act. Especially since we received word that Stanton was gaining access to the lab. You did say to take whatever measures were necessary."

"I know what I said, Mark. I don't need you to recite my words back to me like a tape recorder."

"Sorry, sir."

Waving a dismissive hand Crane said, "Never mind, Mark. Sorry to snap at you. This whole thing has me on edge. I feel like we're in a rowboat a few yards from Niagara Falls. One way or the other, we're going to go over the edge."

"Isn't that what the contingency plan is all about, sir? Making our rowboat into a barrel?"

"I would have preferred a quiet row to the shore, but that option no longer seems possible." Crane stood and began to pace around the sitting area, his hands clasped behind his back. He thought better on his feet, and his chronic pacing was legendary among the staff. "Okay," he said aloud. "Okay, okay." He fell silent again. Adler stood quietly, waiting for the president's next decision.

Finally, Crane ceased his pacing. "I don't see any way around it, Mark. Our hand has been forced. We must activate the contingency plan and not lose a minute doing it. I can't undo history, but I can change its course. Kaster's dead. Nothing will bring him back."

"Yes, sir."

"Make the call, Mark. Make it right away."

"Our people are in position and ready to go."

"Fine. That's fine." Crane started pacing again. "We'll need a cover story for the helicopter accident, as well as a believable explanation as to why Kaster was out there in the first place."

"That may not be necessary, Mr. President," Adler said. "The backup helicopter reports that the crash was ... well, fiery. Identification of the body may be impossible."

Crane nodded. "We can only hope. Using black copters was wise. At least there will be no identifying marks."

"The previous administration was populated by imbeciles," Adler said, "but at least they left us that. Covert military technology used to aid and protect R&D sites has been useful."

"Just make sure it doesn't lead to our downfall."

"I will, Mr. President. I will."

Mark Adler's home was situated in the well-to-do area of Arlington, Virginia. His neighbors included some of the wealthier senators and members of Congress, as well as CEOs and other big business personages. But it was not the plush outside surroundings of Arlington, with its closely manicured lawns, delicately maintained landscapes, and old colonial homes, that occupied Adler's mind, but the other side of the continent—a secret community in California that might not remain secret much longer. That would be a catastrophe for the president, and worse, for himself.

He was seated in a worn easy chair that had been his companion since his first year as an adjunct history professor at his alma mater, Harvard. The chair had sat in his tiny office, and then followed him to his more spacious surroundings as the head of an East Coast university. When he became chief of staff to the president of the United States, he put the chair in the den of his new home. It served as a reminder of his days as an academician. When the world of politics became too grimy and stressful, he would return to his den, sit in the aging brown chair, and remember days when students would furiously write down every word he said. There were no reporters, no self-serving politicos, no cloak-and-dagger FBI, CIA, and DIA men. There was just pure relaxation and thought.

Adler loved his job. He was aide and confidant to the most powerful man in the world. Those who wished to see the president had to first see him; he would then decide if a meeting was in the best interest of the nation and the president. This position of gatekeeper had made him either the enemy or the friend to hundreds of people. There was a certain headiness in being sought out at parties, in being patted on the back and having drinks brought to you. It seemed odd to Adler that he should have developed such a taste for politics. Sure, there were times when he ceased having an appetite for it all, like someone who's been fed a steady diet of fried chicken. The first few days are good, but soon the desire for a change arises.

Still, most days, the appetite was there. Unfortunately, if the president were not reelected, his gatekeeper role would end, and he, like the president, would slip off into oblivion. The president would at least be remembered in the history books, but Mark Adler would not. No longer would he walk the corridors of power and influence. He could run for office, the Senate perhaps, but that would seem like a demotion. Perhaps the next president would be of the same party and offer him a job as an ambassador or even a member of the cabinet, but that was unlikely. The new man would want a new slate of cabinet members. No need to "untrain the old dogs" that way.

As he sat in his chair, he sipped brandy from a large glass snifter, then rolled the brown liquid around in the glass as he ruminated. Crane had been right; they were teetering on the edge of destruction. This was a desperate situation, and it called for equally desperate actions. He supposed he could have told the president the entire truth, that the helicopter had tried to force Kaster's plane into the ground, but that would be unwise. Not because the president would have disapproved, but because as chief executive of the country, he needed plausible deniability—the opportunity to say, "I gave no such orders and knew of no such actions." What the president didn't know, he couldn't confess to. As it was, he knew too much and was too involved. Still, it would be Adler who would take the next few steps, give the next few orders. He was willing to do that, first because he was loyal, and second because there would be a sizable payback.

Adler was too much of a historian not to want to be a part of it—to see that his name was written in the minds and the hearts of others. That would never happen from his present position, and would never happen by running for some lesser office. Since he was not an attorney with sufficient legal training and experience, he could never be considered for the Supreme Court. That left only one position from which to make his mark: the presidency. There were several candidates lining up from both parties to take over the position, but none were more qualified than Adler. He knew that, and the president, if he had any inkling of Mark's desires, would agree. Yet the people knew very little about the man who worked with the president day in and day out. The truth of the matter was, Mark Adler was a nonentity as far as the voting populace was concerned.

"I thought I might find you here," came a sweet voice. Turning his attention to the door, Adler saw the silhouetted figure of a woman, a woman he had known for nearly three decades. "You've got that look again."

"And what look is that, dear?" he asked his wife. She was a stately woman with graying hair that gave her an air of mature beauty without making her look old. She walked like a woman of breeding and confidence. Her eyes projected the Ivy League education that she possessed. Mark Adler loved his wife, an unusual situation for the times and the place that he worked. She had been not only his helpmeet and mother to his two children, who were now grown and on their own, but she had also been an able counselor. Mark had often thought that she would have made an excellent chief of staff herself.

"The look that says you're thinking about the future," she replied. She walked over to the old chair and sat on the arm, striking a seductive pose. Reaching over, she removed the brandy snifter from his hand and brought it to her lips. "Am I right?"

"You know me too well, my dear. Entirely too well." Mark smiled broadly, reached up, and gently drew her face to his. He kissed her with genuine passion.

"Hmm." She moaned quietly and then slowly pulled away. "Let's keep that thought for the near future. For now, I must play the dutiful wife and bring you back to the present. There's a phone call for you."

"Really? I hadn't heard the phone ring."

"You were in the future, remember?"

"Well, I'm back. Who is it that would dare to interrupt my lofty thoughts?" he said with a wry smile.

"Brett Newell."

"It's about time. I've been waiting for the esteemed secretary of defense to return my call."

"Well, he has, and he's waiting for you right now."

Adler rose from his easy chair and walked into the living room. He picked up the phone that was sitting on a small antique table.

"Mr. Secretary," Adler said, "how was your trip to Texas?"

"Not bad, but not especially good either," came the tired voice of Newell.

"I can tell you're tired, my friend, so I'll make this quick. You received the information about Roanoke II?"

"Yes." His voice was heavy with suspicion and concern. "I don't like the way things are going."

"Neither do I," Adler admitted. "That's why I've taken the action I have."

"Which is?"

"It's time to mop things up. Everything."

"We have a lot invested in that facility, Adler. Only a handful of us know just how much."

"That's down to four, now: you, the president, Eddington, and me."

"What do you want me to do?"

"There will be questions from the military establishment. I want you to cover those bases."

"And Roanoke II?"

"I'm taking care of that. I plan to replace the present team with one more acceptable."

"Too bad about Kaster," Newell said.

"None of us are happy about that, or what is about to happen, but it can't be helped."

"I'll cover everything I can from my end; just don't be too obvious."

"Thank you, Brett." Adler hung up the phone and returned to the den. He found his wife there, seductively posed on the couch, holding two brandy snifters. A fire was burning in the fireplace. "You started a fire?"

"Romantic, huh?" she said, grinning broadly. "Now come here and forget world events. It's time to think of . . . domestic affairs."

23 November 2000; 2145 hours
Roanoke II

"It's no use, Captain," Dole said. "My radio is useless in here."

"That's by design," Eddington said. "The concrete and steel reinforcement create quite an effective barrier to electromagnetic emissions."

"I need to know what's happening outside," Stanton said. "How did your people talk to others who were outside the lab?"

Eddington shrugged, then said, "Telephone, of course."

Stepping to a phone that sat atop a gunmetal gray desk, Stanton picked up the receiver and held it to his ear. "I'm getting a busy signal."

"All calls into and out of the compound are run through a central system. The calls were monitored to make sure that no classified information was being conveyed to outsiders. And since everyone is gone, there is no one to clear an open line."

Stanton slammed the phone down. "All right, Dr. Eddington. What do you suggest?"

The engineer just shrugged.

"Will someone tell me what is going on here?" Tulley's tone was tinged with anger and frustration. Stanton knew he was not the only one who felt that way. Everyone outside the lab had seen a small explosion in the distance, but only he, Dole, and a few marine sentries had seen it through powerful binoculars. Nor did the others have radios to hear Kaster's words. They looked confused and frightened.

They were standing in the entrance hall they had first seen through the surveillance cameras. The room had a sofa and two padded chairs, one desk, a coffeemaker, and little else. Stanton was standing by the desk; Zach stood close by. Tulley and Wendt stood opposite them, near one of the concrete walls. Josie stood alone in a corner, rocking back and forth like a metronome.

Sergeants Ramsey and Keagle were by the now-closed door. In the middle of the room were Dole and two of the three marines who had gained access to the lab. The third held a sentry point on the roof. Eddington sat nonchalantly on the sofa. They were all staring at him.

"We received a message from Admiral Kaster," Stanton said quickly. "He's the one who signed off on my orders. He died a few minutes ago." He went on to describe the transmission. "Now our problem is this: Something is happening and we're not in the loop. We may or may not be in danger, but for the moment, I'm going to assume the worst scenario, at least until I can determine otherwise."

"Someone killed Admiral Kaster?" Tulley asked with disbelief. "Who would do that?"

"That's the $24,000 question, isn't it?" Wendt said. "So let me get this right. Somewhere out in the desert is a dead admiral who, moments before he died, told us that we were in danger. And this admiral flew all the way out here from the Pentagon? Isn't there an easier way of getting a message to us?"

"That's right," Tulley said. "How do we even know it was Admiral Kaster?"

"Radio frequency," Dole said. "He had our radio frequency, and that's just for starters. He knew my name and Captain Stanton's; he also knew the location of this compound and that we would be here. Who else has that kind of information?"

"I don't know anything about military matters," Tulley said, "but this doesn't sound right at all."

"So what do we do now?" Wendt asked.

"It's them aliens, ain't it," the old woman said loudly. "You soldiers has been messin' with them aliens, and now they's come for you. There's the Devil in all that. I knows it, I do. The Devil, pure and simple. You listen to ol' Josie."

Stanton had no idea how to respond to the woman, but he did know that things needed to happen quickly. "Dole, I need eyes and ears. A ground battle is your game, not mine. Talk to me."

"Yes, sir. We need contact with my men," Dole began with authority. "I have one man on the roof now, and my perimeter people are still out there. I suggest we find a way to contact my man on the roof."

"What about the air duct?" Stanton suggested. "Can you rig something up through that?"

Dole thought. "Yes, sir. I'm not sure how, but I'll make it happen. The duct is going to give us a different problem, though."

"You're thinking that if we are facing hostiles, they will gain access the way my man did. We need an avenue of retreat."

"Not many of those around, Lieutenant. We're boxed in and—" Stanton stopped abruptly. He turned to Eddington. "Dr. Eddington, it's time you told me where that elevator goes."

"I can't do that—"

Dole crossed the room in two steps, grabbed Eddington by the front of his coat, spun him around, and slammed the engineer into a wall. "The captain has asked you a direct question, Mister."

"Stand down, Lieutenant," Stanton commanded loudly.

Dole, his face red with rage, paused, then released the man.

Eddington backed away from the marine, his eyes wide and his face ashen. Dole had frightened him badly. "Keep him away from me, Captain. You keep him away or I'll have all of you up on charges. Is that clear? Do you understand? Every one of you up on charges."

Dole started forward again, but Stanton held out a hand, touching him on the chest. He could feel the tension in Dole's muscles. Eddington took another step back. "I'm not the enemy here. I'm on your side."

"You've done nothing but drag your feet, Eddington," Dole said. "How is that a help?"

"What do you care?" Eddington shouted. "This is just a job to you. You're here because you've been ordered here. This thing, this complex, is the result of years of my life. I'm the one with the most at stake."

Stanton kept an eye on Dole, hoping that he wouldn't have to step between the two. Dole was thin but as solid as concrete, and trained to handle several men at one time. He was thankful that he wasn't alone.

Dole's jaw tightened with such force that Stanton could hear his teeth grinding. "My brother was stationed here," Dole growled. "My older brother is missing, I think you know why. I think you're the cause."

Eddington blanched. Stanton felt his stomach tighten. This was an explosive situation. Dole was not only a highly trained warrior, but he was also armed. The question was, just how far out of control was he?

"Lieutenant Dole," Stanton said, with the cultured voice of command, "I believe I told you to stand down."

There was a pause as Dole cranked his head sharply to face Stanton. Their eyes locked. Dole's burned with a fury that had been stoked by hour upon hour of suppression. This had been Dole's secret. It was unlikely that his commanding officer would have assigned him this duty if he had known that the lieutenant was emotionally invested in the disappearance. Nonetheless, Stanton was stuck with the man. Until a moment ago, he had shown himself the perfect, disciplined, skilled soldier. Stanton was betting that those qualities would win out.

He turned to better face Dole. "Am I mistaken, Lieutenant?"

Dole was breathing hard enough for Stanton to feel it on his face. The marine narrowed his eyes, inhaled deeply, then said, "No, sir. You are not mistaken."

"Is there anything else I should know, Lieutenant? Any other information you've been concealing?"

"No, sir. I'm . . . I'm sorry, sir. I felt I should be here."

"I, for one, am glad that you are. We'll sort the rest of this out later. Right now, I have other things on my mind. So I need to know: Are you back with me, Lieutenant?"

"Sir, yes, sir," he replied, coming to attention.

"Very well, let's get to it," Stanton said, stepping back, putting a little more distance between himself and Dole. The act was a nonverbal statement that the situation was now resolved. He turned to Ramsey. "Is that door secure?"

"Yes, sir," the big Samoan said. "No one is coming in that way, unless they use a bomb."

That was true, Stanton thought. They had had to break in through the roof. Of course, he had no way of knowing what he was facing. "Mr. Dole, any ideas on how to set up a line of contact with your man on the roof?"

"I have an idea," Wendt said.

"Let's hear it, Agent Wendt."

"There are phones in the offices," she began. "We could use those—"

"It's already been established that we can't call out," Tulley said. "Weren't you listening?"

Wendt cut her partner a harsh glance. "Just listen, Pierce. We can't call out, but we can call in." The statement was followed by a puzzled silence. Wendt sighed. "The phones have an intercom so that a person in one office can talk to someone in another. I'll bet a month's pay that it doesn't go through a computer switchboard."

"Is that right, Eddington?" Stanton asked.

He thought for a moment. "The phone system is a basic office configuration with the exception of outbound calls. I'd have to say that she's right."

"The phone cable is attached to the outside wall," Wendt continued. "Since that wall is solid concrete, the cable couldn't be run inside. It'll take a little work, but we can pull it free from its anchors and run a phone up to the roof through the ductwork."

"Mr. Dole, please assign two of your men to help Agent Wendt. Then join me at the elevator doors. That's our next task."

"Yes, sir." Dole snapped the orders out, delegating two of his four-member team to aid Loren Wendt. To Ramsey and Keagle he said, "You two accompany the captain to the elevator doors. Let's show the navy what marines can do." Dole faced Stanton, his expression stating his thanks and his apology for his behavior.

Stanton answered with a slight nod. There would be no more trouble from Dole.

From the corner of the lobby came a voice, thick with a Southern accent. The words were garbled to the point of incomprehensibility, but Stanton knew what Josie was up to. He could recognize a prayer.

Chapter 14

23 November 2000; 2155 hours
Mojave Desert outside Roanoke II

Dirk Dwyer was chewing gum, clove gum, three pieces. His jaw worked with pistonlike efficiency as he gazed out the front windscreen of the HH–53C Super Stallion helicopter. He wished he was airborne, but he had gone as far as his orders had allowed. Four miles due east of his position glowed the lights of Roanoke II. He wondered what lay across the expanse of scrub and sand. "Talk to me, Truman," he said impatiently.

"You know as much as I do. Headquarters must be chewing pretty hard on this one."

Dwyer frowned. His impatience was fueled by the sight of one of his helicopters falling to the ground in a blazing inferno. Whoever had been flying the plane had gone nuts, killing himself and the two-man crew in the Apache. He had never lost a team member before; now, in the span of minutes, he had lost two. Gazing to the right and then to the left, he saw two additional Apache attack copters and knew the crew in each were chomping at the bit to be back in action. They too had seen their comrades fall.

"I can ring HQ's bell again," Truman said.

"No, let's let it ride," Dwyer replied. "They know we're here; they know about Bravo team. I imagine they're trying to figure out who to blame and how to cover up the wreckage. We'll wait until we get the go-ahead."

"Hurry up and wait," Truman said.

"The motto of the military." Dwyer understood Truman's eagerness. It was tough starting a mission, seeing a tragedy, and then being forced to sit idle. The thirty-eight armed soldiers in the bay behind him had to be anxious. The wait would be easier if they knew why they had been pulled from the sack and told to fly from the hidden base in the Tehachapi Mountains, one hundred air miles east of their position.

"Who tells the family?" Truman asked.

"I don't know," Dwyer said honestly to the pilot. "Things don't work like they did in the military. You know that. We do what we're told, when we're told, and then we forget about it. We get paid big bucks for that and nothing more." Everything was different from what Dwyer had learned in his fifteen years with the army. An infantryman, he excelled at the art of war. He knew all there was to know about leadership, duty, and the technique of quick attack. The army had trained him well, and he rewarded them with hard work and unquestioning loyalty. On the day he was promoted to lieutenant colonel, he was transferred to black ops, exchanging his army greens for solid black BDUs. The work was similar, the hierarchy the same as regular military, but everything else was different. Their equipment, from sidearms to the helicopters they sat in, bore no marks of identification. In the case of the choppers, it was a violation of FAA regulations and military protocol to operate any flying vehicle without proper markings. But then, many things they did were out of the bounds of the law. Still, they served their country as did their counterparts throughout the land and in Europe.

It was with humor that he read the stories written by paranoid civilians of "black helicopters" buzzing schools, dropping chemicals on small towns, and being sighted near cattle mutilations. They were almost as popular among the subset of UFO and conspiracy theorists as little green men and Area 51.

Yet, some of the sightings had been real. Such things were unavoidable. Their secret activities had developed a cult following. Stories abounded on the Internet. Books had been written attributing the activities to the New World Order, the United Nations, and even the Asian military. While none of that was true, they were indeed as secret a bunch as the country had ever seen, or not seen. Operating like the military, and composed of the best the military could provide, they were also very different. They wore uniforms with no insignia; they carried no identification, and there was never an indication of rank. It was a team concept, with each person an expert in his field. No rank was necessary. Everyone knew who gave the orders and who was responsible to follow them.

Dwyer's headset crackled to life. The message was cryptic and unlike anything he would have heard in the army. "Telsor One, you are to go on Roanoke II. Be advised of uniformed resistance. Extreme prejudice. Repeat. Extreme prejudice. Orders on top. Regain and lock target; target is LB1. Maintain confinement. All black. Repeat all black."

"Roger, Telsor Base," Dwyer said smoothly into the microphone of his helmet. "Understand all black." Dwyer looked at Truman, who was staring back with surprise. The enigmatic message had been short, but packed with startling information. "Uniformed resistance" was the code phrase for a terrorist action. A long-held fear of the government had been an armed takeover of a research facility or government building by terrorists outfitted as U.S. military. How would soldiers respond when asked to fire upon people dressed as they were? Could the wrong people be shot? Dwyer had just been told that such was the case. Terrorists, dressed in military garb, now controlled a secret installation. "Extreme prejudice" meant that he and his team were free to take whatever action they deemed fit to recapture the complex or even destroy it.

"Orders on top" meant that approval had been granted by someone way up the chain of command. As far as Dwyer knew, the command came from the president himself. He would treat it as such.

"All black" was the phrase indicating that this was a secret operation. Other military in the area would be left out of the loop, as would local law enforcement. Stealth and speed were the two operative words.

Keying his radio, Dwyer spoke: "Alpha, Tango, we are go. Expect uniformed resistance. This is not a drill. This is not a drill. I want a clear LZ in ten."

The pilots of the Apaches replied. Minutes later, both were airborne. Dwyer's craft lifted off soon after. Within ten minutes, his men would be on the ground and making entrance into LB1, the laboratory about which they had been briefed.

Chewing his gum faster, Dwyer quickly weighed the truth of the situation. People would die in the next few minutes. Hopefully, none of them would be his men. He had lost all he wanted to.

N

"We have communication," Dole said to Stanton. Stanton was standing by the wide elevator doors, studying the security access control. "The phone system works like a charm. My lookout reports all calm. Perimeter is still secure."

"So far, so good," Stanton said. But he still felt uneasy. "Any contact from the outside?"

"No, sir," Dole responded. "I recommend that we contact our base and see what they know."

"Can your man do that from the roof?"

"No, sir. He would have to go to one of the Humvees or have another unit make the contact. Better yet, I could send someone out from here."

"Do it," Stanton said. "Maybe someone can tell us—"

"Lieutenant," one of the marines called with urgency. He was young and wore the chevron of a lance corporal. He held up the receiver of the phone.

Dole marched across the lobby and took the phone in his hand. "Yes." He listened. "Can you identify them?" Stanton could see that Dole was becoming tense but said nothing. Dole would report as soon as he had all the information. "Stand by."

"Sir," Dole said to Stanton, "we have three inbound craft. Night vision surveillance shows them to be helicopters. Two Apache and one larger. They're coming in hot."

"Communication?"

"None. My men have tried to raise them. There's no response."

"ETA?" Stanton asked sharply.

"Two minutes."

Stanton spun and looked at Eddington. "Who are they, Eddington?"

"Why ask me?" His face was drained of color. Clearly, he was terrified.

"If they were part of this mission, they would have made contact before approaching," Stanton said loudly. He had no time for niceties. "This is your complex. You deal with all this cloak-and-dagger stuff. Who are they?"

"I can't help you, Captain," Eddington said.

"I am tired of hearing that, Dr. Eddington," Stanton said hotly. "I am responsible for the lives of the people in this room and the marines outside. I want answers and I want them now."

Eddington fell silent and rigid. He seemed confused, uncertain.

"I want to hear it, and I want to hear it right now." Stanton felt fear turn into fury.

"They're a special secret security force assigned to certain research installations. They don't have a name. I don't know who is responsible for them. I do know that they are not to be trifled with."

"The men outside, are they in danger?" Stanton demanded.

Eddington shrugged. "I can't say. I only know of the security team's existence. I know nothing of their methods or limits. That's all I can tell you."

Stanton studied Eddington, trying to determine if he had told all that he knew or if he was being secretive. Time was ticking by—time Stanton couldn't spare. "Let's take a walk."

"What?"

"You and me, Doctor," Stanton said, as he approached the engineer. "Let's take a little stroll outside."

"No. Why? That doesn't make sense."

"Is there some reason that you don't want to leave this building, Dr. Eddington?"

Again Eddington fell silent.

"Your men are in danger, Lieutenant," Stanton said. "How do we change that?"

"We didn't come equipped to take on Apache helicopters, Captain. Just one of those birds could destroy this complex. I have to pull them off the perimeter."

"Do it. Tell them to take what cover they can. They are free to fire if fired upon. I don't know all that's going on here, but I'm not going to let them sit out there like ducks on a pond."

"I'll make sure we have surveillance and—" A distant popping sound echoed down the open duct. Dole snatched the phone to his ear. Stanton watched as the marine started to speak but was cut off by the man on the other end of the line. "Tell them to fall back," Dole shouted into the phone. "Pull back!" He stopped and turned to Stanton. "The Apaches have opened fire on our perimeter sentries. Heavy casualties. They've returned fire."

Ramsey, Keagle, and the other two marines stepped next to their lieutenant, awaiting orders. "We're ready to go," Ramsey said.

"No," Stanton said. "You'd be easy targets from the air."

"But my men," Dole protested.

The popping sound was louder and more frequent. "Tell your man to get off the roof. I want him down here, *now*." Stanton was outgunned. No squad of men could hold off an Apache helicopter. They would need rocket launchers, something they didn't have.

A new sound snatched Stanton from his thoughts: sharp, rapid thuds against the wall and roof—the sound of 30mm rounds impacting the concrete walls and roof.

"Corporal?" Dole said into the phone. "Corporal, report." He shook his head. "He's not responding." Dropping the phone, he said to his men, "Boost me into the duct, I'm going on the roof."

"Sir," Sergeant Keagle said, "let me. I'm slimmer and can move through the duct faster."

Dole paused for only a second before ordering the woman through. Ramsey and Dole lifted Keagle up to the hole where the duct opened into the lobby. Small pieces of suspended ceiling dropped like snow from the ragged hole where the main supply duct had been split away from the smaller conduits that carried fresh, cool air to the offices. Stanton watched as the booted feet of the female marine disappeared.

"Eddington," Stanton snapped, "no more excuses. Those concrete walls might keep out machine-gun fire, even machine-gun fire from an attack helicopter, but those birds carry air-to-ground missiles."

"Hellfire missiles, Eddington," Dole added angrily. "Those things took out over five hundred tanks and early warning radar sites in the Gulf War."

"Do you hear that, Eddington?" Stanton said. "Just one of those gunships can turn this place into rubble, and you will be lying at the bottom of it with the rest of us."

Eddington was shaking his head slowly from side to side. "This isn't supposed to happen. I could have handled the whole thing. If they had just left it up to me, everything would have been fine."

"Open the elevator, Eddington," Stanton commanded.

"I could have set things right."

"Open the elevator, Eddington," Stanton repeated as he approached the man. He took him by the arm and led him to the security key panel by the large sliding metal doors. "We may have only seconds, Eddington. Maybe not even that. Open the doors."

Stanton had no idea where the large elevator led, nor did he know what awaited him, but he did know what was outside, and it was death. He was responsible for everyone in that room. Aggressors had already taken on armed marines; there would be no hesitancy to take on his small group.

Slowly Eddington began to punch in numbers. "I could have handled it all. Why didn't they trust me?"

Stanton wanted to ask who "they" were, but that would have to wait for later—if there was a later.

The jerry-rigged phone buzzed. Dole snatched it up. He listened intently, then said, "I want you back here, now."

"Bad?" Stanton asked.

"Yes, sir," Dole said slowly as if weighing the truth of his own words. "Keagle reports the roof sentry is dead. She can see other bodies. No one is responding to her radio calls."

"Where's the chopper?" Stanton asked.

"Apparently, it made a pass over us on the way to the far perimeter. She used the sentry's night-vision goggles. They're coming back. It will be here in a second."

A clattering sound announced Keagle's return. She dropped to the floor in a heap but was on her feet a moment later.

The elevator doors opened behind Stanton with a whoosh. He peered in. The cab was huge, large enough to hold a car. The walls of the cab were covered in polished stainless steel. Another pair of doors were situated on the opposite side. "Everyone in! Let's move!"

Only one person hesitated: Eddington. Stanton grabbed him by the front of the shirt and pulled him into the elevator cab with the others.

The doors shut, but the elevator remained motionless.

"What's happening, Eddington?" Stanton asked. "Why isn't it moving?"

With a deep sigh, Eddington looked up and said firmly, evenly: "Mason Eddington, 2250. Down."

The elevator began its descent.

"LZ is clear," Tango pilot reported.

"Roger," Dwyer said. "Hold your position for surveillance." He nodded to the pilot, who moved the craft over the chain-link fence that marked the borders of the compound, and moved over the houses, small businesses, and toward LB1. Below him, illuminated by the amber streetlights, he could see the unmoving bodies of the terrorists. Gazing at the action through high-powered binoculars, he was amazed at how familiar the counterattack of the terrorists had been. If he didn't know better, he would have assumed that those were American troops down there.

Thirty yards from the designated structure, the Super Stallion set down. Immediately, soldiers poured out the side opening and took defensive positions. There was no gunfire. Thirty seconds later, Dwyer stepped from the craft and took in the scene.

One side of the building was riddled, chipped concrete, caused by the onslaught of machine-gun fire from the Apaches. As if he were strolling in the park, Dwyer stepped to the front door and found it locked. He studied the security system, then the steel door itself. The door was marked with black streaks where a torch had been applied.

"They just needed to be a little more forceful," he said to himself. He spoke into the microphone of his radio headset. Instantly his ground troops fell back and one of the Apaches rounded the building and faced the door. As soon as Dwyer was at a safe distance, he gave the order. A firestorm of 30mm rounds erupted from the helo's mounted gun. Sparks flew as the rounds hit the metal door. Smoke poured from the security panel as it was obliterated in a blizzard of bullets.

The door sprung, and the Apache ceased its fire. Followed by his men, Dwyer strolled into the lab, a 9mm pistol in his hand.

Chapter 15

23 November 2000; 2205 hours
Roanoke II

"Quite a party you've thrown here," Hawking said softly, as the elevator began its rapid descent. The walls of the elevator were paneled with stainless steel that reflected their images in a foggy, distorted way, like the mirrors in a carnival funhouse. Stanton studied his friend and felt a sudden wash of regret. His face was ashen, and perspiration stippled his brow. He, like the others, was immersed in barely controlled terror.

"I'm sorry, Hawking," Stanton said. "I never would have called if—"

Hawking waved him off. "How could you know? The question is, what happens next?"

"What was that noise we heard just before the elevator doors shut?" Agent Tulley asked. Stanton and Dole exchanged glances.

Dole answered. "Heavy automatic fire. My guess is that they were shooting their way in with one of the Apache's onboard guns."

"If anyone had been standing by the door, he would have been killed," Wendt said.

"In a very ugly way," Dole responded. "It tells us the kind of people we're up against."

"All right, Eddington," Stanton said. "Game time is over. I have questions, and you will answer them." Eddington looked shell-shocked. His eyes darted about like he was seeing creatures no one else could perceive. His breathing was labored, his skin pale and wet. In any other situation, Stanton would have been moved with compassion, but there were too many lives at stake. "First, who are the guys with the heavy artillery? And don't tell me you don't know."

"They're a security force," Eddington said, just above a whisper. "An elite security force. I told you that already."

"Why are they here?" Stanton demanded sharply.

Eddington raised his head, his face changing from fear to rage. "Because you insisted on coming into the lab," Eddington shouted. His sudden change in demeanor caught Stanton off guard. Eddington continued to shout. "I warned you away from this place. I told you not to come in here, but you couldn't leave well enough alone, could you? You just had to see, didn't you? Well, now your wish is going to be fulfilled, Captain Stanton. Unfortunately, you will not live to report what you've seen to anyone. We're all dead. It's just a matter of time."

"They guard Roanoke II?" Stanton asked, puzzled. "Why didn't they disappear?"

"No, no, no!" Eddington said with agitation. "They don't just guard Roanoke. They are a response team. There are units like them all over the country and in Europe—anyplace where secret labs like this exist. They are supposed to make sure that what is secret stays secret."

"So, they're military," Dole said. "That would explain where their hardware came from, but why would they fire on my men?"

"Wrong again," Eddington spat. "They're not military, at least not like you're thinking. They're composed of the best the military has to offer, but they work for different people; they have different goals and vastly different ways of achieving their purposes."

"Can you call them off?" Stanton asked.

Eddington erupted with laughter. "You've got to be kidding. I'll be shot on sight, Captain, and so will you, and everyone in this elevator."

"All right then, a different tack," Stanton said. "We've been descending for at least two minutes. What is waiting for us?"

"The lab," Eddington said, this time a little more calmly. "The real lab."

"How far down?" Stanton prodded.

"Two hundred and thirty-six feet. Almost twenty-four stories below the surface."

"I hope it is empty," Stanton said. "No secret paramilitary I should know about before those doors open?"

"No. The place should be empty, just like the streets above."

Stanton wanted to follow that comment. There was more there than Eddington was telling, but there wasn't time. Other information had to be ascertained first. "Is there any other way into the lab than this elevator?"

"This is it," Eddington said. "No other way in, and no other way out. I guess it's good news/bad news, Captain. They can't follow us down, but they can make sure we never come up."

"I don't buy that," Dole said. "I've been in underground bases before. They were made with gigantic boring machines. There has to be another access."

"You're wrong, Lieutenant," Eddington said. "The cavern below is natural, not manmade. It's like Carlsbad Caverns. One could set up operations there without doing any drilling at all. That's precisely what we did."

“Next question,” Stanton said. “Can we keep the elevator below? Is there a way to keep it from rising topside again?”

Shrugging, Eddington said, “Sure. It’s just like any other elevator. As long as the doors are open it won’t move. It’s a safety precaution.”

“What about the stop switch on the panel?” Wendt joined in. “Can that be overridden by the people above?”

“They would really have to know what they’re doing,” Tulley added.

“They do, Agent Tulley,” Eddington said. “I doubt they know what’s down here, but they could probably find a way to bypass the elevator circuits.”

“But not if the door is open, right?” Stanton said.

“Correct, Captain. The electronics cannot bypass the mechanics. If they could, then a short or a computer glitch could command the elevator to rise or descend while the doors are still open. That would be dangerous to equipment and people alike.”

“There are two sets of doors here,” Stanton asked hurriedly. “Which are going to open?”

“The rear doors,” Eddington said, pointing to the back of the cab.

“Very well, then,” Stanton said urgently. He could feel the elevator slowing. “Lieutenant, you and your team will exit first and make sure the area is clear. Tulley and I will keep the doors from closing. I’ll throw the switch first, but I want a substantial obstacle in the doorway as soon as we know that the lab is safe.”

“Will do,” Dole said. Before he could say another word, Ramsey, Keagle, and the two other marines moved to the back doors of the elevator. “Ramsey, Keagle, you go first. We’ll follow behind. Make your positions low, and choose your shots, if shots are needed.” The space was filled with the clatter of M16s being readied.

The last seconds of descent dripped by as if time were in the act of freezing. The hum of the elevator cables and machinery dropped an octave as the cab slowed to a stop. There was a slight bounce, and then the doors opened slowly.

"Go!" Dole commanded. Five marines poured from the elevator, weapons pointed and ready.

Stanton stared out the doors, dumbfounded. "I don't believe it," he said. "It's . . . it's amazing."

Through the opening, he could hear the voices of the marines as they searched the area: "Clear. Clear. Clear."

There was a loud, weary sigh, then Eddington's voice: "Come along, Captain. In for a penny; in for a pound. You might as well have the whole tour."

Blinking hard several times, unsure that what he was seeing was real, Stanton reached forward to the elevator's control panel and punched the "Stop" button. "Hawking?"

"Yes?"

"Do you see—"

"Yes, I do."

"Any ideas—"

"Not a one. Not a single one."

Dwyer removed his black helmet and ran a hand across his head. His red hair was cut close to the scalp.

"All rooms are clear, sir," Zeek said. Zeek was the leader of the ground assault team. "We also have a report that all insurgents at the perimeter are dead."

"Good," Dwyer said, replacing his helmet.

"There's something you should know, sir," Zeek said. "All the dead had identification. They appear to be marines from Camp Pendleton."

"Not possible. Whoever they were, they were not U.S. military."

"How do we know that?"

"Because we were told that they were terrorists, and therefore they are. If they went through the trouble to obtain military BDUs and weapons, then they probably took the extra step of fabricating identification."

"If you say so, sir. I would hate to think that we just killed a bunch of good guys."

"Then don't think it." Dwyer stepped through the rubble of chipped concrete, paper, and shreds of metal from the door and steel desk. The Apache had opened the place up like a tin can. Seeing a thick brown cord hanging from the ceiling, he made his way to it. "Looks like a phone cable." He took it in hand and jerked. A clattering sound emanated from the ceiling. He began to pull the cord. A moment later, an office phone fell from the overhead duct to the floor with a resounding crash. Plastic scattered across the floor. "Interesting," he said. "I assume that our radios aren't working in here."

Zeek spoke into his headset microphone. He shook his head. "I can't reach anyone outside. It must be the concrete walls."

"Probably," Dwyer admitted. "The building may have a dampening field around it." He glanced about the room until his eyes fell on the elevator doors. "How many floors does this building have, Zeek?"

The question caught the man off guard. "Sir?"

"Just one floor, right. The one we're standing on?"

"Yes, sir."

"Then why the elevator?" He nodded at the far wall. "I bet there's more here than meets the eye." He walked to the sliding metal doors and examined them closely. He then turned his attention to the keypad next to it. Brute force wasn't going to work this time. He could blow the doors open, but he might damage the elevator or some of its mechanisms, rendering it useless. That would not do. "I want these doors open, Zeek. Make that happen."

"Yes, sir." Zeek hurried from the room and returned a minute later with another man. The man carried a laptop computer and a metal briefcase. Every man on the team was an expert in at least two fields. Some were snipers, others pilots, others experts in explosives. The man with Zeek was an electronic security expert.

"I want in, Benton," Dwyer said flatly. "And I want in yesterday."

"Yes, sir." Benton was a tall, thin Italian man, good with a gun, great with a computer. He set his equipment down and studied the keypad; then, like a surgeon who has done a thousand surgeries, he popped open the metal case and removed a screwdriver. Instead of delicately removing the cover, he jammed the flat-bladed device under the plastic cover and twisted it. The case popped off easily. "Let's see," he said, examining the circuitry. "It's pretty straightforward. There's an embedded processor chip that screens codes. It probably compares them to a computer database somewhere around here. It could be in a different building, though."

"Benton?" Dwyer said.

"Yes, sir."

"Just get me in. You can give me the lecture later."

Benton nodded, turned back to his tool kit, and removed a small gray cable. "First I'll disconnect the modular plug that runs from the keypad to the processor." He reached into the wall and unplugged the connection. "Next I'll hook up the laptop." He took the cable that he had removed from the case and used it to connect the computer to the electronics in the wall. "It's a pretty standard connection, nothing too exotic. Next, we fire up the system and let the computer do the work. It will run random numbers until one hits."

"How long?" Dwyer asked.

"Can't say, sir. It all depends on the length of the number codes used. They shouldn't be very long, though. Too hard for people to remember. They probably use strings of four or five digits. If that's the case, then it should only take—" Benton was interrupted by a beep from the computer. Nothing happened.

"What's going on?" Dwyer asked.

"The computer found a valid code."

"Then why isn't the door opening?" Dwyer demanded.

"Mechanical override, sir. My guess is that the doors won't open unless the elevator cab is in place. You know, to keep people from walking into an empty shaft."

Dwyer swore. "Zeek. Get a pry bar and open these doors."

"Yes, sir."

N

Stunning was the only word that came to Stanton's mind. He was standing just beyond the threshold of the elevator. Behind him, the doors to the cab were propped open by a small metal desk that Tulley had found nearby. Before him was a vast cavern, its ceiling hovering seventy feet overhead. Spherical lights, three feet in diameter, hung from the ceiling by long steel cords, like diminutive suns giving off a gentle ivory light. The air was cool and thick with the smell of brine. To each side was a wall of rock. The cavern spread out before him so far that he could not see the far wall. The sound of running water filled the space.

"Impressive, don't you think?" Eddington said proudly. "There is almost 250 feet of solid rock above your head, Captain, and the cavern is as large as an airfield, carved out by centuries of running water. Nature provided the perfect place for us to set up shop."

"It's unbelievable," Stanton said.

"Amen to that," Hawking added. "What . . . what's that?" Hawking pointed a long, thin finger across the open expanse of the cavern, past three sets of long consoles with built-in computer monitors, and toward a large, undulating mass.

"I'll show you," Eddington said. He led the way across the smooth stone floor. As they passed the computer consoles, Stanton gazed at the work stations. A small bag of honey-coated peanuts lay open on top of one of the work spaces. A Diet Coke sat at another. Half-finished cups of coffee were situated here and there. It was the same vision he had seen above ground: artifacts of a people suddenly snatched away.

"Eddington?" Dole asked. "Our attackers, could they be responsible for the disappearances?"

Eddington shook his head. "No army could do that. No army in the world."

The small crowd of people followed Roanoke's founder. Josie seemed too stunned to speak. Zach clung to Stanton's hand, his eyes wide at the strange sights before him. Ramsey and Keagle followed at the rear, and Tulley and Wendt were on either side of Eddington. The other two marines had been ordered to remain by the elevator as sentries.

"Remarkable," Hawking said. "Utterly remarkable."

Stanton approached wordlessly. Before him was an object unlike anything he had ever seen before. It appeared, at first, to be a ball of undulating, pulsating light, fifty feet in diameter, that hovered three feet above a metal foundation. But that description was inadequate. The thing, the *it*, was not a true sphere, but more ovoid. Stanton tried to ascertain its color, but that eluded him, too. When he first saw it, upon exiting the elevator, he thought it was black, a glowing black, if black could glow. Then it seemed a dark blue. Now it seemed a warm pink. Its surface was strange, rolling, boiling with spots of amorphous lights that blinked on and off, appeared and disappeared.

"I've never seen anything like this," Stanton said with awe.

"No one outside the Roanoke II research team has," Eddington said. Then to the others he prodded, "Spread out. Go on, it won't bite." They did, until they formed a circle around the enigmatic shape. Stanton remained stationary.

"Tell me what you see, Captain," Eddington prompted.

"It's hard to describe."

"Try."

"I see the same thing everyone else does: an egg-shaped mass of changing color."

"Wait a minute," Tulley said. "I don't see that. I see an obelisk with lights running up and down its side."

"Amazing," Hawking said loudly. "I see a wheel spinning on its edge."

"Axis," Wendt corrected. "It's a wheel spinning on its axis."

Hawking shook his head. "No, I said it right."

"This doesn't make sense at all," Dole added. "I see a disk, like a big Frisbee."

"A wheel within a wheel," Hawking said softly. Stanton caught the reference to the Old Testament book of Ezekiel.

"What's going on here?" Stanton demanded of Eddington. "How can we all be looking at the same thing and seeing something different?"

"Let's start with your first assumption, Captain," Eddington said, sounding like a professor. "You're not looking at anything."

"What? Of course I am. It's right in front of me."

"That doesn't matter, Captain. You're not looking *at* something; you're looking *into* something."

"I don't follow," Stanton admitted. Zach stepped closer to Stanton. The object was frightening him. Stanton put a comforting hand on the boy's shoulder.

"First, let me show you this," Eddington said. Stepping to one of the control consoles, he pulled a piece of paper from a legal pad, wadded it up, and then returned to his position next to the enigma. "If I could have everyone stand over here," he said, motioning to his location. The others joined him. When everyone was standing behind him, Eddington tossed the wad of paper into the seething glob of light.

It disappeared and then returned so quickly that Stanton thought it had bounced off the surface of the ovoid-globe-obelisk-wheel thing, but he knew that wasn't the case. The wad of paper landed at Hawking's feet. No one said anything. "Now watch this," Eddington said with an unmistakable pride. Where he had been recalcitrant on the surface, here he was like a teenager showing off his first car.

Returning to the console where he had found the pad of paper, Eddington picked up a pencil. "Gather around, folks," he said. "You will have to be close to appreciate this." Walking to the metal base, Eddington placed his face a mere inch from the boundary of the enigma, then slowly pushed the pointed end of the pencil into the unfathomable shape. Immediately, a thousand pencil points simultaneously emerged all along the surface of the object. To Stanton it looked like a gigantic ball of tiny pencil-point spikes. Hawking gasped and took a step back.

"Here, you try it," Eddington said, removing the pencil and thrusting it at Stanton. Stanton took it in his hand and studied it, like a child might study a magician's magic wand. "Go ahead, Captain. I think you'll be impressed."

"I'm already impressed," Stanton said. "If that's the right word for it." Then to Zach he said, "Stay here." Zach remained in place as Stanton approached the bulbous, pulsating blob of light and gently pressed the point of the pencil into it. He felt no resistance at all. Expecting the same result as Eddington had received, he was shocked at what he saw. No sooner than the graphite point entered the sphere, it reemerged one inch from its entry point. It was as if the pencil had turned in on itself.

"What is this?" Stanton asked in hushed tones, unable to believe his own eyes. He retreated from the object. "Why didn't it multiply like yours? Why did only one point emerge?"

"Not yet," Eddington said with a wry smile. "One more demonstration, first." With no sign of fear or reluctance, the engineer stepped beside Stanton and then walked directly to the orb. He thrust his arm in up to the elbow, which immediately emerged a few inches from its point of entry. It was as if his arm had been broken and turned backwards. The sight was simultaneously amazing and nauseating. Leaning forward, Eddington scratched his nose with his twisted arm.

"Oh, no," Hawking said. "This can't be. It's impossible."

Eddington removed his arm from the sphere and held it out for all to see. "No harm done," he said. "No pain, no broken bones. Just as I designed it."

"I think you had better explain this, Eddington," Stanton said. "And what did you mean, when you said we weren't looking *at* something but *into* something?"

"Fair question," Eddington said. "We're not looking at a thing, but at an event horizon. What looks like an orb, or an egg, or a sphere, or wheel, or obelisk, doesn't really exist. It is the border, the threshold between two worlds."

"Don't you mean dimensions?" Hawking said.

"Quite right," Eddington admitted. "Worlds, dimensions, spatial planes, the term doesn't really matter. The reality does."

"What are you two talking about?" Tulley asked.

Eddington looked at Hawking. "If I have this right, Captain," Hawking said, "Dr. Eddington and his team have bridged the distance between dimensions."

"This sounds like the *Twilight Zone*," Wendt said. "What dimensions are you talking about?"

"Mathematicians and physicists have long talked about the possibility of dimensions higher than ours. By higher, I mean extra dimensions. We have four dimensions: length, width, height, and time. It can be shown mathematically that more dimensions can exist, but while that can be shown on paper, it is impossible for the human mind to conceive of anything greater than our three spatial and one time dimension. That's why the ... the ..."

"We call it the Horizon," Eddington offered.

"Okay," Hawking said. "That's why the Horizon looks different to us, depending on where we stand. Our minds are trying to make something with more dimensions fit into our world of three."

"Three dimensions plus time," Eddington added.

"How far have you gone?" Hawking asked.

"Just six," Eddington said. "But that's enough."

"Enough for what?" Stanton asked.

"Enough to save time, Captain," Eddington said, cryptically. "Enough to save time."

"Again, I don't follow," Stanton admitted. He was growing weary of Eddington's verbal games.

"Then let me lay it out for you," Eddington said. "The Horizon was designed as a transportation device. Imagine this, Captain: A device that could move men, equipment, supplies, and even weapons, any place in the world, without expending an ounce of fuel or wasting a literal second. Imagine if we could send a jet fighter through a Horizon like this and have it appear on the opposite side of the world, where it would carry out its mission, and then return by the same path. It's the ultimate stealth, Captain. One second it's not there, the next second it is. The enemy would have no time to respond, no way to get a fix on the craft. It would just pop in and out of existence. You're a military man, Captain. How would you defend against that?"

"I couldn't."

"Exactly, Captain Stanton. No one could. It's the perfect weapon."

Stanton looked at Hawking. The physicist seemed weak, ill, burdened.

"But it wasn't perfect, was it?" Hawking asked.

"There are a few bugs to get rid of," Eddington admitted. "But as you can see, it works in principle. It's a little hard to control. That's why the captain got a different response with the pencil than I did. It can be a bit unpredictable at times. Sometimes, even I don't know what it's going to do."

"What kind of bugs?" Stanton asked.

"All scientific advances have glitches. It takes awhile to get them worked out."

Stanton looked at Hawking. Eddington was becoming evasive again. "What aren't you telling us, Dr. Eddington?" Stanton asked.

"There's nothing more to tell," he said defensively. "I showed this to you because we are all stuck down here together. Not that it matters. I doubt any of us will get out of here alive."

"Where there is life, there is hope," Stanton said. "Now finish the story."

Eddington turned and began to walk away.

"It wasn't empty, was it?" Hawking asked loudly. Eddington froze. "You thought you could move things back and forth through dimensions higher than ours, like it was some mass transit system—like some multidimensional subway. You expected the other dimensions to be empty, but they weren't, were they?"

Eddington turned back and faced the physicist, then let his eyes travel to the others in the group. His expression was sour, his eyes looked empty. "We thought it would be like outer space," he said, so softly that Stanton had to strain to hear his words over the ambient noise. "You know, huge distances of empty space, but with more than one level of time."

"But . . ." Stanton prompted.

"But it wasn't," Eddington said. He took a deep breath. "It was inhabited. We are not alone. We really are not alone."

"And you learned that from this Horizon?" Hawking said.

"Oh, no," Eddington replied. "That one is too small."

"That one?" Hawking said.

A nod was the only answer Eddington gave.

A realization hit Stanton like a punch to the stomach. He felt a chill race down his spine and spread its icy fingers through his body. "Wait a minute," he said. "You said that you wanted to send an aircraft through the Horizon and have it appear someplace else. But you would need something larger than the Horizon to do that. It's big, but it's not big enough to accommodate a full-size jet fighter. That would mean that you would have to create a Horizon substantially larger than this one. Am I right?"

"Yes," Eddington said. "I suppose you want to see it."

"Oh, Lord," Hawking said with shock. "Oh, dear Lord." The words were more than a release of emotion, of pent-up fear fueled by realization of the impossible—they were a prayer, a genuine plea. "What have you done, Dr. Eddington? What in the name of heaven have you done?"

"I'm afraid heaven had nothing to do with it, Dr. Hawking. Nothing whatsoever."

Captain J. D. Stanton felt weak in the knees.

Chapter 16

24 November 2000
1600 Pennsylvania Avenue, Washington, D.C.

Tell me that the situation has been contained," President Norris Crane said, as he paced around the brightly lit Oval Office.

"Contained and cleaned," Mark Adler said. "Well, more accurately, it is *being* contained and cleaned."

Shaking his head, Crane said, "This is getting out of control here, Mark. How are we going to explain away the deaths of forty or fifty marines? Where did we lose control?"

"Control hasn't been lost," Adler said. "Our men are on the scene. Those who know anything are either dead or soon will be."

"The country will go mad," the president said. "There's no way to keep this quiet."

"I have a cover story all ready, Mr. President. Nothing will get back to you or to me. This is Kaster's fault, not yours. You are simply doing what is best for the country, and the best thing for the country is to make sure that word never leaks out about Horizon."

"But the deaths. The young men who were just doing their jobs."

"Regrettable at every level, sir. I'm not sure why our team opened fire, but they must have had a good reason." Adler hoped his lie wasn't apparent. "Perhaps they were fired on by the marine detail. And you did say to do whatever it took—"

"Stop reminding me of that!" Crane shouted. "I know what I said; I also know what I meant. I can assure you that the slaughter of innocent servicemen was not it."

"Sir," Adler said softly, "this situation is bad, but not out of control. Our men in the field know how to keep a secret. They have to. Their lives are on the line. All we have to do is make sure that all other witnesses are rendered safe."

"Killed, you mean."

"I hope it won't come to that." Adler knew that it would.

"I'm beginning to wish I had never heard of Horizon," Crane said, plopping down on the sofa like a rag doll. "It had such potential, and I was told that it was foolproof. Apparently that was just another lie."

"The concept is brilliant, sir, and you should be praised for having the foresight to see the implications for our military. This device can be the greatest tool in the military, no, in world history. Just think of the nonmilitary uses. We have to stay the course, Mr. President."

"We have to stay the course," Crane parroted bitterly. "Of course we have to stay the course. What else can we do? Anything else leads to disgrace and prison time. I am not going to be the first U.S. president to go to jail." He leaned back and rubbed his eyes, then his temples. "Who else is in the loop on this?"

"Just you, me, the secretary of defense, and the response team." Adler took a seat opposite the president and leaned forward. "Look. Word about the dead marines is going to get out. There's no stopping that. But our cover story will work. We'll announce that a terrorist attack took place. We'll mention a gun battle and explosions. I'm having the bodies moved to a different site. That's where we'll set up the fake confrontation. In the same breath, we'll mention other such attacks that have occurred in the past." He raised a hand and pointed at one finger after another.

"First, we remind the populace of the World Trade Center bombing in 1993 that killed six and injured over 1,000. And then there were those attacks near our embassies in Nairobi and Dar es Salaam. Of course we'll bring up the 1983 fundamentalist suicide bomber who blew up himself and sixty-three others, including sixteen Americans in Beirut. That was followed by an explosion in East Beirut at another U.S. embassy. That one killed eleven. We can throw in others like the explosion that killed nineteen in Khobar, and—"

"I get the idea, Mark," the president said with a wave. "I suppose it could work."

"It will work, but we have to stay on top of this. There's no backing out now."

"Okay, Mark, okay. You're my man on this, but I want to be updated on everything. Actually I would like to know nothing, but it's too late for that." Crane stood, swore, and began to pace again. "First we lose an entire community, then one of our admirals makes a martyr of himself, and now this. Why do I feel like the little Dutch boy with his finger in the dike? If we're not careful, the whole thing is going to give way, and we will all drown."

"I won't let that happen, sir."

"See that you don't. It won't just be me spiraling in. If I go, the whole administration goes. Is that clear?"

"Very clear, Mr. President." Inwardly, Adler smiled.

23 November 2000; 2220 hours
Roanoke II

"Get me a flashlight," Dwyer snapped, as he gazed down the black maw of the elevator shaft. His men had worked effectively and efficiently, relying on brute force rather than electronic finesse to open the large steel doors. Zeek handed the commander a large steel flashlight. Dwyer clicked the on switch and shined the white beam into the ebony hole. A cool breeze ushered up the shaft. "Deep," Dwyer said. "Real deep. I can't see the bottom." He brought the light up to bear on the ceiling above, leaning into the shaft as he did.

"Careful," Zeek said.

"I'm not going anywhere," Dwyer responded nonchalantly. "The cables run past the ceiling. There must be a machine room on the roof. That's to be expected with an electric elevator."

"I thought elevators were all hydraulic," Zeek said.

"Only on small buildings," Dwyer answered, as he redirected the light down the shaft. "Tall buildings use electric motors to raise and lower the car. It's much faster. Of course, this is going down a hole, a deep hole. It's the only way they can do it."

"Can we separate the motors from the control system and bring the elevator up that way?"

"I doubt it. They've jammed the doors open. They're smart, that's for sure. That means we are going to have to be smarter and even more careful."

"So how do we get in?" Zeek asked.

"The hard way," Dwyer replied.

"I don't like the sound of that."

"You don't have to."

"Sir?"

Dwyer turned to see one of his men standing behind him. He was holding out a piece of paper. "This just came from HQ." Dwyer took the note and read it quickly. "Makes sense," he said and handed the note back to the soldier. "Show this to Truman and have him start the process. Then destroy the note."

"Yes, sir." The man turned sharply and jogged from the room.

"They want us to move the bodies," Dwyer said. "Too dangerous to leave them here. I figured they'd do something like that. They have to create a cover story."

"What kind of cover story could explain forty or so dead marines?" Zeek asked.

"It's not my problem, nor is it my assignment. We'll have to let the big boys take care of that. All we have to do is stack up the bodies and fly them back to our base."

"It's a good thing we have the CH–53," Zeek responded coolly, as if he were discussing the transportation of commodities. "The Super Stallion should be able to do it in one trip."

"It had better. I don't want to hang around any longer than necessary." Dwyer looked up the shaft again, then at the cables. "Take some men up on the roof," he ordered. "Make sure the elevator can't come up unless we want it to. Then secure some lines. We're going to rappel down."

"Swell," Zeek said.

"It's just like rappelling from a helicopter," Dwyer said. "I want four teams of four. I lead the first two teams down; the other two will stand by in case we need them. We should be able to access the elevator itself through the ceiling panel. If for some reason there isn't one, then we'll need to blow our way in, so have some C–4 ready."

"Egress?"

"By elevator; otherwise, we'll have to be pulled up. Especially if we have to blow out a portion of the ceiling."

"Won't that damage the cable connections on the elevator?"

"Not if we are careful, and I intend for us to be very careful. Now let's make this happen. We're burning time. Every second that passes gives them more of an advantage."

"Any idea how many people we're facing?"

Dwyer shook his head. "Not many is my guess. The elevator shaft is large which means the cab is large, but I don't think you could get too many in there. Even so, we should be able to handle them. I have to assume that they are armed."

"They have the advantage of position and knowledge of the terrain," Zeek added. "They've been down there for long enough to scope out the situation. They may be able to hide and take sniper action."

"True," Dwyer said. "I want every team member equipped for commando action: vests, stun grenades, all of it."

"Got it."

"Send out a team to locate any air shafts. Send up a chopper too. They have to get air from somewhere; I want to know where."

"Yes, sir."

"Okay then," Dwyer said. "Let's rock and roll."

"Well now," Josie said in her high-pitched voice. "Well, well, well, now. You done did it now, didn't you, Mister? You up and made yourself a pact with the Devil hisself. Yes, sir, ol' Josie ain't got herself much book learning. Not like you anyways, Mr. Dr. Eddington, sir. Not much book learning at all, but ol' Josie, she knows *the* Book."

"Josie, please," Stanton said firmly, but kindly. "We've got several things on our minds here. We need to think things through."

"I guess you do, honey," Josie replied with a laugh. "You got bad guys up there somewhere, and a gate to hell right here befo' yo' very eyes. Yes, sir. I do declare that you do have some thinkin' to do. Real hard thinkin'."

"It's not a gate to hell," Eddington said.

"It might as well be," Hawking said.

"Wait a minute," Tulley said with exasperation. "Will someone tell me what's going on? I'm standing in an underground cavern the size of a small town, with some unknown military group trying to blow us all to kingdom come. Eddington is talking about dimensions, and this crazy woman is talking nonsense. Am I the only sane person here?"

Wendt spoke up. "Try paying attention, Tulley," she said harshly. "This is an experiment gone bad. What was supposed to be a transportation device for military personnel and equipment has gotten out of hand."

"What's this talk about the higher dimension not being empty?" Tulley demanded.

"Just that," Wendt said with exasperation. "If it's not empty, then it must be full."

"Full of what?"

"Of creatures," Stanton said.

Hearing the words spoken aloud brought uncomfortable silence.

"Whoa," Tulley said. "Just a minute here. Hang on one minute. Are you telling me that all the people of Roanoke II disappeared because creatures from another dimension abducted them?" He laughed with disbelief. "Creatures? Little green men? Little gray aliens? The Jolly Green Giant? What? What are we talking about here?"

"You don't believe in the Bible, now do you, Mr. Tulley?" Josie said sternly. "You got the whole world figured out without the Bible. Ain't dat right?"

"I have found no use for such things," Tulley snapped. "I deal in facts and scientific principles."

"Oh, you a real smart one, ain't ya'?" Josie said. "You ain't got no tabernacle in your heart. Ain't nothin' there but emptiness. Nothin' but nothin'."

"Stop your yammering, woman," Tulley said. "We should have left you topside."

"Some could say that about you," Wendt snipped.

"Enough!" Stanton shouted. "We don't have time for this. Right now we have to survive. We'll explain things to you later, Tulley. Then you can believe or disbelieve all you want. Dole?"

"Yes, sir," the lieutenant said.

"If I said we were undermanned and outgunned, you'd agree?"

"Oh, yes, sir. In a big way."

"Okay," Stanton said. "Assess our situation for us."

"Sir, we are secure for the moment. Dr. Eddington has told us that there are no other means of ingress. That's good news, in that we know where the enemy will emerge; the bad news is there is no other way out. We're boxed in. The other good news is that any attack will have to be made on foot. We won't be facing Apache helicopters anytime soon."

"That is good news," Hawking said.

Dole continued, "They will have to carry light arms, since they have to make a vertical descent first, and then make their way through the elevator ceiling and into this area."

"If you were on top, Lieutenant, how would you set up the attack?" Stanton asked, wishing he were on a submarine and this battle was at sea. That was his element. This was an entirely different world. Dole was the key to their survival.

Stanton could almost see the gears of Dole's mind working. Although he looked straight ahead, Stanton knew that he was not seeing the cavern, but the men 250 feet above them. He moved his head slightly to one side, then up and down as thoughts ricocheted around in his head. Stanton did nothing to distract him. Finally Dole spoke. "Strictly a commando operation, sir. I'd first search for all possible entry points. In this case, I'd look for air shafts."

"There are none," Eddington said. "The oxygen is created from the water." He pointed at the wide watercourse behind them. "We also have atmosphere scrubbers, just like on a submarine."

"They don't know that," Dole said.

"They may know more than we think," Stanton said. "We can't assume anything."

"Nonetheless, Captain," Dole said, "the only way in is the elevator shaft. If I were them, I would first try to bypass the circuitry, but since we've jammed the doors, we know that won't work. It won't take them long to figure it out. That means that they have to make ingress through the shaft and through the elevator."

"How do they do that?" Stanton prompted.

"They rappel down to the top of the elevator cab and punch their way through the access panel, if there is one, or use shaped charges to blow out the ceiling."

Stanton turned to Eddington with a questioning gaze.

Eddington nodded. "There is an access panel."

"Carry on, Lieutenant."

"I would then try to nullify any resistance. Stun grenades if I had them. Then I'd drop my team in. I would also have another team close behind. Hit with two or even three waves of attack."

"What would be their first target?" Stanton asked.

"Any obvious foe, but assuming they're hidden, I'd shoot the lights out. Blind my opponent. But only if I have night-vision goggles."

"It was night when they arrived," Stanton reasoned. "Let's assume they have the goggles."

"I would definitely shoot out the lights. That deprives the enemy of one of his senses. I would then establish a position until the other teams are down and in place. Then I go hunting."

"I see," Stanton said. "What are our advantages?"

"We have five marines, counting myself, and two FBI officers. That's five M16s plus sidearms. We can add to that the handguns that Agents Tulley and Wendt have. We also can control the only means of egress."

"Very well," Stanton said. "I want your men a safe distance away from the elevator. If stun grenades or any other kind come rolling out, I want your men safely away. Position them so they can take down anyone who comes out of that elevator."

"This is a shoot-to-kill situation, sir," Dole said solidly.

Stanton hated the thought but knew of no way to avoid it. "You may pass that on to your men. If they're as well prepared as I fear, they will be wearing bulletproof vests."

"Understood, sir. Head and leg shots."

The image sickened Stanton, but he was not the aggressor. Now he had a boy and a woman to protect, beyond his initial team. He nodded his assent. Looking around, Stanton said, "Have your men by the elevator fall back beyond the river—"

"It's not a river," Eddington said. "It's an inlet."

"What?" Stanton asked.

"It's salt water, Captain. The inlet is filled from the ocean."

"The ocean is a hundred miles away," Tulley said.

"Doesn't matter," Eddington replied. "It's still Pacific Ocean water. You see—"

"Later, Doctor," Stanton said, wishing that Eddington had been this forthright from the beginning. Of course, things were very different now. His life was at stake. Stanton turned back to Dole. "Have your men fall back across the inlet and take positions there. They should be able to take decent shots from there and still be safely away from any grenades."

"I make the inlet fifteen yards wide, and it's about another fifteen yards from the elevator to the water. Thirty yards is doable." He shouted instruction to the two marines stationed by the elevator. Then to Keagle and Ramsey, "Escort the others over the bridge. Let's move."

The marines sprang into action. Stanton led the way over the wide metal bridge. The bridge itself was constructed of steel. No doubt it was used to move equipment across the river. Once on the bridge, he paused to look up and down the inlet. At the south, or what he assumed was the south, the water flowed into an opening. To the north it did the same, but much further away. There were no other bridges to be seen. That was good news. Now it was time to wait and time to pray. If he and the others were to survive, J. D. Stanton needed more: more time, more information, and more luck. *Providence*, he reminded himself. *Not luck, but Providence. Only God can get us out of this.*

"Let's do this fast and quiet," Dwyer said, wrapping the nylon rope around the carabiner of the harness he wore. "Once we're through the elevator we will be out of radio contact. I want one man on Team Two to stay on the cab roof to relay messages; everyone else follows me in. Got that?"

Eight men responded in the affirmative. They were ready for action. Dwyer had hoped for an easier, safe entry point, but no air vents or other shafts had been found. This was the only way in. He knew the rest of his crew outside were loading bodies into the Super Stallion helicopter for transport back to the Tehachapi base. He looked down the deep, empty shaft. It was time to earn his salary.

"Let's stay sharp and look lively. I don't want to have to tell any of your mothers why you didn't come home." A small wave of nervous chuckles washed through the room. Dwyer knew that if any of his men were killed the families would never know the truth. A story would be fabricated and dispensed: an airplane accident, auto accident, training accident, or one of a thousand other possibilities. It had happened before; it had been handled. The same would happen here. Fortunately, there was no family waiting for him: no wife, no kids, no parents. Growing up an orphan in a rough Texas orphanage had taught him the power of being alone. It also taught him that he needed no one—no one at all. A family was a liability in his work; it divided his allegiance. He was a better soldier because he was alone and cared for no one.

"Any questions?" he asked his team. There were none. "Let's do it." Dirk Dwyer repositioned his M16, tugged on the rope, and then stepped off into nothing, beginning the slow descent into the darkness. He smiled to himself. This was going to be fun.

Chapter 17

23 November 2000; 2230 hours
Three miles south of Roanoke II

Breathing was difficult. His mouth hung open, and the taste of moist copper covered his swelling tongue. Sticky blood caked the corner of his mouth. Had he been burned? There had been fire. He remembered that much: the orange and yellow flames swirling around his airplane, swallowing it in its fiery gullet, flashing brilliant white for a moment, then dimming to a dazzling mass of churning flame.

That was when the spiral began, the looping, spinning descent from three hundred feet above the desert floor. When he had pulled his aircraft up and into the attacking Apache helicopter, he had assumed that his life was over, that the martyr's act was his final effort in a disciplined, productive life, but he had been wrong. He watched as time slowed to a crawl, his propeller shattering as it dug deep into the metal skin of the Apache on the pilot's side. The prop splintered into pointed projectiles that scattered into the desert night. The right wing of his T-3A Firefly trainer slammed into the copter's skid, tilting the craft on its side. The left wing cartwheeled into the Apache's rotor, fracturing the spinning blades into uncountable shards. For a moment, Admiral Kaster thought the two craft would drop like a stone, an intertwined metal mass ablaze with aviation fuel. Instead, the airplane convulsed from the impact and then bounced away, spiraling downward like a brown leaf of an ancient oak.

Instinctively, Kaster had pulled back on the yoke, hoping to flatten and direct the plane's descent, but it was a useless effort. There was insufficient surface area on the left wing to be of any use; the right wing had been bent, and its flaps were unresponsive. There had been nothing to do but watch the rapidly approaching earth through his broken windshield.

Unresponsive as the T–3A was, damaged as it was, it did not fall straight to the ground. Instead its plummet had been tempered by wind, by bent, fractured wings, and by Providence.

Kaster blinked hard, surprised that he could see at all. He took a deep breath and immediately regretted it. Scorching, pointed pain stung his chest as broken ribs dug into the swelling, tender flesh. He coughed and the pain crescendoed into fiery spasms of agony. Every nerve felt like a conduit of magma coursing through him. He groaned, then whimpered and drew a ragged breath. He was alive, and despite the agony, he felt gratitude for that fact.

An inward darkness, not of night, but of failing consciousness began to close in his vision. Straining, he forced the invading blackness back. He had to remain conscious to fight off shock. If his injuries didn't kill him, shock would.

A new wetness ran down his forehead. It was cool and thin, not warm and thick like blood. Turning his head, fighting a stiff, reluctant neck, he saw broken glass where the window had once been. The wetness he was feeling was from the large drops of rain that had begun to fall from the ebony clouds that covered the sky. Blackness upon blackness, outside his plane, and inside his mind. In the distance was the crushed shell of the Apache. It lay in a lifeless heap on one side. No fire, no movement, just a bent metal box that had once been one of the most dangerous, heavily armed machines ever to fly.

The thought that the two-man crew was dead tugged at his soul. For a moment, in a pain-induced illusion, Kaster thought he could see them walking around their downed craft. Soon, he thought, his ghost would haunt the scrub-covered desert floor with them.

"Oh, man, oh, man." The voice seemed close, yet distant. "Can you believe this?"

"No way, dude," another voice said. "This is too gnarly."

"Be careful, you guys." A female voice. Young. Frightened. "It smells like gasoline."

Kaster struggled to clear his vision. Beams of light danced on the wet desert floor; raindrops reflected like molten silver as they passed through the beam.

"We should call somebody. You know, the police or the military," the first voice said.

"You got a phone on you?" asked the other male voice.

"Back at camp."

"Well, it's not doing much for us there now, is it?"

"Oh, guys, guys, look." It was the woman. "In the helicopter. There are bodies."

"Are they dead?"

"How do I know?" she answered. "I've never seen a dead man before."

Through the gloom, Kaster watched the young trio peer into the canopy of the Apache. He was suddenly fearful that one of them might be injured. If the electronics were still active, they could accidentally activate one of the weapons systems or create a spark that could ignite the spilled fuel. For that matter, any of those things could happen spontaneously.

"Hey . . ." Kaster croaked. His throat was scorched and dry; his voice thready and impotent. He swallowed and tried again. "Hey. Over here. Over here."

"What? Who is that?" the female said.

"Please," Kaster shouted weakly. "Over here."

Flashlight beams converged on him, stabbing his eyes with their brightness. "Look," one of them said. "In the plane. There's somebody alive."

Still fighting back the building pressure of unconsciousness, Kaster watched as the three unknown people approached. "Hey, you okay, man?" one of the men asked.

It struck Kaster as funny. Here he was pinned in a fractured, crushed airplane, and the guy wanted to know if he was "okay." "No," he replied. "I'm injured."

"How bad?" the young woman asked. The flashlight beams reflected off the skin of the plane, illuminating the faces of the three strangers. They were young, barely out of their teens, Kaster judged.

"I don't know," Kaster said. "My ribs are broken and I think my left leg is broken too. The pain is manageable, but I think I may be in shock."

"Can you feel your feet?" one of the young men asked. He was tall with long, dark hair parted down the middle. He seemed older than the other two.

"I can wiggle my toes," Kaster said, "and my right leg moves all right."

"What do you want us to do?" the young woman asked. She appeared to be no older than twenty and had shoulder-length black hair.

"What are you doing here?" Kaster asked hoarsely.

"Camping," the younger man answered quickly. "We have a camp set up about half a mile from here. We heard your plane and the helicopter, then saw the collision. We came over right after."

"How long?" Kaster croaked. "Since the crash, how long?"

"Twenty, thirty minutes," the older man said. "We would have been here sooner, but it's dark and the rain slowed us down."

Thirty minutes, Kaster thought. *I've been unconscious for half an hour*. "Okay," he said. "Do you have . . . do you have . . ." The black of unconsciousness roiled up from the depths of his pain.

"Do we have what?" the older boy asked.

"A . . . a car."

"Yeah, but I doubt if we can drive it out here. It'll get stuck in the mud."

"Well, we can't leave him stuck in that plane in this rain, Jason."

"I know that, Amy," Jason snapped. "But what good is it going to do to have him and us stuck out here in the van? He won't be any better off."

"She's right, Jason," the other young man said. "I could run back and get the van. I think I can get it through the brush okay. I mean, I really know this area."

"If you know so much, then how come you didn't know it was going to rain?" Jason asked.

"Leave Jerry alone," Amy said. "No one could know it was going to rain."

"Please . . ." Kaster said softly. "I don't know how long I can hold on to consciousness. I need your help."

"We have a cell phone back in the van," Amy said. "We'll call for help."

"No," Kaster said. "No . . . no . . ." Darkness slammed shut on him.

“I need to stay with my men,” Dole said. “Keagle and Ramsey will provide support for you while you lead the others away.” Stanton and Dole were standing at the foot of the twenty-five-foot-wide steel bridge. On the bridge stood Eddington, Tulley, Wendt, Hawking, Zach, and Josie. The dog sat next to the boy, wagging his tail, oblivious to the danger they were in. The bridge itself looked sturdy, as if it could hold a tank. The surface of the structure was covered with a coarse, sandpaper-like, slip-resistant coating.

Stanton studied the young marine lieutenant. If he was afraid, he concealed it well. His eyes were fixed and his body steady, but Stanton could tell he was in fight mode. “Very well, but be prepared to fall back when necessary. Take no chances.”

“Understood, sir.” Lieutenant Dole came to stiff attention and brought his hand up in a sharp salute. “Good luck, Captain.”

Straightening himself, Stanton returned the salute. “Godspeed, Lieutenant. Godspeed.”

“After you, sir,” Dole said, motioning to the bridge. Stanton stepped from the rock floor to the metal expanse. Dole and the other two marines followed behind. Before them, the others continued across.

As Stanton reached the center of the bridge, he paused just long enough to look over the three-foot-high metal rail. Below, black ocean water surged in small eddies. He was having trouble believing that the water he was seeing came from the Pacific Ocean, a hundred miles away. But he had no time to think of that now. His mind was occupied with the lives of six civilians and five marines, all trapped in a cavern twenty-five stories below the surface.

Less than twenty hurried strides later, Stanton stood on the other side of the saltwater river. A quick survey of this side of the inlet made Stanton's stomach turn. It was a flat, empty surface where the ceiling of the immense cavern came to meet the ground. It appeared to be a dead end, a box canyon. He would have preferred to see rock formations, or heavy equipment for his men to hide behind, but there was none of that. They were open to a frontal assault with nothing to place between them and an oncoming bullet other than pride and courage. Stanton offered a silent prayer.

Dole wasted no time in ordering positions to the two who would remain behind with him. "Spread out," he commanded. "I want the elevator doors under crossfire." The two marines moved wordlessly to opposite sides of the bridge and lowered themselves to the ground, their M16s pointed at the open elevator doors. To Stanton, Dole said, "There's too much light on this side. As soon as you're out of sight, I plan to shoot out some of the globes. The bad guys probably have night-vision goggles, but maybe we'll get lucky."

"I understand," Stanton said. He offered one more salute which Dole quickly returned, then positioned himself next to the bridge, using its steel frame as a shield. "Eddington," Stanton said firmly. "Where is this other cavern you were talking about?"

"This way, Captain," Eddington said as he marched toward the back wall. "There's a door over here."

"Let's go, everyone," Stanton said as he started after Eddington. The others followed.

Fifty paces later, in the dark shadows, was a metal door, twenty feet high, forty feet wide. Above the door was a large metal grate. "What's that for?" Stanton asked.

"Air exchange," Eddington said. "The register allows air to flow between the caverns. It's necessary. The door causes an airflow problem."

Next to the door was a four-foot-high pillar with an electronic screen that glowed a pale iridescent green. Eddington placed the back of his hand on the screen and said, "Dr. Mason Eddington, 1–2–6–6–7–9. Open." There was a soft beep, and the door slid open on its metal track.

Stanton took a deep breath and walked inside. The others followed, and a moment later the door closed behind them. Five seconds passed, then the sound of gunfire erupted. Single shots fired at leisure.

Dole had just killed the lights. Stanton knew that more than lights would die.

"At least the door will provide some protection for us," Tulley said.

"For us," Stanton agreed. "But not for Dole." Once, while researching a book on submarine history, Stanton had spent a few hours with a sailor who had served on a World War II diesel boat in the Pacific. The interview went well until the man began to describe how his sub had experienced an explosion in the aft torpedo room. Water gushed in, threatening to sink the sub. Bulkhead doors had to be closed, something he did in record time. After securing the compartment he heard a muffled pounding and instantly knew that at least one crewman had been left in the flooding compartment. There was nothing the man could do. To open the passageway was to doom the sub and its crew, to leave it shut was to condemn a fellow sailor to death by drowning. Stanton had watched as the normally stoic man began to tremble as he told the story. Five decades later, he was still immersed in guilt.

"Eddington," Stanton began. "I want this door left open."

"Wait a second," Tulley interrupted. "That would leave our attackers free access to the next cavern."

"I'm not leaving Dole and his men without a means to fall back."

"That's very noble, Captain," Tulley argued, "but they chose to stay. I don't think you have the right to endanger our lives like that."

"Eddington, I said I want this door left open."

"Stay where you are, Eddington," Tulley commanded. "I'm tired of following orders. Look where your leadership has gotten us, Captain. Maybe it's time we had a new man in charge."

Stanton ignored Tulley. He had wondered when the arrogant FBI man would challenge his authority. "Dr. Eddington. Get over here and open this door."

Eddington started forward, but Tulley stepped in front of the engineer, blocking his way. "You stay put," he said to Eddington. Tulley then walked toward Stanton until he was nose to nose. "That door is the only thing between us and armed attackers. Dole made his decision. Now I'm making mine. That door stays closed until we know it's safe to go out there. Have you got that, Captain? Or do I need to make it clearer?" He reached under his blue windbreaker. Stanton knew he was reaching for his gun.

Tulley suddenly disappeared. It happened so quickly that Stanton at first thought he had mysteriously vanished, evaporated into nothing, but then he heard a grunt followed by a blasphemous stream of profanity that lasted for only a second. There was another grunt. Jerking his head around, Stanton saw Tulley suspended above the ground, his back pinned against the surface of the rock tunnel and his feet kicking wildly. Holding him by the front of his coat in one massive hand was the big Samoan, Sergeant Ramsey. Next to Ramsey was Sergeant Keagle, her M16 pressed into Tulley's temple. Keagle appeared tense, ready to fire at the slightest movement of Tulley, if Tulley could have moved. Ramsey looked as calm and emotionless as the first moment Stanton had been introduced to him.

"Wendt," Tulley cried, his eyes wide in disbelief. "Help me, Wendt."

"No can do," she answered. "If you had pulled your weapon, I would have shot you where you stood."

"We're partners," he objected. "How can you do this?"

"That's what I should be asking you," she replied.

"Remove his weapon," Stanton ordered.

"Yes, sir," Keagle said as she ripped back Tulley's coat. She removed a 9mm pistol and quickly ejected the clip from the handle and ratcheted the slide to dislodge the round in the chamber. She handed the gun and clip to Stanton, who placed them in the leg pouch of his BDU.

"Thank you, Sergeants," Stanton said, thankful that they were on his side. "You can put him down now."

Ramsey leaned forward until his face was a mere inch from Agent Tulley's. "When the captain speaks, you listen; when he says move, you move." He let go and Tulley fell to the floor in a heap.

"Sergeant Keagle," Stanton said. "Take the group forward through the tunnel. Ramsey, you bring up the rear. I'll stay with Dr. Eddington until that door is open, but I want you at the other end first."

"Yes, sir," Ramsey and Keagle said in unison. Ramsey threw a hard look at Tulley, who scrambled to his feet and started down the natural corridor.

By the time the group had taken ten steps, Eddington was standing over the biometric security device, waiting for Stanton's order.

As the group moved quickly toward the next cavern, Stanton heard Josie speak. "Good thinkin', ol' Josie," she said to herself. "Gone and got yourself mixed up with a bunch o' crazy people. Sure as God is in heaven, dey is crazy. I shudda stayed home.

Yes, sir, stayed home and paid no never-mind to no lights. Crazy, that's what dey is, just plumb crazy . . ." Her voice trailed off as they walked away.

N

Dwyer and his men had flattened themselves against the walls of the elevator shaft when they heard gunshots.

"What are they shooting at?" Zeek asked.

Dwyer held up a hand to quiet the commando. He listened intently. "I counted ten shots," he said in a whisper. "Is that what you got?"

"About that."

"Lights," Dwyer said. "I bet they're shooting out some or all of the lights. They know we're here and want to blind us. That's what I'd do in their place. I bet they've pulled back and taken up strategic positions."

"With only one way in," Zeek began, "it will be like shooting fish in a barrel—and we're the fish."

"No one said it would be easy," Dwyer said calmly.

"Easy? It looks impossible. What next?"

"Let's take a look." Dwyer motioned to one of the other commandos. The man pulled a small flexible tube and a hand-held television monitor from his pack. Slowly, he lifted the elevator access panel and slid the black tube into the opening. Then with a flick of his thumb he activated the monitor, which he handed to Dwyer. The electronic periscope showed the elevator. "Elevator is empty," he said. "Move right." He moved the fiber optic tube. "There's a metal desk wedged in the door-way. That will provide some protection." He watched the monitor as his man continued to scan the area. "There's a large open bay. Looks like a console of some sort, about fifteen feet from the door. We may have targets behind there." He frowned. "That's all I can see."

"Not much to go on," Zeek complained.

"It's enough," Dwyer said coldly. "Okay, here's how it goes. We use flash-bang grenades and smoke grenades. I go first, Zeek you follow, you third, you forth. When I go in, I'm going to lay down fire. Give me a count of five to get out of the way, then you do the same, Zeek. We do this right down the line. Some lights are still on. My guess is that they don't have night-vision goggles, so they can't see in the dark. That will be our first object. After that, it's seek and destroy. Clear?"

"Yes, sir!" the men replied in unison.

"All right then, let's make some noise."

Zeek and the other men pulled out the specialized hand grenades and readied them.

"Now," Dwyer said, and Zeek yanked up the access panel. One after another they threw their grenades down the access panel and through the open doors of the elevators. The concussive explosion rocked the elevator.

Dwyer stepped forward and dropped through the hatch. A split second later, he opened fire.

Chapter 18

23 November 2000; 2230 hours
Three miles south of Roanoke II

"He's back." Kaster heard the voice when the thick mist of unconsciousness receded. It took a moment for him to gain his bearings. At first he thought he was home, feeling the handmade quilt that had been handed down through his wife's side of the family resting on his chest. Then he moved. Bolts of pain, bullets of agony pierced every inch of his body. He felt as if a thousand hot needles were trying to press their way out of his skin. He groaned through clenched teeth and squeezed his eyelids shut so tight that flashes of colors erupted on his retina.

"Lay still, man. Just lay still. Help is on its way."

Admiral Kaster opened his eyes to see the bleary shape of the tall, dark-haired young man who had been standing next to the plane when he blacked out. Looking around, Kaster saw that he was still in the gruesomely twisted T–3A. Across his chest lay an old green sleeping bag. "Help me get out," Kaster said.

"No way, man," the young man said. "They said to keep you warm but not to move you. As if I didn't already know that."

Kaster struggled to ignore the pain and to focus his thoughts. "They?" he whispered.

"Yeah, we called 911 on our cell phone. They're sending a Med-Flight helicopter. We're too far off the road for an ambulance."

"Oh, no," Kaster said. "You have to stop them. Can't . . . shouldn't fly here."

"What's with you, man? I would think you would want to get out of here. I know I would."

"He's delirious, Jason," a young woman said.

Jason, Kaster thought. He had heard that name before—when they were talking. Jason and Amy and . . . one other. It came to him. Jerry. Jerry and Jason. Brothers? "How long ago?"

"How long ago did we call? Maybe twenty minutes. It took a little while for Jerry to run get the van and the phone."

"Van?"

"Yeah, you need to rest, man. Just take it easy. The experts will be here soon. I think they're sending someone from your base, too. Anyway, we should be hearing helicopters any minute now."

"My base? Which base?"

"They didn't say," Jerry answered. "I saw your uniform and knew you were military. Not to mention, that bird over there is not a pleasure flyer." He motioned toward the downed Apache. "So I told the 911 operator. Pretty soon half the cops in the county will be here."

A new pain entered Admiral Kaster—the cold, penetrating stab of terror.

"You have to leave," Kaster said weakly, but the urgency was clear. "You have to leave now."

"We're not leaving," Amy said. "You're too beat up. You need our help."

He shook his head despite the painful stiffness. He coughed. Blood trickled from his mouth. "Go. You're in danger."

"From the cops?" Jason asked incredulously. "We haven't done anything wrong. We're just camping, that's all. This isn't even private property."

"Go," Kaster ordered as loudly as he could. "They'll kill you, now go."

"Kill us?" Jason said incredulously. "Man, you are messed up."

"You don't understand," Kaster responded. "This was no accident. The Apache was attacking me. They were trying to kill me."

"Apache?" Amy questioned. "There are no Indians around here."

"He means the helicopter, dimwit," Jason said harshly.

Jerry spoke up. "Back off, Jason."

"Make me."

"Shut up, you two," Amy demanded. "This isn't helping."

"Jason," Kaster said. "This is not a joke. I'm hurt and probably dying, so I don't have time to joke around. Leave. Go. Right now. Get in . . ." He was seized by a spasm of pain. "Get in your van and get as far away from here as . . . as possible."

There was silence as the three young people weighed his words. "Please. Please go."

"What do you think, Jason?" Jerry asked softly. "What if he's right?"

"I just don't feel good about it," Jason said.

"But if he's right," Amy said, "we could be in danger."

"Go," Kaster ordered again. "Just leave me and go."

In the distance, under the canopy of night, the thunderous pounding of rotor blades bludgeoned its way through the air.

"Now," Kaster said. Then he began to scream. His broken ribs stabbed him with fierce jagged pain. "Now, now, now." He coughed up more blood.

"Okay, okay. Just relax," Jason said. "We're going."

"Wait," Kaster snapped, as the three turned to leave. "The phone. They can trace the phone. Give it to me."

"It's my mom's," Jason said. "She'd kill me—"

"They will kill you if you don't leave it behind."

Reaching into his pocket, Jason removed the cellular phone and held it close enough for Kaster to take it in his hand. "Take care, man." Jason said. There was a sincere concern in his voice.

"I will," Kaster said. "Thanks for your help. Now go."

The three walked a few steps, then ran to the van. Behind them came the nearing sounds of helicopters.

23 November 2000; 2245 hours

Roanoke II

The rock corridor was only fifty feet long but maintained a uniform width. At the base of the stone walls were marks of cutting. Apparently a crew had evened out the rough edges with pneumatic tools. At the base of the walls was a runner of lights. Overhead hung smaller versions of the lighted globes in the lab area. Eddington was talking nervously as if speaking would keep the danger away.

"The corridor was built by a special team of military contractors. This is actually a crevice between two of the five caverns. We widened it at its base to move equipment. We were quite fortunate, really. It saved us a lot of time. The area is filled with such caverns. These two—the one you were just in, and the one just ahead—are the largest. We were lucky to find them. This whole project sailed along smoothly. Not a single setback; not a single injury." He paused. "Until now, that is."

"How did you find the caverns?" Wendt asked.

"Actually, we didn't," Eddington explained. "A geologist back in the 1940s did some studies in the Los Angeles area. He maintained that channels, tunnels, and caverns ran under much of southern California. No one believed him. No one but the military. They followed up on his work and discovered that he was right. The size and scope of the underground labyrinth is amazing. The navy even sent a small nuclear sub up one of the channels. It never came back."

"What?" Stanton said. "I write books on submarines, and I've never heard that."

"Do you really think that you're so important that the entire military structure feels compelled to disclose everything to you?" Eddington asked. "Really, Captain."

Eddington was right. There were many military secrets swept under the rugs of scores of generals, admirals, and presidents. Not only should he not have been surprised at the revelation, he should have anticipated it. "No one knows what happened to it?"

"No. Obviously, there could be no radio communication. It seemed to sail off the face ..." He paused to rephrase. "... under the earth."

"You didn't find it when you were building this place?" Wendt asked.

"No," Eddington admitted. "Technically, we didn't build this, nature did. We just occupied it and made a few alterations."

"Who cares," Tulley grumbled. "How is this going to save our lives and get us out of here?"

"Not to mention solve the mystery," Wendt said sarcastically. "That's why we're here, or don't you remember?"

"Mysteries aren't solved by dead people, Agent Wendt. I'm good, but not that good."

Keagle, who had been leading the group through the tunnel, stopped abruptly and let out a gasp. Stanton and Ramsey raced to the front, both ready for whatever assault waited them. Like Keagle, they froze. Before Stanton was a cavern larger than he could have ever imagined. Its expanse was breathtaking. Running a hundred feet in front of them another inlet, like an underground river, split the cavern floor. Globe lights hung like spherical pendulums from a ceiling that Stanton estimated vaulted 150 feet above their heads.

Striking as the cavern was, it paled in comparison to the enigma that sat just across the wide inlet. Its magnitude, its size, its sheer grandeur took Stanton's breath away. For a few short moments that passed like hours, he forgot the danger, forgot the armed men that would surely soon descend upon them.

Hawking Striber could only groan in disbelief. "It's utterly amazing."

Josie was not short of words. "It's the Devil's work," she said. "I can see it, I can smell it. You'll be the death of us all. The death of us all, I say."

Eddington was not offended. "Ladies and gentlemen, welcome to Horizon II."

Sounds rumbled down the stone corridor. Frightening sounds of aggression, of weapon turned against weapon, man against man. Blast followed blast, and the retort of gunfire ricocheted off the hard granite.

"Let's move," Stanton ordered. "Everyone to the inlet. Now!"

Dwyer's heart was pounding, not with fear but with exhilaration, as he stepped through the elevator's access panel and dropped to the floor below. Immediately he rolled behind the heavy metal desk that propped open the sliding doors of the elevator. Half a second later he was on his feet, his back pressed against the side wall of the cab. He could feel the Kelvar vest dig into his back. Three rounds flew into the door and pierced the thin metal skin of the elevator's back wall. The bullets struck head high. If his team had not thrown the stun and smoke grenades to confuse the terrorists and conceal his descent, he would be a dead man. Now it was his job to make sure his team didn't die.

Another three rounds entered the elevator. *M16A2 assault rifle*, Dwyer thought. He should know, he had fired that same weapon countless times. Instinctively he thumbed the safety of his MP–5 submachine gun, and then set the weapon for full automatic fire. At that setting, the small weapon could fire eight hundred 9mm rounds a minute. But he would have nowhere near a minute. Any exposure longer than a second would mean his death—body armor or not. Dwyer knew he was up against professionals.

Taking a deep breath, he quickly and smoothly aimed the barrel of the MP–5 out the open door and squeezed the trigger. The 9mm rounds erupted from the barrel in a torrent. Casings flew into the air, landing on the floor in a cascade of brass. Dwyer leaped over the desk and into the cavern, rolling as he did. He let loose another rapid burst of fire and ran to a safe position behind the metal control console. In an oil-smooth, practiced motion, he ejected the cartridge of his weapon and pulled another from his vest. Then he pulled a stun grenade from his vest and, from his position on the ground, threw it with all his might. He was aiming for the bridge he had seen through the surveillance cam. Seconds later a loud, thunderous blast filled the cavern. Dwyer rolled to one side and squeezed off another burst of gunfire.

Behind him came the scream of another hail of bullets—rounds fired from another MP–5. Zeek was through the hatch and into the cavern. Dwyer turned to see his number-two man racing across the rock floor toward the . . . the . . . he had no idea what he was looking at. An oddly shaped sphere hovered over a metal pedestal. It had been too far to one side to have been seen by the surveillance camera, and he had been too focused on remaining alive to notice it when he first entered the cavern.

Zeek was firing across the cavern at targets Dwyer knew he could not see. The terrorists were near, but where? Suddenly Zeek was knocked backward, his feet flying in the air. He landed hard on his back. Dwyer knew he had been hit. Without pausing, Zeek rolled onto his stomach and continued toward the pedestal. Dwyer let loose another burst of gunfire to gain Zeek the time he needed to make it to the pedestal.

"Zeek," Dwyer said into the microphone of his head set. "Zeek, you okay?"

The answer was a string of obscenities uttered in hushed, breathless tones. "Man, that hurts," he said a moment later. "Knocked the wind out of me for a moment."

"Took one in the vest?"

"Yeah, right shoulder. I bet it leaves a huge bruise."

"Guaranteed," Dwyer said. "Their fire has been minimal. They're picking their shots."

"Yeah, headshots," Zeek replied. "How many do you make it?"

"Unknown. My guess is three or four shooters across the river. There's a bridge. At least one of them must be using that as cover. You good enough to throw a grenade?"

"I'll make it work," Zeek said stoically.

"Fragmentation grenade at the bridge on three," Dwyer said, pulling another grenade from his vest. "One, two, three."

Two one-pound grenades, capable of injuring or killing people in a thirty-yard radius, flew through the air. Three seconds later a dual explosion rocked the cavern. "Lights,"

Dwyer ordered. Rolling on his back, Dwyer aimed his weapon toward the ceiling and began shooting the glowing globes. Glass rained down on the ground, and the cavern dimmed with each light that was extinguished. But it wasn't enough. There were lights on the other side of the river. Those would be harder to take out. Of course, he would have to leave at least one globe lit. Night-vision goggles enhanced ambient light but could not work in utter darkness. Outside there was always some light that could be amplified. Here, in a cavern, that was not so.

Another burst of fire exploded from behind Dwyer. It was the third member of his crew entering the elevator. Dwyer turned just in time to see him slip and fall. *The casings*, Dwyer thought. *He slipped on the shell casings. Take cover.* The man rose and then staggered backwards again, but this time for a different reason. The sound of gunfire filled the room at the same time as his man went down. From his position on the floor by the console, Dwyer could see that a bullet had caught his man just above the right eye. He swore softly, then spoke into his microphone. "Send Bravo. Repeat. Send Bravo." In a few minutes the second team would arrive, and if necessary the third. He would like to have had all of his men take the area simultaneously. More eyes and more guns meant swifter success, but with only one point of entry and that through the ceiling of an elevator, such an action was impossible.

In the brief lull of gunfire, Dwyer studied the cavern. It was bigger than he'd imagined; that made his task more difficult. He still had to deal with the lights, but he and his team could do that easily enough, it would just take longer. His real problem was that the terrorists had the choice of position. That gave them an advantage. He had an idea. "I want Bravo team armed with M4s."

The M4 rifle was a shortened version of the M16A2, but it also came with a grenade launcher. Someone was going to pay for killing his man.

Alex Dole could not hear his weapon as it fired. He could feel the butt of the stock press into his shoulder with each round fired, and he could see the spent cartridges as they were expelled from the chamber. But the only sound he could hear was a persistent ringing. One of the concussion grenades had landed a few yards from him. Its explosion shook him, filled him with nausea, and pierced his ears. It took the full might of his will, and the power of desperation, to remain focused on the task. Two men had made it safely from the elevator. The first man had the element of surprise on his side and entered the cavern untouched. He was lucky. The second man had been downed but quickly moved forward. Body armor, Dole reasoned. The third man lay dead in the elevator. This was not the way Dole had hoped things would go. He knew that more men would be on the way, and that he was outgunned. His team had not come prepared for such an onslaught.

Looking to his left, he could see his man facedown on the ground, unmoving. Two fragmentation grenades had been thrown—one landed next to the marine. There was no time to react, not even time to scream. The other grenade had landed near the bridge, its fragments ricocheting loudly off the steel structure. The bridge was the only reason Dole was still alive. To his right, the third man in his team lay prone on the ground, his M16 aimed at the elevator. A few moments before, the man had motioned that he could not hear. Either his radio was out or he was suffering from the same shock of the stun grenade.

A shot. Dole tensed. The cavern became a shade darker. They had taken out another light. Dole had estimated that fifty lights hung from the ceiling: thirty on the other side of the inlet; twenty on his side. They were trying to blind Dole and his men. Exactly as Dole had expected.

"Stay with the plan," Dole told himself under his breath. "Stay with the plan." He leveled his weapon at the open door of the elevator and waited for the next man to emerge.

Seconds oozed by. Sweat trickled from Dole's forehead; perspiration covered the palms of his hands. His breathing was shallow, his heart pounding like a jackhammer. Yet his eyes and hands were steady.

Thoughts, disjointed and confused, flashed in and out of his mind. Nothing, absolutely nothing made sense: people missing in a flash of brilliant light; caverns deep under the desert; an enigmatic object that bent space and time; an attack by a crack commando unit. None of the pieces fit. Nothing in his life could have prepared him for this.

With his eyes still fixed across the inlet and at the open doors of the elevator, he felt a sudden flood of guilt inundate his heart. A man lay lifeless in the cab, his arms spread, his head cocked to one side. Dole wondered if the man had a family. Was there a child waiting for Daddy to come home? A wife patiently waiting for her husband whom she would never see again?

Focus, he commanded himself. *That soldier came down the elevator shaft with the full intention of putting a fast-moving bullet into your head*. The thought did not quench the flame of guilt and confusion. Surely the man was just following orders. *But those orders are to kill me and my team*. True enough. Dole had never killed a man. Now he had and was planning on shooting anything that moved on the other side of the inlet.

The ringing in his ears intensified, and his head ached from the concussive blast of the grenade. More men would be on the way soon. He could bet on that. If only he could get a clear shot, he would take down the attackers regardless of how guilty he would feel after. That was his job, his mission at the moment. He had to honor the orders he had been given. His brother had taught him that.

Guilt was replaced by the frigid cold of sorrow. His brother. Raymond Alexander Dole, First Lieutenant, USMC. Eight years his senior, Raymond had enlisted right out of high school. After boot camp and advanced individual training, he had started college, attending classes wherever he was stationed, whenever he could. His dedication did not go unnoticed nor unrewarded. It took years of hard work, but he earned his commission.

Dole could barely remember his father, who had abandoned the family, leaving them in poverty when he was five years old. Raymond, at the tender age of thirteen, became the man of the house, a job he took seriously. It was Raymond who kept Dole away from the drugs and gangs that permeated every inch of their neighborhood. Twice he had taken a beating from angry gang members because he refused to join their ranks, but only twice. Raymond was a quick study and learned to defend himself. Soon no one would challenge him face-to-face.

Wanting to follow in his brother's footsteps, Dole attempted to enlist as soon as he was out of high school. Raymond had cut him off, insisting that he go to college first, and come in as an officer. "I did it the hard way," he had said. "You do it the right way."

Dole had done just that.

Raymond had been Dole's role model, his hero, and when he learned that something terrible had happened at Roanoke II, the place where his brother had been assigned, Dole made sure that it was his team that led the investigation. Now his brother was gone, and it was looking like he also would die at Roanoke II.

As he thought of his brother, he wondered what Raymond would say and do in his place. "Do your job," he could hear his brother say. "Do it better than anyone else. Do it because it's right, because it is your job, because you can. Do it."

Dole narrowed his eyes and waited for the next event.

Chapter 19

23 November 2000; 2255 hours
Roanoke II

Led by Stanton, with Ramsey and Keagle behind, the small crowd ran to the wide inlet and across a metal bridge similar to but wider than the one they had crossed in Cavern 1. Similar to Horizon I, Horizon II was nearly surrounded by a large console of computer equipment, monitors, and banks of dials. One difference was a wide expanse of concrete that ran from Horizon II and deep into the cavern like a road that had been built from nowhere to nowhere. The concrete street was marked with yellow lines spaced in even increments along its length. Stanton had seen similar things on test ranges where vehicles or aircraft bodies were rammed at various speeds into block walls to measure the effects of collisions.

Most impressive of all was Horizon II itself. Where the first portal appeared like a molten silver sphere, or bubble which changed shape depending on the viewer's position, this one appeared to be a blood-red hole floating in midair. It was as if someone had cored out a giant hunk of the universe and left it to slowly bleed to death. Occasionally the "hole" would pulse, then undulate. It reminded Stanton of a giant esophagus, ready to swallow whatever the mouth wanted to deliver. Stationed around the gaping maw of the dimensional threshold were four columns that ran from their base to the ceiling high above. Each column glowed like burning phosphorus alternating in the colors of the rainbow.

Unlike the first Horizon, this one was not hovering above a pedestal. Instead, the pedestal was recessed into the granite floor. Stanton assumed this was to allow whatever traveled down the runway direct entry into the Horizon.

"Eddington," Stanton said loudly as he stepped from the bridge. "I need a place to hide Zach and Josie, so talk to me."

"There is no place, Captain," Eddington said in a near panic. "There's nothing in the cavern but what you see."

"We've got to do better than that, Eddington," Stanton retorted firmly. "Right now, we are targets in a shooting range."

"I'm sorry, Captain. I truly am."

Stanton thought he saw tears in the man's eyes. "Where does that road go?" he asked, pointing at the wide concrete path.

"Nowhere," Eddington answered. "It's a runway. We were going to send a robot vehicle through, right after the holidays."

"Ramsey! Keagle!" Stanton shouted. The two marines responded immediately by jogging to where Stanton was standing. "Take positions to place the corridor under crossfire. Use the console for protection."

"Yes, sir." They immediately turned and took their positions.

"Eddington, can you shut these lights off?"

"Yes, but why?"

"Because our friends are probably using light-amplifying goggles."

"How does that help us? They'll be able to see us anyway. The Horizon gives off a pale light."

"That's what I'm counting on. I want you stationed by the light switches. When I give you the word, I want you to turn the lights off. Then when I tell you to, I want you to turn them back on. The sudden light should temporarily blind anyone with night-vision goggles."

"The light panel is by my corridor," Eddington protested. "That will put me awfully close to the front."

Stanton thought. Eddington was the oldest in the group and looked far from fit. He needed someone with speed. Keagle and Ramsey were needed right where they were to lay down fire, should the attackers charge forward. That left himself, Hawking, Tulley, and Wendt. Zach and Josie were hovering around Wendt. A bond had developed between the boy and the female FBI agent, which was to be expected. What young boy wouldn't want to be with his mother in time of crisis? Zach's mother was gone, and Wendt was the closest surrogate.

"Tulley," Stanton called. Tulley was standing near the long curved console facing the open corridor. He was unresponsive. "Tulley!" Stanton called again. The FBI man snapped his head around at the sound of his name. He walked to Stanton.

"What is it, Captain?"

"We've got our backs against a wall here," Stanton said quickly. "Would you agree?"

"That's an understatement," Tulley answered.

"Am I going to have any more trouble with you, Agent Tulley?" Stanton's words were pointed and brisk.

"Not down here, Captain. If we live, I'll have a few things to say to you, but down here isn't the time. I have a feeling we're all minutes from death."

"Have you given up?"

Tulley released a humorless chuckle. "Not on your life. If someone wants my life, he's going to have to take it."

"Good." Stanton reached down to the leg pouch of his uniform and removed Tulley's 9mm and clip. He inserted the clip, then handed the gun to the agent. "Eddington is going to show you how to turn the lights on and off. Unfortunately, the switch is near the entry point. That will put you close to the action—too close."

"Lights?"

Stanton explained about the night-vision goggles and his plan to momentarily blind the incoming soldiers. "Feel up to it?"

"You give the word, I'll work the switches."

"It may be the only chance we have."

"I'll make it happen. Just be sure your marine pals don't shoot me instead of the bad guys."

"They won't. Now get going."

Tulley paused and exchanged glances with Stanton. Stanton recognized it for what it was: a silent apology for previous behavior; a statement of support; an unspoken expression of thanks.

As Tulley left, Wendt approached. "We have to get the civilians out of the line of fire, Captain."

"Agreed." Stanton looked around and found nothing to provide security for the boy and Josie.

"Don't you go a-worrin' about ol' Josie. I been in more scrapes than you can count. God always sees that I come through it fine. Ain't no different now. Being underground makes no difference. He's the same God below as he is above."

"You know, Josie," Stanton said, "you're right. If we're going to get out of this, then God is going to have to help."

"Oh, he's a-helpin', all right. He be a-helpin'," Josie said. "You a Christian man, ain't you, son?"

"Yes, ma'am, since I was a child."

"I knew it. You can't fool ol' Josie. I knows these things. Some folk ashamed of that, you know. Like Jesus was some ol' raggedy uncle that nobody wants to see. But not ol' Josie. I don't look pretty, and I know I don't smell none too good, but I am not ashamed of my Lord. No, sir. If I'm gonna to die, I's gonna die singin' his praises." She turned and began signing "Blest Be the Tie That Binds." As she sang, she walked along the concrete roadway.

"Stay with her, Agent Wendt," Stanton said. "Maybe there's something down that way that can prove helpful."

"Do you know what's down there?" she asked.

Stanton shook his head. "Eddington said something about a robot vehicle they were going to use for an experiment. Take Zach with you and check it out." With that comment, Stanton squatted down by the boy. "Are you scared, son?"

His eyes were wide with fright. He nodded.

"Yeah, me too. I want you and Red to go with Agent Wendt. Okay? She's going to walk you down this concrete path. You do everything she tells you, okay, buddy?" Again the boy nodded, then he rushed toward Stanton, wrapping his arms around his neck. Red joined in by licking Stanton's hand.

The sound of gunfire echoed down the stone corridor. Stanton knew his time was short. He hugged the boy. "Go on, son. I'll see you soon. Go on, now." He rose to his feet.

"I'll do everything in my power," Wendt said somberly. She stood erect, her head high in defiance of the fear she felt.

"I know you will," Stanton said. "I know you will."

"Come on you two," Wendt said. The dog barked. "Let's take a walk. Maybe we can catch ol' Josie." They started down the cement path. Stanton wondered if he would ever see them again.

The blackness of the night was punctured by a blinding white beam of light. Philip Kaster looked up through the broken windshield of the T-3A trainer and winced as the light swept across his face. Above him he could hear the pounding of rotor blades. The light from the artificial sun passed the wreckage that trapped Kaster and began sweeping the ground in long side-to-side motions. The helicopter above him moved forward enough for Kaster to see it. In its bright, flashing collision lights he could make out the words Med-Flight. It was an air ambulance, and it was searching for a place to land. For a moment, the despair that had filled his soul lifted.

In the minutes that passed from the leaving of the three young people to the arrival of the evacuation helicopter, Kaster had had time to think. At first he was confused. Why had he been allowed to live? Why had he not died in the plane crash as those in the Apache had? Had there been a purpose? Was this more than a random series of events?

He had no direct answers. Kaster had always been a man of purpose, of discipline, of planning. He had made no time in his life for what he often thought of as intangibles: philosophy, theology, faith, and belief. Such things were best left to others; all things military were his forte. But entombed in the bent wreckage of an airplane, stranded in a remote area of the Mojave desert in a rainstorm, with a body as broken as the aircraft in which he sat, Kaster gained a new perspective. Alone in the dark, as minutes dripped by with maddening slowness, Kaster wondered if some greater power didn't have things in control.

It was too late for him. He knew he was bleeding internally and that it was only a matter of time before shock, exposure, and blood loss caused him to breathe his last. He thought of his wife. No greater woman existed. She had been a military wife more than a score of years, and she remained faithful and loving. Supportive of every move he made, Martha had proven the perfect companion, the perfect helpmate. Helpmate? Where had he heard that term before? It was a Bible term, wasn't it? Something from the beginning. The memory returned to him: Eve was called Adam's helpmate. That's what Martha had been for him, the perfect helpmate. A sadness swallowed him, as he realized that he would never see her again. He could imagine how she would receive the news: the shock; the denial; the onslaught of overwhelming sorrow. How he wished to hold her, to tell her once again of his love and how much she had meant to him, to let her know that she had made him better in every way, and that life without her would have been hollow, shallow.

He had closed his eyes and waited for death to consume him. Then came the light, bright and painful. Accompanying the light was the unmistakable sound of a helicopter. Now he was looking at the Med-Flight, allowing himself a moment of hope. Perhaps there was a reason to hope, to believe. Maybe, just maybe, guys like Stanton and others who professed a Christian faith were right.

Oddly, it had been Stanton's moral stand that had helped Kaster decide to make him team leader. That, and his experience with the *Triggerfish* the year before. The few in the Pentagon who had read Stanton's report about spiritual beings and possession had reacted differently. Some dismissed it as pure nonsense; others wondered aloud how such things could be. The bottom line had been simple: Stanton had saved the lives of hundreds of people.

There had been another reason that Kaster had chosen Stanton, but it was a reason that defied explanation. It followed no rule book, could not be found in a leadership manual, but it was as real as anything Kaster had experienced. He knew that Stanton was the man for the job, a man chosen not by Kaster but by Someone greater. He had quickly rationalized all that away, but now, alone, and near death, it seemed right, seemed accurate. Stanton was a chosen man.

The Med-Flight helicopter circled slowly, looking for a flat piece of desert floor that was clear of Joshua trees, juniper bushes, and scrub brush.

There was another sound. Another thumping of rotor blades. Kaster looked up just in time to see another Apache helicopter fly fast and low overhead. Unlike the Med-Flight, it bore no identification marks and displayed no collision lights. Kaster felt his heart sink.

"You are in a restricted airspace," a voice said over a loudspeaker. The volume was so loud that Kaster could feel the words vibrate the skin of his plane. "Civilian aircraft, I repeat: You are in a restricted airspace. Leave immediately." The Med-Flight stopped its forward motion and came to a hover. Kaster doubted that they could hear anything over the sound of their own aircraft and that of the Apache. The Apache swung in front of the Med-Flight leaving only a handful of yards between the craft. They faced each other, nose to nose.

"Go," Kaster said aloud, knowing no one could hear him. "Just leave me. Go." If the T–3A had power, Kaster would try to tune into the civilian frequency used by the Med-Flight. Of course, if the plane had power, then he would have called for help a long time ago, and announced to anyone who could hear his broadcast that something evil was going on.

The two craft hovered, facing one another like two gunmen in an old western. Kaster knew that the Med-Flight pilot and crew were dedicated people and their mission was to rescue a downed and injured pilot, but they would never stand a chance against the Apache. Then, as if in fulfillment of his unspoken thoughts, the Apache dipped its nose and released a loud burst of 30mm gunfire, which erupted from the chain machine gun. The large-caliber bullets just missed the Med-Flight and pounded harmlessly into the desert below. The message was clear and quickly understood. The civilian aircraft rose straight up and then departed as fast as it could.

A new wave of despair descended on Kaster as the Apache descended to just a few feet above the ground, its rotors kicking up sand that blasted against the fuselage of Kaster's plane and through the open window, stinging his face like a thousand bee stings. Broken, unable to move, and weak from blood loss, Admiral Kaster stared into the machine-gun port, silently said good-bye to his wife, and prayed for the first time in his adult life.

N

Since the entrance of the first two men and the death of the third, they had stopped using stun grenades. It made sense, since the grenade would not make a distinction between friend and foe. Smoke grenades were another matter. Twice more a soda-can shaped explosive had dropped down from the elevator ceiling, exploded, and filled a thirty-yard radius with moss-green smoke. And, each time, two more soldiers dropped through the opening in the elevator ceiling.

Dole and his man had fired into the smoke blindly, hoping to hit their target. When the smoke cleared enough for him to see, Dole counted four dead around the elevator. He estimated that six to eight others had made it through the opening—eight heavily armed soldiers with body armor against two marines with M16s and MK23, .45 caliber pistols, separated by fifteen yards of salt water. The situation was impossible to defend. His only option was to retreat and hope that Stanton had found a more defensible environment in Cavern 2.

The ringing in his ears had subsided and his hearing was returning. At least he could hear the gunfire. He spoke into his radio. "Fall back to Cavern 2. Repeat. Fall back to Cavern 2. I'll lay down cover fire." The marine to his right acknowledged and positioned himself to stand and run, once Dole gave the signal. The signal was simple—Dole would begin firing. Taking three deep breaths, Dole rose to his knees and let loose a sustained burst of fire. The other marine was on his feet and running toward the opening at the rear of the cavern. He had made half the distance when Dole turned just in time see the man jerk, twist, and fall to the ground, as dozens of bullets pierced his body.

Dole had no time for remorse, for he heard something and felt a hot stinging on his right ear. That was immediately followed by an impact on his left shoulder, as if someone had hit him with a bat. He fell backward, landing hard on the rock floor, his helmet skipping across the surface.

Despite his discipline, he screamed in pain, and the faces of his children and wife flashed into his mind.

"I count two down and one unconfirmed hit," Zeek said. "I think that's it."

"Maybe," Dwyer said into his radio. Smoke swirled around his head and clung to the ceiling above like moss. "Report," he said into the radio and then listened as each man stationed throughout the front side of the cavern gave his assessment. To a man, they agreed with Zeek.

"Okay," Dwyer said. "We advance on my mark. Remember, the unknown may still be alive."

Slowly the commando team rose from their hiding places behind the console and advanced toward the bridge, their automatic weapons pointed forward.

"Whoever they were, they put up a good fight," Zeek said.

"Terrorists are better trained than most armies these days," Dwyer said dryly. "And often better equipped."

Step by step, Dwyer led his assault team forward, until they were at the bridge. To the right he could see the bleeding, unmoving corpse of the man killed by the fragmentation grenade. Farther back lay the lifeless form of another terrorist. Dwyer hesitated. He was sure that there had been three gunmen, yet he could see only two bodies. With his MP–5 at the ready, Dwyer led his commandos across the bridge. He motioned four of his men to advance to the opening on the far side of the cavern. "Don't enter, just survey." They broke into a jog.

Dim light fell from the overhead globes, survivors of Dwyer's efforts to blacken the cavern. There had been too many lights and too little time to shoot them out. Squatting close to the ground, Dwyer studied a dark puddle at the foot of the bridge. "Blood," he said.

"Yeah, but where's the body?" Zeek asked, gazing around the room.

"The blood is close to the water," Dwyer answered. "He must have fallen in."

"Again, where's the body?" Zeek asked. "Shouldn't it be floating somewhere?"

"Two possibilities," Dwyer stated. "One, the water has a current, and he was swept to wherever the river leads. Two, he made his way through that opening over there, and we didn't see him. One thing we know for sure: He's not here and there's no place to hide."

"Sir," one of his men called. "Over here, sir."

Dwyer marched from the bridge to where one of the fallen terrorists lay. "What is it?" He looked down at the man who lay on his back staring through unseeing eyes.

"I don't think this is a terrorist, sir. That's a regulation marine urban BDU he's wearing, and his weapon is a standard issue M16A2."

"All obtainable through military surplus or the black market."

Zeek, who had accompanied Dwyer, leaned over the body and pulled the pistol from the man's holster. "Standard issue MK–23, .45 caliber."

"So they're detailed terrorists." Dwyer said. His words were direct and confident, but inwardly, he had doubts. Surely his superiors wouldn't order his team to assault members of the U.S. armed forces. "Remember, the Oklahoma bombing was done by a couple of ex-military guys. Maybe it's some survivalist cult or militia group. This would be the perfect setup." He motioned to the cavern.

"Where are the people, sir?" Zeek asked. "We haven't seen one civilian yet. Not in our flyover, or during the attack on the perimeter."

"The terrorists must have them," Dwyer said heatedly. Something was wrong, and Zeek had been the first to see it. But he could not accept the conclusions. "We have a mission, gentlemen," Dwyer said strongly. "We didn't ask for it; we didn't create it. Our superiors have information that we don't. They know what they're doing and what is at stake. They think; we do. That's all there is to it. Got that?"

"Yes, sir," Zeek and the other man answered.

"Let's move," Dwyer ordered, and his men moved forward. He, however, paused and looked back across the waterway they had just crossed. Something did not feel right. When he had dropped into the elevator and made his way to the cover provided by the wide console, he had thought he'd seen something odd, something unique. But other things occupied his mind—survival topping the list. His vision had been impeded by the smoke grenades and the overhead lights that illuminated the green smoke with a harsh glare. What little vision was allotted him by circumstance he had used to secure cover and identify the location of the shooters.

Still, a vague sight struggled to the forefront of his mind, a vision of a silver, spinning sphere off to his right. Dwyer directed his attention to that corner of the cavern. All he could see was the bullet-riddled console and a two-foot-high platform from which arose thin spirals of smoke. It, like everything else in the cavern, had been a victim of the blistering gunfire. Whatever it was that he had seen out of the corner of his eye was gone. Probably forever.

Chapter 20

23 November 2000; 2315 hours
Roanoke II

The .45 caliber pistol felt heavy in Stanton's hand. It was the weapon that Dole had given him when he first arrived at Roanoke II. He wondered if Dole was still alive. Down the stone corridor rolled the loud bangs and pops of automatic fire. Louder, more disturbing blasts had occurred, too. Explosives. Three men attempting to hold off attackers who came armed with grenades. An ache, hot and deep, erupted in Stanton's stomach.

He studied the gun he held. He had fired handguns before during his training. A great many years had passed since then. Another image came to his mind, one in which he saw himself firing an older but similar weapon to protect himself and a fellow officer in the *Triggerfish* incident. A man had died then, killed by the gun in Stanton's hand. Stanton had never questioned his actions; he was right on every account and placed in the same situation he would repeat his actions. But the shadow of that day had never left him.

"I hope you're not trying to figure out how to use that thing," Hawking said. Hawking was seated next to Stanton, as was

Eddington. They had taken a position at the rear of the long computer console. It was the only area of protection available. They were as close to being fish in a barrel as men could be.

"No, it's not that," Stanton said.

"What then?" Hawking asked softly. He struck Stanton as a man who had reconciled himself to death. Hawking was a man of deep and abiding faith. A scientist by training, a Christian by belief, Hawking was, Stanton found, kind, insightful, confident, and perhaps one of the smartest men alive. Now he sat on the cold rock surface, hidden behind a heavy sheet metal console. Next to them was the massive hole that Eddington called Horizon II.

"Our situation is not good," Stanton admitted. "Any minute, I will be called upon to level this gun at a living, breathing human, and pull the trigger."

"Don't think you can do it?" Eddington asked.

"I can do it. I will do it. I'm obligated to do my best to complete this mission and care for those under my command. So when the time comes, I'll do my duty. It's just that men are dying out there, and more are going to die."

Hawking nodded his understanding, but Eddington was nonplussed. "Oh, come on, Captain. You used to skipper a nuclear submarine. Your boat had torpedoes on it, didn't it? I'll even bet that you had several torpedoes with nuclear capabilities."

"That's true," Stanton said. "It's odd, I never gave that a second thought. On several occasions, we followed Soviet subs and were fully prepared to do battle. My boat was an attack sub; that's what we were trained to do."

"But this is different," Hawking said. "It makes sense. In the sub, you never had to see the enemy. Now you have to meet them face-to-face."

"I suppose you're right," Stanton said. "I've read that World War II bomber pilots could carry out their duty without question as long as they didn't have to see the destruction they left behind. Several who had seen the death and carnage they had helped bring about could no longer do their jobs." Stanton pushed aside the growing feeling of uncertainty and asked Eddington, "Why does Horizon II look different than Horizon I?"

"It doesn't matter," Eddington said sullenly.

"If there's one thing I've learned in my life," Stanton said, "it's that in an emergency anything and everything could be important. Horizon I changed shape. It looked like a sphere, then an obelisk, then something else. This one hasn't changed."

"As I said," Eddington replied, "it doesn't matter. The grave doesn't care what you know."

"Power," Hawking said. "They're using more power and have established a control grid over the threshold. The voltage must be enormous to be able to open and maintain a dimensional corridor like that."

"It's not a corridor, Dr. Striber," Eddington said. "You should have surmised that. It's just a hole. Pass through there and you step up a dimension. A corridor has width and length. Horizon II has neither. It just is."

"I stand corrected," Hawking said. "My guess is your power source is somewhat erratic. You had a spike in the voltage, the containment field grew beyond the confinement grid, and it sucked everything living into it. But that's only a guess."

"Since it happened while I was gone, I can only guess too," Eddington replied. "What you say makes sense. We use an underground nuclear power plant not far from here. That's why these caverns were so ideal. The saltwater inlets are used to cool the reactor. The ocean water makes a great heat sink. Most of the time the power is constant, but the reactor has been known to spike. Before I left, I was told that the problem had been solved. Apparently it hasn't."

"Has anyone ever gone in the Horizon?" Stanton asked.

Eddington shook his head. "No. With Horizon I we sent in small video cameras, but it never worked. The Horizon was too small. We'd mount a video camera to a pole, plunge it into the Horizon, and it would come out someplace else around the threshold. Nothing was ever recorded. So we built Horizon II. We knew more by that time and could stabilize the opening. We were scheduled to send the robot vehicle in right after Thanksgiving. The mechanics had to finish a few adjustments on the remotely operated vehicle."

"I'm missing something," Stanton said softly. "I'm overlooking something."

"There's no more that you can do, Captain," Hawking said. "You have positioned your people to defend against attack the best you can. All we can do is wait to see what happens next. We've done everything in our power."

There it was again, a disquiet in Stanton's mind as if he should be seeing something that he wasn't—something obvious. He prayed, *Lord, clear my mind. Let me see it, whatever it may be.*

Hawking leaned forward. "What is it, Captain?"

Stanton looked at the wide expanse of water as it ebbed and flowed. It struck him hard. He turned to Eddington. "You two were talking about the power necessary to stabilize Horizon II. Where are the power cables?"

"Power cables?" Eddington said. "Underground, of course."

"Underground?" Stanton was confused. "This is solid rock under us."

"We cut a channel in the rock, laid the cable, and covered it over with metal panels."

"Can we get to it?" Stanton asked.

"I guess so. Why?"

"Show me." Stanton was on his feet and a moment later was dragging Eddington up by the collar. "We don't have much time."

Hawking stood too. "I hope you're onto something good."

"I hope so too, Hawking," Stanton said. "Better yet, I *pray* that I'm onto something good."

Dole shuddered as wave upon wave of chill rolled through his body. The cold came less from the water that covered him to the waist than from the wounds he had received. The salt water swirled around him and occasionally splashed the open, bleeding bullet hole in his shoulder. The pain was excruciating and it took every ounce of will, every fiber of discipline, to refrain from groaning. He had been in the briny flow for five minutes, but it had seemed to creep by like hours. After seeing his last man go down and then feeling the bullet graze his ear and puncture his shoulder, Dole knew that he had only one chance at survival. He would never make the corridor, but he could slip into the water. Maybe they would think that he was towed under.

The water moved lazily around him, tugging at him with each surge, as he hung by his right arm from a support girder underneath the bridge. He had bought himself some time, although he was uncertain that it would do any good. He was too weak from blood loss to put up much of a fight. To make matters all the more dark, he had lost his M16 in the water. Unable to hold on to both the girder and the weapon, he had let it slip beneath the dark waters. That left him only his sidearm. That would do little good since by his count there were now eight commandos at the opening to the corridor. He might be able to shoot a few, but he would be dead soon after. Still, he couldn't watch a slaughter take place. He had already lost all but a few of his original team. No, he would not stand idly by.

Now all he needed was a plan. A plan and a miracle.

The down draft of the powerful Apache helicopter beat against the torn and battered carcass of the crashed T-3A. Inside, Admiral Kaster painfully raised an arm to shield his face from the wind and sand kicked up by the rotor blast. It felt to Kaster as if he were confined in a sand-laden wind tunnel with nothing but his bare skin to protect him. The forty-eight-foot rotor, driven by 1,857 horsepower engines, was creating its own sandstorm, and Kaster could do nothing but endure it.

It remained motionless for several long minutes as if hung in position by an invisible cord. To Kaster it seemed as if the crew was confused about their next step. Perhaps they were awaiting orders. If they were going to kill him, he wished they would get on with it. Being shot by the 30mm machine gun would almost be an act of mercy. The rounds were so large and would fly from the gun in such number that he would never know what hit him. He would be a mangled mess of death before the gunner could think to release the trigger. It was that power that had made the Apache one of the most significant weapons of the Gulf War.

As the seconds rolled by, Kaster realized the problem. The Apache had no place to land. Kaster had crashed in the midst of high desert shrubs and Joshua trees. The Joshua trees stood like eight-foot-tall, gnarled gargoyles, their thick, twisted branches reaching skyward, their needle-sharp pointed leaves spread out like hundreds of knives.

Suddenly, the thunder of the Apache increased as the engines increased in power. The craft rose straight up and pulled away.

It began a slow, lumbering spiral around the crash site. *Looking for a place to land*, Kaster thought. He was right. A few minutes later, he watched as the dark painted helo descended a hundred yards away. He heard the engines power down.

The crunching of sand under boots told Kaster that he was no longer alone. He could see two men approaching through the stygian dark. They paused at the downed Apache and shone a flashlight in the cockpit. One of them spoke, but Kaster could not make out the words. Slowly they approached the plane. Rain began to fall again.

At first, Kaster was tempted to close his eyes and play dead in the slim and ridiculous hope that they would go away and let him die in peace. That desire passed quickly. Kaster's character demanded that he face his enemy with pride and aplomb, at least as much as possible in his present condition.

"Did you do that?" one of the men asked. He was a six-foot-tall Caucasian with a thick neck and a Texas drawl. Kaster looked for a name tag on the man's flight suit and found nothing. Nor were there any patches on his sleeves. The man flew a military helicopter, but he was not part of any military unit known to Kaster.

Kaster coughed painfully. More blood trickled from his mouth. "Let's say it's something we did together."

"Those men were my friends," the man said.

"Who are you?" Kaster asked.

"Just a man doing his job." With a nonchalant motion, the man pulled his sidearm from its holster, chambered a round, and aimed it at Kaster's head.

"Wait a minute," the second man said. "I know him." He was an inch or two shorter than his partner and his face was as black as the night that surrounded them. His eyes moved quickly as he took in Kaster's appearance. He had an intelligent look about him.

"So?" the man with the Texas accent asked.

"Kaster?" the black man asked. "Admiral Kaster?" He turned to his partner. "That's Admiral Philip Kaster of the Pentagon. He spoke at my graduation at the Academy. We need to get him some help."

"No help," Texas said. "He's the cause of all this. Our orders are to eliminate him."

"We can't do that. He's an admiral in the United States Navy. He's no terrorist."

"Orders are orders. Besides, we're not military anymore. Not technically."

"I didn't sign on for this," the black crewman said. "I've done some weird stuff for this outfit, but I didn't sign on to kill an admiral."

"You just helped kill a couple of dozen men in uniform," Texas countered.

"Terrorists. They were terrorists who had overrun a research facility."

"They were no terrorists," Kaster said. "Those were marines. You massacred your own kind. They were your brothers in uniform."

"No," the black man said, shaking his head. "No, we were told they were terrorists."

"You were lied to," Kaster shouted, but a mere whisper emerged from his lips. "You murdered brave men sent on a rescue mission."

"That's not possible," the black man said. "I don't believe it."

"What you believe doesn't matter," Kaster said, making eye contact with the man. "You murdered marines and left them lying in the dirt. I don't know what outfit you're with, soldier, but the U.S. military doesn't do things that way."

"You'd be surprised, Admiral," Texas said. He pulled back the hammer on the pistol and took new aim at Kaster's head.

The gunshot echoed along the desert night, and it surprised Kaster that he heard it. He heard something else—a long stream of cursing, followed by: "Have you lost your mind?" The man with the Texas accent was struggling to get to his feet. In less than a second, the gun had been pushed aside and the second crewman had knocked his partner to the ground.

"There's no way I'm going to let you shoot the admiral."

"Maybe I should just shoot you then," Texas said hotly. He raised the gun and pointed it at his crewman. "You always were a little soft on these kinds of missions. Always questioning. Always reluctant. Don't make me kill you. We've been buddies for a long time. Don't make me choose between you and duty."

"Duty? Look at you," the black man shouted. "Is this why you signed on? To kill people? To shoot them in cold blood?"

"Yes," he replied flatly.

"You're not here for him," Kaster said, trying to draw the gunman's attention again. He was sure he was going to die. It didn't matter now if it was by bullet or by his injuries.

"Shut up!" Texas yelled. "I have time for both of you."

"How are you going to explain his disappearance?" Kaster asked. "There are two seats in that Apache, and both were filled when you left."

"That's less of a problem than you might think," the man said. "The loyalty factor is very high in our group—at least for those who follow orders without question." He spoke to his partner: "What's it going to be? You with me on this or not?"

"Not."

"Too bad."

A rock the size of an orange sailed out of the night and struck Texas on the left temple. His head snapped to the side, viciously. He turned to see where the stone had come from, then dropped to his knees and then onto his face.

"Bull's-eye!" someone shouted. Kaster recognized the voice. "Right on the money!" It was Jason.

From behind the brush emerged the three Good Samaritans who had first come to Kaster's aid.

The Apache crewman pulled his own gun from its holster and pointed it at the three young people. "Stand where you are," he shouted. They froze in their tracks. Stepping forward, and with his eyes still fixed on the three, he picked up the gun that had a moment before been pointed at his chest.

"Hey, man. We just saved your life," Jason said incredulously.

"I know them," Kaster said. "They tried to help me earlier. I sent them packing when you showed up."

"Yeah, but we didn't go very far," Amy said. Her black hair was matted to her face and scalp by the falling rain. "We saw what happened to the Med-Flight. We knew they didn't have time to get you. We couldn't leave you out here in the desert."

"I knew we couldn't outrun a helicopter anyway," Jason said. "So we drove about half a mile with our lights off, then walked back."

Kaster laughed softly, then coughed. "You don't take orders very well, do you?"

"We're not in the military," Jason said. "We don't know how to take orders."

Amy started forward.

"I said, stay where you are," the Apache crewman shouted.

"Stand down, soldier," Kaster ordered as loudly as he could. "Secure that weapon."

The man looked at the admiral, then complied. He did know how to take orders. "Sorry, Admiral. I'm a little confused."

"Understandable, son," Kaster said. He rolled his head back and closed his eyes. The cold night, the wind, the stress, and his injuries were pushing him beyond his endurance. "What's your name?"

"Riggins, sir. Charles Riggins."

"I have a thousand questions for you, Riggins, but I don't have time to ask them now."

"We have to get you to a hospital, sir," Riggins said.

"What about your helicopter?" Amy asked.

Riggins shook his head. "It's a combat helicopter. There's no place to lay down."

"He's not laying down now, and he looks real bad," Amy countered.

"Moving him could kill him," Riggins said.

"Leaving him in the rain *will* kill him," Jason said. "We can run get the van, but the drive isn't going to do him any good. How fast can that chopper of yours go?"

"About two hundred miles per hour," Riggins said.

"Well, that's faster than my van, and you can fly in a straight line," Jason said. "You're his only hope."

"Let's do it," Kaster said. "I've got nothing to lose."

Chapter 21

23 November 2000; 2325 hours
Cavern 1

Like most, Dole had seen his share of movies and read his share of adventure novels. He had watched unquestioningly as the hero, wounded and battered, fought back with skill and heroic determination. Now, with a hole in his shoulder from a gunshot, it was taking every ounce of his strength not to faint. Nausea plagued him, cold embraced him, pain stabbed him with each movement. He hung from the underside of the bridge, knowing that one slip would be his last. The sound of his falling in the water would be enough to draw the attention of the commandos. They would find him and kill him on sight, if the water didn't wash him into some earthly conduit where he would drown.

Holding on to the bottom of the box frame construction with his injured arm, he reached out with his other hand until he grasped the next lateral brace. The pain was piercing and ragged. Each movement caused such excruciating torment that he had to bite his lip until it bled to keep from releasing screams of agony. But he reached out again, and again. When his desire to quit grew irresistible, he thought of his missing brother, of his own children, of his wife—and then he reached for the next girder, then the next.

Hours seemed to pass, but Dole knew that it had been only minutes. The inlet was fifteen yards across, just fifteen good steps for a grown man if he was walking—just forty-five feet—but it seemed like miles. Slowly he reached forward again, grasping the supports and letting his body move smoothly through the water until he hung vertical underneath the frame. Then he reached forward again.

By the time he reached the end of the bridge, he was covered in icy sweat. His arms, normally firm and powerful, shook like leaves on a tree. He wished he could be like the hero in the movies, fighting off injury as if nothing had happened, but this was no movie.

Clenching his teeth until he was sure his jaw would snap, Dole pulled himself up. His injured shoulder protested, ligaments threatened to give way, muscles reached the threshold of failure; but Dole pulled anyway until he could lift his right foot out of the water and onto the flat stone floor that was six inches above the surface. Contorting, pushing, pulling, he eased himself out of the inlet and onto the side of the bridge, then onto the firm rock.

His first impulse was to lie down, to rest for a moment, but there was no time. While the attackers had moved to the far end of the cavern, any one of them could return and find him. He was in no condition for one-on-one combat. He had two advantages: one, the attackers were a good distance away, preoccupied with the corridor and how to make their way down it safely; and two, they had shot out most of the lights on this side of the cavern. Staying as low as possible, he crawled toward the console, making each movement as quietly as possible. Silent stealth was the key. Any noise louder than that made by the humming of the Horizon's electronics and the sound of the running water in the inlet would echo off the hard stone walls of the cavern, drawing attention to his activities. He had been trained well for this, except this wasn't an exercise. It was real. One mistake would mean doom for him and for the others.

Although easier than moving along the underside of a bridge, the silent scrabbling along the cavern floor was arduous and taxing. Dole had spent his physical resources crossing the inlet. Only determination to fulfill his duty to his men and his country kept him moving forward.

Upon reaching the console and concealing himself on its far side, Dole paused long enough to inhale deeply. The air was still thick with acrid smoke, but it tasted sweet to Dole. Unconsciousness hovered over him like a demon, calling him to rest, to sleep, to surrender to dark nothingness that contained no pain and no fear. Dole refused.

Positioning himself on his knees, Dole took in the sights before him. Two men lay dead a few feet away. The elevator cab contained three corpses, the best he could tell. The large metal desk blocked much of his view. He wondered if other soldiers were waiting on the ceiling. It didn't matter. What he had to do, had to be done.

Moving toward one of the dead men, he found what he was looking for—an automatic weapon. It was an MP-5 submachine gun. He lifted the gun and silently ejected its clip. It was nearly full. The man had scarcely fired a shot. But would one clip be enough? He crawled over to the second fallen man and ejected the clip from his weapon. It too was nearly full. Two clips, that would have to do. Now all he had to do was find the safest position that would allow him the greatest latitude for shooting. He would need a retreat, too, just in case some men lived through the attack, or he had to change clips.

Peering through the smoke-saturated air, he saw his spot. It was far from ideal, but the cavern offered few opportunities. The base of Horizon I rose two feet above the floor. He could position himself just to the right of the base, make his shots, and roll behind it for cover, if necessary.

That was it, then. It was time to make things happen and accept whatever consequences came.

N

Dwyer stood two feet to the left of the corridor, his left shoulder near the wall. He sighed as if he were stymied by a crossword puzzle, not involved in a life-and-death operation. "We can't charge down the tunnel. They'll mow us down."

"How do we know they're still there?" Zeek asked. "Maybe there's another way out."

"Perhaps, but do you want to be the one to walk up there and find out?"

"No. At the moment they have the advantage." Zeek, who stood on the other side of the opening, peered around the edge of the corridor. A shot ricocheted off the edge of the passageway, splintering off a small piece of rock that struck the commando on the chin. He yanked his head back and swore. Blood trickled down his neck.

"That seems to answer the question," Dwyer said. "You all right?"

"Yeah, just peachy," Zeek snapped. "Someone is going to pay for that."

"Go ahead, take a shot or two."

Zeek shouldered his weapon and let loose a quick burst of fire down the hall. Dwyer listened but heard nothing. "Feel better?"

"No. How are we going to get in there?"

"We're not," Dwyer said. "I have another idea." He stepped away from the stone wall, turned his back to the others, and spoke into the microphone of his headset. The signal would never have made it through the surrounding rock to the surface if a relay transmitter had not been placed in the elevator.

"Why don't we just throw a few grenades in?" Zeek asked.

"Corridor is too long. Someone would have to stand in the opening to get a good angle on the throw. Anyone doing that would have more than a scratch on their chin to show for it.

"If they had another way out, they would have used it by now. We must have them outnumbered, or they wouldn't have left just three men behind to defend their retreat. Drawing a line in the sand here doesn't make sense. They've dug in because they have nowhere else to go."

"Tear gas? Grenade launcher?"

"No. I'm putting an end to this right now."

Dole froze at the sound. It came from the elevator. Another soldier had descended the elevator shaft. His first instinct was to take aim and fire as the man dropped into the cab, but the shot would give away his presence. He would be dead minutes later. Instead, he flattened himself to the ground, laying his body over the submachine gun. His best chance was to play dead, and his blood-stained uniform would make the act all the more believable. He only hoped the newcomer wouldn't wonder why Dole was wet or why his BDUs differed from the others.

Lying face down by the Horizon I base, Dole slowed his breathing, turned his face toward the elevator, opened his eyes in a death stare, and waited.

The man who came through the elevator access panel was tall and in his late twenties. He carried a satchel the size of a small backpack. As he stepped from the elevator, he paused at the site of the carnage and said, "Unbelievable." He leaned over one of the fallen commandos and swore. Apparently the man had been a friend. He then straightened himself and jogged toward the bridge and the others.

Dole remained as still as the ground he lay upon, waiting to see if any others should appear. None did. Stealthily, he moved along the floor until he had found a position near the metal base above which Horizon I had once hovered. Sighting down the barrel, he planned his shots. A level sweeping motion would afford the best opportunity to hit all the attackers. The clip would empty quickly and he would have to replace it, hopefully before any survivor could return fire.

Stanton moved close to Keagle. "Hold your fire until you're sure of your shot, Sergeant. Our ammo is limited—far more limited than theirs."

"Understood, sir," she replied. "Sorry, sir. I guess I'm getting antsy."

"We all are, Sergeant. We all are." He looked across the inlet, the empty expanse of cavern floor, and down the corridor. "What have you seen?"

"Not much, sir," Keagle said. She didn't sound antsy, but the epitome of calm. "Several men crossed the far end. They're armed, but we already knew that."

"Could you tell how many men?"

"It looked like four, maybe five. I'm too far away to tell for sure. There seemed to be soldiers on both sides of the opening. They've made no attempt to come down the passageway."

"It's a standoff, all right," Stanton said.

Keagle cut her eyes to the bridge. Ramsey, Tulley, and Hawking were working at a feverish pace. "May I ask what they're up to?"

Stanton glanced over at the bridge. "A shot in the dark, Sergeant. I've been asking myself how they plan to attack. It seems that their choices are limited. We can hold them off for a while, but I doubt they're going to give up."

"I saw you pulling up the access panels in the floor. You're planning on doing something with the electrical."

"Right. There are two unused power lines that Eddington had placed for future equipment. He's nothing if not forward thinking."

Stanton watched as her eyes moved from the open channel in the floor, where several thick black cables ran to the bridge. "A barricade," she said softly. "You're going to use the guardrails on the bridge to make a barricade across the passageway opening, and you're going to electrify it with one of the power cables."

"Exactly," Stanton said. "The guardrail is bolted onto the support structure of the bridge. There was a full set of workman's tools near the ROV. If the attackers charge us, they'll run into the barricade."

"No one in their right mind would charge down a corridor like that," Keagle said.

"They might. If they charge with weapons blazing we won't be able to fire back. Even if we do, we may not get them all."

"It would be risky on their part."

"Agreed, but no more risky than dropping down 250 feet of elevator shaft and entering Cavern 1. There are other things they can do. Sergeant Ramsey thinks that they might use—"

"A grenade launcher," she said evenly.

"That's right," Stanton replied with some surprise. "You read minds, too?"

"No, it just makes sense. I've been sitting here wondering how I would formulate an attack. That would be my first choice. Of course . . ."

"Of course, what?" prompted Stanton.

"It all depends who they're taking orders from and what their mission is." Her eyes shifted back to the corridor and remained there. "If they were here to capture us they wouldn't have attacked our men topside the way they did. My guess is that they are to stop us no matter what. No one is to know about this place. We weren't supposed to be ordered in. Your commanding officer got ahead of somebody's game plan."

"What are you getting at, Sergeant?" Stanton asked.

"Sir," she began, "if I were them, and I couldn't get in, I'd make sure no one got out. I'd seal the opening, let us starve, and dig it out later."

A deep chill ran through Stanton. "Why didn't they do that in the first place? Why not seal the elevator?" He paused, then answered his own question. "Sealing us in is the last resort, and they don't have orders for that."

"I think you're right, sir."

"My barricade wouldn't be worth much then."

"No, sir, but we don't know that they have the explosives to do the job or if they're even thinking of that. Your barricade is the right idea at the right time."

Stanton didn't feel comforted. It was a last-ditch effort on his part, but one he had to try. Sitting, waiting, and wondering were eating at him. He had to do something. "Thanks for your honest appraisal, Sergeant."

"I wish I could do more."

He patted her on the shoulder. "Stay alert. If you see something, holler. Ramsey and the others will be there to help you out."

23 November 2000

1600 Pennsylvania Avenue, Washington, D.C.

President Crane paced around his office, his hands clasped tightly behind his back. "That seems extreme," he said to Mark Adler.

"It can't be any more extreme than what's already been done," Adler said. "Fate has scripted this for us. At this point, we're just along for the ride. All we can do now is cover our tracks."

"The bodies have been taken care of?" Crane asked.

"Yes, sir, and the remaining members of the investigation party are trapped in Cavern 2."

"But if we bury them, we may never get back to Horizon II, and we're too close to let that happen."

Adler listened carefully, not so much to the president's words as to his tone. Over the years, Adler had learned to read the fine print of the president's speech. Despite his protestations, Crane was approving of the plan. He hated it, loathed the messiness, but he would approve it. All he needed was a little more prompting.

"There is only one other option, Mr. President, and that is for our men to shoot their way in. They have the means of launching several grenades in—"

"No!" Crane said emphatically. "That could destroy Horizon II. That's too much to lose, much too much to lose."

"Very well, sir. I'll take care of the communication."

"We're on a slippery slope here, Mark. Don't let us slide to the bottom."

"I'll make sure that we don't."

Chapter 22

23 November 2000; 2340 hours
Cavern 1

"No," Dole said under his breath. He closed his eyes, squeezing the lids hard, then opened them again. Blurry. His vision was fading, rendering his normal 20–20 sight to a foggy haze punctuated by splashes of bright color. He tried to sight down the MP–5, to take aim at the enemy who stood gathered together near the opening of the corridor, but the gun sights seemed to waver back and forth and up and down. Even though he lay prone next to the base of Horizon I, the weapon propped up on his injured arm, the butt extension pressed into his good shoulder, the gun still swayed like a conductor's baton. The nausea had returned, burning in his stomach and filling his mouth with the pungent, gagging taste of bile.

His head dropped forward and he immediately snapped it back. "Not now," he whispered. "Not now. I need a few more minutes. Just a few . . . more . . . minutes." He had been watching his targets work. His failing vision made it impossible for him to see just what they were doing, but he knew that it wasn't good. If only he could see better, if only he were a little stronger, and if only his mind wasn't so foggy with pain.

An ache, deep and hot, radiated from his wounded shoulder. Something wet ran down the inside of his arm. Blood. He didn't have to look; he knew the wound was still bleeding, and with every ounce of blood lost, he came closer to losing consciousness. He fought back the encroaching blackness, willing it away, wishing it away, and it would recede for a moment, then make a new assault, like heavy waves beating against the pylons of a pier. Dole knew that no matter how strong his will, how determined his heart, he would sooner or later succumb to the ebony dark of unconsciousness. What he had to do, he had to do now, or forever give up the cause.

He lowered his head and took three deep but ragged breaths; holding the last, he sighted down the barrel again. The gun steadied for a moment. Dole pulled back on the trigger with a smooth, even motion. He had set the weapon to full automatic, which meant it was capable of firing eight hundred rounds in a single minute. Unfortunately, the men he planned to kill carried the same weapon, and there were eight of them. That was 6,400 rounds a minute. Of course, no clip held 800 rounds, but that was a moot point. He was outgunned, outnumbered, and in no condition to fight. Dole understood that he would probably be dead within a few minutes of firing his first burst. That was acceptable. He would probably bleed to death before help could arrive, anyway.

The men were moving away. It was time. He squeezed the trigger a little harder until it engaged. Dole swept the gun from left to right, hoping to hit each man and at least incapacitate them, if not kill them outright. The MP–5 jumped in his hands as the rounds flew from the barrel.

There was no more pain. There was no more nausea. There was just the mission. Just him and eight killers.

N

Dwyer had watched his men work. They carefully removed the packages from the satchel the new man had brought down the elevator shaft with him. Gently they had removed the plastic explosives, wired them with detonators, and placed them as far in the corridor opening as they could reach without exposing their heads or torsos to gunfire. Ideally, Dwyer would like to have placed the C4 in the middle of the passageway, but that was impossible. One or more people in the other cavern had a direct line of fire. A man would not make it a yard up the corridor before being filled with holes. This was the best he could do, and it would be enough.

"All set, sir," Zeek said. "The corridor should cave in nicely."

"Very good," Dwyer answered. Tapping his radio headset, he said, "I've received the go-ahead. Let's fall back to a safe distance. We'll push the detonator when we're in the clear."

Zeek turned to the men and started to speak, but instead of hearing words, Dwyer heard the rapid popping of gunfire. Instinctively he turned to see its source. That's when he was hit. At first he thought someone had kicked him in the legs, knocking his feet out from under him, but the scorching, boiling pain came next. He started to scream when he realized he was falling backwards. He landed hard on the floor, his helmet striking the rock. His head bounced off the stone ground and then hit again.

"Take cover!" Zeek shouted.

Dwyer rolled over on his side, just in time to see Zeek pull his weapon from his shoulder where it had been hanging by its strap. With practiced smoothness he brought the weapon round and began to level it in the direction of the gunshots. He never got his finger to the trigger. Three rounds hit him: two in the chest which, despite his body armor, pushed him back. The third round struck him in the bridge of the nose. He fell lifelessly to the floor.

Wide-eyed, Dwyer watched as two of his men instinctively jumped into the corridor, only to stumble back after being shot by a marksman in the other cavern. Both fell dead, one shot just under the helmet, the other, judging by the radiating patch of red, had been hit just under the arm, an area not protected by body armor.

Dwyer's weapon had slid a few feet away from him when he fell. He reached for it but it was a full two feet beyond his reach. He tried to stand, but his legs would not respond. Pulling his sidearm, a Beretta 92 FS, from its holster, he unleashed several rounds in the direction of the gunfire. Dwyer had no specific target.

Two more of his men went down, but quickly rolled over onto their stomachs, alive because of the vests they wore. The trail of bullets from the other side of the inlet continued on its course. Several rounds caught one of his men in the head. Another kill.

Who was doing this? Dwyer wondered. They had cleared the cavern, and no one else could have gotten by his men on the surface. It hit him hard. The missing man! The unaccounted-for corpse that he had assumed had fallen into the inlet. Somehow, someway, he had found a way to hide and was now attacking.

Another burst of fire went over Dwyer's head, the bullets bouncing off the stone wall behind him. The shots seemed erratic. Either the man was panicked or injured. There had been blood where the body was supposed to have been. Why didn't he just have the decency to die?

Dwyer fired a few more rounds in the general direction of the gunfire. Another burst erupted. *Gotcha*, Dwyer thought. "There!" he shouted to his men. "There!" Dwyer fired again; this time he was joined by the remaining soldiers. He crawled toward his automatic weapon and as he did, he took stock of the situation. One shooter, probably injured; four of his men dead; one unconscious from bullet impacts on his vest; three returning fire. Counting himself, that made it four to one. He, however, was wounded—his legs were not responding at all. Probably broken, he surmised. If it weren't for the adrenaline coursing through his veins, he would be mad with pain. That would come, but hopefully not for another few minutes.

The cavern echoed with gunfire; bullets ricocheted over the stone walls.

Several more shots came down the corridor. "Stay away from the opening," Dwyer shouted. This was as bad as it could get. They were pinned down by a man who had clear shots at all of them, and they had no cover. At any moment, attackers could come down the corridor and pick them off easily. Well, there was something he could do about that. He reached for his machine gun, flipped off the safety, and let loose a dozen rounds at the sniper. Still on his belly, he turned and began to crawl toward the detonator. As he did, he saw one of his men pull a fragmentation grenade, yank the pin, and hop to one knee ready to throw it. Another burst of gunfire crossed the inlet and hit the man square in the chest; the bullets, which were traveling faster than the speed of sound, bowled the man over. The grenade dropped by his side. "Watch it—" The grenade exploded, sending pieces of hot metal flying outward. Several pieces struck Dwyer—one hit his arm, several bounced off the stone floor near him, and several struck him in the legs. A quick look revealed that the wayward grenade had killed not only its owner, but the man next to him. Now there were only two left to fight: himself and one other. He had no idea how long the unconscious would remain so.

Another round of fire from the far side. This time the spray was fifteen feet over Dwyer's head. The attacker was losing it. Maybe he would pass out. Better yet, maybe he would just die and save Dwyer the trouble of killing him.

Dwyer had three goals at the moment: stay alive; call for reinforcements; trigger the explosion. As he crawled toward the small detonator, he keyed his microphone. "This is Dwyer, come in." Nothing. "This is Dwyer," he repeated. Still nothing. He paused just long enough to pull the radio from his belt. Maybe the headset was damaged when he fell. It wasn't the headset. In his hand he held the plastic case of the radio which had a clean hole through it. He looked at the back—blood, his blood. He wished that all his men had been equipped with communications, but only he and Zeek had carried them. Too many radios on the same frequency made communication impossible. He would have to make his way back to Zeek and use his unit. Between Dwyer's location and the lifeless body of Zeek lay the detonator. He would accomplish two things at once.

Stanton, his pistol in hand, dropped to the ground next to Sergeant Keagle. Three feet to his right was Sergeant Ramsey. "What have you got?" he asked. He had heard the gun fire from the other cavern, then heard the explosive report of Keagle's weapon.

"Two men entered the corridor," she said softly but firmly. "I fired at each. I think I got them both."

"Anyone else enter the corridor?" Stanton asked.

"No, sir, but something big is going on over there. First they were doing something around the mouth of the opening. I was trying to make it out when I heard shots. Next thing I know, there are two men in the corridor. I fire and they stumble out."

"Assessment."

"I don't know, sir. I can't see much beyond the other opening."

"All right, Sergeant, how about your best guess."

She paused without taking her eyes off the passageway. "Someone opened fire on the commandos. Caught them off guard."

"That's good news," Stanton said. "Maybe it's a rescue team."

"I hope so—"

The explosion sent concussive waves of air and dust out of the corridor. The ground vibrated with the force of the blast. Stanton's ears began to ring loudly and dust filled his lungs. Seconds ticked by as he waited for another blast. *Grenade?* he wondered, but dismissed that idea as soon as he could see down the passageway. Where once light had filtered through the long tunnel, there was nothing but darkness.

"Oh, no," Keagle said. "They wouldn't."

Ramsey was on his feet and moving cautiously over the bridge and toward the opening. He took a position next to the corridor's mouth and peered in. Then he stepped into the passageway itself. Less than a minute later, he reemerged. "We're sealed in, sir," he reported. "They blew it up."

Tulley and Eddington walked over to Stanton. They, like Ramsey, had been working on fabricating the barricade. "It doesn't look like we're going to need the barricade," Tulley said sullenly.

"No, Agent Tulley, it doesn't."

"What now?" Eddington asked.

Stanton shook his head. "I have no idea."

The explosion caught Dole off guard. It had been the last thing he had expected. It made no sense. Why destroy the only access into the next cavern? Through the sludge of grogginess the answer came. The attackers could not go in, so they made sure no one could come out. Whether death came by gunshot or starvation it would still be death, and their mission would be complete.

Sadness enveloped Dole. In the back of his mind there had burned a flicker of hope that somehow, Stanton and the others would find a way to gain the upper hand. That tiny flame of optimism went out like a match in a tornado. He lowered his head, partly in sorrow, partly because keeping it up took so much effort. Dust from the explosion filled the air and began to settle in the still cavern. It brought with it silence. The return gunfire had stopped.

Lifting his head, Dole tried to focus his eyes. The hanging lights swung in pendular arcs, causing shadows to dance wildly on the floor and walls. Forcing the muscles in his eyes to cooperate, he peered through the haze, searching for movement, for any sign of danger. There was nothing. *Maybe they blew themselves up*, he thought. *Maybe I got a break*. The thought brought him no joy. Even if he had gotten a break, his friends hadn't. And there was still the matter of the soldiers above.

Uncertain of how much longer he could maintain consciousness, Dole decided to test the awareness of his opponents. Aiming the MP–5, he pulled the trigger of the submachine gun. A burst of three rounds was released. He waited for reprisal. There was none. He repeated the test. Again nothing. Was this a trick or was the battle over? Now he faced a decision. Every brain cell pleaded with him to rest, every muscle begged to be left alone, but Dole knew that if he rested too long, if he fell asleep, he might never open his eyes again. Despite the protestations of his body, Dole turned and crawled away from the raised base of Horizon I. On the way, he exchanged his MP–5 for that of another fallen soldier. He was too weary to care if he crawled over bodies, just as long as he kept moving. Once he reached the end of the console, he fired off another few rounds. Again they went unanswered.

Looking across the bridge, Dole knew the rest would have to be covered on foot; there was nothing that could offer protection in a firefight. Had he been well, or just moderately injured, he would have been happy to wait for the others to make their move first, but Dole doubted he had much more time left.

He stood and started forward.

Dwyer inhaled a ragged breath of acrid air, air burned by plastic explosives and made bitter by smoke from the gunpowder. His legs raged in pain, and his ears buzzed so loudly that he raised his hands to cover them, as if the act could quiet the noise in his head. The concussive blast had damaged his hearing, maybe even broken his eardrums. As a child, he had become fascinated with pirates and battles at sea fought by wooden sailing ships. He had once read that a cannonball could injure a score of men without touching them. The vacuum caused by the ball's speed could inflict painful damage to ears. The explosion in the corridor had done that to him.

The pain was increasing, radiating up from his lower extremities. He wanted to stand, but knew his damaged legs would never allow it. Blood. How much blood was he losing?

He turned slightly, ignoring the agony of the act, and looked down at his lifeless, unresponsive legs. A trail of bright red marked the distance he had crawled to reach the detonator. The blood loss was significant. He had to stem its flow.

He tried to sit up, knowing that it would make him a better target, but that no longer mattered. He would die anyway, if he didn't stop the flow of blood. His strength failed. No matter how he tried, he could not raise himself. He turned to his side, an effort that was more difficult than anything he had ever done. The pain was excruciating. Reaching down, he took hold of one leg of his pants and pulled the injured extremity up in hopes of reaching the wound. It was like pulling a bag of sand. Despite his iron will, he groaned at the agony, then let go. His strength was gone.

He rolled over on his back and stared at the dark ceiling above. He was helpless. His men were dead or gone. The men above were out of reach without a radio. And he was bleeding to death. Letting his hand drop, he felt his pistol. He took it in his hand and waited. Maybe, just maybe, the shooter would come looking for him and he could squeeze off one more shot . . . just one . . . more . . . shot. He released his grip.

The smoke above him began to swirl and twist, becoming a vortex. Then it began to glow, and spin faster. Dwyer watched, enraptured by the sight. Through the incessant buzzing in his ears he could hear something, faint at first, but becoming louder as the seconds passed. Time grew slower. Seconds seemed to stretch to minutes and minutes to hours.

The vortex lowered, inch by inch, and Dwyer felt as if he were looking down a long, spinning train tunnel—no, a funnel. That was it. A long spinning funnel. His breathing slowed, his eyes darkened. In the ill-defined distance, originating someplace beyond the cavern with its cold floor, and now acrid air, was the voice. Calling him, whispering to him ... beckoning ... reaching ... drawing.

The voices became louder, turning from whispers to screams, to ululations of agony and torment. The funnel descended like the open mouth of some gigantic eel, opening, sucking, swallowing. Screams layered upon screams, pain breeding pain, torment, agony ... hell.

"I don't want to die," Dwyer said with childlike pleading. "I don't want to go there. No. Please. No."

The massive maw descended until only darkness filled Dwyer's eyes. He took one heaving breath and then felt his heart throw one last beat.

Each step came with great difficulty, as if he had been immersed in an ocean of molasses, left to trudge his way through the viscous mass. But Dole plodded on, with the muzzle of the MP-5 pointed ahead of him. He staggered across the stone floor, making his way to the bridge. The metal span had a slight rise from its foundation to its midpoint. To Dole it looked like a rise of a dozen feet when he knew it was no more than a foot.

The air seemed thicker now, the cavern darker. The ground beneath his feet seemed to move, to undulate with each step, as if he were walking on a waterbed mattress. He was struggling to breathe, to inhale the thick dust-and-smoke impregnated air. The ringing in his ears continued, first from the half-dozen stun grenades that had poured from the elevator, then from the gunfire that was amplified by the solid rock walls.

He took another step, then another, as he stepped upon the steel bridge. Reeling, tottering, he forced his mind to focus on the arduous task of remaining upright. Had he climbed Mt.

Everest, he would have been no wearier. How he remained standing was a mystery to him. Something deep inside, a sense of duty or pride or even fear, kept him going, dragging one foot after the other.

When his right leg gave out, he stumbled to the side, kept from falling headlong into the inlet by the guardrail. Despite himself, he coughed, destroying any chance of a covert approach. *What was I thinking?* he admonished himself. He was standing straight up in the middle of the bridge in full view of anyone in the cavern. But no one shot at him, no one approached. It was as if he were the last person on the earth.

In the earth, he corrected himself. *You're not on the earth*, *you're in it.* The thought struck him as funny, but he didn't know why. He giggled, then chuckled. "Quiet," he said to himself, then giggled again. Starved for oxygen-rich blood, his brain began to shut down.

Leaning over, Dole stared into the black water that churned under the bridge. Black, cool, inviting. Suddenly, unreasonably, he longed to fall in the saltwater stream, to float on his back until the water pulled him under and took him wherever it wanted. There would be no guns, no grenades, no explosives. Just quiet. Just peace.

Lieutenant Alex Dole turned on his heels slightly, dropped to his knees, then fell forward on his face. Darkness swallowed him.

Chapter 23

23 November 2000; 2350 hours
Cavern 2

Only two sounds broke the silence: the gurgling of the inlet and the hum of electronics. Stanton sat at the computer console in front of Horizon II. He was rubbing his temples, thinking, praying, at a loss for direction.

"Well, this is another fine mess you've gotten us into, Ollie," Tulley said in his best imitation of Stan Laurel—except Stan Laurel had never come close to matching Tulley's sarcasm.

"Knock it off," Wendt said. After the explosion that closed off the only access into Cavern 2, she, Zach, and Josie had joined the others. Zach sat on the ground next to Wendt. His eyes were wet with tears and he shook from fear. "You're not helping."

"If you haven't noticed, *Agent* Wendt," he said, "we are beyond help."

"The very least you can do is be professional about it," Wendt snapped.

"Professional? Professional?" Tulley shouted. "This goes beyond professionalism. There was nothing in my training that prepared me for an assault of commandos and being sealed in a cavern. Give me the tire off a criminal's car and I can scrape the treads, analyze the soil, and tell you where it's been. I can read DNA printouts, use lasers to lift fingerprints, but I'm a little out of my league facing a slow, agonizing death surrounded by the idiots who got us here."

"Watch it," Ramsey said.

"Or what," Tulley taunted. "You going to shoot me, or something? It would be a faster death than what we're facing. So go ahead. Shoot me." Tulley spread his arms. "What's the matter? Chicken?"

Ramsey, who had been sitting on the floor, rose to his feet. He stood four inches taller and weighed seventy-five pounds more than the FBI agent. Stanton looked up in time to see the fury in the Samoan's eyes.

"Stand down, Sergeant," Stanton said firmly.

"Come on, you moose," Tulley taunted.

"Stop it," Wendt called. "You're acting like a child."

Ramsey took a step forward. Tulley reached inside his jacket.

Stanton was on his feet and crossed the distance to Tulley in three steps. In a fluid motion, he interposed himself between the two men, grabbed Tulley by the front of his jacket, and yanked him forward. As the agent's weight shifted forward, Stanton took one easy step to the side, placed his right foot behind that of Tulley's, and pushed. Tulley, who was already pulling back to keep his balance, tumbled to the ground. Stanton had not let go. Instead, he dug his knee into Tulley's ribs. The man winced in pain.

Releasing his hold on the jacket, Stanton reached in and pulled Tulley's gun from the holster, then checked its safety. It was on. With his knee still firmly placed on Tulley's chest, he released the clip, which fell to the floor, and pulled back the slide so the chambered round was ejected. Stanton then stood, turned toward the inlet, and hurled the pistol, then the clip and free round, into the water.

Hearing something behind, Stanton turned sharply on his heels. Ramsey had resumed his approach, his face a cloud of fury and determination. "Stand down, Sergeant." Ramsey continued his approach. "I gave you an order, Sergeant. You will stand down!" His voice reverberated off the cavern walls and ceiling.

Ramsey shifted his gaze from Tulley, who still lay on the ground, to Stanton. Again, Stanton positioned himself between the two men. He was no match for the big man who had to be fifteen years his junior, but he was not going to let Tulley get pummeled, no matter how much he deserved it. Ramsey stopped short. His fists clenched, looking more like mallets than hands. "Sergeant. Don't test my patience."

Closing his eyes, Ramsey inhaled deeply, then released it in a gush of air. He repeated the process. Stanton wondered if he were snorting like a Brahma bull ready to charge, or making an effort to calm himself. He prayed it was the latter.

"Sorry, Captain." Ramsey closed his eyes and took in another bushel of air. "It won't happen again."

"Very well, Sergeant. Let's put this behind us." Stanton turned to Tulley, who sat on the floor rubbing his chest. He looked pale.

"You nearly broke my ribs, Stanton," Tulley complained.

Taking one long step toward the FBI agent, Stanton grabbed him by the front of the coat again and jerked him to his feet.

"Hey," he protested. "Take it easy."

Stanton didn't take it easy. He was furious and doing everything he could to contain himself. He walked to the console dragging Tulley with him. If he were going to maintain control, he had to deal with the matter forcefully. The console had six high-back leather chairs. Stanton approached one and threw Tulley into it.

"I said watch it!" Tulley shouted.

Leaning forward, Stanton put his face uncomfortably close to Tulley's, so close that he could watch the man's pupils dilate. "I am going to say this once, and once only," Stanton growled. Tulley pushed himself back in the chair. "We are in this together. We are alive. We are intelligent people. I am going to see that we get out of this—"

"How?" Tulley asked.

"I don't know," Stanton said. "But you will never do what you just did again. If you do, I will have Sergeants Ramsey and Keagle hog-tie and gag you. Is that clear?"

"And I'll help," Wendt said angrily.

Tulley looked around. He was surrounded by enraged, seething faces. "I understand, Captain," he said softly.

Stanton stepped away. This was a crucial moment. If he was going to maintain leadership, then he must, absolutely must, establish control now. "Listen to me," he said with an unwavering voice. "If we panic, we die. If we divide ourselves, we die. If we turn against each other, we die. Is anyone not clear on this?"

No one answered.

"Good. Now let's get to work." He began to pace. "We've all looked at the corridor and agree that it's useless. Whatever they used caved the walls and ceiling in. Our radios are useless in here, and even if they did work, there's no one left on the surface that we can call a friend. Our advantages are few: First, the attackers will assume that we're dead or trapped forever. At least there won't be bullets flying in here; second, we have plenty of air."

"But no food and water," Wendt added.

"True enough," Stanton agreed. "We do have power and light. That's a plus."

"Great," Tulley quipped. "We can watch each other die." Stanton cut him a flint-hard glance. "Okay, okay. I'll shut up."

The tension had been mounting. The explosion had caught them off guard, leaving them stunned and shaken. Stanton had been the first to race to the passageway, and the first to realize the hopelessness of clearing it. The rock face had crumbled in boulder-sized chunks too large to move by hand. Even if they could combine their physical effort to move the heavy stones, it would be a useless effort. All but ten feet of the corridor had collapsed. This Stanton easily deduced. The men who set the charges had not come up the passageway. Keagle could testify to that. That meant that the explosives had to be set near the opening. Since only ten feet of the corridor were still clear and several dozen feet were buried under the rubble, they would need another way out.

As each member of the team came to realize the impossibility of clearing the debris, a heavy depression set in, like a thick fog that swallowed all before it. Without saying so, they each had concluded that only a slow death awaited them. Their families and friends would never know what happened to them. They had scattered around the cavern, each lost in his or her own thoughts. Silence prevailed until Tulley's outburst. Even Stanton had been consumed by the overwhelming sense of doom. But no longer.

"Let's focus, people," Stanton barked. "Let's use our skills and training and see if we can't get out of this mess."

"There is no way out, Captain," Eddington said softly. He was sitting in one of the chairs at the console. "I know this place. I chose this place. I have personally examined every inch of this cavern. The only way in and out was through the corridor. We are entombed here like Egyptian mummies."

"I don't buy it," Stanton said.

"Well now, that ought to change things," Tulley said sarcastically. "If the good captain doesn't buy it, then it must not be true."

Hawking spoke before Stanton or anyone else could reply to Tulley's cynicism. "What is the chance of rescue? Could other people come looking for us?"

"No chance," Eddington answered quickly. "Those people out there who did this, did it for a reason. Their goal is to keep Horizon II a secret. Their bosses merely have to wait thirty or forty days until they're sure we're dead, then bring in a crew and equipment to reopen the cavern."

"Just who are their bosses?" Stanton asked. Something was percolating in the back of his mind. It was amorphous, unrecognizable, but it was there nonetheless.

Eddington shrugged.

"I want a better answer than that, Doctor," Stanton said. His voice carried power and conviction with it. "Your loyalty is misplaced. Remember, they trapped you in here too."

"I'm expendable," Eddington replied.

"Obviously," Wendt said.

"Who are they?" Stanton demanded.

"People, just like the people who gave you your orders, Captain. And the soldiers out there are just like you."

"I wouldn't bury a group of people in a cavern to die," Stanton objected.

"Wouldn't you?" Eddington said. "Wouldn't you really? Not even if ordered to? Tell me, Captain, when you were on your submarine and an order came through, did you routinely question it?"

"Of course not."

"So if you were ordered to fire upon any and all Russian ships, would you have done it?"

"If those were my orders."

"Merchant ships carrying a crew guilty only of being sailors?" Eddington prodded. "You'd put a torpedo in their midsection and condemn them to die in the cold ocean waters?"

Stanton stood in silence. He had been thankful to God that he had never been asked to do such a thing, but that was exactly what he had been trained to do—to kill other subs and ships.

Closing his eyes, Eddington rubbed his forehead. The strain was wearing on the elderly man. He sighed loudly. "As you can tell, they're a commando team," he said suddenly. "As I said earlier, they're a black operation. Everything they do is secret. They're military trained and then recruited from the different branches. Only the best are sought out. They exchanged their uniform—navy, army, marine, or whatever—for a new one, one without patches and rank indicators. They fly in unmarked aircraft and do whatever they are told to do."

"Such as?" Stanton prompted.

"Such as fly researchers from one research and development location to another. Protect sensitive sites. Carry out maneuvers that might have some bearing on research. Spray chemicals on unsuspecting farmers and their livestock. Track down and remove people who have become security risks."

"Men in black?" Wendt asked.

"That's television and myth from the UFO cults, but essentially, that is right."

"Everything you describe is illegal," Stanton said.

"Yeah, so?" Eddington replied. "You sound surprised."

"I am."

"Then you're naive," Eddington chastised. "And a man with your background should know better. Governments break the law all the time. Ours does; everyone's does."

"This is all very interesting," Tulley said, unable to keep quiet as promised. "But how does it help us? At this rate we're just going to die better informed."

The amorphous, ill-defined thought that had been haunting Stanton's mind suddenly took shape. "When we first entered the elevator, when the commandos opened fire on the lab blasting the door down, I asked why they were doing this, and you said because we had entered the lab."

"That's right," Eddington admitted. "So what?"

"How did they know we had entered the lab?"

"I . . . I don't know what you mean," Eddington stammered.

"Our team was the only one in Roanoke II," Stanton said. "How did your covert army know we were here?"

"Someone, presumably their superiors, must have told them," Eddington replied. His face was a mask of puzzlement.

"That begs the question, doesn't it? How did their superiors know?"

"I don't know," Eddington admitted. "There is no direct monitoring outside the complex. There was no way for them to see in."

"Satellite surveillance," Ramsey suggested.

Shaking his head, Stanton said, "No. Even with real-time, heat-sensitive surveillance they wouldn't be able to see through the cloud layer. It's been overcast since we arrived."

"Well, then," Wendt said, "if they couldn't see what was going on inside the compound, then someone on the inside must have been calling out."

"I've told you," Eddington said. "The phones don't connect to the outside directly. All outbound calls had to be cleared and manually connected. That was a security requirement. And since there was no one available to do that, no one could call out."

"Maybe it was one of Dole's men," Tulley suggested. "One of the guys on the perimeter, I mean."

"Not a chance," Ramsey said tersely. "I knew almost every one of those men out there. They were my friends."

"So what," Tulley snapped back. "I work for the FBI, remember? We are constantly doing background checks on people in the military, and you'd be surprised what you learn."

"I have to agree with him, Sergeant," Wendt said. "Background checks was one of my first assignments."

"And let's not forget that some of the most famous spy cases in recent history have involved military personnel," Tulley added. "The same can be said for the CIA and even the FBI. No group is exempt. Not even your precious marines."

"That's true," Eddington said quickly.

"Would you mind standing up?" Stanton asked Eddington.

"Why?"

"I'd consider it a favor," Stanton replied. He walked over to where Eddington was sitting. "Don't make this difficult, Doctor Eddington. Please stand up."

Slowly Eddington complied. "What do you have in mind, Captain?"

Without answering, Stanton put his hands on the engineer's shoulders and turned him around 180 degrees. He then began to pat the man down like a police officer about to make an arrest.

"This is an outrage," Eddington protested loudly, his words rebounding off the cavern walls. "What do you think you're doing?"

"Please remain still, Doctor." Stanton continued, but then stopped as he felt something hard and rectangular in Eddington's coat pocket. He reached in, took hold of the object, and removed it.

"Stop it. That's mine," Eddington shouted as he spun around to face Stanton. It was too late. Stanton held the object in his hand. It was made of black plastic and was very familiar in form. Opening it, he studied the cell phone. He held it up for the others to see.

Tulley jumped to his feet. "Why, you—"

"Sit down, Tulley," Stanton ordered quickly. Tulley ignored him and started for Eddington, who was backing away. "I told you to sit down." Stanton's voice boomed.

Tulley pulled up short. "But—"

"I will have no more trouble from you," Stanton said. "Now *sit down.*"

Like a scolded child, Tulley returned to his seat at the console.

"I know what you're thinking," Eddington shouted, "but you're wrong. It's not that way at all. I didn't call anyone. I didn't tell anyone we were about to enter the lab."

"There were several times when you were alone," Stanton said. "I can think of two times when you sat alone in the Humvee, while we were occupied with other things."

"That means nothing," Eddington countered. "Tulley and Wendt were alone at the house. Remember? They could have called."

"Not true," Wendt said. "That was long before we tried to make entrance into the lab."

Stanton looked at the phone again. "Direct satellite connect is my guess. Am I right?"

"Yes, but that doesn't mean anything."

Anger welled up in Stanton. Once again, Eddington had been holding back. Cell phones weren't carried on this mission because they were too easy to monitor, and too easy to track, and yet, here was Eddington with a state-of-the-art satellite communication device. Admiral Kaster's last words had been "This whole thing is dirty. Be careful who you trust." Was he referring to Eddington? "I want a straight answer, Doctor Eddington," he said. "Did you, or did you not, call your superiors telling them we had entered the lab?"

"I did not."

"Then why the phone?" Tulley called out. "You're the only one here with those kinds of connections. You're the one who stands to lose the most. You had motive, means, and opportunity."

"This isn't a trial," Wendt said.

"Who asked you?" Tulley snarled back.

"Shut up, Tulley," Ramsey said. Tulley swore.

"Don't make no difference now, do it?" Josie said. She had remained quiet, standing away from the others.

"Excuse me?" Stanton said.

"He weren't on no phone when I first laid eye on him in dat big fancy automobile he was a sittin' in. But it don't matter if he was. We're still here, no matter who made what call."

She was right, Stanton decided. Whether Eddington made the call or not was really secondary to survival and escape. He had to focus on that.

"And," Josie continued, "dat fancy phone don't mean dat he used it. I got plenty o' things I don't use, but I still has 'em."

"Thank you for your deep insights," Tulley said, "but why don't you leave the thinking to those of us who are equipped for it."

"I ain't got no learnin', mister," Josie said with a near toothless smile. "But I is smart enough to know dat just about any of these here people would be happy to give you the wuppin o' yo' life."

Ramsey laughed, as did Wendt and Keagle.

"That's enough," Stanton said. "Josie, you are right. Our first task is to get out of here." He tossed the phone to Ramsey, who deftly caught it in one hand. "It's a shame that thing won't work down here."

"Prayin' is a good start," Josie said.

Stanton smiled. "I've been doing a lot of that lately, Josie. An awful lot."

"Well, you keep it right up. Best thing you can do. God will see us through this. You bet, he will. He'll see us right through. Ol' Josie knows these things. You'll see."

"I think you're right, Josie," Stanton said. "I think you're right." He turned back to Eddington and said, "You're off the hook for now, Eddington, but if—when—we get out of this, I'm going to want some answers."

"Captain," Eddington said solemnly, "I did not make any calls."

Stanton studied the man and wished he could believe him.

Chapter 24

24 November 2000; 0030 hours
Cavern 2

"You've been awful quiet," Stanton said as he approached Hawking. The physicist was standing next to Horizon II, gazing intently into the angry-looking hole. Like everyone in the cavern, he was covered with thick, clinging dust.

"It's amazing," Hawking said softly. "I've been studying it for some time now, and I still can't wrap my brain around it. It has no edge, yet I perceive one. It hovers there like someone has scooped out a huge hunk of reality."

Stanton studied the enigma. Up until then, he had been too distracted to pay much attention. The thing, the event, the threshold, whatever it was, hung fixed in midair, surrounded only by the four glowing pillars spaced equidistant around a sphere of nothing. It was crimson, like an angry, open wound, and it seemed to pulse, if something that wasn't there could pulse. No matter what direction Stanton looked, it seemed as if he were peering at the center. It reminded him of those trick concave images that seemed to follow the viewer as he moved. Inside the sphere was nothing. Even the term *sphere* seemed wrong. At a distance, it looked like a giant bubble hovering above the ground, but up close it seemed the opposite—an anti-sphere, if there was such a thing. Stanton had never heard of one. Like Hawking, he could make no sense of what he was seeing.

"As frightening as this thing is," Hawking admitted, "I'm fascinated by it. For years I've known of other dimensions, at least on paper, but I never dreamed that I would ever see one. Not like this anyway."

"I owe you an apology," Stanton said quietly.

"Oh? For what?" Hawking seemed surprised.

"For getting you into this mess, of course. I had you snatched from your warm bed, dragged you here in a helicopter, and promptly placed your life in danger."

"No apology is necessary. I wouldn't have missed seeing this." He paused as he continued gazing at the object. "I wish it didn't exist. It scares me to think what may be on the other side of this portal, but it also intrigues me."

The two men stood in silence, bathed in awe and wonder. Finally, Hawking spoke again: "I take it Dr. Eddington didn't have any ideas."

"None," Stanton admitted. "The corridor was the only way in. I asked him about the inlet. I've noticed that it is rising some. He said it was purely tidal force and that it led nowhere. We would drown trying to make our way out in that flow. Most of it courses through underground channels with no area above the surface for a man to breathe. Apparently there's a stiff current that runs underneath. Anyone who gets into the water would be dragged under and drowned in short order."

"I thought as much," Hawking said. "It looks pretty grim, doesn't it?"

"That's putting a positive spin on it," Stanton replied. "All we can do is wait for a rescue team to dig us out."

"Do you think one will show up?"

Stanton shrugged. "I don't know. I have no idea what is happening in the other cavern. Whoever is responsible for the attack may make sure that we stay here until we starve. That would be the easiest thing to do."

"So we sit by and see what happens next," Hawking said, coughing to clear his throat.

"I'm open for ideas."

"I'd give you some if I had any."

Returning his attention to the portal, Stanton said, "Would this have really worked?"

"Yes," came a different voice. Turning, Stanton saw that Eddington had joined them. "We were close, Captain. Very close. We have sufficient power, we have stabilized the opening. It would have worked."

"You really think you could send a jet or a tank through that and have it instantaneously reappear someplace else?"

"I'm convinced of it. The only problem that remained was the point of exit. We don't know where it leads."

"Trouble, dat where it leads. You take it from ol' Josie. Dat ain't nuthin' but a bunch o' trouble for you and the whole world. God never meant for the likes of us humans to go messin' with his creation like you done." The derelict woman had come up behind the three men. In the dim light of the cavern and the red glow of Horizon II she looked frightening, like Medusa exiting her cave.

"Madam, please," Eddington said. "This is a scientific experiment, not some spiritual mumbo jumbo."

"Go easy on her, Doctor," Hawking said. "She's right."

"I expected better of you," Eddington said.

"And I of you," Hawking said. "There are factors here that you've not even begun to understand, and because of your anti-spiritual bias, you can't see them. What you've created here is not new. It's not original."

"Of course it is," Eddington objected. "No one in the world has done this."

"You know very little of me, Dr. Eddington. All you know you learned from the brief introduction you had when I first arrived, so let me fill in the gaps. I have a Ph.D. in physics from a reputable, accredited university. Science has been my passion since I was a child and the second most important thing in my life."

"Second?" Eddington asked.

"I, like Captain Stanton, am a man of faith. I view the world through the eyes of faith. I have made the Bible my guide and Jesus my Savior. Everything I see, everything I experience is colored by that commitment, and I have found my faith to be true in all aspects."

"I know'd it," Josie said. "I just know'd it."

"Spare me," Eddington said with exasperation.

"It explains many things," Hawking said, unperturbed by Eddington's sarcasm.

"Such as?" Stanton prompted.

"Let's take the biblical examples first. The folks of Roanoke II are not the first people to disappear. In Genesis, there is the account of Enoch, who walked with God and was no more, for God took him. Have you ever wondered where he went?"

"He went with God," Josie chimed in.

Hawking gave her a quick smile. "That's right, but just where is that?"

"I've always assumed that it was heaven," Stanton offered.

"And where is heaven?" Hawking continued. "Is it out there somewhere?"

"It's everywhere," Josie said.

"Correct again." Hawking turned to Eddington. "There are scores of accounts in the Bible that can only be explained if God exists in dimensions higher than ours. Heaven itself would have to exist in dimensions higher than ours. Christ, after his resurrection, walked through a locked door to appear to his disciples. That's a miracle of higher dimensions. Moses and Elijah appeared to Jesus and three of his disciples on the Mount of Transfiguration. Remember, according to the Bible, Elijah never died."

"Ol' Elijah, he went up in a fiery chariot," Josie contributed. She was clearly excited.

"What's all this have to do with Horizon II?" Eddington asked.

"Elijah and Enoch are two men who never died. God took them from our puny world of three dimensions—four if you want to count time as a dimension—and translated them into his dimension, where death doesn't apply. In a sense, they disappeared like the people of Roanoke II."

"Are you saying that God took the residents of this research community?" Eddington asked harshly.

"Not at all, Dr. Eddington. What I'm suggesting is that you have, through your engineering, forced open the door that you had no business opening."

"Rubbish. Nonsense," Eddington fumed. "I'm tired of being blamed for everything. I'm tired of being pushed around." He stormed back to one of the consoles and sat down.

"You said you'd start with the biblical examples," Stanton said. "Did you have other examples in mind?"

"There are many stories of people disappearing," Hawking said. "Sometimes they're individuals, other times groups. There are eye-witness accounts, too. I suspect that portals like these occasionally happen by accident."

"Accident?"

"Ours is an imperfect universe," Hawking explained. "God created it perfect, but it has been damaged by sin. The apostle Paul said in the book of Romans, 'We know that the whole creation has been groaning as in the pains of childbirth right up to the present time.'"

"Accidental portals?" Stanton thought about that for a few moments. "There are case histories of such things?"

"Of mysterious disappearances," Hawking corrected. "I know of no case where someone actually saw what we're looking at. There are, however, cases like the *Iron Mountain*, a steamboat that disappeared off the Mississippi and was never seen again. The passengers of a downed plane in the northwest went missing. Nothing was ever seen of them again. There are many such events."

"So they what? Fell into heaven?" Stanton asked.

"Heaven? Probably not. Heaven is just one of the possibilities. The Bible speaks of heaven as being a place. The apostle John had a vision of it and recorded what he saw and experienced in the book of Revelation. But there are other places. Sheol and Tartarus are the most obvious. Do you remember the story of the rich man and Lazarus?"

"I do," Josie said. "Jesus told of a rich man who had everythin' and poor ol' Lazarus who had nuttin'. Dey both die, and dis rich man, he goes to a place of torment, but Lazarus, he goes to a different place, a place called Abraham's bosom."

"Lazarus was at rest in Abraham's bosom," Stanton said. "But that's not heaven, is it?"

"No," Hawking said, "and the rich man wasn't in hell. They were in Sheol, the place of the dead. Lazarus was in the place of the righteous dead, the rich man in a place for the unrighteous dead."

"But I thought that when a Christian died, he or she went immediately to be with the Father in heaven," Stanton said.

"That's right," Hawking replied. "But remember that Jesus is telling this story prior to his death on the cross and his resurrection. He's giving a real-time illustration. When Jesus was hung on the cross, there were two thieves crucified with him. One repented and Jesus told him, 'I tell you the truth, today you will be with me in paradise.' Paradise is probably the same place that Lazarus went. After the Resurrection, all that changed. Today a believer dies and is immediately with the Father."

"Absent from the body; present with the Lord," Stanton paraphrased. He looked at the enigma again. "So I wonder where this thing goes."

"I shudder to think—"

An electronic shriek pierced the air. Stanton turned on his heels. The sound was coming from the console where Eddington sat. Quickly, he crossed the distance that separated the console from the gaping hole that was Horizon II. "What is it?" he demanded.

"An environmental warning," Eddington said quickly. He was scanning the computer monitor in the console. "It's the air scrubbers. They're failing."

"Failing? Why?" Stanton asked.

"Look around you, Captain," Eddington snapped, his face lined with concern. "Dust. Massive amounts of dust from the blast and cave-in. It's probably more than the scrubbers can handle."

The others, having heard the alarm, gathered around. A pall of silence fell over them.

"How long before we run out of air?" Wendt asked.

"Normally we would have time," Eddington replied. "This is a big cavern and there's plenty of air for a while. Maybe a few days, even a week. I can't know for sure."

"What do you mean, normally?" Stanton asked.

Eddington nodded toward Horizon II. "It uses air."

"What?" Wendt asked, astounded. "It's a machine. How can it use air?"

"Air is composed of matter, Agent Wendt," Eddington said as if lecturing a high school science class. "The air we breathe is made up of oxygen and nitrogen molecules. The Horizon is designed to transport matter. It doesn't care if it's a car or free-floating molecules, it lets the material pass."

"This just gets better and better," Tulley said.

"When we first arrived in Cavern 1, didn't you tell me that there were no air ducts to the surface and that all the oxygen needed was made from seawater in the inlet?"

"Yes, Captain, I did," Eddington replied. "I also told you that we used air scrubbers. Between the two there was more than enough air. But Cavern 1 was the only cavern with the device that converts the water into breathable air. As long as the corridor was open, we had a fresh exchange of air. But the corridor is no longer open."

"Why didn't you mention this sooner?" Tulley asked harshly.

"What difference does it make?" Eddington snapped back. "I figured the scrubbers would keep us alive for awhile. As long as they worked, we would be fine for several days."

"You're not making sense, Eddington," Hawking countered. "Once the tunnel was sealed, the volume of air in here became finite. If a portion of it is leaking through the Horizon, then the scrubbers would have nothing to clean, no CO_2 to convert to O_2. We would have had a problem whether the scrubbers failed or not."

"Is that right, Eddington?" Stanton demanded.

Eddington blanched. "I . . . suppose so."

"You suppose so?" Tulley shouted. His brow was furrowed with anger and he stabbed at the air with his finger like it was a knife. "You suppose so? What kind of an engineer are you?"

"One who shouldn't be here," Eddington shouted back. "I'm not a military man. I'm not used to running for my life, being shot at, and having explosives go off in my vicinity. I'm not a young man. This is all too much for me."

"Your stupidity is too much for us all," Tulley fired back.

"Leave him alone," Wendt snapped. "It's not like you've come up with any brilliant ideas to get us out of here."

"Josie," a small voice said.

"I have had enough of you," Tulley spat and turned to face his partner.

Ramsey took a step toward him.

"Josie," the small voice repeated.

"Hold it," Stanton said loudly. "Everyone be quiet. This isn't helping. We've got a problem, and that needs to be our first priority. If we get out of this you can spend the rest of your lives pointing fingers."

"Josie."

"What?" Stanton said. He looked around for the strange voice.

"Josie is going away." It was Zach. He was standing behind Wendt and pointing toward Horizon II.

"He's talking," Wendt said with surprise.

"I see why the FBI hired you," Tulley said.

"What about Josie?" Stanton asked. He had barely been able to hear the boy over the loud voices of the adults.

"Going away." He raised his hand and pointed at Horizon II again.

Spinning around, Stanton saw the old woman standing at the edge of the bubble. "Josie, no!" he shouted. "Don't go in there." He was on the move, sprinting the thirty feet between the control console and the enigma. He was too late.

Josie stepped forward into the nothing and was instantly gone.

Chapter 25

24 November 2000; 0100 hours
Cavern 2

"Unbelievable," Wendt said. She was staring first at the enigma, then at three balls of light that danced near the ceiling of the cavern. The spherical lights were about a foot in diameter and glowed a pinkish white. They skipped around the ceiling as if they were airborne ballet dancers. One disappeared into the ceiling as if it wasn't there only to return a few seconds later.

Stanton was stunned with astonishment. No sooner had Josie stepped into the void than the luminous globules appeared. "What are they?" he asked, as all three globes melded into one then separated again.

"Artifacts," Eddington said flatly. "That's the most I can tell you."

"Holding out again?" Tulley asked pointedly.

"Not at all," Eddington replied. "That's all I know. We first noticed them with Horizon I. If something of sufficient mass entered the portal, these things came out."

"How come we didn't see them when you were demonstrating with Horizon I?" Stanton asked softly.

"Like I said," Eddington answered, "it all has to do with mass. In Cavern 1, I used a wad of paper, then a pencil, and finally my arm. All pretty small, really. If I had thrown a chair in you would have seen smaller versions of these."

"The unknowns that Edwards tracked on radar?" Stanton prompted.

"Big versions of these. The mass of fifteen hundred people is substantial. They're amazing, aren't they?"

Before anyone could answer, one of the spheres rocketed down from the ceiling at a speed that was almost impossible for Stanton to follow with his eyes. It struck Tulley in the chest. The man screamed and jumped. The globe had exited his back a fraction of a second after it had hit him.

"Tulley!" Wendt shouted.

Agent Tulley staggered for a moment, his hands clutching his chest. He took a deep breath, then lowered his hands. His eyes were wide with fright and the blood had drained from his face.

"Odd sensation, isn't it, Mr. Tulley," Eddington said. "He's all right. It's more illusion than reality. The spheres display attributes of high dimensionality. While it appeared that it had burrowed a hole in Agent Tulley, it merely passed through the space."

"That's why the radar report showed the objects of Roanoke II as crashing into the ground and then reappearing," Stanton said.

"Exactly," Eddington said, then added, "It is also the reason they appeared on the radar during one pass and not the next. We're seeing them in our dimension, but they really exist in another."

Suddenly the three lights blinked out. Stanton waited for them to return, but Eddington put an end to that. "They're gone now."

"Wow," Tulley said. "That was . . . interesting."

"Where is Josie?" Stanton asked.

"I have no idea," Eddington answered. "No idea whatsoever. No one has ever done what she just did."

"Make a guess," Stanton said.

"I can't. At least not a reasonable one." Eddington scratched his chin. "With Horizon I, everything came back into the room. That unit lacked sufficient power to really open a threshold. This one is different. We have more than enough power. That wretched woman could be on the moon, in France, or at the bottom of the sea. There is no way to know."

"She's in none of those places," Hawking said.

"How can you know that?" Wendt asked.

"Basic logic," Hawking said. "You need a portal to get in, you need one to get out. It's not a tunnel that we're looking at. It's a door to a different universe. She entered into something, not passed through something."

"But she is alive?" Stanton inquired.

"Who knows?" Eddington responded slowly. "Who knows?"

"Well, we are going to find out," Stanton said. "We have a big problem here, and we are not going to sit around waiting to die. Eddington, it's time you earned your keep."

"Anything?"

"Nothing."

Truman looked down the long, empty elevator shaft. "And you say it's been thirty minutes since their last report."

"That's right." The man to whom Truman spoke stood next to him, also gazing down the shaft. "Jenkins took the plastic explosives down twenty-five minutes ago. Twenty minutes after that, we heard the explosion. Then came the gunfire. It's been silent for the last five minutes. I haven't been able to raise Dwyer, Zeek, or anyone. The transmitter relay must have gone out or been hit by a wild bullet."

"Maybe it wasn't a wild shot," Truman said.

"We sent enough men down there to take over Fort Knox. I don't see how anyone could withstand our team. Besides, they radioed that Cavern 1 had been contained."

"Then why haven't they radioed in?" The man didn't answer. "All right," Truman continued. "Select two other men. The four of us are going in. And get me some body armor." Truman was third in command, following Dwyer and Zeek. He was primarily concerned with helicopter ops, not ground attack, but the mantle had now fallen to him. "I want us on down the shaft in ten minutes."

"Got it."

"And it's fully functional?" Stanton asked. He was looking over the Remotely Operated Vehicle, the ROV. To him, it looked very much like a half-sized version of a mutated Volkswagen Beetle. Hawking Striber stood next to him, eyeing the oddly shaped device. The chassis was composed of inch-and-a-half tubular steel painted in bright bands of rainbow colors. Two arcs of the same tubular steel rose from the back of the device and spanned the distance to the front; they reminded Stanton of a safety cage on a race car. Four two-foot diameter tires supported the frame.

"The engineers were finishing the fine-tuning over the holidays," Eddington said. Despite the dire circumstances, he still beamed with pride. "We call it Rover. Not very creative, but ROV seemed far too clinical."

"Why all the wild colors on the frame?" Hawking asked.

"We're dealing with a great many unknowns, Dr. Striber," Eddington said. "We have no idea how things are perceived in higher dimensions. The alternating color bands will help us determine that. Each color reflects light at a very specific wavelength. That's something we can measure." He tapped a box mounted between the curved arcs at the top of the ROV. "There's a camera in her that is focused on the frame. Once Rover is on the other side, it will take measurements of the reflected light. We can measure and record any differences. There's a great deal of information that can be gathered that way."

"Let's keep moving, Doctor," Stanton said. "Please continue the tour."

Eddington stepped to the front of Rover. "It's a simple device, really. It carries its own power source in the form of onboard batteries. Here on the front"—he pointed to two cylindrical white enamel cases with clear plastic lenses on the front—"are video cameras. They work together, and their individual images are melded into one through a computer. This gives us binocular vision. Since we are working with other dimensions, we have no idea what to expect. The images that come back may be jumbled or may be as clear as a postcard. We have no way of knowing. Follow me, Captain." He led Stanton to the rear. "Rover receives its commands and sends back its images through this fiber optic cable. It's shielded to minimize the effects of the strong magnetic field that holds Horizon II open."

Stanton studied the cable for a moment. It was a full inch thick and covered in black insulating rubber. He guessed that a metal shield surrounded the optic fiber. Running alongside, and bound to the black cable, was a quarter-inch thick woven steel line. "What's the steel cable for?"

"Two reasons. First is to protect the fiber optic cable. If Rover were to repeatedly tug at the line, it could damage glass fiber.

The steel line keeps that from happening. Second, it's a high test anchor," Eddington replied. "It's possible that Rover could enter Horizon and immediately cease functioning. We want to be able to pull it back."

The image reminded Stanton of something his pastor had said in a sermon. The ancient Jewish priests used to tie a rope around the waist of the high priest when he would enter the Holy of Holies in the temple. Once a year, such an entrance was required to make an annual sacrifice. Since the Jews believed that God was resident in the Holy of Holies, and since God could not tolerate sin, they feared the priest could be killed. The only way to get him out, if such a thing happened, was to pull the man out with a rope tied around the priest's waist.

"You operate all of this from the control console?" Stanton asked.

"That's the idea."

"Do it," Stanton ordered. "Let's make the most of the time available to us. I want to know what happened to Josie."

"Is that all you're thinking?" Hawking asked.

"No," Stanton admitted but offered no explanation. "Dr. Eddington, I have one final question: How does Rover enter the Horizon? Josie was able to lean in, but Rover can't do that." He pointed at the round hole, the anti-sphere. "It looks like only the top part of Rover would make contact with the threshold horizon."

"There must be a hidden ramp," Hawking said. "Maybe the floor rises."

"Close, Dr. Hawking. Close." Eddington led the two men to the console and punched a button. The computer screen came to life. The words ENTER PASSWORD appeared. Eddington quickly typed in a word. The image on the monitor changed to an image of a circle. Sitting down in the console chair, the engineer made a few more quick keystrokes. "Instead of raising the floor, we lower the portal."

A mechanical roar filled the cavern and the floor began to vibrate. Stanton watched as the foundation of Horizon II, which had been flush with the floor, began to descend. With it descended the glowing red orifice. At first, Stanton thought the entire foundation was lowering into the ground, but then realized that a six-foot-wide section had remained in place, spanning the newly formed pit. It was a narrow bridge, and the spherical hole descended upon it, swallowing the bridge.

In utter amazement, Stanton walked to the Horizon. The bridge that matched the small roadway that the Rover would travel disappeared into the opening as if the threshold had bitten off the bridge in one gigantic bite.

"It's still there, Captain," Eddington called out. "We've run this portion of the experiment many times. Now, if you will please stand back."

As soon as Stanton returned to the console, Eddington activated the Rover with a series of keystrokes. "Batteries are fully charged, motor is responsive, steering is functional, and . . ." He entered another command. The computer monitor changed from a command screen to a picture of Horizon II. The angle was low. Stanton realized that he was seeing it from the perspective of Rover. "Tallyho," Eddington said as he took hold of the computer mouse at the side of the keyboard.

With excruciating slowness, the automated vehicle crept forward. Its electric motor whined as it cranked its thick rubber tires. Stanton realized that he was holding his breath. He glanced at Hawking, who had his eyes fixed on the monitor as if hypnotized.

Forward the go-cart–sized vehicle moved, covering the distance in just over a minute, a time span that seemed just short of an eternity to Stanton. Foot by foot it approached the pulsating cavity. When Rover was a foot away from the opening, Eddington inhaled noisily, released it, then said, "Let's see what no one else has seen before."

N

"Move the cameras up," Tulley demanded.

"I know what I am doing," Eddington replied coldly.

"Then why don't we see anything?" Tulley asked.

"I don't know. Now shut up and let me do my work." Eddington's face had grown increasingly red, embarrassed, and frustrated over the snowy, imageless picture on his monitor.

"Swell," Tulley said, flinging his arms in the air. He and the others had gathered around Stanton and Eddington when Rover began its slow roll forward. "Another engineering feat by the great Dr. Mason Eddington."

"Give it time," Wendt said.

"I've had enough of you, Agent Wendt," Tulley said. His face was lined with stress, his eyes brimmed with fear-laced anger.

"And I've had enough of you," she spat back.

"Knock it off," Stanton said loudly. His voice echoed down the cavern. The two FBI agents fell silent. "Let's stay focused, people. If you don't have anything helpful to offer, then keep quiet." He turned to Eddington. "Tulley's question is a good one, Doctor. Why don't we see anything?"

Eddington shook his head. "And my answer was truthful. I don't know. All the systems checked out before we sent Rover in. You saw that. We were getting a perfect video feed right up to the moment that the ROV entered Horizon. After that, nothing but this video noise."

"Maybe the strong magnetic field damaged the video equipment," Hawking suggested.

"No," Eddington said. "We know exactly how strong that field is and we took the proper precautions. Everything that needed to be shielded received it, plus a ten percent fudge factor. We're not stupid, you know."

"I'm not suggesting that you are," Hawking replied evenly. "I'm just brainstorming out loud."

Eddington pursed his lips. "It doesn't make sense. I'm not getting any readings. It's not just the video, but every sensor on Rover. Nothing is responding."

Raising his head, Stanton looked at the iridescent red hole. The cable that trailed behind Rover traveled along the ground and disappeared into Horizon. It looked as if someone had cut it off with an axe. Yet, it moved forward, dragged by Rover, so Stanton knew it was still connected.

In exasperation, Eddington pushed back from the console. "It's hopeless."

"Bring it out," Stanton said.

"Why bother?" Eddington asked coarsely.

"We can double-check the systems and see if there has been any damage," Stanton answered.

"There's no damage. The systems work fine; there's just nothing to see." Eddington walked away.

"I think I can do it," Hawking said. "I was watching him work the controls. It seems simple enough."

"Great, Hawking," Stanton said. "Let's bring Rover back." He was thankful the physicist was with him. At times, he seemed to be the only other thinking person in the cavern.

Sitting in the chair just vacated by Eddington, Hawking studied the monitor for a moment and then began tapping keys on the keyboard. He shook his head. "I have no bearings to go by. I can't tell if Rover is turning or not, or even how far. It could be going in circles for all I know."

"Can you disengage its power? Maybe we can drag it out."

"That's a good idea." Hawking made a few more keystrokes. "There, that ought to do it."

"Ramsey, Keagle," Stanton called. "Help me with this cable." He walked briskly to the long electronic tail of Rover and picked up the fiber optic cable and the steel rope to which it was attached. Ramsey and Keagle shouldered their weapons and joined Stanton. A moment later they were pulling. Hawking joined the effort. The cable withdrew from Horizon with surprising ease. After pulling twenty-five feet of the cable back through the opening, Rover appeared, its bright colors shimmering in the overhead lights.

"That's good," Stanton said, once the full body of Rover had reemerged. "Let's take a look."

The examination was brief, for there was nothing to see. Rover was unchanged. Eddington, who could not resist examining Rover, joined the others. He checked and rechecked every sensor, every camera, and even examined the rubber tires, and found nothing.

"I'm sorry," Eddington said softly. "I'm sorry."

Stanton patted him on the shoulder. "You gave it a try," he said.

"It looks like we're back to waiting for rescue," Hawking said.

"Yeah," Tulley said sarcastically. "As if that's going to happen in time." The FBI man walked away. A few seconds later, Wendt left. One by one, depressed and discouraged, they each retreated to their own thoughts. Only Stanton, Hawking, and Zach remained near Rover. Even Red sulked off and laid down.

"I'm out of ideas," Hawking said slowly, as if uttering the words was painful.

"I'm not," Stanton said. "I want to try one more thing."

Chapter 26

24 November 2000; 0130 hours
Cavern 2

"You're not serious," Hawking exclaimed in hushed tones. "I know things are serious, but—"

"They're more than serious, Hawking," Stanton interjected in equally hushed tones. "We have no idea of what is going on in Cavern 1. The place could be crawling with commandos and even if it isn't, and a rescue team were working their way to us, there might not be time. I have to do this and do it while I can."

"But you don't know what's over there."

"And I won't, unless I go in." Stanton sighed. "Look, Hawking, I don't have a hero complex. This is not my idea of adventure, but I owe it to my team, to everyone in here." He looked down at Zach and offered a reassuring smile to the boy. After his short outburst, the boy had fallen mute again. "It's something that has to be done."

"Then let me be the one to go in," Hawking offered.

"I can't do that."

"Why not? I'm as fit as you, and I have some understanding of dimensionality. There's an old joke that says the only people who can comprehend higher dimensions are physicists and children. I'm the physicist, remember?"

"I know that, Hawking, but you're also a civilian in a military operation. It would be inappropriate for me to let you cross that threshold."

"Nonsense," Hawking said firmly. "There has never been a case like this before. There is no precedent, and therefore no established rules can apply—military or otherwise."

Stanton put a hand on his friend's shoulder. "I appreciate the offer, Hawking, I really do. But I'm in charge here, and that means the decision is mine. Besides, if something happens to me, I need you here to provide some balance. Ramsey can take charge, but he will need someone who understands the science and engineering behind all of this. Eddington is too flighty. We can't count on him."

"But—"

"No." Stanton's voice was as solid as the rock floor on which he stood. "This is the way it is going to be. End of discussion. Now just give me your best guess as to what I'm going to see and experience."

"No one knows," he said flatly. "How can we know? It's all math and speculation."

"Take a stab at it," Stanton prompted. "And put it in layman's terms."

"Okay, okay." Hawking rubbed his eyes. "Here are the basics in a few sentences. We live in three spatial dimensions and one time dimension. I can move forward"—he took a step closer to Stanton—"or to the side, or up and down." He lifted himself up on his toes then lowered himself again. "All those directions are ninety degrees to each other. A fourth spatial dimension would be ninety degrees to those three."

"How can that be?" Stanton asked. "There's no way for another ninety-degree direction."

"Not in our world," Hawking agreed. "At least not that we can see and measure. That's going to be one of your problems. I don't know how many dimensions Horizon II spans, but everything you see—if you can see anything—will be out of place. Direction may have no meaning for you. There may not be an up and down, left and right, like you're used to. It could be entirely different."

"So my sense of direction is going to be off?"

"You can bet on it."

"Why do I feel like you have more bad news?"

"Because I do," Hawking said without humor. "There's the problem of time. Time may not pass in the same way."

"I don't get it."

"We live on a half line of time," Hawking explained. "Yet we think on a full-line. I can talk to you about yesterday and you immediately know what I mean. Your mind holds memories of events that happened in time past. But does that past time exist?"

"Not in reality," Stanton said.

"That's right. None of us can move backward in time. All we have is the present and the future, and we have to wait for the future to arrive. We can't speed it up. As kids, we would wish with all our might that Christmas would arrive sooner, but it never did. We move through time at a constant rate. Our perception of time changes. As we grow older, time seems to pass faster than when we were ten years old. Events alter our perception of time also. Half an hour in the dentist chair is vastly different than half an hour at a football game. Well, in higher dimensions, the time line may be different. There may not be a difference between the present and the future, for example."

"That would explain a few things about eternity."

"Exactly right. Have you ever wondered how God can hear all the prayers of the world at once?"

"Yes," Stanton admitted. "But what does that have to do with this?"

"Let me show you." Hawking led Stanton back to the console and found a pad of paper and mechanical pencil left by some worker. He drew a horizontal line and put an arrowhead on each end. "This is the typical time line we learn in school. On the left is the past, on the right, the future." He drew a dot at the middle of the line. "This is our present moment. As I said, we can't move backward along this line. The past doesn't exist. But what if it did? What if in higher dimensions there is an extra half line of time?"

"A being might be able to move forward or backward," Stanton answered.

"Perhaps," Hawking said. "It is equally possible that the time line would be a point and not really a line, at least from the being's perspective. Past, present, and future would be the same. That's what we mean when we say God is eternal. He exists in the present, but also in the past and in the future. Most likely God sees the past and the present and the future as the same moment. You're familiar with a globe," Hawking said. "As you know, lines of longitude are those that run from pole to pole. Imagine that the equator is our time line. If we could sit at the North Pole and look down toward the equator, we would see a moment in time. If we look to our right we might be looking into the past, to the left, the future, but what time is it at our position at the North Pole?"

Stanton thought for a moment. "It's all the same time."

"Exactly." Hawking returned to the horizontal line and drew a vertical line up the page, perpendicular to the first one, so the drawing looked like an upside-down T. "What if one of the additional dimensions was another half line of time. That's what this vertical line represents. For those of us on the normal time line, time passes by at a consistent, measurable rate. But if we could travel up this new line of time, then it would seem that time has ceased."

Stanton furrowed his brow. "I'm not following you."

"This vertical line is a second time line. If God exists in that time line, then he could hesitate, indeed dwell, in any split second of our time. He could hear six billion people pray if he wanted to, and hear them all in less than a second."

"Okay, you're saying that I may have no sense of time."

"Precisely," Hawking answered, then modified his position. "Well, that's not quite right. If there were no time, there would be no movement. Imagine that you're saluting. Your hand travels up from your side to just over your eye. The movement requires time. So if you can move, there will be the passing of time. It may just be different."

"How so?"

At that question, Hawking just shrugged.

Stanton thought deeply about what he had heard. Any other time, and any other place, it would have been fascinating, but this was real. He was about to step across a threshold into something he didn't understand—possibly *couldn't* understand. "What should my greatest fear be?" Stanton asked stoically.

"Insanity," Hawking said with mock clinical detachment. "It is quite possible that your brain may not be able to understand what it sees."

"No chance that I'm stepping into heaven?" asked Stanton with a weak smile.

"I doubt it. Maybe heaven can be described as existing in higher dimensions. It sure would explain a great many things. Still, I doubt any human effort could create a portal to heaven itself."

A churning ocean of uncertainty immersed Stanton. He struggled to think of some other way of saving the people for whom he felt so responsible, but no ideas came to mind. Not one.

"I should have a line tied to me," he said. "If, as you suggest, my sense of direction may be unreliable, then I'll need something to follow back."

"That might not even work," Hawking said. "Our physics may not apply over there. Still, it couldn't hurt."

"If I don't return in ten minutes, then you guys can pull me out like we pulled out Rover."

Hawking nodded. His face was clouded with great concern, and he was having trouble making eye contact with Stanton. "There are some things that must be left up to Providence, Hawking. This is one of them. A year ago, when we first met, I was pretty hard on you. I thought your ideas about the *Triggerfish* incident were nothing more than nonsense, but you were right. You challenged the depth of my belief. I realized then that my faith had been set firmly on the shelf, attended to only when I needed it. Because of your direct words, I had to face the truth that my faith is a daily commitment, not just some personal, historical event. It's that faith that tells me to go with this now. The rest we leave in God's hands."

Hawking looked up and nodded.

Turning, Stanton called out to Ramsey and Keagle. Both made their way to him. "It's time," he said to Hawking.

"Do you remember what Eddington said when we first saw Horizon I?"

Stanton nodded. The conversation was fresh in his mind. "You mean his comment about it not being empty over there? I believe you were the first to say that."

"I was," Hawking said. "Not that that matters. Just remember, you may—"

"Not be alone," Stanton finished Hawking's sentence.

N

"Nothing," the soldier said, his eyes fixed to the small LCD monitor. "I haven't seen any movement at all."

"There's a mixed blessing," Truman said. He was standing on the roof of the elevator watching as one of his men directed the electronic spy camera through the access panel in the elevator cab's roof. They had been patiently watching for the slightest sign of activity. "No sign of our team?"

"None. And no sign of the enemy."

"Open the panel the rest of the way," Truman said. "I'm going in."

"Should one of us go first?" the man asked.

"Nope. It's my call and I'm taking the honors." He readied his weapon. "You three wait here until I call for you." He took a deep breath. "Open the hatch."

One of the soldiers pulled back the metal access door. Truman sat down, hung his legs in the hole, then slipped the rest of the way in. He landed hard on one of the bodies of the earlier team. The sound and thought made Truman nauseous, but he had no time to be sick. Every second wasted could be his last. With the MP-5 pointed ahead of him, he rose quickly and placed his back against the elevator's metal surfaced wall. He listened, but heard only his own shallow breathing. Slowly he peeked around the front of the elevator and through the doors. The cavern floor was littered with bodies of men dressed in the same black uniform he wore.

Careful of his footing, Truman stepped over the desk that propped the elevator doors open and moved forward, alert to any movement, any sound. He heard nothing and saw only the lifeless bodies of men and the smoke-filled air. He keyed his radio. "Clear," he said. Two minutes later he was joined by the other three soldiers.

"I don't like the looks of this," a soldier by the name of Berger said.

"Me either," said one of the others.

"Okay," Truman ordered. "Let's fan out. Check the bodies. Someone may still be alive. If you find Dwyer, I want to know."

The men quickly complied. Truman walked through the middle of the cavern. The air was acrid with the smell of spent gun smoke. The light was dim, and the floor was littered with shards of broken glass from the overhead lights and brass casings from the firefight. As he walked past bodies, he couldn't help stepping in the sticky flow of blood that emanated from the men he had served with. This was not going to go over well with his superiors. As the new senior man, he would be asked to give an account, and he had no idea what to say. A crack, highly trained team of commandos had been eliminated by a group of terrorists.

No, this wasn't going to go over well at all.

He had heard voices. Dole tried to open his eyes a little more, but they were too heavy. His eyelids were mere slits that allowed only a little sight in. He could see the edge of the bridge upon which he lay; he could see the dark, brackish water of the inlet as it quietly churned in its natural rock culvert. Nothing about his body worked anymore. His arms wouldn't move, his head felt as heavy as a mountain, and his lungs could barely draw air. Blackness repeatedly swept over him. He kept pushing it back, but each time it lingered longer, seemed darker and thicker. His tongue was swollen, and he was so very, very thirsty. If only he could sit up. If only someone would bring him water, cool, silky water. Then maybe he would survive. Then maybe he would have the strength to open his eyes, to see who had been talking.

Perhaps they were friends. Rescuers who had come to his aid and that of his team. Perhaps. Perhaps. The darkness was returning and it was blacker than before, an obsidian cloak. It had texture, like old wet wool. It was covering him. It was calling him. It caressed him.

The formerly terrifying blackness now seemed comfortable, welcome. Dole wanted to release to it, to surrender to its gentle call, its loving caress, its unrelenting beckoning. To rest. To sleep. Too tired. So weary. Thirsty. Cold. So alone.

A pair of booted feet stopped two inches from Dole's face.

N

J. D. Stanton stood one foot away from the spangled, undulating hole that was Horizon II. A gentle but steady breeze brushed past his face and fell into the threshold, a reminder of why he was going to such an extreme as to step from one world, one he knew and loved, to another that he couldn't fathom.

They had each tried to talk him out of it. Even Tulley had made a case against the foolhardy act, but none could convince him. Deep in the well of his being, Stanton knew this was a step he had to take. He didn't know why, but he was certain that it was correct.

Up this close, he could see the Horizon's edge, that indefinable line between what was the world as he knew it and that which was a world not seen. There was an odd, unexpected anomaly at the "surface" of Horizon II, although he knew that the event had no true surface. Still, it was there—his reflection. He stared into his own weary eyes and saw fear, but he also saw determination. He blinked and his reflection blinked at him.

Focusing his vision further into the enigma, he suddenly felt as if he were falling. The spherical hole made him feel as if he were hovering over a gigantic bowl, or parabolic dish.

"You okay?" Hawking asked.

"I'm . . . yes, I'm fine," Stanton replied with a stammer.

"The cable is attached," Hawking said. He was the only one speaking to Stanton. The others, sensing their close friendship, had fallen silent. The steel rope had been removed from the fiber optic cable, lessening the weight that he would have to pull behind him. Ramsey, Keagle, and Hawking held the cable in their hands. They were to feed the line in as Stanton entered the field. Since no communication could be carried on once he was through the threshold, the cable would be their only contact. Tugging on the line twice would be the signal to start pulling, assuming that such tugging would be felt on this side. A time limit had also been established. If Stanton didn't reappear in ten minutes or less, they were going to drag him out.

"Is it comfortable around your waist?" Hawking asked.

Stanton looked down at the chrome colored metal line. It had been wrapped around his waist and then coupled to itself by two U-clamps taken from the extensive tool chest. "No, but that's all right."

"We're ready when you are," Hawking offered. "But take your time."

Stanton inhaled deeply, as if he were about to dive underwater. Then he closed his eyes and offered a simple but heartfelt prayer. Images flashed in his mind, pictures of his wife, his friends, his home. He wondered if he would ever see them again, or if his next step would be his last. He longed for his wife, to hold her, to whisper his love, to smell her hair. Tears began to fill his eyes. He could hear her voice and see her smile. The desire to step back rose volcanically within him. No one would blame him if he stepped away, if he said, "I can't do this." Each of them had tried to persuade him otherwise. There wasn't a man or woman in the world who would consider him cowardly for turning around. But he wouldn't. It was no more possible for him to back away than it was for him to make the sun set earlier, or to cause the stars to stop shining. He was going in, no matter what. It was not heroics, it was his destiny. He was as sure of that as he was of his own name. When he opened his eyes again, he heard Hawking speaking.

"'Where can I go from your Spirit? Where can I flee from your presence? If I go up to the heavens, you are there; if I make my bed in the depths, you are there. If I rise on the wings of the dawn, if I settle on the far side of the sea, even there your hand will guide me, your right hand will hold me fast.'"

"Psalm 139," Stanton said softly. "One of my favorites. Thank you, Hawking."

"God bless you, J. D.," Hawking said softly.

"'How precious to me are your thoughts, O God! How vast is the sum of them!'" Stanton said, quoting the same psalm. He took one more deep breath, and whispered, "Deo Volente." With no further hesitation, he lunged into the threshold.

Chapter 27

24 November 2000; 0150 hours
Cavern 2

Cold washed over him like an icy shower. Stanton shivered. Then waves of heat danced off his skin. A thousand sharp, needle-like pains pricked at his body, his scalp, his fingers, his eyelids; all pulsed with the combined pain of a million ant bites. His flesh seemed to crawl; his hair stood on end and waved in wisps, as if a sudden storm had arisen, but he felt no wind.

Instinctively, he clutched his arms around his body in a self-hug. His heart pounded like a symphony full of kettle drums. He was immediately aware of everything in his body. He could feel the blood course through his veins with such accuracy, with such perception, that he felt he could identify each red and white blood cell if he tried. In every movement he made he could sense the ligaments, the cartilage, the muscles working in tandem. The gas exchange of oxygen and carbon dioxide was measurable in his mind. Nothing happened in his body of which he was not aware. Every eyelash, every pore on his skin, every hair on his body was known, and the information was driving him mad.

He opened his eyes and saw nothing, everything. Before him was a grayness the tone of cold ash at the bottom of a fireplace.

Fragments, flakes of gray swirled through the air, spinning, churning, like flecks of dirty snow made drab by centuries of pollution. His brain cells fired endlessly, agitated by the confusing, amorphous near-nothing before him. Reaching out, he tried to capture a flake of gray. It passed through his hand as if it weren't there, as if he were a ghost, a spectral image of his one-time self now void of substance or reality.

"My hand," he said aloud. The words emanated from his mouth but sounded distant, as if someone else had spoken them. His eyes were fixed on his hand. Something was wrong, something out of place. It took several seconds for him to realize it was backwards. Facing the palm of his right hand, he saw his thumb projecting to the left, the way his left hand should have done. He raised that arm. The left hand was backwards, too. He forced his eyes closed again, squeezing them as hard as he could, then opened them again. "Calm," he said to himself, "calm." Forcing back the tsunami of terror he felt, he focused his attention on his surroundings, trying to get his bearings. He saw nothing but the gray flecks.

Wanting to start with the basics, yearning for something he could recognize as reality, he looked down to the ground. He was standing, therefore there had to be ground, a floor, or something. There was nothing, at least nothing he could see. His feet hovered above a vast chasm of emptiness, a void of gray specks. Yet he felt something substantial even though he couldn't see it. The pit of his stomach dropped. He had never gone skydiving, never done a bungee jump. He hated heights. He was a man of the sea, not of the air.

He was falling.

In panic-induced frenzy, Stanton turned sharply and reached for the portal through which he had just passed, but it was too far away. He could see it in the distance. It was a dozen yards away—no, it was closer—farther. Distance made no sense. While he could perceive the oxymoronic concave sphere, he could not judge its distance. He reached for it. His arm seemed to stretch like an elastic band. He screamed and pulled it back. It responded by shrinking to normal size.

Stanton screamed. He could not recall a time in his life when he had ever screamed before, but he was screaming now. The sound of his voice materialized some distance to his right.

He wasn't falling. He wasn't rising. He just was. A curled-up ball of a man. His overstimulated brain tried to bring reason to the unreasonable, to force a framework of reference on what he was seeing. He found no such framework.

Willing himself to be calm, he froze all movement. "This was to be expected," he told himself. "Hawking warned me of this." He took in a deep and ragged breath, and felt each alveoli fill with air molecules. Air molecules? In the back of his mind a tiny flicker of recognition blazed for a moment. Slowly he opened his eyes and gazed back at the portal. It glowed red, like a gigantic ember. From it streamed a million flecks of gray like those that surrounded him. It reminded him of mechanical snowmakers that he had seen ski resorts use. But what could be flowing in from the other side, his side, in such unrelenting abundance?

Air.

"Of course," he said aloud to himself, ignoring the misplaced sound of his own voice. He was seeing air molecules. Not the actual molecules as they existed in his world, but as they appeared in this place, with its additional spatial dimensions. How that could be, he had no idea. He couldn't even be certain that was the case, but it somehow made sense.

Unwinding himself from the tight ball that fear had compelled him to make, Stanton stood, doing his best to forget that he was standing on something he couldn't perceive. Forcing himself to think logically, he began to look around. The gray mist was pervasive. He thought of Josie. She had entered at the same point. Could she be nearby? Time was passing quickly, or so it seemed. He had set a limit of ten minutes at the end of which Hawking and the others would begin pulling him back. Looking at his watch, he paused. The second hand showed twelve seconds past the minute, then eleven seconds, then twelve seconds, then eleven.

Something moved. Stanton cut his head to the right. Nothing. He snapped his head to the left. Still nothing. There it was again. Another movement, just out of sight, hidden by the fog of colorless flakes. It happened again. A shadow, or a flicker. Something was there with him, near him. Turning around, he looked behind him, in the direction of the threshold. The threshold was gone. His heart began to race again; his blood flowed hot like magma. Where was it? He hadn't moved very far, hadn't taken any steps. He spun around again, still nothing. Slowly turning, he examined everything in the 360 degrees of his sight, if there were that many degrees here. No threshold.

A sudden, powerful sense of loneliness buried him. He was cut off, adrift in a sea of gray, an ocean of nonsensical Alice in Wonderland-like confusion. "The cable," he shouted to himself. "I must still be attached to the cable." Reaching behind him to where the cable should be, Stanton probed, clutched, frantically grabbing for the lifeline. It was gone. "No," he said. "That can't be." Oddly, he still felt its presence, its weight.

Something touched the back of his head. He jerked with a start, and quickly spun around, his hand in front of him, as if to ward off an attacker. Nothing. He was touched again, and once more he flinched and turned. Once more, he saw nothing. The powerful pounding of his heart increased.

Again the touch. Again nothing.

At the next touch to his head, Stanton responded differently. Instead of turning, he reached behind his head as quickly as he could. He got it. It felt hot and cold to the touch. He pulled hard. It was the cable. But why would it be touching his head? It had been attached to his waist. Looking up, Stanton saw the red orb of Horizon. Somehow it had moved, or he had moved, and now it appeared to float above his head.

"It's confusing."

The words startled Stanton. Until that moment, he had not realized how silent the place had been. All he had heard were his own words.

"There's no need to be afraid," the voice said. It was familiar, yet distinct and very different.

"Where are you?" Stanton asked.

"Right next to you."

Stanton turned to his right. A figure was there, startling him so much that he stumbled over his own feet and fell backwards. At least he thought he fell. He no longer had any sense of up and down, right or left.

The figure smiled. It was nearly as tall as Stanton and was bathed in a soft, barely perceptible aura of rainbow colors. Familiar. Different. Close. Distant.

"Don't you recognize me, Julius?"

There was a hint of an accent. "Josie? Josie?"

She smiled a full-toothed beaming grin. "I's a lil' different, but it's still ol' Josie."

Another figure emerged out of the gray.

"Dole?" Stanton said, nonplussed. "What are you doing here?"

"I have no idea," he replied.

"I count three dead bad guys and close to twelve of our own," Truman said. "That includes Dwyer and Zeek. What a mess."

"How could three men take out so many of our guys?" Berger asked. His face was ashen.

"I have no idea. The two dead on this side are armed with M-16s. The guy on the bridge had one of our MP-5s. He must have run out of ammo and snatched up one of our weapons to keep fighting."

"Tough guy," Berger said.

"Not tough enough," Truman remarked. "Dwyer got the explosion off before being killed." He paused and surveyed the mayhem around him. "Our superiors are not going to like this one bit."

"I know I don't like it," Berger said. "What now?"

"Clean up," Truman said. "We need to get teams down here and remove both bodies and weapons. I want it done fast. The longer we sit around, the more likely something could go wrong."

"Where shall we take them?"

"Same place we took the dead terrorists. Someone else is going to have to sort all this out." He started back to the elevator. "Help me move the desk, so the elevator will work. I'm going to radio for instructions. In the meantime, start collecting weapons and shell casings. I don't want anything that can be tied to us left behind."

"That's a huge job," Berger said, as he and Truman reached the bridge.

"I'll send down lots of help." He paused for a moment at Dole's body, then stepped over it. "Let's get to work."

Josie was remarkable. Her tangled, matted black hair was smooth and orderly; her deeply lined skin seemed younger, supple. Where once her mouth had been devoid of all but a few teeth, she now possessed neat, white, immaculate teeth. She had been made over in a miraculous way. "I don't understand," Stanton confessed.

"I knows you don't, dear, but it's all right. Yes, sir, better than all right." She held out a hand to Stanton. For a moment, he thought it might stretch, too, but it remained as it should. He took it. Her hand was warm, smooth, and firm. Somehow he expected it to be different, to be cold, unsubstantial, like ectoplasm. The old woman's touch felt fine, and it filled Stanton with a sense of relief. He was not alone.

"Why did you enter the Horizon?" Stanton asked. "You knew it was dangerous."

"I did at dat," she confessed. "I just knew that I had to go in. I felt it deep in my soul. Can't say no to somethin' like dat."

"But it didn't hurt you," he said with bewilderment, remembering the first few painful moments he had spent on this side. "You look . . . revived."

"It did hurt, Captain. It hurt real bad."

"But you seem okay, now."

"That's cuz I is dead." The emotion in her voice remained constant. She said it as matter-of-factly as if she were talking about the weather, or whether or not she liked peas with her dinner. "I had me a bad heart. Had it a lotta years. Walking through as I did was just too much for it. But it don't matter none, now. I'm better off."

"Dead?"

"That's right, child. That thing that Mr. Eddington done built, killed me. But don't let that fret ya' none. Dying was the best thing that ever happened to me."

Stanton glanced around at his surroundings. A sick uncertainty filled him. "This isn't . . . I mean this is not what I expected of . . ."

"Heaven?" Josie laughed, and her laughter was sweet and clear like brass bells. "Child, this here ain't heaven. No, sir. Not by a long shot."

"Then where are we?"

"I can't say that I rightly know, but I know it ain't heaven. I've been there and I'm going back. But you can't go. It ain't your time, or so I'm told. No sir, not close to being your time."

Stanton looked at Dole.

"It ain't his time, neither."

"Captain," Dole said bewildered. "I don't . . . I don't understand. I was shot. I was bleeding to death . . . that's the last thing I remember. Where am I?"

Sadness and guilt filled Stanton. He had ordered Dole to stay behind while he and the others retreated to the second cavern. It had been his hope that Dole and his men could hold off the others, since there was only one entrance point. Things had gone downhill from there.

Forcing himself to face the brave man, Stanton noticed that Dole too looked different. Just how was hard to describe, but his formerly pockmarked skin was smoother, his eyes brighter. "We're in a higher dimension, Lieutenant. Josie and I came through the second portal."

"But I didn't go into a portal," Dole said.

Stanton struggled with words. He wanted to say just the right thing.

"You is dead, son," Josie blurted. "They done killed you out there and now you are here."

There was no sadness in Dole's eyes, just confusion. "Dead?" He raised a hand and looked at it. "I'm a ghost?"

Again Josie laughed. It was an easy, sweet laugh that carried no derision, no malice. "Son, there ain't no such things as ghosts. I certainly ain't one and neither is you."

"But—" Dole began.

"Ain't no use in trying to figure it out now," Josie said. "It ain't neither of your times. When it is, then you'll know. Now come with me." She turned and started to walk away.

"Josie, wait. Where are we going?" Stanton asked. She didn't answer. After exchanging glances with each other, Stanton and Dole followed.

The mist of gray granules dissipated. In its place was a vast field of white. Stanton felt as if he were in a snowstorm, in whiteout conditions, yet there was no snow. Unlike the area just this side of Horizon, there were no flakes filling the air. Stanton's mind raced with what he was seeing, and not seeing. He had no sense of travel, even though he was walking; he had no sense of direction, even though he was standing. Josie had said that they were not in heaven. He could believe that. There was nothing here that spoke of beauty and peace, just immeasurable distance and confusion.

Hawking had spoken of Sheol and Tartarus. Sheol, the place of the dead. Stanton was familiar with the Hebrew term. It appeared many times in the Old Testament. Depending on the context, the term could refer to the literal grave, the hole in the ground, or it could refer to the place of the dead. Hawking had used Luke 16 as an example of Sheol. The rich man and Lazarus. Lazarus, after a life of poverty, found himself in a blissful place of rest called Abraham's bosom, a euphemism for Sheol; the rich man was in a place of torment. But this place was neither of those. There was no bliss here, but neither was there any torment. It was just empty.

His friend had also spoken of Tartarus, a place mentioned only once in the Scriptures. Their conversation had been interrupted by the alarm announcing the problem with the air scrubbers, but it didn't matter. Stanton knew the passage to which Hawking had referred, 2 Peter 2:4: "For if God did not spare angels when they sinned, but sent them to hell, putting them into gloomy dungeons to be held for judgment ..." It was one in a series of illustrations that the apostle Peter used to describe the future of the false teachers that troubled the early church. Most translations rendered the Greek word *Tartarus* as hell, since there was not a corresponding English word. From his many history classes at the Academy he remembered that the ancient Greeks considered Tartarus to be the lower parts of hell. The basement of hell. The theological question had been: What did these "angels who sinned" do to be bound in such a place? The companion passage in Jude 6 stated that these angels "abandoned their own home."

Stanton thought back to a Bible study led by his pastor, who said that many scholars think that these angels were the ones mentioned in Genesis 6 as the sons of God who cohabitated with women.

"No," Josie said.

"What?" Stanton asked.

"No, this ain't the place you is thinking 'bout," she answered, still walking into the white nothing. "It's kinda like it, but it ain't."

"You can read my mind?" Stanton asked, feeling more vulnerable than ever before.

"Sort of," she replied easily. "Communication is easier over here. Especially in heaven. Nothing to hide there. No sorrows to tuck away so's peoples don't see; no selfishness, no, none of that."

"I see."

"No, you don't. Not really. But you will. Not now, but you will." She slowed as she talked. "This is kinda like that there Tartarus place, but it's different, too. The Creator made a great many places, but all believers need concern themselves about is heaven. This here place is just what that Mr. Doctor Eddington fella was looking for. It's an in-between place."

"So he did find it," Stanton interjected. "But I thought he said it wasn't empty. This place looks as devoid of life as is possible."

Josie nodded. "I didn't say he found it. I said this is the place he was a-lookin' for. What he found was different. It was bad. His machine don't work none too good, either. It moves from place to place and it don't stay the same size. It's like a door that gets bigger and smaller."

"I didn't see it change size," Stanton said.

"Yo' can't see it with yo' eyes, honey," Josie said with a smile in her voice. "Not most times, anyways."

"Most times?"

"Them people you is looking for? They is gone because that Eddington fella's machine went haywire. That there portal done got real big and then small again. It took the people with it."

This did not surprise Stanton. Although he didn't know how it happened, he was sure that Eddington's Horizon II had been the culprit. "Where are we going, Josie?"

"To somethin' I want you to see."

Chapter 28

24 November 2000; 0150 hours
Cavern 1

The elevator doors closed, and the cab began to move smoothly up the shaft. Truman felt heavy, weighed down by the carnage he had just seen. In front of his men, he had presented himself as calm and unscathed by the body-littered battle area, but alone in the cab, he allowed himself the luxury of slumping against the wall and releasing a loud, long sigh. At his feet were the unmoving bodies of two of his team. Both had sustained bullet wounds to their heads and necks. It was worse than any horror movie he had ever watched, worse than any nightmare he had dreamed. Even though the elevator was the largest he had seen, it seemed small and confining. The air was thick with death. Letting his eyes travel down, he stared at the fallen soldiers. Their sightless eyes stared forever forward, unresponsive to the light overhead.

He felt sick. His stomach burned, nausea boiled within him. Instinctively, he wanted to flee, to put as many miles between him and the gore as possible, but his training restrained him. There was nothing left for him to do but make a radio report, clear out the bodies, and evacuate the area.

What a lousy job this had turned into. The early days had been filled with excitement. There was a thrill in belonging to a group so secret that not even the military, apart from a few in the Pentagon, knew of its existence. Flying night missions, carrying out covert ops, and never having to leave the country. It was ideal. That feeling was gone now, forever marred by the sights of mayhem and death. People he called friends lay dead in a deep cavern, never again to be seen by their families. The worst part was that their wives and children would never know what truly happened. That information would be confined to just a handful of people. The rest would remain in ignorance. He envied them their innocence.

The trip up seemed far too short. He longed for additional time to gather himself, to reconstruct his military persona. That time was not available. The shiny metal doors parted, and he stepped out. Four men stood in the lobby of the upper lab. Each turned at the sound of the opening doors, each swore when they saw their dead comrades.

"They're all dead," Truman said, without preamble, and without noticeable emotion. "Remove these two bodies and prepare them for transport. Then go below and help the others. Take a trash can. There are cartridges everywhere. Also—" He stopped as his radio crackled to life. He listened for a moment, then ran outside. His men followed.

There was thunder in the air, but not from the storm. This was all too familiar to his ears. He ran from the building, waving his arms in an up-and-down motion. "Up," he called into his radio microphone. "Get those birds up. I don't want them caught on the ground."

It was too late. A deafening noise pealed across the sky, hammering the night. A dark but unmistakable shape shot over his head and abruptly turned around. It was joined by another, then another. Within seconds three Army RAH–66 Comanche armed reconnaissance helicopters were hovering overhead, each with enough weaponry to handle a small army. Truman was staring down the barrel of one of the three 20mm Gatlin guns that each helo carried. The weapon bay doors on the side of the helicopters were open and extended, revealing mounted missiles. In the dark, Truman couldn't identify the type of missiles, but that didn't matter. They were all killers.

One of Truman's soldiers raised his weapon to fire. "*No!*" Truman screamed into his microphone. The man would not be able to finish a single burst of fire before being sliced to death by the powerful onboard guns of the Comanches. "Secure your weapons. Repeat, secure your weapons."

His men complied, then looked to him for instruction. Slowly Truman sank to his knees, then to his belly, his arms stretched out before him. It was an act of surrender and the only sane thing to do. His men followed his example. Their work was over.

"That's . . . that's a steamboat," Stanton exclaimed. Before him was a 180-foot-long white steamboat, its large paddlewheel moving slowly at the stern.

"Yes, sir, it is," Josie answered. "Right off da' Mississippi. You see dat man with da black and gray beard? Dat be Captain Beecher. A fine, godly man. He come here back in 1872."

"1872?" Stanton said in disbelief. "He has spent the last 127 years standing on the bridge of that boat?"

"Oh, no sir. He just got here."

"What? Josie, that doesn't make sense," Stanton said.

"Why not?" she asked. "As far as he is concerned, it is still 1872. It don't always work dat way, leastwise dat's what I am told. It's different for him." She pointed. "Dat man dere, well, he knows time's been a passing, he just don't know how much."

The man was yelling. "Help. Help me please."

"How long has he been here?" Stanton asked.

"Dere you go again, Julius," Josie said without exasperation. Her tone was that of a mother directing the thinking of a child. "It's not da same here as where we is from. It's different. You understand? He come here back in 1880, but to him just a few hours have passed. It's different for different folk. I don't know why, so don't ask. It just is."

"Is it that way in heaven?" Stanton asked.

"Oh, my no, child. Heaven is a wonderful place. You'll see, when yo' time come. Dis here place weren't meant for no humans. No, sir. Weren't meant for nobody."

"Then why does it exist?" Dole asked, breaking his silence.

"Only God knows. Maybe he has a plan for it. Maybe he don't."

"I don't understand how they came to be here," Stanton said. "And what's going to happen to them."

"Da world ain't a perfect place. Sin done seen to dat. When God was done a-creatin', the world was fine, real fine. But sin, now dat changed everything. We got earthquakes and hurricanes and tornadoes. Da Father, he don't go and make all dem things, leastways da way dey work now. Dey is just part of what is, part of what the world is. Well, sometimes dere's an opening 'tween there and here. Don't happen real often, I'm told, but it do happen. And every once in a while folk like that get caught up in it. Sometime, it's just plain folk like Mr. Lang over dere; sometimes it's a whole bunch of folk like Captain Beecher's boat. Been entire villages show up here from all over da world and all across time itself. Even dead people, once."

"What is going to happen to them?"

"Dey is going back." Her words were confident.

"After all these years?" Stanton said.

"Ain't no years here. I done told you dat."

"But why wait so long?" Stanton asked.

"So you could see 'em," Josie said succinctly. "So you could see 'em. So you could know how wrong dat Eddington fella is. Someone has to stop him and his work before he goes and opens the gates of hell itself. God, he has his own time for things. Ain't nobody knows just what dat is, and ain't nobody gonna mess with it."

"I . . . I feel funny," Dole said suddenly. "I feel strange."

"What do you mean?" Stanton asked.

"I don't know. Just like I don't belong here."

"You don't, honey. It's time for you to go back, but dere is something you has to do. It's important."

"I couldn't move," Dole protested. "I couldn't even open or close my eyes. I was dying."

"Yes, you were. Yes, you are, but you are gonna be finer than frog's hair. But you gotta do something." She reached to him and stroked his cheek. "It's gonna be hard, child. Real hard. The hardest thing you ever did before."

He looked at her, then at Stanton, then back to her. "Yes, ma'am. I'll do it."

"I have one more thing to show you," Josie said, and then turned. "The Father wishes to bless you." The sea of white dissolved like a fog before a warm wind. In its place, but at a distance was . . . was . . . Words failed him. Thoughts failed him. His mind was ablaze with the image. He could feel his heart pound like a jackhammer. He gasped, then held his breath as if breathing no longer mattered. It was majestic. It was peace personified; joy realized. The sky shone with a color Stanton had never seen, and he prayed he would never forget. None of the images of heaven he had seen looked like this. By comparison they were drab old tintypes. What he was seeing vibrated with beauty, resonated with peace. It was magnetic in its draw, hypnotic in its appeal.

"Oh, oh," was all Stanton could say. All the sunsets he had seen, all the blue skies, all the snowcapped mountains were ugly dregs of something far more splendid. Creatures moved in the distance. Some were human, some were straight from the pages of the Bible. All seemed active yet at peace. There was another quality Stanton could not define, an attribute that no language could explain. The people fit. It was where they belonged, it was what they had been created for. For them to have been any place other would have been a travesty of misalignment, round pegs in square holes, orchids in fields of weeds. A soft gold haze filled all that Stanton saw without diminishing any color, without distracting from any image. Stanton wondered if he was seeing God.

Stanton slumped to his knees. It was wrong to stand in the presence of such glory. Tears of profound, inexplicable joy streamed down his cheeks; his lips moved in silent prayer.

Suddenly the image was gone, replaced by the stark white of the world before. "No," Stanton said with a sorrow he had never before felt. He ached inside for the image to return, if just for a moment. "Please, no. A little more."

Dole was weeping profusely.

"Soon enough," Josie said. "Soon enough."

N

The red hole in space-time disgorged Stanton. He carried the aged body of Josie in his arms.

"You found her!" Ramsey blurted. He stared at the woman for a moment, then asked the question that Stanton knew was on everyone's mind. "Is she . . . dead?"

"Yes," Stanton said with sadness. He knew that her soul flourished, but holding her lifeless corpse was sobering. She was an odd woman, unpleasant in appearance and quick with her opinion, but she was one of them, made a part of the group by the danger they faced.

"How could you have found her so quickly?" Eddington asked. Even his tone was subdued.

"What do you mean, quickly?" Stanton said, as he stepped away from Horizon II. Gently, he set Josie's body down on the floor. Kneeling beside her, he brushed back a lock of tangled, matted hair. Ramsey stepped behind Stanton and began removing the metal safety cable. He had him free in moments.

"You couldn't have been in there more than two or three seconds," explained Eddington.

Stanton stood, his eyes still fixed on Josie. Instead of feeling sad, he was awash with warmth. A smile crept across his face.

"No, I'm sure of it," Eddington said forcefully. "The others will tell you the same. You weren't in there more than a few seconds. Less time than Rover—"

"What happened?" Hawking asked, cutting Eddington off. He was eyeing Stanton suspiciously.

"This," Stanton said with a broad grin, "is something you have to see for yourself. But there is one thing we have to do first." He stepped to the console and sat down at the control monitor. He started pounding keys.

"Hey," Eddington said. "You don't know what you're doing."

"I do now," Stanton said. "I do now."

Air rushed into Dole's lungs. It was thick and rich, despite the pollution of a gun battle. Another breath. He blinked, then blinked again. Pain began to race up and down his body, and with each lap it increased in intensity. He groaned and wished for the sweet relief of unconsciousness, to relive the dream he had just experienced. It had been so very beautiful.

Was it a dream? What else could it be? Still, he could see the black woman, see her smile, hear her words. Then there was heaven. If preachers could describe what he had seen, every church in the world would be full.

But it wasn't a dream. It had been real, and the reality of it began to set in.

Dole rolled over. The act wearied him more than any drill he had experienced in the marine corps. His heart was pounding in triple time to move what little blood he had left through his body.

"What was that?" To Dole the words seemed a continent away. "I thought I heard something."

"You're imagining things," another voice said.

"No. It sounded like a groan."

"They're all dead. We checked. Remember?"

"Yeah, I remember. This place gives me the creeps."

"Me too, buddy. Where's our help? Didn't Truman say he was sending people down to help?"

"That's what I heard."

A ding sounded. "Good, there they are now. Help me with this—"

The elevator doors parted and eight Army Rangers poured out, M16s pointed ahead of them.

"What the—" the first man said.

"Down, down, down!" one of the Rangers shouted. "On the ground. Now!" His voice was loud. Others were shouting the same thing. Dole rolled onto his side in time to see two commandos dressed in black drop to the floor.

"Make a sweep," the Ranger with a loud voice shouted. The men fanned out.

"Help," Dole said weakly. "Help me."

A soldier approached Dole carefully, pointing his weapon at Dole's head. A second later he pulled it away. "Major. Man down over here."

Looking up, Dole saw a uniformed man in brown BDUs. On his sleeve he wore the insignia of the U.S. Army Rangers. His name tag read "Getz." "Take it easy, son. We'll have you out of here in a few minutes," he said. Then he called out, "Medic! I want this man evacuated immediately."

"Wait," Dole said. "Help me up."

"You're not going anywhere except on a stretcher, Lieutenant. You've been hit pretty bad."

"I have to do something first. I have to get up and do something."

"Lie still, Lieutenant. Everything is under control. We have everything topside secured. There's nothing to worry about."

"No, you don't understand," Dole protested. "It's a matter of life and death. My friends—"

"Your friends will be taken care of," Major Getz said.

With all the strength he could muster, Dole reached up with his good arm and grabbed a handful of the major's uniform. "Sir, I must get to Horizon I. I will not leave here until I do."

"What is Horizon I?"

"The consoles. Help me to the consoles, or my team will die. Please, Major." Dole watched as the major's eyes studied him. The request was insane. Dole was far too weak to stand, far too weak to be moved. "Come on, Major," Dole said as forcefully as he could. "I have to do this now! I don't know how much longer I can remain conscious." Dole released the major's uniform.

"Sergeant," the major said loudly. "Help me with this man."

"But, sir."

"Do it, Sergeant."

The sergeant was a tall, thickly muscled man. Instead of helping Dole up to his feet, he reached down, slid his arms under him, and lifted him off the ground as if he weighed no more than a child. "This will be easier on him and us, sir."

"Take him to the consoles."

"The platform," Dole whispered through clenched teeth. Pain ripped through him, as if someone was cutting him open with a serrated saw. "The metal platform on the other side of the consoles."

The sergeant carried Dole, who could feel each footstep with searing agony. The distance was crossed in seconds. "Now what?" Major Getz asked.

"A cable has been broken. We . . ." Dole coughed harshly. "We have to reconnect it."

"Why?" Getz asked.

"Because it will save the others," Dole screamed, but the words came out impotently. "There," he said pointing. "There, do you see it?" Dole was staring at a thick black cable that ran along the ground and to Horizon I's raised pedestal.

"It's a power cord," the sergeant said. "It's probably still hot."

"Put me down," Dole said. "I'll do it."

The sergeant didn't move.

"That's an order, Sergeant," Dole snapped. Still the army man remained motionless. Dole watched as he made eye contact with Major Getz.

"Put him down," Getz said. "Be easy about it."

As soon as Dole's back touched the floor, he rolled over. His face screwed up into a pain-driven grimace.

"No you don't, Lieutenant," Getz said. "You stay still. I'll do it."

"Let me, sir," the sergeant said. "My dad's an electrician. I spent my summers working for him."

"Good. But let's not waste time. I want this man on the surface right away."

"I need to kill the power first." Dole watched through fogging eyes as the man followed the cable to a gray box mounted on the wall a dozen feet away. He opened the large metal case. It contained circuit breakers. "I don't know what they do here, Major, but they sure use a lot of power." After a moment's study, he tripped one of the large black switches, then returned to the damaged power cable. "Looks like a bullet grazed it," he said. "Cut the positive lead right in half. The rest of it looks fine." Removing a knife from its sheath at his side, he quickly cut away half an inch of heavy insulation from the two ends and then twisted them together. The whole process took less than a minute. The sergeant stepped briskly back to the circuit breaker box and flipped on the circuit.

Horizon I came to life with a buzz and whine that circulated through the cavern. The shape-changing hole in reality rematerialized.

"What is that?" Getz asked in utter astonishment.

"You wouldn't believe me if I told you," Dole said in a forced whisper. Relieved at the sight of the enigma, he laid his head back. He had expended the last ounce of energy he possessed.

Horizon I changed colors and pulsated.

"What's it doing?" the sergeant asked.

Flash. A blinding light split through the gloom of the cavern, pushing back the twilight for a moment. When it blinked out, Stanton, Hawking, Eddington, and the others were standing around the pedestal. They all had tears in their eyes.

"It was . . . it was amazing," Eddington said. "I never believed . . . would never believe, but now I know." Ramsey hugged Keagle; Wendt hugged Tulley. Eddington slapped Hawking on the back. Their joy was uncontainable.

Zach looked up at Stanton and said, "Wow! Double wow!" Laughter erupted from the team, and Stanton reached down and picked up the boy. Red, who had emerged last, barked.

"What is going on here?" Getz demanded.

Stanton turned to face the army major. He offered a salute. "Major, I am Captain J. D. Stanton, United States Navy, and this is my team."

Instinctively, Getz returned the salute. "Where did you come from? How did you get here? What is that thing?"

Raising a hand, Stanton said, "All in due time, Major. Right now I need your help. Please have all your men move back to the walls."

"What?"

"Have them clear the area. Line them up against a wall. I don't want them on the floor when it happens."

"When what happens? Never mind." Major Getz gave the order, and his men backed away, until each stood with his back to a stone wall. Eddington, Hawking, and the others followed suit.

Stanton looked down at Dole, who flashed a grin that seemed to reach from ear to ear. "You did it, Lieutenant. You did it."

Dole offered a weak salute.

"I need to move you," Stanton said with concern.

"Let me do that, Captain," the sergeant said. "I'm an old hand at this." Stanton yielded to the younger man, and stepped back. Again, the big sergeant hoisted Dole into his arms. To Dole, he said, "Hang in there, Lieutenant. You're going to be okay. No one dies on my shift."

Dole offered a weak smile, then made eye contact with Stanton. "It doesn't matter, either way, Sergeant. It doesn't matter to me at all. Not anymore."

Stanton knew exactly how Dole felt. The entire team did.

Flash. The bright light exploded with blinding intensity. Ripples of warm energy washed over the area. For a moment Stanton felt as if every nerve in his body was firing at one time. The cries of startled men echoed off the walls of the massive cavern. A second later, new sounds began to waft through the air. Voices. Voices of people. When his stunned retinas cleared enough for him to see, Stanton saw a dozen men and women in white lab coats milling around, stunned and confused. Several people gasped at the blood and bodies that still lay strewn about. One, a middle-aged man with a thick gray-and-black beard, approached Eddington, confusion deeply etched into his face.

"Dr. Eddington, what . . . what are you doing here? I thought you were going out of town for the holidays."

Eddington smiled warmly, slapped him on the shoulder, and said, "Welcome back. Welcome back. I'll explain everything later, but first I need to know something important: Was anyone, anyone at all, working in Cavern 2?"

Stanton had wondered the same thing. If everyone was being returned to their places like Josie had said they would be, then there were several people trapped in the thinning air of the other cavern. They would die in short order.

"Welcome back? I haven't gone anywhere."

"Was there anyone in Cavern 2?" Eddington asked again, the urgency clear in his voice.

"No, Dr. Eddington. No one. I had gathered everyone in here for a staff meeting."

Eddington let out a long and loud sigh. "That's good. That's very, very good. Please gather your team in the elevator."

"I'm confused, Dr. Eddington. The bodies . . . the soldiers . . . when did this happen? How did this happen? Why don't I remember any of this happening?" The man's face was ashen gray, made all the more pale by the dim light emitted from the few remaining lights above.

"Any explanation I give you right now will only heighten your confusion," Eddington said. "I promise to fill you in, but it's very important for you and your team to leave. Now please follow my instructions and get your people out of here." After the man left, Eddington turned to Stanton. "Captain," he said softly, remorsefully. "I lied to you. I did make that call. I called my contact in the Pentagon when I knew you had found a way into the lab. I'm sorry. I never anticipated this. I thought that someone would order you off the site. If I had known that so much death and destruction was going to take place ..." Tears brimmed in his eyes.

"There was no way you could know," Stanton said. He placed a hand on the engineer's shoulder. The nonverbal gesture was all he could think of to do, and it communicated what words could not.

"Sergeant," Major Getz said. "Get that man on the surface. I want him in a hospital as soon as possible. Understood?"

"Yes, sir."

To Stanton, Getz said, "Captain, I'm ready for an explanation."

"Major," Stanton said. "If I told you, you wouldn't believe me."

Getz groaned. "Why does everyone keep saying that? People have died down here, Captain. I believe an explanation is warranted."

A profound and cold sadness filled Stanton. Men, brave men, had indeed died, and there was nothing he could do about it. "It's a long and convoluted account, and I'm certain I will be explaining things many times. But there is something that I must see to first. Dr. Eddington, if you would, please."

"My pleasure," he said. He walked over to the circuit breaker panel and shut off the power to Horizon I. The threshold blinked out. He then returned to the pedestal, knelt down, opened a panel, and removed a large printed circuit board. "The mother board," he said, holding it up. He then propped it at a forty-five degree angle between the floor and the pedestal.

Bringing his foot up, he stomped down on the delicate electronics. It shattered into three pieces, which he picked up and carried to the inlet. Stanton watched as the engineer tossed his life's work into the dark water. There had been no reluctance.

"And Horizon II?" Tulley asked.

"Programmed to shut down five minutes after we entered," Eddington answered. "The rest will have to be taken care of when we can get back in there."

Stanton approached Major Getz and shook his hand. "Don't get me wrong, Major. I am very glad to see you. How did you come to be here?"

"An Admiral Kaster was flown by an unmarked Apache helicopter to Fort Irwin. He was weak and close to death, but he made sure the base commander knew a few things. Next thing I know, we're on our way to retake this place."

"Kaster's alive?" Stanton said with joyous surprise.

"Yes, sir," Getz answered. "He insisted on briefing me before he would let the doctors work on him. He's one tough bird. Especially for a navy man."

"I'll overlook that, Major," Stanton said with a laugh. "Now, if it's all right with you, I'd like to put some distance between me and this place."

Topside, Stanton, who carried Zach in his arms, and the others exited the elevator. The ragged pieces of rubble created by the relentless fire of the Apache's guns reminded him how close he and the others had come to death. Stepping through the ragged remains of the door and into the cool night, Stanton caught sight of Eddington's engineers standing in stunned silence at the carnage that surrounded them.

Stanton could only imagine the mystification that was swirling in their minds. One moment below ground doing work that they had done day after day; now standing in the remains of battle with no knowledge, no recollection that such a conflict had occurred. There would be others who would be confused, too. Those in restaurants would wonder why their food was cold and dry. Some would look out windows and wonder when it had rained. Those who had been watching television when the event happened might wonder when the program changed. Clocks would be the most baffling. Most would be aware that time was missing. The clues were all around them, and nothing in their life experience would be able to explain away the puzzle.

"How do I explain all this?" Eddington asked softly.

"Carefully and slowly," Stanton said. "That's not very useful advice, but it is nonetheless true." Stanton turned to Getz. "Major, I need you to secure this area. No one in, except Dr. Eddington and his team. Also, some of your men can help by patrolling the streets. I think you may find some people who will have a great many questions."

Getz nodded. "I'm afraid I don't have any answers."

"I'll explain what I can as we drive," Stanton said.

"Drive?" Getz questioned.

Stanton set Zach down. "I know a boy who might like to see his parents." He rested a hand on the boy's head. "How about it, son, you ready to go home?"

Zach smiled. "Yes. I know my address and everything."

A broad grin crossed Stanton's face. It was only the second thing he had heard the boy say. Looking up to the heavens, Stanton saw the thinning clouds part like a curtain on a stage, revealing a canvas of brilliant stars, and was reminded how big God was and how he could bring healing out of chaos.

Epilogue

28 November 2000; 1830 hours
Home of J. D. Stanton

"Your wife is a great cook," Hawking Striber said, as he took another bite of food. "I've never had a turkey taco before."

"I've been eating turkey since I got back," Stanton said. The two men were eating dinner in the living room of Stanton's home. *Monday Night Football* played on the television. Neither man paid much attention to it. "It's a tradition around here. Turkey for Thanksgiving, then it's turkey soup, turkey and eggs, turkey Mexican style, turkey and pasta. My wife knows more ways to fix turkey than the navy has ships."

"Sounds like paradise to me. Of course I'm single and have to fend for myself."

"You're welcome here anytime," Stanton said, setting his plate on the coffee table. "What's in the envelope?" He motioned to a large brown package next to Hawking.

"I've been doing a little research," he answered. He stopped eating long enough to hand the envelope to Stanton. "It's not much really, but I had a couple of my people track down a few things. Do you remember that steamboat we saw?"

Stanton nodded. Josie had been there when the entire team entered through Horizon II. She had patiently explained the same things she had told Stanton. Then heaven appeared again, this time larger and closer. To a person, they fell on their knees in awe and amazement. None would ever be the same. "I remember. I remember everything we saw."

"I don't think we'll be able to forget, not that anyone would want to. Anyway, we searched the historical references and found a mention of the *Iron Mountain*, a steamboat which disappeared off the Mississippi in 1872. There is only one reference to the disappearance: an article in a Vicksburg newspaper. There may be other records such as cargo manifests and the like, but that would take a lot of digging to uncover."

"So they sailed into a higher dimension somehow. Josie mentioned that that occasionally happened."

Hawking nodded. "Here's the kicker. A later newspaper report said that the *Iron Mountain* reappeared the next morning. They quoted a man who lived on the river as saying that it just reappeared. There's no mention of her after that."

"I can imagine. That's a hard story to believe. If I hadn't seen what I did, I wouldn't believe it."

"That's just the beginning. I wondered how far back this could go, so I checked some prehistory records."

"Prehistory records?"

"Sounds oxymoronic, doesn't it?" Hawking said with a smile. "I'm talking about petroglyphs. Prehistoric cultures used to make rock carvings. I searched several university databases on the Internet. There were some good sources and pictures of petroglyphs. One from near Roanoke II showed the stick fingers of a family and what appears to be spheres floating overhead. I immediately thought of what Eddington said about the glowing artifacts we saw when Rover went into Horizon II. You had no way of knowing this, but the same thing happened when you went in. I think you are right in assuming that Edwards Air Force Base was trying to track those artifacts. It may be that the larger the mass that passes through the threshold, the bigger the lights."

"Josie mentioned that even dead people had crossed over," Stanton said. "Their bodies, I mean."

"That puzzled me, but my researchers came through on that too. Back in 1947 a plane crashed on Mt. Rainier. When rescuers arrived, they found evidence of injury, but no people. No bodies and no footprints in the snow. They were just gone." Hawking took another bite and chewed his food contemplatively. "We came across a book written by a reporter back in 1959. His name was Frank Edwards and his book was titled *Stranger Than Science*. It's an interesting read, and he mentions a few cases like this. Unfortunately, he didn't document his sources, so we have little to go on.

"And then there is that Mr. Lang you said Josie introduced you to. We found two newspaper accounts on him, also. One mentioned his disappearance and the subsequent search; the other his sudden reappearance eight months later to a stunned and happy family. He had no explanation for his disappearance. Soon after that, according to the county records, he sold the farm and moved away."

"So there could be a handful of cases, or hundreds," Stanton said. "Well, at least we know the Roanoke II people are back, albeit without any memory of the event."

"That's for the best, I'm sure."

"Why do we remember?" Stanton asked.

Shrugging, Hawking said, "I can't be sure."

"Well, I think it's because we needed to put a stop to the project. That was part of our mission. It sure turned Eddington around."

"Have you talked to him recently?"

"Yes, he called this morning to say that the rubble had been removed from the tunnel and that Horizon II is no longer functional. He didn't explain beyond that. It took a lot of courage for him to set Horizon II to shut down five minutes after we entered. All he had to go on was my word."

"We didn't have a lot of choices," Hawking said.

"I think it goes beyond that. He seemed genuinely moved by Josie's lifeless body. Deep down, Eddington is a good man. It took everything we went through for him to see the danger of his project. There are some things that humans aren't meant to mess with."

"That's certainly true. Speaking of Josie, what happens to her now? Her body, I mean."

"Eddington said that he did some researching. Josie had no family. He's taken it upon himself to give her a decent burial."

"Josie was quite an enigma," Hawking offered. "At times she seemed positively crazy, but you couldn't help but see her faith."

"She was unusual, all right," Stanton agreed, "but she displayed more faith than any of us. That's why God sent her our way."

"I've been thinking about that, and the more I think about it, the more I see God's hand in it all. I don't think a single one of us was there apart from his will."

"I've struggled with what we've seen," Stanton said somberly. "I've been trying to make it work in my mind. I know the Bible mentions people who have had visions of heaven, people like the apostle Paul and the apostle John in Revelation. Is what we saw the real thing or a vision?"

Hawking shook his head. "I don't know. It seemed real, but then that's what a vision is. The person actually participates in the action of the vision and carries on conversations. Such events happened to Isaiah, Ezekiel, and others. What took me a while to understand is why God would let unbelievers like Tulley and Eddington to glimpse heaven. Then it hit me."

"What hit you?"

"Several things actually," Hawking said, becoming more animated with each word. He quoted, "'The Lord is not slow in keeping his promise, as some understand slowness. He is patient with you, not wanting anyone to perish, but everyone to come to repentance.'"

"Second Peter 3:9," Stanton said. "That verse came to me as well."

"I also started thinking about the ways in which God dealt with unbelievers or disobedient believers in the past. There is no biblical record of an unbeliever seeing heaven, but there are a number of cases where God used visions or manifestations to get an unbeliever's attention. The story of Joseph and Pharaoh's dream is one example. The handwriting on the wall in Daniel is another. God has often done the unusual to get his point across. Unusual from our perspective anyway. Just think of Balaam and the talking donkey. Unique, but direct and to the point. But the real clincher for me was Luke 9:6."

A small Bible rested on the coffee table. Stanton picked it up, found the reference, and read, "'So they set out and went from village to village, preaching the gospel and healing people everywhere.'" He thought for a moment, then said, "I don't get your point."

"Jesus is sending out the disciples," Hawking explained. "He sent out all twelve. That means that Judas went out with them, preached, and healed. The Scripture never says that he was precluded from doing the same work. Yet we know that he was not a believer. At least, most scholars would say that."

"I get it now. People benefited from the disciples going out even if one of them was Judas. The point being that God is good, even if people aren't."

"Exactly," Hawking said. "The bottom line is that God can do what he wants. We can see his pattern of work throughout the Scripture, but we also see events where he does something extraordinarily different."

Stanton nodded his agreement. "Whether we saw a vision of heaven or heaven itself, I know one thing: I will never be the same, and I don't think any of the others will be either."

"What do you suppose will happen to Eddington?"

"I don't know. This thing goes deep into the Pentagon and the White House. I visited Kaster in the hospital. He says the president is tied up in all this."

"President Crane?"

"Yes. Admiral Kaster is calling for a congressional investigation of the White House and the Department of Defense. If anyone can make that happen, he can."

"How is he?"

"Pretty beat up. That crash should have killed him. They expect him to leave the hospital next week."

"God is good."

"Very good." Stanton relayed the story of the three young people who helped Kaster, and how one of the commandos recognized him.

"As busted up as he was, he flew in the back of an Apache helicopter to Fort Irwin?"

"He didn't think he was going to make it, but as you said, God is good."

"And Dole?"

"He's doing great. I spoke to him on the phone. He thinks he'll be back to active duty in two or three months. He's a changed man."

"I bet he was happy to see his brother again."

"He was, but his brother is confused about it all. Like the others, he has no memory of the disappearance."

Hawking took a long sip of coffee. "It's the boy that puzzles me the most," he said. "He and that dog. I can understand how Josie missed being taken since she lived three miles away, but what about Zach?"

The mention of Zach brought a broad smile to Stanton's face. "I spoke to his mother today. She said he won't stop talking. By the way, his real name is Aaron."

"Aaron was initially the spokesman for Moses."

"Ironic, isn't it? Anyway, she explained what happened. His father was one of the guards stationed at the front entrance. His watch was almost over when friends of the family brought Aaron to the front gate. He had spent the day with them and they were returning him home. Since his father was going home in a few minutes, they left Aaron with him. That way, they didn't have to be cleared to drive on the compound. They had taken the dog with them. Apparently they have an Irish setter, too."

"Was the dog's name really Red?"

"No. I had assumed that dog was a male, but he is a she, and goes by the name of Guinevere, or Guinny for short. After Zach—I mean, Aaron—had been dropped off, he waited for his father just outside the front gate. There's a small field there, well within sight of the guard shack. Aaron was throwing a ball, and Guinny was chasing it. They were just killing the last ten minutes of his father's shift. That's when it happened. The portal expanded enough to take in all of Roanoke II, but not much beyond it. It just missed the boy. All of a sudden, he was alone. He watched his father disappear."

"No wonder he was so traumatized," Hawking said.

"Yes, but he's fine now."

"That's great. What about Agents Tulley and Wendt?"

It was Stanton's turn to shrug. "They left soon after the debriefing, but it was pretty easy to see that they had been changed for the better. Seeing heaven must have softened Tulley's heart. He apologized for his attitude a hundred times over."

"He didn't make things easier, that's for sure."

"He even suggested that we get together for an annual reunion. I like the idea."

"Count me in," Hawking said. "Just so long as we don't meet in a cavern."

Stanton laughed. "Amen to that. Amen to that."

Author's Afterword

The story you have just read is speculative fiction. As such, certain liberties were taken for the sake of the story. Most of the disappearances mentioned in a historical framework were based on events reported to have actually happened. However, as is the case with such accounts, finding definitive proof is impossible. The stories of David Lang, the *Iron Mountain*, the crash on Mt. Rainier, and others are based on such reports. Oya is purely fictional. Frank Edwards and his book *Stranger Than Science*, which are mentioned in the epilogue, are real.

Discussions of extra dimensions and how they relate to life and faith are taken from numerous discussions and sources from the scientific and theological communities.

While this is a work of speculative fiction, I have made every effort to avoid offering explanations or descriptions that would be contrary to Scripture while simultaneously examining what might be. As for what is, we have the Scripture to guide us, and the blessed hope that awaits us. As the apostle Paul said in 1 Corinthians 2:9, "However, as it is written: 'No eye has seen, no ear has heard, no mind has conceived what God has prepared for those who love him.'"

Grace and peace,
Alton L. Gansky

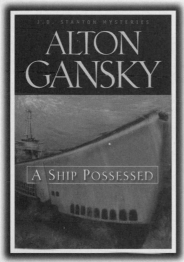

We want to hear from you. Please send your comments about this book to us in care of the address below. Thank you.

ZondervanPublishingHouse
Grand Rapids, Michigan 49530
http://www.zondervan.com